The Cockroach Catcher

Am Ang Zhang

Bauhinia Press

NewYork 2008

This book is a work of fiction. Names, characters, and incidents are the product of the author's imagination. Any resemblance to events or actual persons, living or dead, is entirely coincidental. However, references to real people, institutions and organisations that are documented in the footnotes are accurate. Footnotes are real.

Published by Bauhinia Press, New York

ISBN 978-0-6151-8628-3

To My Family

Contents

Chapter 1 Seven Minute Cure

❝This is the Captain again. I hope you have enjoyed the view of St. Lucia. It is unusual to have so little cloud. Anyway, in seven minutes we shall be able to come into view of Barbados. We should be coming in from the north side where you will be able to see Port St Charles. Then we shall go round the west coast. With any luck you will be able to see Sandy Lane, the best hotel in the world. So, in seven minutes. Barbados. The temperature in Barbados: 83 degrees Fahrenheit, with scattered clouds."

In seven minutes I would start my life of leisure in this Paradise Island in the sun.

Seven minutes.

Seven minute cure. My famous seven minute cure. It was the making of me at the Adolescent Inpatient Unit. It was the pinnacle of my career. The most defining seven minutes in my career.

And Candy really helped me launch myself into it.

"It is our view that clinically it was wrong for Candy to be transferred at this stage. It was wrong for the NHS to accept her back and in our view Candy is in serious risk of – quite frankly – dying."

Those were more or less the words said at the transfer meeting by the nurse from the private hospital where Candy had been for the past eighteen months. She had been compulsorily detained twice and she had been put on Olanzapine. Olanzapine is one of a new group of drugs licensed for Schizophrenia and has been found to induce a voracious appetite especially the bingeing of carbohydrates. Some psychiatrists have started using it for this specific effect. In Candy's case she managed to fight the biochemical effect of Olanzapine.[1]

---

[1] Olanzapine – (Zyprexa-Lilly) Anti-psychotic drug. Eli Lilly agreed on Jan. 4, 2007 to pay up to $500 million to settle 18,000 lawsuits from people who claimed they had developed diabetes or other diseases after taking the drug. Lilly denied any wrongdoing. In its statement, Lilly said the settlement did not change its view that Zyprexa is a safe and effective treatment for mental illness.

Lilly's internal documents show that in Lilly's clinical trials, 16 percent of people taking Zyprexa gained more than 66 pounds after a year on the drug, a far higher figure than the company disclosed to doctors.

Olanzapine-induced weight gain may be secondary to excessive ingestion of food due probably to an inability to increase plasma glucose and leptin following a glucose challenge.

The F.D.A. added a warning in 2003 to the label of Zyprexa and other new antipsychotic drugs about their tendency to cause high blood sugar.

http://query.nytimes.com/gst/fullpage.html?sec=health&res=9f00e5db1430f936a35752c0a9619c8b6
3

http://www.medscape.com/viewarticle/418312_3

http://www.obesityresearch.org/cgi/content/full/14/1/36

Candy was just two days free of tube-feeding, which apparently was the only way to get her weight to a less frightening level.

Ethics in medicine has of course changed because money is now involved and big money too. What was in dispute in this case was that the private health insurance that sustained Candy through the last eighteen months had dried out. The private hospital then tried to get the NHS to continue to pay for the service on the ground that Candy's life would otherwise be in danger. The cost was around seven hundred pounds a night. Some would argue: since we as a state hospital would not be getting the money, why should we take the risk? After all, the consultant in charge would be in the dock if the patient did die. Nowadays, patients and their families are trigger happy and complain even if the patient becomes better. God help us if they die.

I argued the case in the opposite fashion. We shall help the authorities without precondition and who knows, I may be able to get them to give us something when the time is right.

Cynics at the unit looked at me as if I had just dropped off another planet. Get something out of the Health Authority? When were you born?

A quick calculation gave me a figure of over a quarter of a million pounds per year at the private hospital. No wonder they were not happy to have her transferred out. Before my taking up the post, there were at one time seven patients placed by the Health Authorities at the same private hospital. Not all of them for Anorexia Nervosa, but Anorexia Nervosa required the longest stay and drained the most money from any Health Authority. I have seen private clinics springing up for the sole purpose of admitting anorectic patients and nobody else. It is a multi-million pound business. Some of these clinics even managed to get into broadsheet Sunday supplements. I think Anorexia Nervosa Clinics are fast acquiring the status of private Rehab Centres. Until the government legislates to prevent health insurers from not funding long term psychiatric cases, Health Authorities all over the country will continue to pick up the tabs for such costly treatments

The poor nurse did not realise what hit her. That was my first week. I am never threatened. I like the challenge of difficult cases and definitive statements like – the patient will die. I like to prove it otherwise.

The nurse concerned was not naïve either. Far from it. She based her judgement not on what she knew about me. It was only my first week after all.

No, she based her judgement on her knowledge of the unit, as she used to work here. She was once its lead nurse. Alas, poor pay and bad conditions coupled with the deteriorating consultant leadership prompted her to jump ship. I could not blame her for that.

The unit went through a difficult phase until the last consultant was finally suspended. Even before that, other consultants started refusing to refer patients here, and the two main Health Authorities that the clinic served had to fund ECRs (Extra Contractual Referrals in the then re-organised Health Service lingo) to mainly private hospitals.

Then the unit had a locum and the operation was scaled down drastically. Bed availability dropped to less than half the normal capacity and the waiting list for admission grew. Unlike elective surgery, some patients in psychiatry cannot wait. Beds had to be found and often they were placed with adult psychiatric patients. It was not ideal even for the psychotics and certainly inappropriate for Anorexia Nervosa. Private Hospitals had to be used.

My first task as the new consultant in charge was to ask the Charge Nurse what would limit our ability to admit to full capacity.

"Your time," was his reply.

So we aimed to move to full capacity, not overnight but within the following three months. The shock on the faces of the managers as this was announced at a meeting gave me such an adrenaline rush.

Or, did they think, "What a fool!"

Fool or no fool, one needs to enjoy one's work, even in the NHS.

This perhaps is one thing that the government has conveniently forgotten. Many of us do what we do because we enjoy it. Otherwise why should anyone want to teach in universities when they can earn ten or twenty times more in industry? We may also decide to dedicate more time to work for personal pride and satisfaction. During the few years I worked at the inpatient units I spent in excess of a hundred hours a week there, one man doing the job of at least two. In addition to that, I was still looking after two outpatient clinics.

With increased capacity, we were ready to take on transfers. At that time the Health Authorities still had decent managers not yet blinded by directives and performance targets. For a start these managers did not interfere with clinical matters. For our part we were free to exercise our clinical judgment. Unfortunately many consultants abuse this privilege of clinical independence, often making excessive demands for treatments and investigations, and managers have learnt to ignore them. Worse the government set up this organisation called NICE (National Institute for Health and Clinical Excellence) to try to deal with such behaviour.

"It is our view that clinically it was wrong for Candy to be transferred at this stage. It was wrong for the NHS to accept her back and in our view Candy is in serious risk of – quite frankly – dying."

The nurse was probably unwise to make such a declaration, as my mind was already made up to take on Candy regardless.

What if the private hospital did not exist? It would have been down to us then. So to me that was no big deal. After all, most private hospitals are notorious for transferring their dying patients to NHS hospitals so as not to mess up their pristine mortality figures. What was so different here?

"Shall we meet the family?" I said, trying to break the ice.

There had of course been a pre-visit by our Charge Nurse and his team.

"This one is difficult and I think you may have a problem with father."

Candy led the three-some. She gave me such a look as if to say, "Wait till I give you all the trouble." She looked out of the window for the rest of the time. Mother was warm but worn. Eighteen months had taken its toll and she was gracious enough to be pleased to meet me. Father on the other hand seemed to show some anxiety. In fact, he was a quite a powerful negotiator, and had managed to persuade the insurers to agree to extend the private medical care for another six weeks on a shared cost basis, either with the parents or with the Health Authority. He was still quite keen on the private treatment, and was half hoping that I would refuse to take Candy on clinical grounds and then the Health Authority would pick up the bill from then on.

To be fair, eighteen months was a long time even for Anorexia Nervosa. Perhaps someone else should have a go. NICE had not yet come up with a standard treatment and I certainly would challenge them to do so. Tube feed everybody? That would be the day.

Mother was more intuitive and I think she got the measure of me very quickly. "Darling, perhaps we should give Candy a new start. The new doctor might work in a different way."

"It is the nurses that did most of the work." A final and desperate attempt by the nurse from the private hospital to set the record straight was missed by the nervous family. The rest of the world still looked up to the consultant, perhaps not for much longer but until Armageddon, I was going to enjoy it.

"I will give it my best shot."

So on a rather unusually beautiful sunny Tuesday morning, we received a soon to be dead Anorexia Nervosa patient who had been abandoned by her insurer to the unsafe NHS. What a challenge! Some of those at the meeting must have considered that I was delusional. I believed that money should not be part of the consideration for the best health care and I was determined to make sure that my delusions should remain true for me. I had to maintain a good service in my little corner of the NHS.

Perhaps I was able to capture mother's heart and gain her confidence through mine. She decided that they should give us a try.

Do I tube feed her straightaway or do I wait?

I am no coward. So let us wait.

Adolescent units are notorious for making life difficult for authority figures. This is perhaps due to severe professional rivalry. To most of the nursing staff, the only difference between the psychiatrist and them is that the psychiatrist is licensed to prescribe. If a patient is not on medication a psychiatrist would barely be needed. Over time various mechanisms have been introduced to minimize the input of the psychiatrist even when he is supposed to be in charge. Many psychiatrists gave up the fight a long time ago just to survive. A patient's stay in hospital involves a large number of multidisciplinary meetings that often lead to half-baked treatment plans that have little hope of success. Surprises are unwelcome and generally discouraged.

I have found this kind of "consensus" approach a serious problem. It is simply not my style. Perhaps one of the reasons I stayed as an outpatient consultant all these years was to continue to enjoy the independence from such approach.

Now all eyes were on me.

On that Tuesday I felt as though the whole unit was putting me through a trial. It was like living through a reality show. Everybody was watching me, and I would have to deliver or perish. My reputation, the reputation of an alien psychiatrist, was at stake. I needed to act fast and I did not have eighteen months. Otherwise I would be packing and leaving this jungle, house or whatever reality show I was in.

Apart from true madness, Anorexia is the only condition where one can use the Mental Health Act to detain and if necessary force feed against the patient's wishes, although little is known about how effective this aspect of our law is. There is still a rather high mortality rate, even in acknowledged centres of excellence like the Maudsley[2]. Tube feeding does not seem to be saving lives. It also hurts our pride if we have to succumb to tube-feeding. It means that we have failed as psychiatrists.

Then I remembered my own golden rule about parenting. When all else fails, try bribery. And that is what I did, but not with Candy.

Any nurse that could get Candy to start eating would get three bottles of nice wine or two cases of beer. It might not be strictly against the rule, but I am sure a few eyebrows were raised. Candy refused to eat or even drink.

I had to be in London for a Royal College meeting that Friday. My mobile rang. Day 4: Candy was still refusing to eat or drink.

"No tube feeding, just check her blood chemistry" was what I decided should be done. People do not die so easily even with

---

[2] Anorexia mortality: http://bjp.rcpsych.org/cgi/content/abstract/175/2/147
Anorexia nervosa is a mental disorder with a high long-term mortality. Detained patients gained as much weight during admission as voluntary patients, but took longer. More deaths among compulsory than voluntary patients (10/79 v. 2/78) were found 5.7 years (mean) after admission. CONCLUSIONS: Compulsory treatment is effective in the short term. The higher long-term mortality in the detained patients is due to selection factors associated with an intractable illness.
The British Journal of Psychiatry 175: 147-153 (1999)
© 1999 The Royal College of Psychiatrists.

committed fasting. We had got time, and nobody was going to get my wine or beer, I told myself.

By Sunday, there was a major concern that Candy, having not eaten for five days, might be at some risk. A quick electrolyte check showed normal sodium and potassium levels. I left instructions again not to jump up and down and worry too much. I was quite sure she must have been secretly drinking, perhaps not from her own jug. Often other patients would "help", not quite comprehending how their "help" might indeed be a "hindrance". I have even seen nurses "helping" to dispose of patient's food or even eat it. Anorexia stirs up funny emotions.

By the time I got in on Monday, Sophie, Candy's nurse said to me, "I think you had better see Candy. There has been no change at all." This was in some ways quite unusual as most of the time the consultant in charge only gets involved in family meetings and reviews that are pre-planned. Junior doctors deal with the day to day checking on patients. Perhaps she was somehow hoping that I would give in and put Candy back on tube-feeding.

I think if there had been a NICE guideline[3], I might not have been given this chance. Instead some on-call doctor over the weekend would have put her on tube-feeding as per protocol. After all, that had been her mode of feeding for weeks.

We would use the law if and when it became necessary.

However, that would have defeated the whole point, as she would have been stuck with the old ways forever.

Stubborn patients deserve stubborn doctors.

Candy came in.

---

[3] NICE guidelines for eating disorders were not issued until January 2004, some years after this case.

"Aren't you going to tube feed me?"

"No."

"Then I will die."

"So I will be very sad but we do not tube feed here." At least I don't.

"You can't do that. I want to be discharged."

These are more or less verbatim reports. My mind was racing fast trying to come up with an answer.

"I want to be discharged!"

"Candy, it is actually possible."

I can still remember the look of horror on Sophie's face: "Is this doctor for real?"

"You mean discharged today?"

"Yes. I mean today."

I could see Sophie was in complete shock. "What planet did this consultant drop out of and how is he going to pull this one off?"

"Well. If you start off by drinking one carton of Ensure Plus and some squash, then eat your lunch and have another Ensure Plus in the afternoon, you will be discharged home and you can come back daily."

When I used this case in my teaching sessions with junior doctors, they invariably showed incredulity that I offered this to Candy just like that, without consulting her parents or her nurse. I knew that if there had been any discussion it would never have happened. There would have been objections from somewhere. That is the trouble with consensus.

But you see, it was important for Candy to know that I had authority. Many adolescent units have gone too far the other way, and they really are a reflection of dysfunctional families where the adolescent rules the roost. A totally democratic approach will never produce the thunderbolt and deliver the sustainable therapeutic effect.

A strange bond was developing between me and Candy. I gave her a way out and she would oblige. I had no doubt at all she would be compliant.

Sophie then went to fetch exactly what I told Candy she needed to consume. When Sophie came back, the drinks went down in seconds. I could see the relief and disbelief in Sophie's eyes.

That took seven minutes.

And now the real work began: the details. I told Candy she would be discharged as an inpatient and would need to come in every day as a day-patient. A trick you might say.

She did not object.

She never expected to be discharged in her state. The important thing was that I took control. For her it was a relief. She never protested that I perhaps tricked her. It too was a relief for her to have something in her stomach. What was more important was I saved her face and she, mine.

I was to stay on in the show.

How could I justify sending a fragile fasting patient home on the first day of resumption of eating?

For five days we achieved nothing when she was in hospital.

What about the parents?

In fact I phoned mother in front of Candy straight away. I played a trick on her. I just said, "Candy is coming home." A long silence indicated how shocked she was. Then I told her of our seven minutes.

"I knew you could do something. That was what I told my husband, but I did not know it was going to be this quick. I did tell him you were OK."

You can wait for years for a case like this. It is like a hole-in-one. You just know the moment the ball leaves the tee. With one such case, I could now put up with anything anyone cared to throw at me.

At least for a while.

To Candy, it was like a heart transplant. She had been stuck for too long and was probably pleased to get out. Hospital was not like home and she had not been home for a long long time.

So where is Candy now?

She was eventually discharged to attend a state school but that did not work. She eventually went to an agricultural college where she worked mainly with horses and did extremely well. Her weight was well maintained. That took another fourteen months.

But she remained a day patient throughout except for a long weekend when her parents went away for their anniversary. At Candy's request, she stayed in the hospital that weekend.

Chapter 2   SARS, Freedom and Knowledge

Thirty years ago, I saw mountains as mountains, and waters as waters.
When I arrived at a more intimate knowledge, I came to the point
where I saw that mountains are not mountains, and waters are not waters.
Thirty years on,
I see mountains once again as mountains, and waters once again as waters.

Adapted from Ching-yuan[4] (1067-1120)

In 2003 the world was in the grip of a new plague that challenged our knowledge of medicine to its limit.

For the first time, doctors and nurses who were normally in the forefront of the fight against diseases were fighting for survival from SARS[5] (Severe Acute Respiratory Syndrome), a new and

---

[4] Adapted from a famous Zen saying by Zen Master Ching Yuan about perceptions before and after enlightenment.
http://www.geocities.com/dharmawood/mountains_and_rivers.htm

[5] SARS: see WHO guidelines for the global surveillance of severe acute respiratory syndrome.
http://www.who.int/csr/resources/publications/WHO_CDS_CSR_ARO_2004_1.pdf

dangerously contagious disease. The alarm was first raised by its first victim, Carlo Urbani[6]. He was an Italian physician employed by the World Health Organisation (WHO) and based in Hanoi, Vietnam and he gave the disease its current name. It was as if this newly mutated virus knew what it was on about. Get the doctors as they would be the first who could deal with you. Urbani died. So did some of the medical staff that attended the first few patients.

Doctors often thought that they would be immune, a God given right I suppose. Not so this time! The virus obviously knew what it was doing.

Our knowledge base was in total chaos. What we knew was obviously not good enough. Nor were the most up to date antiviral drugs. Even then in some places they were sold out as rumours spread. There were rumours too of vinegar and certain dietary items giving protection to certain ethnic groups, notably Koreans[7] . The lack of knowledge about this new infective agent led to the great proliferation of myths that were soon spreading like wild fire on the Internet. Anyone with cold symptoms was treated as if he was carrying the plague. It was the plague, the new plague.

Without any sound knowledge authorities took draconian measures – any measure anyone could dream up. Some worked well if only to raise public awareness. One actually caused more harm and unfortunately deaths. That was the restriction of movement in one of the tower blocks in Hong Kong – a true

---

[6] Dr. Carlo Urbani of the World Health Organization died of SARS
http://www.who.int/csr/sars/urbani/en/

[7] Korean remedy for SARS: It is believed that the eating of "Kimchi" may have helped.
http://news.bbc.co.uk/2/hi/asia-pacific/4347443.stm

quarantine. In the absence of insight into how the infection was spread, more people were infected. Some broke the law and fled the buildings before the quarantine. Unfortunately 321 people were infected and 42 died. Eventually someone was sensible enough to move them to another quarantine site. Otherwise there would have been more deaths.

Canada's hasty decision[8] to declare its virus free status when so little was known about the virus proved costly and further eroded the public's trust in governments and people in positions of influence. Clinicians' view no longer seemed to hold any sway where commercial interest was more important.

Except in Canada, one advice was almost universally adopted – the wearing of a mask. During this time, I was in correspondence with many of my medical colleagues and relatives in Hong Kong and Canada. One thing was clear: even the most difficult child complied and wore a mask. To this day one still needs to wear the appropriate mask to visit someone in hospital in Hong Kong, on top of having a dollop of alcohol gel to sterilize one's hands. Many clinics require patients and staff to do the same.

Now this must be the clearest lesson to every parent in every land. *Where life and death is concerned, there can be no compromise.*

So it started me thinking about my practice, specifically Anorexia Nervosa and other difficult cases that I have encountered. Take Anorexia, it may have been unnecessarily classified as a mental illness, given that it is the result of the parents giving the individuals concerned too much right and freedom for self

---

[8] Globe and Mail, Toronto May 31 2003 SARS: A Costly Error
http://www.healthcoalition.ca/sars2.pdf)

determination. If a child can be made to wear an uncomfortable mask, why can parents not make a child eat?

The answer may lie with our view of freedom. Many parents of Anorexia Nervosa sufferers are highly educated, and some hold high positions in big corporations and even in Health Authorities. Many are professionals. Many have a great respect for individual freedom and self-determination and unfortunately they get caught in a bind of not being able to be authoritarian as far as their own children are concerned. It is not difficult to see why many parents of Anorexia Nervosa sufferers are not prepared to give up being a modern parent, and until they do, we psychiatrists will have to soldier on with the difficult task of treating what need not necessarily be an illness, let alone a mental one.

My second thought is that when something as familiar as chest infection can turn out to be a deadly new plague called SARS, we need to examine again the relationship between our existing knowledge and medical practice. We have to keep an open mind. What we know from the past should be an aid, not a hindrance. Otherwise *we shall never see the mountains and waters for what they really are.*

Chapter 3   Barbados and Retirement

Barbados, as everyone knows, is an island in the Caribbean. We had never taken a holiday in the Caribbean and it was a shock to friends and colleagues when news broke that we were moving there.

It may seem ironic given my love for my work that I could give it up so easily. The truth is that the unrelenting re-organisation after re-organisation in the NHS had finally taken its toll. I first arrived on this tropical island to accompany my wife to take up a two year posting with her employer less than a week after September 11. We had no idea where the world was heading and if there was going to be any world conflict Barbados seemed to be far enough away from where those conflicts might be. We first stayed in a hotel right by the sea on one of the loveliest beaches in Barbados that to this day remains our favourite.

We arrived in the evening, and in Barbados when the sun goes down it becomes pitch black immediately. Imagine the surprise in the morning when I pushed open the door to the small balcony overlooking the beach and saw the loveliest blue sea that only the white coral sand and Caribbean September sky could conspire to provide. Pure white coral sand tinged with pink and beckoning palm trees complete with gentle surfs was a sight too much to resist.

There is a Buddhist saying: *Better save one life than build a seven-storey pagoda.* I felt that I had done my duty as a doctor, and could now retire and let the younger generation take over. It would be dishonest of me not to mention my frustration with recent changes in the NHS – no, not changes for the better. The havoc on my physical health together with events of September 11 were the final straw.

I remember bumping into one of the neurologists who retired a year earlier from my hospital. We more or less started at the hospital around the same time and most years we managed to meet up at Glyndebourne.

Glyndebourne is one of those places that started life as a private opera house. The small and intimate opera house proved too small and eventually a new opera house with much bigger capacity was built in its place. Fortunately the gardens were left relatively intact and every year from late spring to late summer operas are performed every evening with an extended interval so that patrons can have a nice champagne picnic in the grounds. Most patrons continue with the Black Tie tradition and the few dissenters just look out of place. It was during one of the dinner intervals as I was ready to open a bottle of champagne when I saw the neurologist. When he learnt that I too was contemplating retirement, he exclaimed, "There is a hell of a lot of life after the NHS, you know."

It was not necessary for him to have said anything as my mind was already made up. On a sunny afternoon in the beautiful setting of Sussex countryside cows grazed on the other side of the ha-ha. How many hours do they have to graze in order to produce a pint of milk for the coffee that we nicely dressed humans consume? Is there a lesson there somewhere?

It is not that difficult to decide that there is more to it than to continue to toil under politicians all purporting to do their absolute best. We all started off with high hopes. Hope for a better health service. Hope for humanity and mankind.

As my first guru and mentor in England put it when I called him with the news of my consultant appointment, "You now only have your retirement to look forward to." How right he was.

Chapter 4   The Cockroach Catcher

The ability to dissect out a full set of cockroach salivary glands was a prerequisite requirement for medical school entrance in Hong Kong in our days.   It is almost a 180 degree turn around nowadays when many young doctors have no idea about the biological world we live in. Nearly all Medical Schools in England no longer specify biology as a prerequisite subject for anybody who wishes to embark on the study of the human body. As we are so intertwined with the rest of the living biological world I find this policy quite extraordinary.

Do you think that there is a conspiracy to limit our knowledge so that everything can be kept under control? Or do you think political correctness has run amok and medical schools dare not exclude people for their dislike of the natural world?

But why should there be a conspiracy about anything at all? Foolhardiness is sometimes seen by too many clever people as conspiracy.

I have my own theory of cockroach salivary glands.

In our days in Hong Kong, there was only one single medical school and many bright pupils fought to get a place. So it was highly competitive. Most years the intake was for about sixty five as there was a limit in the anatomy dissection room. Dissecting the salivary glands requires not only anatomical knowledge of the said cockroach but also a degree of manual dexterity.

So there you have it. Manual dexterity is required in many branches of medicine. Little did our teachers know in those days that those same salivary glands are now being studied for neuro-transmitters. Without this knowledge, there would have been a delay in the creation of Prozac. Would that have been a blessing or a curse?

Insects, on the other hand, are very much enjoying a comeback. Come to think of it, they have never gone away. True to form as a good predator, they are not only capable of transmitting diseases, but are also able to do so without even causing much discomfort in their prey sometimes for as long as twenty years. You may think this happens only in Africa or deep in the rainforests of South America and East Asia. Not so. What about Blue Nile in Manhattan; Japanese encephalitis in Hong Kong; and Dengue in a wide tropical band that spreads from Hawaii to Indonesia?

There is always Malaria.

So do we believe that we can be doctors without knowing too much about insects[9]?

As it happens, when my family eventually left the city of Kowloon for the rural New Territories in the early fifties, we rented a semi-restored village stone house half way up the hill in a small village called Kam Shan (literal translation being "forbidden hill", although some years later it was changed to "beautiful hill" as the two Chinese words sound very similar).

We had lived in town for at most three months, and in some ways the move was a bit of a relief. Our home in town was on the third floor, directly above an abattoir. The noise started at four in the morning and I once woke up to have a peep and realised how somebody had to work for our meals. Witnessing the slaughtering once was quite enough for a five year old. The apartment was in many ways restrictive and it was in the market place of Kowloon. A rough area so to speak. So much is made of uprooting children nowadays. I was pleased that we moved.

Many years later, I ventured back to the same street. The buildings were still there, just about. But the abattoir had long since moved to modern premises. There used to be areas in Kowloon that no developer would imagine developing, but that has changed, with the old Kai Tak airport moved and height restrictions lifted. I would not be too sorry to see that part of Kowloon redeveloped.

---

[9] Doctors do not have to know about insects: a number of Medical Schools in the UK no longer require A level Biology. Johns Hopkins Medical School still requires Biology so did the majority of US medical schools.

http://www.ucas.com/candq/curr2000/medical06.pdf

http://www.hopkinsmedicine.org/admissions/apps.html

In fact, the new home in the New Territories remained my home for the whole of my growing up years. Certain features about it still invoke some fond memories.

It was originally a two storey house, but the roof and first floor probably fell into disrepair and the owner basically removed the top floor and rented out the place as a one storey dwelling. A tin roof of various combinations was put on to keep out the rain. There were some corrugated asbestos sheets as well. Asbestos sheets were widely used for roofing in those days. Some were just corrugated iron sheets which of course rusted with time. I have a suspicion that once upon a time the house had a proper old fashioned tile roof but that was most likely destroyed in a typhoon. The house consisted of two units side by side, in a semi-detached fashion, and my father managed to persuade our neighbours from Swatow to move into the other one. That is one sure way of maintaining your neighbourhood. We stayed as neighbours until all the children had grown up.

In many ways it had a feel of a Chinese village house typical of the south that I later came to recognise through my travels into China. Each unit had a giant wooden front door that had huge wooden shutters on the inside to secure it at night. On the outside you could lock it by a push bar and padlock. The kitchens were in a separate one floor building separated from the main house by a narrow open but walled courtyard. It kept the place safe, and also gave us free access to our neighbours' house through the back doors, which were never locked.

Being in the countryside meant that we were about five minutes by train to a nice little beach in Taipo. For many years, that little beach was the main recreational spot for the family and for those of our relatives who lived in the city but came to visit. I can remember snorkelling at an early age and anyone who knows about Hong Kong will agree that in those days the water was unpolluted with fishes a-plenty. A little stream flowed across the bottom of the hill in front of us and we spent many weekends fishing there, especially during the winter when it was too cold to swim.

Without a proper job, my father, who managed an airport in China before fleeing to Hong Kong, decided he would like to try his hand at poultry farming – ducks, pigeons, chicken and turkey. The farm was right by the river and so it was convenient for us children to be engaged in fishing or exploring the nearby ponds. At the time I had no idea that my school friends in the city did not have such activities and more importantly such fun.

I later realised in medical school that I was probably amongst three or four of the poorest in the class. I never felt out of place in secondary school as I attended a government school (the equivalent of a state school in U.K. and a public school in U.S.). Rich kids normally attended subsidised or private schools. Medical school was where I had the first shock to my system.

At the time, two of the porters at the Airport where my father was general manager also came to Hong Kong with him. They built a hut at the farm and basically they were the main workers for the farm.

The farm was to be closed rather unexpectedly. There was nothing wrong with the running of it; and business was good. But "Bird Flu" struck and it struck bad, literally wiping out our whole stock. No farm along the river was spared. The sight of dead poultry was horrible. I do not know how they were cleared, but cleared they were, probably by the government.

Thus my father's little entrepreneurial venture came to an abrupt end. I do not think he really ever recovered from that as he never went into another business venture and became very cautious. He first found a job at a camera shop through one of my uncles, the husband of the aunt with the heart condition. Thus I was introduced early to cameras and photography. However, this job lasted only a few months as he soon found work in a major insurance company. As my father was English educated it stood him in good stead with a British firm. He was to stay with the same firm until he retired.

The two porters were grateful my father gave them some breathing space at the farm. I was not to know until much later that the good deed my father did to have them running the farm was to be very important for my medical career later. Life comes round in mysterious ways.

After the disaster at the farm, they moved to Shek Kip Mei and squatted where most refugees did. They then opened a small grocery shop and later they opened a second one. The great fire of 1953 of course destroyed their shops. Luckily they managed to get re-housed and continued to run grocery shops. They continued to come to visit my parents and our neighbours during Chinese festivals and Chinese New Year. At Chinese New Year they always showed up. It is considered disrespectful if you do not go and see relations during the Chinese New Year period.

Much later these same people were to lend money to my father interest-free to see me through Medical School. It was an age when nobody put a price on favours. There was no expectation of any "return" – a favour was just a favour, without pre-condition. What I never realised was how much money two totally uneducated individuals eventually made. They owned a number of apartments and became quite well off. Yet they started in a shanty town, living in cardboard huts with no water or sanitation.

Not that we had mod cons in our home either. At least we had tap water, but for a long time we did not have electricity. Toilet was essentially a spittoon, which some years later was replaced by a slightly more civilised bucket with a toilet seat on top. What luxury at last. I shall not bore you with methods of emptying and so on, but will just say that the contents would be emptied into a huge earthen container right at the back of the house. This in turn we paid for someone to empty at regular intervals. That was when we children would rather be out somewhere than face the stench.

Perhaps that was why I only ever had one girl friend and her first and only visit (which she insisted on) was probably more traumatic for me than for her; but she did become my wife despite all that. Perhaps that was a real test of love.

The lack of electricity meant we had to be without a fridge. Food was not such a problem as my mother used to go to the market twice a day. However, my father had a good job in China, and the family was used to some luxury before coming to Hong Kong. There were evenings in China when ice-cream making was the fun highlight. In our new home, we no longer had the old fashioned ice-cream churner that we had in China, so the next best thing for the children was jelly. As I became older I was allowed to go to the market to buy an ice-block for eighty cents. I would also be given an extra ten cents to ride at the back of a bicycle back to prevent too much melting of the ice in the heat. The others would have stirred the jelly mixture and all would be eagerly waiting for the ice block to turn up. My father had got everything down to a fine art. A wash-basin would be commissioned for the purpose and the whole set-up would be covered by a lid of sorts to be further insulated by layers of rice sacks. Invariably someone would take a peep now and again and announce the readiness of the jelly. This was to be shared by all the children and I cannot really remember if the adults ever had any.

We had fun and we never complained that we were bored. Looking back, I realise that we did not have a chance to get bored. We were so close to nature. Fly-catchers and other exotic plants were in abundance. We had guava, banana, papaya and we still kept chickens and turkeys.

We once even encountered a python, not to mention other poisonous and not so poisonous snakes. None ever really bothered us.

One main disadvantage of living in the countryside was the omnipresence of insects. We slept under mosquito nets all the time, which also helped to keep out the other insect which was really the topic of my earlier discussion – cockroaches. Cockroaches would even nibble at toes if they touched the net.

Any food in the kitchen had to be kept in a special home-made cupboard that had netting all round, and had legs standing in tins filled with water. To prevent rotting of the wooden legs, small jam jars were used to protect the wood. Each jam jar was in turn put in a tin – normally milk powder tins. This device kept out both cockroaches and ants.

Each night when the kerosene lights were blown out, within minutes the cockroaches would be out in force. They would be after any leftover crumbs, rice or any traces of cooking oil or sauces. Leftover food inside the food cupboard still attracted cockroaches, which attached themselves to the netting in their eager attempt to get in. They could spend a long time trying and such insect behaviour was closely observed by me from an early age.

I still vaguely remember the few times when the family returned to our ancestral home in the village of Chun Nim. The excitement of the new environment meant that I would refuse to fall asleep. The maid at the time would carry me on her back in a silk sling. She would alternate between singing a Teochiu[10] lullaby and producing her ultimate weapon – a huge live cockroach kept in a match box. Just as well they did not have child psychiatrists in those days or I would have been pronounced traumatised for life with a specific phobia of cockroaches.

As it turned out I became a cockroach catcher. I developed different ways of catching them without causing any damage and the best was to use milk powder tins. Some left over rice used to do wonders.

---

[10] Teochiu dialect – Teochiu, also called Chaozhou, Teochew, Teochiu, Tiuchiu, or Diojiu, is a dialect of the Chinese spoken variant of Min Nan, spoken in the Chaoshan region of eastern Guangdong. Both my parents originated from this region.

You would not be surprised that these same cockroaches put me ahead of others in my ultimate pursuance of a medical career. Inadvertently, I became the sole purveyor of huge live cockroaches and the sole supplier to the rest of my class. I also became the unofficial guide for our class biology field trips. Our biology teacher used to leave it to me to take her and the rest of the class to prime sites for the study of wild plants and pond life.

I did secretly practise on the dissection of the said insect and getting good marks for biology was never a problem.

Chapter 5   The Village

I had two friends from my village in the New Territories who were my inspiration. On school days they used to play Bridge on the train, to a very high level too. Their parents would have been horrified to see that, and yet despite all this time not spent on studying, they both got a scholarship to the university. At the residential hall in university, they also played Bridge regularly, but only for a brief time after dinner.

While attending university we all gave private tuition to aspiring future university hopefuls. There was a belief amongst the wealthy families that the number one choice for someone to tutor their child would be a medical student. One of my two friends was so popular that he ran out of time and passed two of his pupils on to me.

My other friend knew how tight my financial situation was and lent me the half skeleton that we all needed to have until we passed the Anatomy examination which was at the end of the first year.

How our family came to live in the village I never know. Price must have been a key consideration. It would have been much cheaper to live there than in town in Hong Kong or Kowloon. For many years, to get into town required a commute by train. We went through the age of steam to diesel and of course nowadays it is electric.

One of our aunts who must have been around sixty at the time came from China to Hong Kong with us. She was a great help to my mum, doing most of the cooking, washing and cleaning chores. She spoke our Chinese home village dialect of Teochiu and, seldom venturing beyond the front of the garden, never managed to learn the Cantonese dialect commonly spoken in Hong Kong. My mother paid her some pocket money and occasionally she went down the hill to the corner store. It was years later when she was admitted to hospital in a diabetic coma that we realised that she had been hoarding sweets and jars and jars of sugar. I had just graduated from medical school then and I still often blame myself for not spending enough time at home during my medical studies to recognise that. She was one of the few women I knew who had bound feet – a fetish allegedly ascribed to the Chinese men that I, as an open minded psychiatrist, fail to comprehend; and how quickly the fetish died.

It was perhaps unusual but we and our neighbours got along well. Traditional Chinese courtesy probably saw to it that nobody took advantage of anybody. I think most friendship that lasts is when no party tries to take advantage of the other. There was a lot of give though. Now the children have all grown up and some of the older generation have passed away. We do not see one another that often, but when we do we are still very close. During Chinese festivals there was always much sharing of food, and that was traditional style Teochiu food that I have come to miss. And I miss them a great deal too.

I remember going out to the fields with my mother to pick certain "weeds" for want of a better word. These were pounded and mixed with rice flour to make one of the best tasting desserts. These cakes filled with sweet red bean paste were steamed and left to stand in piles. When visitors came round during the Chinese New Year, some would be fried and served. They were supposed to cleanse your system which I am not sure about. I know one thing though: it beats wheatgrass drink any day.

There is so much in the natural world that we have not yet fathomed. But before we have a chance to think about it, developers come in, concrete the place up and what might one day be a cure for some illness is wiped out. This reminds me of the story of Artemesinin[11], now reckoned to be the most powerful anti-malaria drug. It was recorded in the Chinese book of Herbal Medicine, which is over a thousand years old, as treatment for

[11] Artemesinin is derived from the plant Artemisia annua that has been used in China for at least 2000 years for a variety of conditions including swamp fever. To date it proved to be highly effective and is relatively free of side effects and the build up of resistance. It is now the recommended drug by WHO in combination for the treatment of malaria.
http://www.who.int/malaria/cmc_upload/0/000/015/364/RBMInfosheet_9.htm
http://www.msf.org/msfinternational/invoke.cfm?objectid=2F169856-4D66-4E90-B49E02C3EAE4F496&component=toolkit.report&method=full_html

swamp fever. Its rediscovery by China was met with scepticism until it was noted that during the Sino-Indian conflict Chinese soldiers were not dying from the malaria that was rampant in that part of the world. For a long time, the Chinese did not share the findings with the rest of the world. By chance along the banks of Potomac River, specimens of the plant were found. It took some years before the drug was developed. By now it is the standard treatment of choice.

I know how lucky I was to have the opportunity at an early age to be exposed to a world still very much in its raw state. It set up for me a life long interest in living things and the environment in which we live. Our good neighbours had two boys and two girls whereas I had three younger sisters. We were never allowed to play in the streets though, and as a result I was not what you would call streetwise.

Our local government primary school did not start until the fourth year. I have now worked out that it was the government's crafty way of selection. Education was not compulsory then. This became a kind of perpetual embarrassment to the then British Colonial Government in later years. The fact that education was not compulsory was generally brushed aside in any official documentation. Parents had to pay school fees for their children in any school, government or privately run. The Government schools were cheaper but in fact had higher standards on the whole, unless you could afford the elite schools which were generally run by the Anglican or Catholic Church.

Being late for the year's entrance, my father had to enrol me in a rather rough school in a rough neighbourhood quite far away.

A good half hour's walk. My three sisters were younger than me and so I was the first to go to school.

My father had good martial arts training and my wife always maintained that his good posture and good health were partly due to that. He lived to ninety two. In his wisdom he taught me some martial arts moves for self defence purposes.

Well, I lasted in that school for one half-day. Dressed in a pristine white school uniform, I realised that I was in some sort of a peculiar environment. These boys were a head taller than me. They looked dirty and they looked rough. I kept my head down and tried to work out what to do. I cannot remember a thing about the teacher except she sounded tired and was always shouting. At break time this boy wanted to know what was in my pencil box. I declined to show him and he tried to punch me in the stomach. It is strange how something that is still fresh in your mind can rush to your defence. I put my father's martial arts lesson to immediate use. Not only did I avoid getting punched, but I even managed to return his "compliments".

Unfortunately, my defensive move was seen by the teacher. She kept me to one side and at lunch time when mum brought my lunch, the teacher told her I was too violent for her school. She returned the month's school fees and off we went.

Most parents would have given me a wallop and a good telling off. My mother only asked: are you all right? It is so good to have parents who know and trust you. Even then I knew I was not wrong, and so did my mother. My father actually had a good laugh with our neighbour. They all agreed that it was too rough a school and I did not start school again till the next September. In any case I was not even six and back then children did not start school till six, although private schools would take your money whatever.

My father was still running the farm then. He decided to teach me and get me to recite classical Chinese texts at home. I had been to Kindergarten (nursery school) in China and was already reading and writing and had good number sense. I do not see this as something unusual – our grand niece of four in Hong Kong can do the same. Some of the Classical Chinese I can remember and recite to this day. An excerpt from one of these I incorporated in the eulogy at my father's funeral.

Temporarily freed from school, I had more time to do other things and to get to know the village and our new home.

Across the farm separated by a river was the railway. The railway track was elevated so there was a slope of at least 30 feet which ended in a 12 feet wall of granite blocks that held the river embankment together - very solid engineering indeed. The embankment was the best place to fish and we had to cross the river to get there. There was a man-made crossing of boulders, but it made for a very interesting crossing as only the older kids had long enough strides. The younger ones had to be carried. Only the older children were allowed to handle the hooks and bait but we all had fun. A bamboo stick was used as the rod and a fishing line was tied to one end. The best places were the side tributaries where the flow slowed down. In the stagnant bits of water could be found abundant little fishes, mosquito larvae and rich pond life. We used a small net to get the smaller fishes and kept them in little fishing bowls complete with other plants that we found in the river. When they died off we replenished the bowls with new ones. Some of the best things in life are free.

During weekends in the summer the whole family often took the train to Taipo Kau for a beach outing. Back in Swatow in China, we had a very nice beach resort and in the late forties it was well equipped with a huge cabana built of bamboo and timber. I am not sure if one needed to pay but I remember having great pleasure learning to swim and playing with the sand. That tradition continued with the discovery of this little cove in Taipo Kau, Kau being the Chinese word for cove. It used to have a government built swimming hut but that had been left to rot. Nevertheless, the beach was attractive in many ways. We improvised and constructed our own special awning with a big square piece of cloth supported by four upright bamboos. The bamboos were held to the ground by two strings each. That gave us shelter from the sun. The beach proved to be a major attraction for the relatives who first gave us shelter when we came to Hong Kong. In fact they were relatives of my aunt in Bangkok. Three or four families were involved and very few would miss such a Sunday outing in the summer season.

One of the main drawbacks of the beach was that a few places had rocks that were stuck with oyster shells. These had sharp edges and they could easily cut a wandering foot or arm. Soon enough the grown-ups mapped out where these were. These outings must have lasted a good dozen years and are still remembered fondly as highlights of our childhood. Such outings also fostered the friendship between the children. Our neighbours often joined us with their four children. Their mother was a good swimmer and I used to admire how she could cover great distances without much effort.

This cove was also where I first learned to snorkel. In those days we had snorkels that had a ping pong ball at the top end – a sort of umbrella handle at the top with the ping pong ball inside a little cage so that it floated up to stop water coming in.

As time became taken up with studies such beach activities came to a stop. The sea became rather polluted with the increase in population, and the water no longer clear for snorkelling. Going to the seaside became an activity for an annual class outing and later something to do with one's girl friend.　Now the beach has been filled in and 20-storey high buildings stood where we once snorkelled and swam.

When I moved to U.K. snorkelling became a thing of the distant past. Imagine the shock when we went to the Great Barrier Reef some years later and were given snorkels that bore no resemblance to the ones I used in childhood[12]. There was no ping pong ball in a cage and there was a drain at the bottom. The top was slightly curved with a clever design so that water from waves could not get in. Any water that managed to get in was drained away at the bottom. I looked at it and smiled. One must always question traditional beliefs. We can be blinded by what looks like a most sensible and reasonable approach – ping pong ball in a cage.

---

[12] Snorkel - Some modern snorkels have a sump in the mouthpiece to allow a small volume of water to remain in the snorkel without being inhaled when the diver breathes. Some also have a one-way output valve in the sump, which automatically drains the sump as it fills with water. http://www.wisegeek.com/what-is-a-snorkel.htm

Our house looked down into a fertile valley of small holdings of orchards and other poultry farms. A large part of the whole area was covered by rice paddy fields.

Yes, I was fortunate enough to have seen the traditional Chinese paddy fields and observed the full sowing to harvest cycle. We passed these fields on our way to the farm. The cycle started with the seedlings which were grown tightly together, then the transplanting when the seedlings were pulled and spaced out in rows. Rice started life with flooded paddy fields. An ingenious flooding system was in place and where required special foot operated water transporting systems were installed. These were like stationary cycles and they were mostly operated by women. Nowadays modern people pay a high price to do the same in a gym. They were mainly Ha Ka women (the Chinese equivalent for Aboriginals) and they wore traditional black wide rim hats and black silk pant suits. The same black silk is now used in haute couture with a high price tag. I have never worked out the reason for the black colour but perhaps it is 100% UV opaque.

Fresh seedlings were beautiful before planting out. They had a fresh green colour that was so attractive that the image was permanently imprinted in my memory. Think Wheatgrass next time you see it at a juice bar and then spread it out to two or three fields. Two or three fields are all you need for your imagination.

Before the planting out, there was the ploughing. As rice was mostly grown in clay soil, the ploughing was done when the fields were flooded. The plough was pulled by a huge "Water Buffalo", a very clever animal that could heed verbal commands. There was no John Deer or Toro and no petrol or diesel fumes either, but always a young boy who looked after the buffalo. He was responsible for taking the buffalo to its grazing field. He rode it as depicted in many Chinese paintings and he was known as the "Watch Buffalo Kid". What about school you may ask. Remember? There was no compulsory education.

The planting out was interesting for the speed with which it was done. As if by magic what were just rectangular sections of water-filled fields became suddenly dotted at regular intervals with little green plants. The first bit of growing was quite boring visually. When the plants got to about two feet the beautiful green colour returned, only more so and more spectacular. As the wind blew you could imagine a beautiful green sea. This only lasted a brief time, before the rice field was drained dry and the ears formed and turned golden.

Then came harvest – no Combines either. Everything was done by hand. Special bashing stations were set up so that the rice stalks could be thrashed in the fields to separate the rice seeds. The stalks were bundled up for fuel and rice seeds put into carts and taken to various village houses where they were spread out to dry. After that they were milled to get rid of the husks and to produce the best tasting "new rice" of the season. These farm houses also had stone mills to grind the rice into flour for making the best cakes. The millstones were made of granite and the mills operated by foot. Our immediate neighbour on the left side was one such farm house and we used to get flour from them for major festivals. Rice flour is speciality flour in the west, but for us it was a standard ingredient.

We sometimes ventured deeper into the village up the gentle valley. At the end was a quite well known Taoist monastery. We took many visitors there to have pictures taken. On the way we passed through thick wooded areas where the sun could hardly peep through. There fresh mushrooms of the Chinese variety were grown – one use of the rice stalks mixed with horse manure, I was told. These too were very pretty and mysterious at the same time. The mushrooms were sun dried before being sold. Now fresh Shitake is gourmet food. Further up the valley across the small mountain range was the village of Lam Chuen, where the source of our river was. Lam Chuen was where we often went later as boy scouts to camp. We camped away from the villages and used water from the river to cook and make tea. It made the best tea in the world.

Further on from Lam Chuen was Shek Kong, where the British Air Force in Hong Kong was based. The sight of a Vampire[13] doing tricks in the air was our regular entertainment.

Going up the back we saw other villagers pick firewood. There seemed to be an unwritten rule. People picked just enough firewood for their own use. They did not harvest it to the exclusion of others. For a while we used firewood for cooking in our kitchen. The kitchen was also equipped to use straw, but straw was rather

---

[13] The Vampire is not one of the "hottest" jets ever built, many faster, better and bigger aircraft have seen the light of day since 1943. But unlike those huge and often ugly supersonic beasts the pesky little Vampire never fails to take my breath away when I see one. The Vampire has been a favourite with modellers for decades since it became the first jet aircraft operated by a very large number of air forces around the world and remained in service for a very long time. The Vampire T11, first flew in1950 and served in Britain until 1968.
http://www.brushfirewars.org/aircraft/dh_vampire_rhodesian/dh_vampire_rhodesian.htm

http://www.vampirepreservation.org.uk/aircraft.htm

smoky. That was why at meal times smoke could be seen coming out of different chimneys, not an unpleasant sight in the sunset.

Kite flying was a source of great amusement. Kites were made with special paper and split bamboo. Some boys coated the lines with ground glass and glue in order to cut other people's lines. We tended to fly ours when the big boys were fighting elsewhere. Now and again there might be an encounter but if you moved away they tended not to bother you. You might still lose the kite to the trees or to the power lines. It was great fun though.

At the back of our house was a couple of huts and then wilderness. It used to be the favourite place to climb up when we had visitors. These visitors were the same relatives who went swimming with us. When it was too cool to swim they came to our house. With fresh farm poultry and various fresh vegetables that we grew we always had great parties. From all these fairly regular meetings with relatives, we were able to glean the wider family history. The continuity provided by such contacts was, on reflection, of great value to me. There were things that your own parents might not want to talk about but other relatives might, and slowly I was able to build a better picture of life in the past, life in the Chinese village, life during the war, life in Shanghai, and life in Swatow.

After lunch the whole party would go up to the top of the mountain for a panoramic view and that view was good. The top was not difficult to reach as technically it was only a hill. Hill and mountain are the same word in Chinese. Only one aunt would have difficulty. I found out later she had Rheumatic heart disease, a crippling condition caused by a strain of Haemolytic Streptococcus.

A school friend of ours had it and several of my cousin's children had it too. The modern day drive to get doctors to cut down on the use of antibiotics may have one major effect and it is not a healthy one. There is now a resurgence of Rheumatic heart disease, Rheumatic fever and related conditions and in child psychiatry the emergence of PANDAS[14]. Perhaps these microbes have their set pattern. Such early exposure to other people's illness planted questions in my mind and I had wanted a solution. Somewhere in my heart, I wanted to be a doctor as I was very fond of that aunt.

[14] PANDAS, is an abbreviation for Pediatric Autoimmune Neuropsychiatric Disorders Associated with Streptococcal Infections. The term is used to describe a subset of children who have Obsessive Compulsive Disorder (OCD) and/or tic disorders such as Tourette's Syndrome, and in whom symptoms worsen following strep. infections such as "Strep throat" and Scarlet Fever.

Chapter 6 Medical School - The Beginning

On a bright Monday afternoon of September in 1963 I queued up outside the Registrar's Office of the University of Hong Kong to register for medical school admission. It was still hot at that time of the year in Hong Kong although the temperature was off the peak of the humid summer.

Even in those days the London Examination Boards' standards were considered at least two notches down and the University of Hong Kong decided in their wisdom to run their own matriculation examinations. Politicians seem to think that lowering the standards of public examinations to fit their political agenda is enough to fool the unsuspecting voters, who if they happen to have a child sitting the exam are only too pleased to receive the accolade of ever improving grades. The truth is indeed miles away. The average IQ scores for many populations were rising at an average rate of three points per decade during the 20th century with most of the increase in the lower half of the IQ range: a phenomenon called the Flynn effect. It is disputed whether these changes in scores reflect real changes in intellectual abilities, or merely changes in calibration.

This is not to say that examinations are the be all and end all of all things, although it was generally seen as a major achievement to be one of the sixty or so freshmen admitted at that time to the only Medical School of the colony. Only a small percentage of those school graduates who aspired to study medicine were lucky enough to get a place. The elite subsidized schools might fare better overall but the variations from year to year were enormous. The year above us in our government grammar school achieved over 50% admission and that was exceptional by any standard.

Of course a bit of luck was involved as well. Quite a few of our classmates who did not make it have done very well overseas, mainly in U.S. and in Canada. There were too few places and in a race, someone was going to be left out – loss to Hong Kong but gain for other countries. With a high concentration of families who had the vision to escape Communist rule, one could expect a higher than average concentration of high achievers amongst their descendents.

So there I was with my classmate. In our class of twenty two, we were the only two accepted. Although feeling outnumbered, we were quite excited to meet for the first time our future "window-mates" for the next five years – in Chinese to study together is described as sharing the same windows. Although time has washed away some less memorable past, my first encounter with some of my fellow medical school students was quite permanently imprinted. The quiet ones would remain the quiet ones and the flamboyant and rather manic ones would stay so. I remember meeting one of them who was very friendly and introduced himself. After a near twenty year gap when I returned to Hong Kong he called to refer a patient to me and he sounded exactly like he was when I first met him.

It was an interesting time. Most of us in Hong Kong were "refugees" from the communist uprising in China. There were those from families that had recovered quickly through running their own business. There were a few whose families were based in Hong Kong and survived the Japanese occupation. They prospered ahead of those like my family who arrived after 1949. Other families might have been able to get money out of China before the final collapse. In all it was a curious "mixed up" society where the class structure was quite different to that of say Britain.

Here I was, standing outside one of Hong Kong's finest examples of colonial buildings, ready to take the first step into a future that I had not even started to imagine.

Unlike some other courses, Medicine was a pretty tough one and required a good deal of difficult memory work for which there was no short cut. Being clever helped but not if you did not work.

The registrar was a most formidable lady and we felt like school boys again. No. Here. No. There. No respect for the future doctors, we all thought. When I look back now, she was right. We were sky high and someone needed to bring us down to earth and she would not be the last one either.

Now we were ready.

Or were we?

Medical schools around the world at the time were still using traditional methods of teaching, as Problem Based Learning (PBL)[15] was still very much in its infancy. One of the first rites of passage for any medical student was the *cadaver*. The very first lesson ever was Anatomy Dissection. To access the dissection room we had to go through the small anatomy museum where partly dissected cadavers preserved in formalin filled casings greeted us as we hurried upstairs. We all tried to put on a brave face although there was no hiding the fact that even for future doctors this was a momentous time. Years of traditional belief in ghosts and after-life in our collective psyche could not help but be at play. We were confident in only one thing. We needed the knowledge to serve humanity better. The poor souls of these unclaimed bodies that formed the main source of the cadavers were not aware of the critical role they played, but for that we were grateful. At least they would be given a proper burial at the end of our five terms of detailed study.

With hindsight, I cannot be entirely sure that the dissection was an essential part of our medical education. Could a formalin hardened shrunken cadaver teach us more than a modern computer

---

[15] Problem-based learning (PBL) in medical education began with the Faculty of Medicine at McMaster University in Canada in the mid 1960s. From the origin at McMaster thirty years ago where the model for student-centered, problem-based, small-group learning took shape, adoption of PBL at other medical schools experienced a slow, though gradual increase through the 1970's and 1980's. Now, however, we are seeing an explosion in the use of PBL in its various adaptations. Today, most US medical schools and many in almost every country of the world are implementing (or are planning to implement) PBL in their curricula to a greater or lesser extent.
From: Problem-Based Learning: A Paradigm Shift or a Passing Fad? Gwendie Camp, PhD
http://www.med-ed-online.org/f0000003.htm

generated 3-D realisation of human anatomy? However, I am sure surgeons will agree that there is no comparison with live bodies, even if those of animals, for work like heart transplants or delicate brain surgery.

Soon we got over the initial shock and got on with the cadaver dissection. Fortnightly viva examinations did not allow time for contemplation and then there were the other basic subjects of physiology and biochemistry to learn.

However, for most of us, Anatomy remained the most unforgettable initiation, not least because the professor was one of the most awesome characters we were to meet in our whole study, perhaps equalled only by the professors of medicine and surgery who taught us later on, but the first one was bound to be most memorable.

Our anatomy professor from Cornell was in his senior years by the time we became his students. He had a stony face and wore a pair of old fashioned gold-rimmed eyeglasses that would take another twenty years before being re-popularised by Armani. Then, most of us had fashionable acrylic frames, mostly black for men and fancy coloured ones for ladies.

Early Parkinsonism did not help to soften his formidable look.

His first task in the morning was to lock the lecture room door and then take the roll call. As far as I knew, no one dared to be late or absent, so no one really knew what he would do if you were – a lesson parents could all learn.

Rumour had it that over the years he had been collecting data on *handedness* in men and the way the scrotum hang. As we all know, one side of man hangs lower than the other. The subjects were, yes you have guessed right, medical students. More interestingly he had a project on ladies too - breast asymmetry - which gave rise to his nick name of Zhai Lo, Zhai being the Cantonese slang for breasts, female breasts, not chicken ones.

What was his research tool? A camera.

We were all resigned to the fact that we would be called to his office and be photographed. Of course none of that happened and I could not find any of the immediate seniors who had their pictures taken either. The nearest to Zhai I personally witnessed was when he demonstrated the effect of tensing the Pectoris Major[16] on the breast of one fellow female medical student. He never touched her and she complied most gallantly.

All for the sake of science.

Another thing we shall all remember of our anatomy professor was how he arrived at the lecture theatre one Friday morning in 1963. He did not lock the door and did not carry the roll call book. He could hardly hide his emotion when with his crackly voice announced: "The President of the United States has just been killed. There will be no lecture today," and left the room.

We were all stunned. Some looked tearful. Others were in disbelief. Has the civilised world come to an end? Is there going to be a world war? We looked up to the world's most democratic country that had hopefully moved on from the Lincoln years. What happened?

---

[16] Pectoris Major - Pectoris Major is the muscle that goes across the front of the chest

It was some years before we had another similar earth shattering experience. Two in fact: one the discovery of the VAMP[17] cure for one form of Leukaemia and the other Barnard's heart transplant, both in our final year. Luckily these events, unlike the Kennedy assassination, gave us hope.

So went the preclinical years. The majority of us survived, and we moved on.

---

[17] VAMP treatment - VAMP is named after the initials of the chemotherapy drugs used in the treatment, which are vincristine, doxorubicin (originally called Adriamycin®) and methyl-prednisolone, which is a steroid.

Chapter 7 Morrison Hall

Robert Morrison [18] was one of the first non Catholic missionaries in China and the Chinese Missionary Society built a residential hall for the University of Hong Kong in his memory.

For "green horns" (or freshmen, a reference to a young buffalo calf so young that its horns are still green), Morrison Hall was reputed to be one of the toughest in the University. Rumour had it that some left after a month. Since my seniors from my

---

[18] Morrison Hall: Morrison Hall was the third men's hostel built for Hong Kong University students. It was established by a religious body, the London Missionary Society, in 1913 and located on Hatton Road. Rev. Robert Morrison, after whom the hostel was named, came to China in the early nineteenth century. He was an early missionary of the Society and the first translator of the Bible into Chinese. Morrisonian boys were renowned for their outstanding team spirit and sporting achievements. In 1948 after the Second World War, the Hall underwent restoration. It was used until 1968 when it was demolished. A new Morrison Hall was re-established in 2005 with the aid from the old boys.

school all joined the same Hall, I thought what was good enough for them must be good for me. There was also a matter of economics - it was the cheapest to stay in.

The biggest widely known "secret" was the ragging. Ragging was in every hall and most lasted from a few days to two weeks but ours lasted a full four weeks. It was a way of humbling the new entrants to the university and everybody said it was character building. As it was a voluntary choice to join a hall you more or less agreed to the ragging.   In those days, it was not compulsory for a freshman to stay in a residential hall.

As it turned out, the ragging was not that bad and it is something I remember with a certain degree of fondness. There was, as far as I knew, no physical or sexual side to any of the ragging.

Any senior could summon a junior, who was addressed as Green Horn, to ask him questions. It is in effect a peculiar way for the senior to get to know a junior. In reply, the "Green Horn" could only address himself as "small i" as oppose to the usual "I". Anybody who forgot had to eat a square meal, having to make the chopsticks trace a square before the food picked up could reach his mouth. The delay so caused meant that in the communal style of eating, the Green Horn would not get to eat much for that meal.

The other rather major punishment for the Green Horn was to run around wearing his shoes round his neck.

The ragging took place around the dinner table and for about an hour afterwards when the seniors played Bridge. If you were smart enough to answer well, you could get exemptions so that other seniors would not bother you for the rest of the day – a bit like Big Break on the Golf Channel. The rules of engagement were applied fairly, and juniors and seniors would in four weeks become great friends. That was the theory.

Entering Hall the first time was quite a daunting experience. One of my friends from the village advised that my parents needed not go up as it was near the peak and not accessible by public transport. What was the point of spending on the extra taxi fare that my family could ill afford? So they escorted me to as far as the Star Ferry and then I was put on a taxi to start my life as a medical student.

I did not cry when my father put me, aged four, on the plane to Hong Kong all those years ago, and I did not cry then. You could not if you were going to be a doctor. Other things helped. Hong Kong was indeed a small place so you would not be hundreds of miles from home. When our daughters went to university, they did not cry either as they had already spent some years at boarding school. Some of the boys, yes boys, were inconsolable.

I was dropped off at the front door where the male servants lined up to help and to welcome the returning Morrisonians and the Green Horns. It was such a majestic building with pillars and an entrance that was very classical English in style. There was a covered veranda all round the building. The Warden had his own flat on the south side of the building over the Chapel. Yes, a Chapel is part and parcel of the college tradition at Oxford and Cambridge, and we were no different.

For me, the contrast in living condition was phenomenal. Most people nowadays go to university to face a spartan room and in the first year you might even have a room-mate. At that time, my family home still had leaking roofs and we did not have a refrigerator, a telephone, or a flushing toilet. It was the first time in my life that I slept on a mattress. I grew up sleeping on boards with a thin rattan mat, and it was good in the hot summers but rather cold in the winters even with a layer of quilting. It was, I suppose, a welcome change.

We were each assigned our own servant, who each looked after six residents. He carried our luggage and showed us to our room. At meal times he was responsible for refilling our rice bowls or getting extra dishes that we might care to order. Those cost extra though, and the favourites were dry fried pork, beef or chicken. Whatever you ordered you had to share with the whole table of eight. I cannot remember any Green Horn daring to order extras. We kept our secret supply of food in the room such as blocks of Kraft's Cheddar, which was handy for filling hungry stomachs and required no refrigeration.

The servant also took care of the laundry. Every other day the laundry would come back nicely folded on your bed and those clothes items that needed hanging would be found hanging in the corner wardrobe.

This was in the early sixties, and there were some strange rules. If any girlfriend wanted to spend the night the mattress had to be out of the room. I never saw one in my three years stay. If you actually left your mattress outside your room, you would be inviting an audience and no self-respecting girl would ever agree to that.

In any case, the rooms were not all that private as most were separated by only partial partitions. We could actually shout to our friend in another room about some study problems. Noise was never a problem. Most of us in fact studied hard. There were just a few quite private rooms but they were reserved for the most senior at the Hall.

The freshmen stayed mostly on the ground floor and a few rooms were big ones that accommodated up to three. Round by the dining hall, on the shortcut route to the toilet and showers, were four rooms with full walls that went up to the ceiling, as opposed to partial partitions. That corner was dubbed the Russian Corner, in memory of four Russian students who were unfortunately killed fighting the Japanese during the Japanese invasion. It was rumoured to be haunted and frequented by tall ghosts - they were tall Russians.

One of the first year Malaysian engineering students managed to get one of the rooms. Within a month he had a severe manic episode. So the ghost story never went away. The student eventually went back to Malaysia. It is surprising that the Chinese philosophy of "if in doubt believe it exists" had such a strong hold even amongst the educated. Mainly those with strong religious beliefs would agree to stay in these rooms, but most did not stay for more than a year.

The north side faced the games field. Morrison Hall was located in the upper Mid-levels of Hong Kong Island, where the extreme rich lived. Yes. One of the then richest men in Hong Kong had his grand villa just opposite our entrance. Now and again we would see his Rolls Royce pull up. Of course quite a few of us would eventually achieve incomes that would put them in the 100 richest in Hong Kong, alas not those of us who went to work for the NHS in U.K.

On the south side the Warden's flat faced two tennis courts. I had a few lessons from some fellow Morrisonians who had had expensive lessons before coming to university, but never went beyond how to hold the racket and serve.

The rooms were on the west and north side looking into a central garden. The services such as laundry, kitchen and the servants' quarters were on the east side. Just at the end of the drive into our Hall was one of the many access paths to Victoria Peak, the small mountain that dominates the small island of Hong Kong. Some weekends when we were tired of studying a few of us would walk up the peak and admire the view of possibly the most beautiful small city of the world. I would not say most beautiful city, but most beautiful small city would guarantee unanimous agreement.

We had a perfect environment for studying. Daily chores were taken care of, and for physical activities there were tennis courts, a football court, and a games field for track running, and long and high jump.

Green Horns had to go into training for the annual Sports Day, one of the key events being the ten mile Inter Hall relay. Gyms or fitness centres were not widely popular as they are now. Running had to be practised on the streets. The half way mark where we turned round was the house of one of our medical classmates. They had this prestigious address because his father was a doctor. Doctors were, and still are, part of the social elite in

Hong Kong. It was a training that I enjoyed and the tough test was at the end, when we had to go up two hundred steps. Nobody was exempt unless they had a medical certificate, and nobody had one.

In the end most of us saw ragging as something positive. There were ridiculous things such as memorising the constitution of the Hall. Personal pride came in and no self-respecting university student would have a problem, except of course we had to recite the first line backwards. To this day I can still remember it even in my sleep: Club Hall Morrison Called Be Shall Club The Of Name The. You can work that one out.

One of the first year medical students refused to partake in ragging and he was left alone. He did not pass the four weeks interview and left. He still became an accomplished doctor although even in class he did not talk to anyone.

Chapter 8   Medical School -The Clinical Years

Now that the hard work of memorising where every single bit fitted within our body was over, we thought we would at last get into what we entered medical school for – seeing patients.

Another shock awaited us.

"We are starting medicine at the end," the Professor of Pathology declared as he held up the scalpel, "and we are the final arbiter!"

It would be another year before we came into contact with live patients. This of course was medicine as it had always been taught. First, dissection of the cadaver; followed by post mortem of dead patients. It is very different from some modern day medical schools where first year medical students are given an unconscious patient on assisted breathing. I am really not sure which the better way is. In any case, we did not have a choice then and we were happy for what we got.

Every day at eleven after our various lectures in the morning we were down at the mortuary for the "live" demonstration of post mortem – every day except Saturday and Sundays. Our white coats which used to reek of formalin in the preclinical cadaver dissection days now began to acquire a different stink.

Was it that surprising that whenever we went home our mothers looked worried? "Why are you getting thinner?" Not that we could afford to go home that often, what with studying and the need to grab every spare moment to be with one's girlfriend. It was a great relief to be able to get home, leaving behind those newly acquired smells and the pages and pages of medical books and graphic images of bodies on stainless steel tables. It was a relief to breathe a different air and taste food that we had taken for granted for years through our childhood.

Then there was Bacteriology at 2 p.m. The Electron Microscope was still in its infancy. The best our microscopes could do was to get to 1000X with oil immersion. Lectures were conducted with a carbon-arc lantern slide projector with its rather noisy hum. Given the then low profile of Bacteriology and the monotonous delivery of our Professor, only the highly motivated stayed awake during the postprandial period. It was time to catch up with our sleep. It has been suggested since that such cat naps are good for the brain and we started practising young. Whether it was the effect of sublimal learning that we discovered by chance, most of us managed to pass the Second M.B. examination in the subjects of Pathology and Bacteriology.

It was never my ambition to become a pathologist and be the final arbiter. Little did I know then that the months spent at the mortuary would pay off later in my career. As on-call Medical Officer at Hong Kong's only Mental Hospital, we had to perform post mortem on any death that occurred during our duty period. I was only once called to perform the job, and in front of the much experienced technicians I at least knew my way round. I was thankful that was the only time, and it was pneumonia and not something that had to involve forensics.

On to real patients.

"You might be wearing a white coat. You might look like doctors. But here you are the lowest worm!"

So our terrifying Professor of Medicine put us on the pecking order, lower of course than the cleaner and the porter. Fortunately most patients in those days had little understanding of English.

I do not think teachers nowadays can get away with comments ten times milder, not with student assessment through the Internet and unofficial blogs. Yet the few teachers whom we respect and remember most are these formidable non "politically correct" ones. Of course they would not have been respected if they had not been brilliant clinically.

Lectures on Internal Medicine by our Professor overshadowed all other lectures. First we had to be sure we studied the subject at least the night before the actual lecture. God help the few naïve enough to turn up at a lecture knowing nothing about the topic. You may ask then what the point of the lecture was. Yes, I struggled with that too. Now I realise that by that stage we were supposed to have moved beyond the spoon feeding days and we were there to interact.

There was a sort of pecking order even on where you sat. The front row was always occupied by the elite of the class, the hopefuls who expected to participate in the Distinction Viva in the finals. However, only about half of them would ever make it. There was the odd one who had little insight. We nicknamed one Dr Keen. He would choose to sit on the front row too and in time the Professor learned to avoid his gaze and ignore his eager hand. He subsequently became a very successful gynaecologist. His keenness obviously paid off.

There was the hard core who never learned that sitting at the back row was simply an invitation for embarrassment. Did they really think that the Professor in all his wisdom was not going to the back?

The rest of us were happy to take the middle ground, the second row to the last but one. We might still get asked the occasional question by the Professor, but generally it was show-off time for the elite of our class and to be fair we did learn a lot from them. We are forever grateful for that.

Now Surgery was totally different. The flamboyant Malaysian Chinese was more concerned that his students knew the answers, and having very early on identified the few that could provide the answers, he would hardly risk asking the rest of us. His surgical skill was legendary and we tended to forgive him for all his shortcomings. Legend had it that he had sliced a few ulna nerves[19] of his senior lecturers in fits of temper in theatre. I have yet to meet one to confirm that myth. It requires a robust personality to become a surgeon although the financial rewards are high for surgeons in private practice.

Instead of a towering figure, our Professor of Obstetrics and Gynaecology was so short she needed steps specially made for the operating theatre. She was small in stature but not in any other way. It would be fair to say that almost single-handedly she brought Obstetrics in Hong Kong to lead the world with Japan in terms of low infant mortality, which held true from our medical student days to the present day. From very early days we had a dedicated seven storey maternity hospital that could in an emergency get a baby out by Caesarean in four minutes, five being the acceptable time after which brain damage is considered irreversible. The little glitch in an otherwise exemplary mortality record was due mainly to re-used drip sets. Their replacement with disposable ones helped bring Hong Kong medicine up to world standard.

Her reputation was way ahead of her and we never realised how small she was until we saw her in person. To fast forward to the end of my story about her, I had the great honour to have her as my finals practical examiner. It was the accepted wisdom that if you got the professor you were either borderline for failure or for distinction. I never did manage to find out which, though I did not consider that I did badly at all in my Obstetrics and Gynaecology

[19] Ulna nerve - The ulna nerve is a nerve which runs from the shoulder to the hand, at one part running near the ulna bone. It is the only exposed nerve in the human body (it is unprotected for a few centimeters at the elbow)

papers. I was given a patient where an internal examination was deemed necessary. Having to discard the Professor's step platform might have unnerved me, but when I realised we had a cervical polyp of some size, I duly described in metric terms the closest to my estimation, namely 2.5 cm diameter. Horrified, she looked at the notes in front of her from her most trusted senior lecturer – 1 cm. Re-questioning did not change my mind as I was confident of my estimation. With the said Senior Lecturer in tow she put on her glove, dipped into some KY and stepping on the platform that the Senior Lecturer duly replaced, she performed her own examination.

"It must have increased in size overnight."

Fair was fair, and I was grateful for that. I was glad I stood my own ground – a lesson I shall always remember for other aspects of medicine. *Always trust your own assessment.*

Tsan Yuk Hospital (the Chinese name meaning promoting birth) was where we learned about venipuncture (drawing blood from the vein) and vaginal examination, and had our other initiation – delivering a baby.

Without much public health education, most mothers in Hong Kong knew the importance of antenatal care, and attendance at antenatal clinics took on a scale that has seldom been seen in the western world. Expectant mothers queued from as early as four in the morning and by the time our little group of ten gathered around 8 a.m. on our first day for the Senior Resident's briefing, there were already hundreds waiting in the line. By the end of the morning clinic we were experts in venipuncture. We of course approached vaginal examination in a most doctorly manner and the main surprise was to the female members of our group. They never imagined the variety.

It was only a matter of days before we delivered our first baby and the only words that echoed in our mind were from our Professor of Medicine: we were the lowest life form. There was so much we could learn from experienced mid-wives and so much about humanity from others.

There is of course so much I can write about our clinical days, so much about serious illnesses that seemed to form the main part of our curriculum and so little about mundane day to day colds and illnesses that the majority of us are destined to deal with.

Two important events that I mentioned earlier marked the highlights of our clinical years. It was the era of Love Story and the tragic death from Leukaemia, and I still remember the day my friend came to where I sat in the university library and exclaimed: they found a cure. That was VAMP and what a change it brought! The other was the historic breakthrough of Christiaan Barnard and the heart transplant from South Africa[20], a country shunned by the rest of the world for its apartheid regime. Whatever the merits of what we know of the man later, what he accomplished then was monumental. It was a good time to be graduating as a doctor. The new age of Modern Medicine has arrived!

On a lighter note, our final year in medical school also saw the arrival of the mini-skirt. I could remember one day on the

---

[20] Christiaan Bernard and Heart Transplant: On December 3, 1967, South African surgeon Christiaan Barnard conducted the first heart transplant on 53-year-old Lewis Washkansky. The surgery was a success. Eighteen days after the operation, Washkansky died of double pneumonia.

veranda of our library chatting with some of my group before a seminar when the last member of our group walked down the slope leading to our library.

She was wearing a mini-skirt.

There is fun in medicine after all.

Chapter 9   After the Examinations

The examinations were finally over and I was back home in the village that I had more or less abandoned for the most of the last five years.   I could not remember skies as bright and temperature as high, but it was a nice interlude from the mad preparations and the nerve-wracking examinations.

We had an unusually dry May. The worst of the 1966 rains seemed like a distant memory and the crisp blue skies somehow made the heat tolerable. Even back then we seemed to be complaining of the ever rising temperatures in Hong Kong. The way we had been complaining about the rise ` every year, the temperature should really have reached 110 or more by now. The air-conditioning of offices, followed by that of private homes, necessarily led to the feeling of higher ambient temperatures in the streets.

The garden was filled with the fragrance of the white tropical jasmines. That fragrance is only second to that of the Osmanthus (Gui Hua)[21], the flowers of which are tiny and appear more towards winter. We used to collect the Osmanthus flowers, dry them and use them to flavour our best teas. Jasmine is more a late spring and summer flower and we had a big bush. By nightfall the cooling hill breeze brought with it occasional whiffs that made you want summer to last forever.

It was a peculiar time for those of us who had lived in or around the university for the past five years. We left home as school children and now we were back, and with any luck the majority of us would in a few weeks become fully fledged doctors ready to apply our skills.

We had changed and the rest of the family probably not as much; and yet it was a time to savour – the last of the old before embarking on the new and brave.

It was good to be reminded of the fine cooking back home, of an older and more sedate time when shopping was done twice a day for fresh ingredients. This practice of course still continues in some parts of the world.

It was good tasting again eggs that tasted like no others in the five years in between or since. These were expensive eggs as they could have been sold to chicken farms at a premium price. Not only were they free-range but they were extra healthy and fertilised

---

[21] Osmanthus (Gui Hua) - Osmanthus fragrans is a flower native to China that is valued for its delicate fruity-floral apricot aroma. It is especially valued as an additive for tea and other beverages in the Far East.

by highly priced chicken of the best Chinese breed. They could fetch upwards of two dollars per egg when one could get a dozen for the same price in the market.

Then there was the chicken, freely running and on a truly magnificent diet that allowed for such fine taste to develop – the original A.C. (Appellation Controlee)[22] chicken of Taipo. These chickens were so special that I used to be given the task of delivering to my father's retired boss and his family during Chinese New Year two live ones, in double extra strong paper shopping carriers fitted with a bamboo handle. This family lived near the University and I only had to make a special stop on the bus en route. It was more trying and required more skill than you ever imagine, talking to two fully grown chickens to keep them happy on the train and bus journey.

Father's now retired boss and his wife and two daughters were relatives of the cousin who was brought up by my father. They had done well for themselves and they visited our "country home" many times. The chicken and other fresh produce might have been the main attraction, but one must not be unkind. He set my father up to work at the British insurance company where he was the highest ranking Chinese manager. My father eventually rose to his position before he too retired but that was some years hence.

I would normally arrive at around five on a Sunday afternoon. There was always some food as I am sure they thought we did not

---

[22] A.C. Chicken - *Appellation d'Origine Contrôlée* (AOC = Protected Designation of Origin) French designation to protect and therefore guarantee the origin of products. The origins of AOC date back to the 15ᵗʰ century in France, when Roquefort was regulated by a parliament decree. Widely used on wines and now extended to other products including Bresse Chicken. Seen by most as a guarantee of quality.

get decent food at Hall. Then true to Chinese custom they would give me a red lucky money package. I am sure they could get ten chickens for the same money but alas not the quality or the thought. My mother always assured me that I should use the money for whatever purpose I saw fit. I suspect she knew I did not get much pocket money and tried my best to skip some meals at Hall in order to get some refund – we could get up to ten percent refund for uneaten meals if we remembered to sign out. I suspect too that she knew that with a girl friend I should be paying for some of the dates.

The guavas were not quite ready but our own giant papaya tree seemed capable of fruiting through the year. These were yellow fleshed and delicious though without the special fragrance associated with the red variety. Bananas too grew wild and bunches were cut when ready and suspended from a tripod for indoor ripening. It was too risky to let them ripe on the tree as various animals and birds would have had first claim.

Mother always bought fresh fish from the market, often a Pompano which when fresh has tender flesh with a delicate flavour and makes a popular Teochiu dish. It is perhaps very apt that the first fish I caught in Myrtle Beach some forty-five years later was none other than a Pompano.

I also remember she brought back a huge lobster one day. The fisherman, learning that her son the future doctor was back, gave her a special deal she could not refuse. The lobster was first steamed and then left to cool before being shelled and presented as cold slices – a different approach to serving lobster. Some years later I tried serving lobster in the same way to some close friends in England, much to their surprise.

By then we had a fridge, though only a second hand model. My years of medical school had probably drained every cent my father could earn, subsidised by the eggs the hens could lay and hours of sewing my mother could do day and night. By then hand-stitching of sequins must have been in fashion in the U.S. and a home industry had sprung up in our village. Each top fetched about the price of ten eggs but any income was income and that was how the likes of our mothers were exploited. But without this how could she contribute to her own son's education?

The fridge was a LEC, a good name, I believe. It was green and was rather battered on the outside. It had the lovely curved door and cooled perfectly. One of the uncles was getting a new American fridge and decided to give his old one to my father. He and his family were regular visitors and he liked his beer cold. Without a fridge it was rather a struggle for my father to keep the San Miguel's and Carlsberg's cool. This uncle worked for an aluminium company and one day he had one of his company vans and staff deliver the fridge.

The fridge meant no more bike rides to get ice for jelly and we could even have ice cream in the freezer. It did not change my mother's habit of food shopping twice a day though.

We still had no phone and I either had to go to the grocery store at the bottom of the hill to buy some groceries and borrow their phone or I had to write, as I was then in love and my future wife was working full time. Staying in the Cote d'Azur forty years later reminded me of the Basildon Bond azure paper and envelopes she used. No land line; no cell phone; and definitely no Email. Kids nowadays feel so hard done by if they lack even one of these three essentials.

I was given a hardback copy of Gone With The Wind to occupy my mind and keep sane, together with a model of a formula one car to assemble. Weekends I tried to see her in town. It was the longest few weeks of my life. I have a lot of sympathy these days for children waiting for their examination results.

The day the exam results were announced at last arrived. We passed! We were the few close friends who studied together. With the results came the scramble for good house jobs. I had to be on Kowloon side to secure a job at a rather prestigious medical unit at Queen Elizabeth Hospital. I made arrangements to phone one of the few who went to look at the actual posting of results. He wanted a job at the University Paediatric Unit and was well placed to scan the results. I cannot remember how we agreed to make contact as mobile phones were not even on the drawing board. I suspect I called his brother's office as two of them were Senior Lecturers. Paediatrics, or more specifically Neonatal Paediatrics, was to be his chosen career, and he rose to become one of the foremost international pioneers in Neonatology.

My other house job was Obstetrics in the University department as I felt that it was one branch of medicine that dealt with the beginning of life and might suit me well enough. Who was to know at that time that child psychiatry would become my career and in many ways my passion? The working of the mind fascinates me and the only regret I have in choosing this specialty is how little science we have for it, and that what we do have is often so unreliable. It is disappointing how, with so little scientific backing, the government and bodies like NICE now see fit to prescribe treatment that is unproven, unsound and often dangerous. I am sure this is the modern problem with a number of specialties in medicine. Child psychiatry just has it worst.

Chapter 10 First Encounter

In the winter of 1972, something happened that sealed my fate to stay in England forever. I was appointed Registrar to a world famous clinic.

By then I already had one of my higher qualifications (D.P.M. – Diploma in Psychological Medicine) and was in the process of sitting the first ever examination of the Royal College of Psychiatrists. At last we could achieve the same standing as colleagues in most other disciplines - a membership, not just a diploma. I had moved to London to take the examination for this most prestigious psychiatry qualification. My wife had accompanied me for what we thought was a year abroad.

On a cold October morning I made my way to one of these old mental hospitals which was running the first ever training course for the Royal College Membership examination. It would be foolish not to be there as most of those who ran the new College were on the teaching panel.

As you drove into the main gate of this rather imposing Victorian beauty or monstrosity, you got the same feel as in most mental hospitals of the same era. There was the odd one working the kerbs and gardens. A small group might be shepherded by a nurse to cross a road on their way to their morning's appointment. Many had the typical shuffling gaits from the antipsychotics they were on.

The last of the summer's Hydrangea flowers still tried to hang on. They looked tired and ugly. I would never have hydrangea in my garden.

The Post-grad place was easy enough to find as you just followed the majority of the cars. Wow, with half an hour to go, the car park was already nearly full. I suppose we all wanted to have a nearby spot to park on such a chilly morning.

I liked to be nearer the front as chances of falling asleep would be much reduced. I spotted a gap, made my way in and before I could sit down, someone offered me a hand.

"I am Gail. I am from the Tavistock."

The Tavistock? Many others would think this was the place they had pop concerts, and doctors would know that the British Medical Association was at Tavistock Square, London. But I knew. I was too astonished. I did not know what to say. Then I managed to utter my name and said that I would be going to the Tavistock, and that I had just been appointed a Registrar there.

Where I came from no longer seemed so important.

Synchronicity[23], you see. Gail put her thumb in her mouth and started sucking it vigorously.

"Sorry, my mother's fault and she has already paid for my analysis for the last three years. Between you and me, I preferred my thumb. Who is your analyst?"

"Haven't got one."

"Oh, yes. Dr Collinwood is the odd one out. Her registrar does not need to be in analysis. However, one good thing the thumb sucking did was to get me my job at the Tavi. I was already in analysis."

Analysis for thumb sucking? I thought to myself. Never! Whatever next? And a sought after job in London?

What did I do wrong, or right to get my job?

"Ah, you see you are Chinese. You don't need analysis. Your predecessor was Greek. She had the collective culture of the Ancient Greeks."

Perhaps her next registrar would be Egyptian.

Over the next six hours or so, I began to understand the scale of her problem. It was really like having sex in public and she could be so engrossed in it. It would be wrong to suggest that she tried to reach orgasm but sometimes from the sound she was producing it was not far off. Now and again she noticed that I was paying more attention to the thumb sucking than to the lectures. She stopped and apologised.

---

[23] Synchronicity – In *The Structure and Dynamics of the Psyche* Jung describes how, during his research into the phenomenon of the collective unconscious, he began to observe coincidences that were connected in such a meaningful way that their occurrence seemed to defy the calculations of probability. Unfortunately it is often quoted as a scientific basis for astrology and other improbabilities.

It would be odd to have gone through years of training at a place where the perceived wisdom was that all problems big and small could be traced back to our childhood and more particularly to our sexual development that I should write about my work without any reference to these aspects. It would also be peculiar if I, having been brought up in a Psychoanalytic Centre of world class reputation, could pretend that sex did not play a significant part in human psychopathology.

My first encounter with my future colleague certainly shocked me. What was I getting myself into? Was I going to see even crazier people?

The staff, not the patients.

My start at the Tavistock was straightforward enough. They had a good introductory pack. I was first briefed by Miss Frys the social work team leader. She was the nicest person one could meet and work with. Warm, kind and she listened carefully. She looked normal enough. I found out later that she was a Quaker and she came from a family where every female member lived to over a hundred. She looked like she was heading that way too.

She told me Dr Collinwood was very fond of her previous registrar who was a Greek girl. She was going back to Greece to have her first child before starting a Child Psychiatric clinic there.

"We are rather fond of Greeks here right now, as there are two others whom you will meet probably at lunch."

One later on became a Health Minister in charge of Psychiatry and the other started the Athens Psychoanalytic Society. I too became very fond of both of them and continued to meet them occasionally at international congresses.

Miss Frys had some impressionist prints on the wall and they just seemed to match the colour of her hair. A peculiar picture with coloured squares was by the cupboard and was obviously not hers.

"Ah, an imposition here. You see, our local library is very good. They have all these prints they lend out to clinics and public offices. This one seemed to be the one left when everybody else have had their pick. I thought, well it is not my type of picture, but it is mathematical and perhaps a Chinese would appreciate it."

There were not as many Chinese in the U.K. in those days, and multicultural understanding was almost non-existent.

Well, it is not in my nature to speak my mind, not at a first meeting with someone who seemed to ooze wisdom and kindness. I took another look and asked, "Who is the artist?"

"Mondrian."

"Very neat," I said.

"It is rather, I think you should have it in your room." Miss Frys replied.

"Thanks." Had I managed to resolve some irresolvable conflict or had I been categorised already? In any case the Mondrian would be fine on its own.

Years later I found out that even the Tate rejected Mondrian, but then the Tate also rejected Picasso.

Now I am going to be cultured as well.

"Do you like music? The library has a superb collection of records and they get every thing new as well. I live very close to the Festival Hall. I must take you to a concert there some time unless you have been already."

I must confess that with all that studying and preparing for the arrival of our first baby, concerts seemed like a lot of trouble; but I would certainly try and get the records as I had a very good sound system. Radios and electronics had been my hobby from the age of nine, and over the years I had built at least eight systems of my own, starting with a simple crystal radio set, then graduating to a triple valved receiver system and ultimately to a high fidelity amplification system with EL84[24], which remains the gold standard of the industry.

It was not until some years after her retirement that I finally took up her offer and met up with her at the Royal Festival Hall. There is no better place to be in London on a late June evening when the light never seems to want to disappear.

"So you are having a new baby in March. Dr Collinwood is very pleased because you will be able to observe your own baby's development. It will save a lot of time. But I shall arrange for you to do your nursery observation about three streets away.

"Now here is Dr Collinwood, I can hear her coming down clanging two cups. She had this kidney stone problem years ago, and her doctor advised her to drink lots. So she takes two cups of coffee instead of one. Oh, I see the coffee lady is bringing down two more. I presume one is for you and one for me.

"We have this coffee lady who comes in at ten to make coffee. I do not think they pay her very much, but the clinic is

---

[24] EL84 - a vacuum tube (a.k.a. valve) of the power pentode type. It has a 9 pin miniature base and is found mainly in the final output stages of amplification circuits, most commonly now in guitar amplifiers, but originally in radios and many other devices of the pre-transistor era. However, even now, hi-fi connoisseurs still prefer sounds produced by valve amplifiers to digital transistor sound.

thinking about instant coffee and tea-bags so that they can save some money. She has been here twenty two years, as long as I have been, and is part of the fixture. We are all writing letters."

I greeted Dr Collinwood, my consultant. She put the coffees down and shook my hand. She looked less scary than the first time I met her. There were now more smiles. What was she making of this young Chinese doctor from across the globe, I wondered.

Her first concern was the baby. Well she was a real children's doctor. I later found out that she had worked for years with Winnicott. Winnicott is someone I still have a lot of time for. He was really a paediatrician but his psychological understanding of children and mothers was nearer to my heart than many of the Viennese psychoanalysts such as Sigmund Freud, Anna Freud, and Melanie Klein etc. Dr Collinwood continued to show great interest in both our children and after she retired the whole family had spent quite a number of summer holidays at her retreat in Suffolk. One time the grand parents came with us too.

I knew straight away that I would be fine at the Tavistock.

"There is this case I need to talk to you about. We missed the last two case presentations (maternity leave and all that) and I promised that we would try and do one six to eight weeks after your arrival.

"I do not normally give my new junior any old case to take over but this is a nice boy and you might get on with him. I shall continue to see his mother."

Meeting with the psychotherapist was another really nice experience. There was so much gesturing that I later discovered was a Jewish thing. But Miss Horowitz you cannot fault. Her father was a famous child psychiatrist and she was really an Anna Freudian[25]. Not so much of the penis envy or bad breast good breast stuff that Gail kept talking about.

We had twelve cupboards all with individual keys. Each therapy patient got assigned one and they could put their first name on it. There were packs of toys that the other psychotherapist sorted out and it included drawing material. Drawing paper was multicoloured and we tried not to let the children take their drawings home as a rule, as they were important material for analysis.

All that medical training and exams and so on had not prepared me for what I had to do. I had to start from scratch. I was not even going to take a history. The first session with Michael would be a play oh, sorry psychotherapy session.

---

[25] Anna Freud - Anna Freud moved away from the classical position of her father, who was concentrating on the unconscious Id (a perspective she found to be restrictive) and instead emphasized the importance of the ego, the constant struggle and conflict it is experiencing by the need to answer contradicting wishes, desires, values and demands of reality. By this, she established the importance of the ego functions and the concept of defense mechanisms. Focusing on research, observation and treatment of children, Freud established a group of prominent child developmental analysts (which included Erik Erikson, Edith Jacobson and Margaret Mahler) who noticed that children's symptoms were ultimately analogue to personality disorders among adults and thus often related to developmental stages. At that time, these ideas were revolutionary and Anna provided us with a comprehensive developmental theory and the concept of developmental lines.

As such, the formation of the fields of child psychoanalysis and child developmental psychology can be attributed to Anna Freud.

"......I think that a psychoanalyst should have...interests...beyond the limits of the medical field...in facts that belong to sociology, religion, literature, ,[and] history,...[otherwise]his outlook on...his patient will remain too narrow. This point contains...the necessary preparations beyond the requirements made on candidates of psychoanalysis in the institutes. You ought to be a great reader and become acquainted with the literature of many countries and cultures. In the great literary figures you will find people who know at least as much of human nature as the psychiatrists and psychologists try to do."   *Anna Freud*

http://www.freud.org.uk/fmanna.htm

"You will be fine, although it would have been better to learn on a new case."

All the Nation's pride and glory was up to me now. I could only succeed.

Michael turned out to be a very nice boy as I was promised. He had two problems: nightmares and soiling.

The nightmares annoyed mum but she really could not stand the soiling.

"There must be something physical, Dr Collinwood. He has already seen the Greek doctor for six months and now you want him to see this China man?"

"Oh, very nice to meet you," she said, putting her unlit cigarette back in her big handbag. She had a very Jewish look with a very Cockney accent. If I knew what I know now, she looked exactly like one of those handing out drinks in one of the New York Hassidic Jewish camera stores. The way her eyes were scanning she did not miss a thing.

"I brought his pants from school. He soiled it again. I thought the doctor might want to see it."

I was beginning to "like" her. Such consideration!

"Sorry mummy."

"There is no need to show Dr Zhang. I hope with a few more sessions we may get to the bottom of the problem."

Dr Collinwood was confident. I was not sure if I was. But my tough medical training saved me – the important rule of using long words and never expressing doubt. I did not hesitate and said, "Sure we are going to."

Mrs Green was evacuated during the war. Dr Collinwood and Miss Frys were trying to put a series together on the effect of evacuation on problems for mothers with the next generation. It was quite unique in its way as hopefully there was not going to be another war and perhaps evacuation would not be used if there was one.

Her husband was probably Jewish as well and was on Incapacity Benefit as a result of some illness or other.

Michael soiled only at school and almost always just before going home or coming to the clinic. He often woke up screaming in the middle of the night and insisted that mother should go and see him. She now put him in bed with her to save getting up, she told Dr Collinwood. Mother cleaned for the school so Michael stayed at home with father.

Mrs Green was so fed up that the previous week she took Michael up Archway Bridge ready to jump. She called Dr Collinwood instead.

At least in those days we did not have tons of local authority social workers around you once something like that happened. Nowadays Michael would probably have been placed with another family at some point.

Michael got into a routine pretty quickly. First, we played football - a soft ball. I kept goal three times and he three times. Then we wrote the score on the little black board. He wrote his name on the card provided for the cupboard but insisted on putting three black lines round it. What would Miss Horowitz say? Then he played with the animals and then arranged the family dolls around the table. Mother, father and a little girl. A boy would probably be too close to home.

Though he was eight, he was more like six in size and was very timid. He asked permission for just about everything.

He would then finish with a game of draughts. I made the mistake of leaving the pieces as they were. He saw me three times a week, and he was my first and only patient then. He asked if I saw anyone else. I quickly learned to put some names on the other cupboards and tidied up the draughts. An obstetrician delivering his first baby must not let the mother know it was his first.

He soon started drawing. Mother, father, and a baby girl in the middle. We religiously put all these in his cupboard.

"I like that drawing," he pointed to the Mondrian, "So neat." He was right.

We saw mother and son separately at the same time for fifty minutes twice a week. Mum always said goodbye to Michael outside my door, with a kiss and darling this and that. One day after a few sessions, as she walked with Dr Collinwood to her consulting room, she said very loudly, "Is your new doctor any good? He seemed quiet and sensible, but Michael tells me he only plays football and draughts with him."

It was much later that I realised that children are equipped with defences so varied that it sometimes takes one a while to understand what has happened. Michael was an intelligent boy. He had set up decoys. He had now established with mum that I only played football and draughts with him. No wonder we only ever played for a few minutes each time and no wonder it did not matter if the draughts game finished.

Now instead of putting the girl in the family group, it was a boy, and he no longer drew a girl on his pictures. He drew a boy.

He kept putting the father in the toilet in the doll's house.

One day Michael drew me a picture that I could no longer hold back from Dr Collinwood until supervision time. I intruded into her fluid loading time.

Michael drew a naked mummy complete with big boobs and pubic hair. The boy in the middle was naked too and had a rather large tool on him. Father was in his pyjamas and Michael drew tears down his face.

We made the case presentation. It was well attended by nearly everybody including those from the other teams. Word must have got out that Dr Collinwood had a case that had sex features.

Father suffered from severe diabetes and had been impotent for years. Mother had very bad abuse history from the evacuation days and had become rather needy of sexual gratification. In a desperate attempt to shame her husband she slept stark naked and put Michael in the middle. She would get Michael to have an erection and then say to her husband, even your eight year old can do better than that. She would not contemplate leaving him, as the benefits were good and she got to drive his car. Dr Collinwood did not mince words on erotic stimulation etc. etc. All the way through, Gail never sucked her thumb. We passed around the drawings. Freudians made their bid with Oedipus and all that. Kleinians[26] insisted on bad breast. To me it was just an abused

---

[26] Melanie Klein - child psychoanalyst who worked in London (as the US required a MD degree to practise psychoanalysis) had a strong following and some severe critics too. Her theories – (as portrayed in *Nicholas Wright's 1988-Mrs Klein*) include references to: "good breast" and "the bad

mum having a bad time and using the boy to get back at her husband. But it was only my first case.

Gail gave me a thumbs up (the other thumb) approvingly afterwards and said I passed the test. I told her that attending Dr Collinwood's case meetings could save her lots of money. "It's my mother's anyway," she said.

Michael continued to see me for the best part of the rest of my stay at the Tavistock. His nightmares disappeared and he stopped soiling. Nobody knew if his mother stopped fiddling with his penis but to me it was an eye-opener. At least being Jewish she had no qualms about bringing Michael to the clinic three times a week for his therapy sessions. Since then, I have collected quite a few other similar cases, but I shall always remember Michael and Mondrian.

---

breast"; "symbolic urine"; playing the violin as "a repressed masturbation fantasy"; automobiles being penises and mountains being breasts.

http://query.nytimes.com/gst/fullpage.html?res=9E0CEEDD153FF937A15756C0A964958260

Chapter 11 Faking is Not All Bad

It has to be one of the few most enjoyable things in life to be able to watch wildlife in its natural habitat. Most will agree that going to the zoo, watching Discovery or National Geographic channel is not going to be the same. Others argue that your presence alone or with a group of like minded people would have made the situation unnatural. I have no argument with the latter view, but there can hardly be a better alternative. If more of us can see wildlife in its most natural setting, then we can begin to see the need to preserve nature for the generations to come, not just building zoos or aquariums and ignoring the natural environment in which these animals thrive.

Nature is of course not about beauty or beauty alone. Beauty is both deceptive and subjective. To love only the beautiful and good and dislike the ugly and bad is missing the point and in our recent history has probably led to the inappropriate management of National Parks the world over.

Wildlife is just wildlife. Not good. Not bad. Just survival.

The little cute Robin that graces many Christmas cards is in fact one of the most vicious birds of that size and does not even spare its own kind in defending its territory[27]. Many of the cute looking frog species in the tropical forests are amongst the most poisonous on planet earth.

I believe that watching nature often provides us with some unexpected insight into human nature. Having spent my working life trying to figure out how children's minds work, in my travels I not only marvel at sights but also tend to relate them back to my work. This has become second nature. After a visit to Yellowstone I related what I heard from one ranger of how coyotes[28] hunt in packs to something we were trying desperately to understand: how even quite young children can become so vicious in a group and can even kill. In the huge farewell card on my retirement someone drew a coyote to remind me of that episode. That was nice.

On a recent trip to Costa Rica we had the opportunity to be amongst fairly well preserved natural National Parks. The difference between a National Park and a Zoo as I see it is that we

---

[27] Robin - As is well known, the robin is pugnacious, fighting with its own kind and attacking other birds such as greenfinches.

[28] In Yellowstone National Park, with the unwise removal of wolves, coyotes began to fill the wolf's ecological niche, and hunted in packs to bring down large prey. Re-introduction of wolves may begin to redress the balance. This is one of the most quoted incidences of how modern men could be misguided in matters of ecology and nature.
http://www.yellowstone-bearman.com/wolves.html
http://www.nps.gov/yell/

are in some small space looking at the animals in the wider space. In Africa, you may be in a Jeep or some safe safari lodge. In Costa Rica, you are often on a small boat.

Another difference is that in a Zoo, you are bound to see the animals. In a proper National Park, there is no such guarantee and that makes the trip more exciting. We are still an intrusion and some animals do not like it. Some are used to it and a few might even be attracted by it. Luckily with the banning of feeding in most such places the animals generally stop coming forward for food. Some monkeys still try in a few places and that often is due to poor control over the presence of food.

Some will argue that even the National Park concept is wrong. I would disagree. What is the point of preserving nature if nobody knows about it? It will only lead to more ignorance and in the end inadvertent destruction because of the lack of will to preserve such places for future generations to enjoy. The answer may lie in the limitation of the numbers of visitors allowed per day to control the impact of humans. This can be done by actual limitation, as is practised in some parks, or by zone limitation. For coral reefs zoning works well with a four year rotation of a quarter of the reef being accessible at any one time.

Men will in the end be part of the eco-system, contrary to the belief of some ecologists. The disaster at Yellowstone has been well documented, when nature was left to its own devices and men were banned from a level of hunting that has kept a nice balance in the diversity of wildlife. Africa is now facing a major catastrophe from the over-abundance of elephants[29]. Kruger now has over twice the population of elephants that it can sustain and a culling program is being actively considered. Elephants have to be culled in families as otherwise they become too distressed but the process is distressing to the Park Rangers. We really are very primitive in our understanding of ecology and the delicate balance of nature. What appears right may in a few years prove disastrous.

In Costa Rica we are on the verge of witnessing one of the main defining features of Homo Sapiens, the most unique and only species known that is capable of extinguishing another species, the Leatherback Turtle[30]. In the meantime other lower profile battles between species continue with or without help from us. I was privileged enough to witness one such small battle.

---

[29] The irony is that the explosion in animal numbers is due to the success of conservation projects, and measures to counter poaching and ivory-smuggling. The repopulation of elephants since culling was stopped in 1994 has been so dramatic that it threatens other species, and the elephants' own well-being.
http://news.bbc.co.uk/1/hi/world/africa/4392800.stm
http://www.southafrica.info/ess_info/sa_glance/sustainable/culling-150807.htm

[30] Leatherback turtles - Peter Popham: Race is on to save the leatherback turtle. In 1980 there were more than 115,000 adult female leatherback turtles, but today there are fewer than 25,000 worldwide. In 1988, 1,367 female leatherbacks came to nest on Playa Grande in Las Baulas, the national park on the coast of Costa Rica, which is their last bolt hole on that coast. In 2001 there were only 67.
Costa Rica is not to be blamed, far from it. It remains one of the few major breeding grounds of the Green Turtle, which by all accounts is doing very well thanks to efforts by the environmentally aware government. Some may argue that Costa Rica has selfishly realised the benefits of Eco-tourism and is trying to preserve a fifth of the country as National Parks. The Green Turtle uses the Caribbean side and the Leatherback the Pacific one. The Leatherback, which can be as big as 2000 lbs, survived whatever that wiped out its contemporaries over 65 million years ago, but is now on the verge of extinction. This is despite it being equipped with a rubbery shell enabling it do dive far deeper than other turtles, and being "so fertile" that it lays tens of thousands of eggs. Evolution alas is no match for pelagic longlines, a form of fishing net set by fishermen with 4.5 million hooks every night, the equivalent of 100,000 miles of barbed wire in the oceans. Drift nets unfurled like huge underwater fences off the coasts of Peru and Chile. These together with shore developments and bright lights have helped to write another sad chapter for our achievement in extinguishing another species although I doubt if we would ever learn the true reason or reasons, or indeed learn from it.
http://www.independent.co.uk/environment/wildlife/article2461407.ece

One of the most exciting birds to watch is the Anhinga[31]. In Costa Rica, they are fairly easy to spot as they dry themselves on a branch or tree stump over the water after their fishing endeavour. The reason it has to dry itself is because it has no oil gland. Some commentators say that the bird is primitive and has not really evolved. Is that so? Without oiling its feathers like most other birds do, it can swim underwater without trapping air and causing a turbulence to slow itself down and to disturb the fish it tries to hunt. Why fix something when it is working well? Unlike the eagle, it does not need to be circulating on top of thermals. To be able to catch fish is more important than anything else.

Its ability to swallow fairly good size fish has been observed and with fish stock not always available, it has the uncanny ability of swallowing a fairly high number of fishes. However, they seem to prefer to kill the fish first. A struggling fish in the stomach may not indeed be the most pleasant thing even for the Anhinga.

There seems little the poor fish can do when faced with such advanced credential in the evolutionary war. That the Anhinga has survived without much evolving is a clear endorsement of its hunting skills. I wonder if its stripy wings mimic shoals of fish under water thus giving the real fish a false sense of comradeship.

In Tortuguero National Park of Costa Rica, we were fortunate enough to observe a catch by the Anhinga. A seven inch fish was the latest victim. The said Anhinga found a little piece of river bank and started to flick the fish. The neck of the Anhinga is

---

[31] The Anhinga is a member of the darter family, The Anhinga's feathers are not waterproofed by oils like those of ducks, and can get waterlogged, causing the bird to become barely buoyant. However, this allows it to dive easily and search for fish under the water. It can stay down for significant periods.

strong. I suppose it has to be with all the work-outs under water. The fish seemed exhausted. You could see from the way it looked. Another flick and all was quiet. Cameras clicked and videos zoomed to get a good view.

The fish looked truly dead. In normal circumstances, one flick was enough. It had two. Or was it three?

The bird was now relaxed. Why rush when you can wait till the previous fish is fully down? Spread your wings a bit – there is a huge audience of tourists. It was a beautiful sight – a female Anhinga spreading out its wings. It was indeed a sculpture of exceptional beauty. More cameras clicked and more video whined.

Suddenly, very suddenly, the little fish came to life, made a couple of strong wriggly movements, slid into the water and swam off. By the time the Anhinga realised, it was a split second too late. The fish disappeared into the mangrove roots.

We all spontaneously clapped. Support the "under-dog". Or should it be "under-fish"?

The oldest defence: faking. Not just faking, but faking death.

After the Anhinga experience, I tend to look at faking in a different light, no longer as a matter of moralistic right or wrong.

Chapter 12 Wrong Foot

"Behaviour is not – and cannot be – a disease, except in psychiatry.
Controlling behaviour, with or without a person's consent is not
– and cannot be – a treatment, except in psychiatry.
And faking illness is not – and cannot be – an illness, except in psychiatry."

Thomas Szasz[32] 2001

There is a widely held view that children are born pure and innocent and it is society that contaminates them.

There were two schools of thought in old China: one where one is born with a pure and clean mind; and the other that one is

---

[32] Thomas Szasz (born in Budapest in 1920): He is Professor of Psychiatry Emeritus at the State University of New York Health Science Center in Syracuse, New York, Adjunct Scholar at the Cato Institute, Washington, D.C., author and lecturer. His classic The Myth of Mental Illness (1961) made him a figure of international fame and controversy. Many of his works--such as Law, Liberty, and Psychiatry, The Ethics of Psychoanalysis, Ceremonial Chemistry, and Our Right to Drugs--are regarded as among the most influential in the 20th century by leaders in medicine, law, and the social sciences.
http://www.szasz.com/intro.html

born with an evil and wicked one. This posed a lot of problems for the ancient education and legal systems.

Fortunately for families and for society most of us are probably born pure and innocent.

Professor Winston of the test tube baby fame once did an experiment. A train set was hidden under cover behind a little boy, who was told he must not turn round and take a peep at all. The boy of course took a peep when no one was around, but he managed to lie blatantly when questioned in front of a camera. Professor Winston's view was that the boy's act was indeed a mark of intelligence.

Now we know this was in a documentary broadcasted by the BBC[33] and so it must be true!

Anyone who claims that they never lie probably has some serious problems.

Children indeed fake illnesses - both physical and mental, but more often physical. Until we are prepared to accept that, such children could be put at risk, the risk of being prescribed medication they should not have.

How do parents cope?

With great difficulty.

Parents nowadays seem to prefer it if their child suffers from some named condition – even if serious and incurable. You might think that I exaggerate. Not a little bit.

---

[33] "First Steps" the third in BBC's "The Human Body" series, shows how children cram huge achievements like walking, talking and being socially aware into their first four years..... Around 70% of three-year-olds who are told not to peek at a new toy when an adult leaves the room do so and then lie that they have not looked.
http://news.bbc.co.uk/1/hi/special_report/1998/05/98/the_human_body/103007.stm

Autism is by and large considered incurable at least by those on this side of the Atlantic. Do parents have problems with that? None whatsoever.

We have more trouble telling parents that their child does not have a mental illness, which is of course difficult given that DSM IV [34]now includes almost every condition. Of every category, there is the NOS - Not Otherwise Specified. It is therefore quite difficult if you want to explore the family dynamics before coming up with a definitive diagnosis.

The main drawback of not giving a diagnosis is that the parents will somehow demand it and eventually get it from elsewhere. I need not labour the point on ADHD which attracts certain State benefits, and we all know about compensation illnesses.

Can we really blame kids for wanting or needing to fake illnesses? I am afraid not. In most cases, it may not necessarily be a wilful act. It could well be part of their genetic endowment, a survival instinct so to speak.

My worry is for the psychiatrists who do not recognise the fakes. In 1971 a journalist sent some "fake" patients to attend a famous psychiatric clinic and most of these patients were not recognised as fakes. The clinic and their psychiatrists were furious and asked for a rematch. This time no fake patient was sent but nearly 30% were "recognised" as fakes. That does not induce a lot

---

[34] DSM IV - Diagnostic and Statistical Manual of Mental Disorders, 4th Edition, Text Revision, also known as DSM-IV-TR is a manual published by the American Psychiatric Association (APA) and includes all currently recognized mental health disorders. The coding system utilized by the DSM-IV is designed to correspond with codes from the International Classification of Diseases, commonly referred to as the ICD.

of confidence in our patients, if one is truthful. Most medical students with any emotional problem do not seek help from their psychiatric department but from the professor who drives the most expensive car.

What about the children?

Again, my main worry is for the professionals: the kids might think we are fools because they have been faking and we do not even know.

How does one deal with that?

Tommy

I once had this boy Tommy who developed a limp on his right foot. This prevented him from participating in sporting activities at school, much to the school's annoyance. It upset their rules. He then refused school, complaining of severe pain in both legs. He was admitted by my consultant for observation. I was at the time Senior Registrar. He was about eleven. His mother suffered from Multiple Sclerosis and it was not difficult to see that the limping was from observing his mother's gradual deterioration. She was by then in a wheelchair and yet still pleasant and cheerful. Tommy was a very well brought up boy. I felt at the time he was expressing his fear that he would one day be like mum and if he presented his symptoms early we might be able to do something. Others felt it was more a kind of sympathy pain given mum was now unable to walk. He was in fact a very good table tennis player and represented his school until recently (hence the school's annoyance). One day I was having a game with him after lunch and noticed that he was limping on the wrong foot. So before my next serve, I said to him: Tommy, wrong foot. He saluted me and said thanks and went back to limping on his right foot again.

It was an encounter that I remember with some fondness for how I dealt with it and how he took it. From then on we had a great therapeutic alliance and he eventually made good "recovery" and is now a swimming instructor at a local public pool. His mother has since passed away. Whenever I see him at the pool he would start limping for old time's sake.

Chapter 13 Hiccup Boy

Johnny was referred by his GP to me because he had been having non-stop hiccups for the better part of six months. It was unusual for the problem to have gone on for this length of time before being referred to me. His doctor was one of those who seldom referred anyone. He tended to believe that there must be a physical reason, especially for a condition like hiccups. The boy had even been to the National Hospital for Nervous Diseases at Queen Square and Great Ormond Street. Both sent him back to the GP saying that his problem was probably psychological and perhaps the local psychiatric clinic might be of help.

At the time my junior doctor Dr Zola was a girl from South Africa who decided that, given the new situation in her country, she wanted to emigrate to Israel where her doctor father, mother and three brothers were. She was an eager learner and would follow me to every single case I saw and even to meetings. She truly shadowed me. I had no complaints at all and she still writes to the clinic every year to tell us how she is doing. After training with us she was able to get into the professorial child psychiatric department in Jerusalem.

For what I did to her on this hiccup case she would never forgive me and to this day she will still remind me of it.

Johnny was an unattractive obese boy of twelve with a similarly unattractive obese mother. Together they looked a picture, an ugly one.

This led me to draw my first impression: he was a "bullyee", i.e. someone who would be a target of bullying – in school, in the streets, in football matches and in fact everywhere.

He was holding a big bottle of Coke - the two litre bottle, and so was mum. It was August and England was having its unusual heat wave.

This led me to draw my second impression: (no, not about obesity – that is too obvious) he did not hiccup when he was drinking from the bottle.

So within the first few minutes, I knew what to do.

"Dr Zola, would you mind taking mother to the other room to get some history?"

I knew from her look she was reluctant. She had heard of my many magic cures and she knew she was about to miss one. But she had also come to like my style and my work. She really had no choice but to take mum to another room. Meanwhile Johnny was happily hiccupping away between sips of Coke.

I have often said to many of my juniors that *child psychiatry is not about asking questions, but about feeling the answers.* It is a discipline where empathy rules. It is important that you know within ten minutes or so what is wrong.

Dr Zola, I think, felt it too. She knew I was going to perform one of those cures.

By the time I asked both of them to come back the hiccups had stopped and I had a mother who looked both surprised and embarrassed, and Dr Zola looked as if she would not talk to me till after the next Sabbath.

After sending the patient and mother off with instructions and another appointment date, I had to deal with a very unhappy junior.

"What did you do?" she demanded to know.

"You really want to know?"

"Yes, I need to learn."

"Something unorthodox."

"Did you hypnotise him?"

"No. Maybe I shall tell you another day as I am not sure if he will sustain his recovery."

I did like to tease some of them. Dr Zola was having none of that. It was Friday and I knew she had to leave early for Sabbath, but sunset was later in August.

I asked if she noticed that he could take long sips of Coke without hiccups and this often did not happen with true hiccups.

Dr Zola said, "I thought the Coke was one of the factors for his and his mum's obesity."

That was obvious but I decided not to say it as it would be too patronising.

What happened was I said to Johnny, "It is school, isn't it?" He nodded. "Now if I sign you off school as of now, do you think these hiccups might go away?" He nodded.

Dr Zola said, "That's it?"

"That's it. But I really do not think he would have stopped had anyone else been there. I gave him a sense of security. His secret was safe with me."

I think in the end Dr Zola understood, but to make a boy who sustained the hiccups for so long stop without resorting to heavy medication like Chlorpromazine or Haloperidol is indeed one of life's sweet events.

I do not think my secretary ever got over it when she typed my notes and letter.

It is often better though if you can somehow get the parents to do the magic cure.

Chapter 14 Who Are You?

Jemima got up one morning and turned to her younger sister and asked, "Who are you?"

It is strange how when you move to a new clinic some unusual case is bound to turn up. It is as if the local doctors and your new staff want to see how you are going to fare. This was particularly scary when the previous consultant psychiatrist was female and had an extremely good reputation. She also happened to be a good friend of mine. Her retirement was met with some dismay amongst her staff and the local GPs. The Management had difficulty finding a replacement and somehow managed to persuade me to cover that clinic. It was in some ways an attractive clinic to work in because it was truly "county" and did not have the problems of the so-called "new towns" like the one where my previous clinic was located. That new town had over 50% of ex-South Londoners, who brought with them the inner city problems.

The rural communities have their fair share of problems but they are different. Many London commuters moved to these rural places for better environment and better schools. This market town has one of the county's best schools. The more correct description should be that these schools have some of the brightest pupils in the county. The performance of a school is sadly more a reflection of demographics than the absolute quality of teaching. To be fair schools in nice areas do attract better quality teachers in the end and so it would be unfair not to give credit somehow.

Unlike in the new town, poverty and deprivation are not the main causes of problems here. Many parents, especially the fathers, work in the City in important jobs. Many of the mums are well-educated but stay at home to bring up their children. They help local charities and raise funds for schools and churches and other worthwhile causes. Many have health insurance that will pay for private medical care.

These families have nice big houses and go on at least two holidays a year. A skiing and a seaside one seem to be the norm. By the time they came to see us some sort of investigation would have been done on how good I was and whether I was the right person. It helped that we shared similar values and lifestyles. The race problem was often not perceptible even if it existed.

In fact, being Chinese sometimes gave me some advantage with this group of upper middle class patients. They were simply unable to put me in a class they knew. There was the mystique of the Orient with all the ancient wisdom attached. You might think that medicine is without frontiers but the fact that a fair number of doctors in the U.K. are ethnically Chinese is of some credit to our traditional values and family expectations. In more recent years, since the boom years in the City, more Orientals choose to study accounting and finance. Other more romantic ones shift to design.

What parents did professionally was of great interest to me and I never missed the opportunity in the first session to find out one way or another. Quite often I could even guess it much to the annoyance of some juniors. This was because they felt they had to learn everything from me, but this was not something you could learn.

In the case of Jemima, I had no such insight but it had some bearing on her predicament in a perverse kind of way. I think I shall let you know after I have told you Jemima's story.

Jemima and family had just returned from a two-week holiday in the Costa-del-Sol area of Spain. She had just finished Junior School and would be starting at Senior School in a couple of weeks' time.

Everybody enjoyed the vacation and there was another family at the same resort. The other family had a girl who was Jemima's best friend but unfortunately she would be moving to a private school. The two families arranged to have their holidays overlap by a week so that the two girls could have a good time together before separating. They lived quite near each other. The dads played some golf - the Costa-del-Sol is now officially also known as the Costa-del-Golf. The mothers enjoyed their reading and sun bathing and in Spain nobody needed to cook.

It was a bit of a shock that after their rather late flight from Malaga Jemima woke up not recognising her own sister.

Father made some phone calls to his contacts and the consensus was that with such problems it would be better to take Jemima to the local clinic than to drag her to Harley Street. I discovered later that the family also checked my credentials with their own GP, who told them she was happy with the outcome of the few cases she sent me.

As the story unfolded it was clear that Jemima, who was not quite twelve, now thought she was three and a half. She started talking in a babyish manner. She also said that her main home was in Spain and she had a nice big swimming pool there. At first everybody thought she was just joking when she asked who her sister was. Then when they realised that she meant what she said they were alarmed and her sister later became rather distressed. Little sister was only seven.

She claimed she did not know what the parents were talking about when they mentioned her best friend's name.

She believed that she had never been to school and asked mum, "What is School? Is it a School of Fish?"

I was pleased mum told me that. I knew what to do.

Father told me he had the highest level of health insurance cover and he had already checked. There would not be any problem with payments for MRI[35] scan, EEG[36] or anything at all that I felt

---

[35] MRI - magnetic resonance imaging, is a non-invasive method used in medical imaging to demonstrate pathological or other physiological alterations of living tissues. Lauterbur and Sir Peter Mansfield, pioneers of MRI, were awarded the 2003 Nobel Prize in Physiology or Medicine. http://nobelprize.org/nobel_prizes/medicine/laureates/2003/

might be necessary, not that he wanted to tell me how to do my job.

With this kind of case, it is often so easy to fall into the trap of jumping in with a lot of unnecessary investigation even if it would not cost the tax payers a penny. It does not give the parents any confidence if you just fire off straight away like a machine gun. If I ask for an investigation I need to justify it to myself. Over-investigation can itself cause strange problems and may perpetuate psychologically based symptoms.

On the other hand I have never seen such a case before and it is not in any book either. A colleague once made a case presentation of a very bright boy who suddenly could not walk, eat or drink on his own. He was in a wheel chair and tube fed for the better part of a year. Then one day after a regular family meeting everybody except him left the room to discuss the next step as there was total lack of progress. The video was left running and they saw through the monitor that he got up from his wheel chair to look at the camera to see if it was still recording. That was the crunch point and he went back to school and had been fine since.

My case was obviously very different in manifestation but the differences were only superficial.

So when the parents asked if I had seen such cases I was able to say with confidence:

"Yes!"

---

[36] EEG - Electroencephalogram, a neurophysiologic measurement of the electrical activity of the brain by recording from electrodes placed on the scalp or, in special cases, subdurally or in the cerebral cortex. Electrical currents are not measured, but rather voltage differences between different parts of the brain. The EEG is a brain function test.

School seemed out of the question but I said I would look into home tutoring straight away. Mother tried to explain to Jemima that school was a place of learning and where children started going at five.

I could not believe how quickly she adapted. She really thought Jemima did not know that.

"So, you don't go to school when you are three and a half?" was Jemima's loaded question.

I could only laugh to myself whilst putting on a straight face.

It is interesting how many of these parents could not simply say, "Don't be ridiculous. Of course you know what school is!" In her trusting way, mother adjusted too quickly to the new situation. She was now sucked into Jemima's system. Jemima must be having such a good laugh about it.

Mum doubted if Jemima would even accept a tutor.

Right then my priorities were different.

If a child says that there is a monster in the bedroom, do you play along and look everywhere to prove that there is no monster? Many parents do, and they may have the same problem again night after night.

Is it not simpler to say: "There are no monsters. Go to sleep."? Mother should know best, and it inspires confidence. In such cases, "playing-along" to me is never the "best" way.

The girl knew what a school of fish was, for goodness sake, I thought to myself.

Jemima proved to be a hard nut to crack. She complied with most things. A plan was set up for her to attend the clinic once a week for a one-hour session. Part of the session I would leave her with her mother or both parents as father tried to attend at least once a month. Jemima would mostly try to play with very childish toys as if she was really under four.

The only giveaway was her drawing, which was extremely good, and she was drawing portraits of her mother in profile and three dimensional buildings to show off. On the Draw-a-Man test she would be well over her own chronological age.

One day, within a few weeks of the sessions starting, both parents turned up for one of the sessions. Father said on seeing me that something strange happened when Jemima got up that morning. Both her upper arms were "paralysed". They had to feed her breakfast. He suggested it might be necessary to get some MRI or Scan done as he felt it might be something serious.

Jemima looked her usual cheerful self except for the inability to use either arms or hands. Father was looking rather tense but kept quiet whilst I continued the session as I had done before, except I was the one playing with the toys.

When asked if she would like to do some drawing, Jemima said yes and proceeded to do so. Only she picked up the Marker Pens with her mouth, took them one after another to mum to get the cap off and did some rather beautiful drawings.

I would have to deliver, I thought to myself. These parents were giving me till the end of the hour and that would be it. Harley Street and various neurological investigations would be next.

No, I did not want to lose Jemima now as she was proving very interesting.

What should I do?

Then I remembered one Sunday some years ago when we had visitors to our house. Our good friends had two little girls very similar in age to our two and we were just having a nice outdoor meal with a good barbecue on one of England's rare summer days. Then it started to drizzle. The grown ups looked at one another and without any prompting said: "RAIN? WHAT RAIN?" and carried on. The drizzle soon stopped and the children thought that the highlight of the Sunday was: RAIN? WHAT RAIN? And they even wrote it in their journal for school, much to the amusement of their teachers.

Talk about the power of suggestion – but we all had a great time and nobody minded a bit of wet.

So as time moved on I suddenly asked Jemima to let me look at her left hand. As I was examining it, I flicked her thumb and exclaimed:

"JEMIMA, IT MOVED!"

Jemima looked at her left thumb, moved it herself and said:

"YEAH, IT'S MOVING."

From the corner of my eyes I could see two totally amazed parents.

I repeated the same with the other arm and both arms were now moving freely and she finished her drawing with a big grin.

I was not entirely sure if I could repeat this too often. There was no more talk of London, MRI or scan.

I was going to continue as Jemima's doctor.

The tutor played the game too by starting Jemima on some preschool books and moving her quickly through the years, all the time saying she was a bright girl for her age. Jemima took the bait and was soon doing work more appropriate for her age.

Months went by and nothing much happened. One day I happened to stumble upon Jemima's favourite toy.

She boasted to me that she had a collection of over seventy Barbie Dolls.

"Seventy!"

"Yes," mother confirmed, "perhaps more."

"And I can remember their birthdays." Jemima told me.

She apparently gave them individual names and she treated the date when each doll was bought as its birthday.

Got you, Jemima.

I told Jemima that for next time I would be most interested to have all their names on a list complete with their birthdays.

Jemima did not turn up the next time.

As these dolls were bought over at least an eight-year period, Jemima knew she had been found out. When she returned the following week it was about preparing her to attend school as she was now ready. I did not ask about the list but simply told her that the tutor thought she was all set. She did not object and in fact did eventually do extremely well and went to Art Foundation course and Art School.

You may all be wondering what father's occupation was. He worked for a major insurance company in their loss adjustment department dealing mainly with malingerers.

He thought on day one it was embarrassing.

Chapter 15 Miracles

It is not my intention, either as an individual or as a scientist, to express an opinion on religious visions and miracles. Science has generally failed to understand these phenomena and many religions on the whole have tended to ignore scientific explanations.

For the religious amongst us, a close study of the history of religion would have seen deliberate attempts a couple of millennia ago to trick people into believing certain things supernatural. In a recent visit to Ephesus, we heard tales of how early "Christians" were duped and "cured".

The commercial success of fictional works such as Da Vinci Code, Angels and Demons and latterly Labyrinth gave us an indication of worldwide interest in not only the supernatural but also in attempts over the ages by those in positions of power and influence to suppress science and knowledge in order to bolster primarily the income and perhaps also the power of their institutions.

When the Western World was in the tight grip of the Catholic Church, the Jesuits were generally regarded as the greatest scholars. They brought Western culture and religion to the East. They must have had a glimpse of the Chinese understanding of the universe and the world[37]. Yet for so long the religious view of Flat Earth held true. Did the Jesuit scholars know the truth or did they pretend not to in order to avoid persecution and possible death? We shall never know.

Many "visions" have proved to be the work of errant brain waves due either to epilepsy or brain tumours. Yet the Church continued to celebrate these phenomena.

One of my earliest lessons on "miracles" is from none other than our eminent yet formidable Professor of Medicine, Professor MacFadzean, "Old Mac" as he was "affectionately" known by us,

---

[37] J. Needham: History of Science and Mathematics in China.

Joseph Needham's multivolume Science and Civilisation in China is recognized as one of the great works of historical scholarship in the twentieth century. The conception of world history that frames and shapes its arguments, however, has gone unnoticed. To sketch Needham's ideas on world history, one must go to scattered discussions and suggestions in Science and Civilisation, as well as to numerous papers that Needham wrote as his masterwork moved forward. Needham conceived of world history as shaped by a dialectical relationship between China and the West, and he believed that synthesis of the two cultures would be furthered through Science and Civilisation. Moreover, Needham thought that such a synthesis would help realize what he called "the world co-operative commonwealth," a global communist society, a "Kingdom of God on earth" that would be permeated by humane values nurtured in traditional Chinese society. Needham's idiosyncratic views and political passions thus inspired Science and Civilisation, which is not only a monumental exposition of Chinese science and technology, but also, in the judgment of its creator, a force within world history itself.

http://www.cambridge.org/browse/browse_all.asp?subjectid=1225755

the affection having most likely been preceded by awe for most of us. The "elite" medical students probably never feared him as we mere mortals did, but that is a different story.

The two things Old Mac taught us right from the start were:

One - One patient, one disease. It is far better to assume that a patient is suffering from a single disease, and that the different manifestations all spring from the same basic disease.

Two - Never say never. One must never be too definitive in matters of prognosis. What if one is wrong?

Medicine has moved on a fair bit since our student days, and yet for me, the concept of one patient one disease has served me well. It is not written anywhere that this should be so, but it offers the patient such great benefit for a clinician to think one disease only, be it psychological or physical.

For the second concept, he quoted his own story. A "miracle" in fact.

First Miracle

When Professor MacFadzean first arrived in Hong Kong a few years back, he was consulted on a middle-aged Chinese man, a fisherman who had a huge lymph node under his left arm pit. Investigations showed that it was a secondary from a primary in the lung.

The man asked him, "How long?"

"Three months. Maximum six."

Two year later as the Professor was crossing the harbour on Star Ferry, a man came up to him. It was not difficult to spot him anywhere in Hong Kong as he was at least a head taller than most, with a bright red face that Scots seem to acquire in Hong Kong.

"Professor. Professor. Remember me?"

The man pointed to his armpit.

No mass.

"Three months. Remember?"

It turned out the man sought the advice of his fortune teller in Shatin on the third day of Chinese New Year, and he had a good "fortune" telling him about an illness disappearing.

"Now it has disappeared!"

What a miracle! Fortune telling has been a major growth industry in Hong Kong. Recently, the richest Chinese business woman left all to her fortune teller.

"Never be definite about prognosis, especially if it is a bad one. Spontaneous cures have been recorded regularly, especially with lung cancer."

To the patient, it was old ways triumphing over modern medicine. It was his "miracle".

Second Miracle

The second "miracle" I am going to recount was again not experienced by myself but occurred none other than where most miracles happened.

Jerusalem.

And in the 20th Century.

I heard about it at a World Congress on Infant Psychiatry held in Chicago.

Generally the big plenary sessions at nine in the morning were reserved for the big presentations. Given that it was an Infant Psychiatry Congress, one was surprised to be having a presentation of a case of an older child.

Yet this was a presentation by one of the most respected professorial units in Jerusalem. The hall was packed and word must have got out that this was going to be good.

The professor was himself on stage. He was already rather old, but when he spoke he did so with authority and a certain air of natural arrogance. It was the kind of arrogance that came as a matter of course to one who had made a discovery of some kind that none of us in the hall, except his team, had heard of. Perhaps pride is a better word to describe it, but no matter. Something big.

His presentation involved the showing of some film clips, one of which was from the BBC archives.

This boy suffered from severe epilepsy from a very early age and was on four different medications. He never acquired speech, ever.

He had a younger brother, bright and very advanced, who was reading well before the age of three, not unusual for Jewish boys you might say, but unusual given his brother could not speak.

His mother sought help for him over the years, and by the time he was twelve, most specialists she consulted told her there was a critical period after which a child would never acquire speech.

She had said her fair share of prayers at the Synagogue.

One day, unbeknownst to her, her genius toddler took an overdose of his brother's medications. He was found in time and his life was not threatened. For four full days after he came out of intensive care, he stopped talking altogether.

It suddenly occurred to her that it could be the medication that was holding her son back.

She immediately secured a consultation at a top hospital and the consultant said that it was possible to use other methods to control the epilepsy.

But it would be drastic, as it involved removing nearly half of his brain.

"Without medication would he learn to speak?"

Now this was where the BBC film cut to a big picture of the lady consultant who said, "Never. He is beyond the critical age. He will never learn to speak. Never ever."

The Professor in a very solemn voice said from the podium, "She is not one of ours."

The boy had the operation. He was now free from epilepsy and free from any medication.

Mother decided to emigrate to Israel and seek help in the Promised Land.

"What a wise move." The Professor interjected again.

The boy now came under the Professor's care, and a big team of different therapists started working on him.

And mother's prayers were at last answered.

The boy now spoke fluent Hebrew and reasonable English. Not one but two languages.

I remembered what one Rabbi said to me at our friend's son's Bar Mitzvah, "You know our God will give, but we must work hard."

And Old Mac: Never say never.

Third Miracle

The third miracle is closer to home. I did not perform it either, but it happened to the mother of one of my patients.

Over the years, I was blessed in my work at different clinics with interesting secretaries. They had always managed to fill me in with the latest gossip, teenage trends ranging from fashion to music to leisure pursuits, and local news, all of which was so important in my work. In thirty years I have been to the local pub no more than five times. Without my secretaries I would probably have very little understanding of the main group of families that I dealt with most of the time. I cannot, by any stretch of imagination, claim to be able to move amongst that circle. Only rarely did I come across a family that shared my interests in art, music and culture in general.

I have certainly come across a child psychiatrist who could hold his own in any pub and was able to switch into Cockney at will and who became a professor at a very young age.   But, that was not me and I have no hope of changing that.

This particular clinic was in a "new town" which was established after the war to take in south London inhabitants as part of the great Social Engineering endeavour of the post war government. Having worked in three totally different localities in the same county, I can safely report that the morbidity rate in the new town far exceeded that of the other two locations, one of which has recently been classed as amongst the five most liveable towns in the whole of England. Off the top of my head, the rate of disturbance is between two to two and half times of that in the other two localities.

As far as I am concerned, the only slim chance of success of Social Engineering would be in a totalitarian state.

It was therefore a bit of a shock for me to hear about this miracle in the "new town".

This particular morning my secretary showed me a copy of the local paper. I never bought the local papers. I used to find them so intellectually de-stimulating that I had an unspoken fear of reading them. The clinic though had an extremely long tradition of ordering not one but both papers and that tradition continued. I often wondered when, in the new world of NHS management, someone would take that away to boost the manager's performance related pay.

On the front page was a big picture of the mother of one of my patients.

"Miracle Cure" was the headline.

One could not miss her as she was amongst the most obese patients I had ever met.

I was half expecting to see a seven stone wonder on the inside page. Instead it was a picture of her church complete with members holding a candlelight vigil.

'After a 49-night vigil, she was cleared of all cancer,' it was reported.

It could not be. My trusting parents normally told me these things. She never looked like she was ill and if anything, she seemed to have continued to put on weight in the six months I had known her. I always remembered her as being overweight by any standard.

"Doctors could not find any cancer cell!" The report continued.

She was apparently given only three months to live and had been on morphine for some weeks before she joined the church. Now her specialist told her that there was no longer a single cancer cell in her.

As she was due to attend our clinic, my social worker said she would make some phone calls to the Family doctor and gently enquire about it. She had in the past mentioned something about painkillers but never cancer.

My social worker's enquiries drew a blank. They had read the same paper and were equally puzzled. She was certainly not receiving any treatment for cancer and definitely not on painkillers.

During the session she told my social worker that she had private health insurance and produced a card to prove it. She was told that she only had three months to live. In desperation she joined the local church and the rest we knew. Also, her son's soiling had stopped as well.

There was no further need to attend our clinic.

We were all amazed.

Chapter 16 Autism and Entrenchment

In 1943 Leo Kanner[38] published a paper that would, with Asperger's work[39] a year later, form the basis of present day understanding of Autistic Spectrum Disorder. He considered five features to be diagnostic. These were: a profound lack of affective contact with other people; an anxiously obsessive desire for the preservation of sameness in the child's routines and environment; a fascination for objects, which are handled with skill in fine motor

---

[38] Leo Kanner (1894 – 1981) was an Austrian-American psychiatrist and physician known for his work related to autism. He was the first physician in the United States to be identified as a child psychiatrist and his first textbook Child Psychiatry in 1935, was the first English language textbook to focus on the psychiatric problems of children. His seminal 1943 paper Autistic Disturbances of Affective Contact, together with the work of Hans Asperger, forms the basis of the modern study of autism.

[39] Hans Asperger was an Austrian physician who first described the syndrome in 1944 that was later named in his honour. In Asperger's Disorder, affected individuals are characterized by social isolation and eccentric behaviour in childhood.

movements; mutism or a kind of language that does not seem intended for inter-personal communication; good cognitive potential shown in feats of memory or skills on performance tests, especially the Séguin form board[40]. He also emphasized onset from birth or before 30 months.

The observational approach to clinical diagnosis creates a problem when there is little understanding of the actual cause of the symptom. This is a problem for modern medicine as a whole but a good deal more so for psychiatry. Today there is a better understanding of brain physiology and biochemistry, thanks mainly to the advances in imaging techniques and nuclear medicine. Through our knowledge of neurotransmitters we are getting closer to understanding some of the most serious psychiatric conditions, but we are still a long way off.

Any diagnosis based on symptom manifestations is likely to end up with controversies especially with the shifting of diagnostic criteria. What seemed like a straightforward set of criteria when I was training has been subjected to revision after revision. In the beginning, diagnosing Autism based on Kanner's strict definition was clear-cut. With subsequent changes in diagnostic criteria it became harder and harder to the point that the diagnosis essentially became a matter of opinion. To the parents, the opinion counted at first if it was from an expert, then from a well-known expert, but as

---

[40] The Seguin Form Board Test is used to assess visual discrimination and matching and eye-hand coordination. Test materials consist of ten differently shaped wooden blocks and a large form board with recesses corresponding to these shapes. The child is instructed to put the shapes where they belong as fast as he/she can. Three trials are given, each with similar instructions, and the child is instructed to go faster on each trial. Time, in seconds, and number of errors were obtained for each trial. A significant decrease in response time from Year 1 to Year 2 was found. Results indicate that cognitive-perceptual abilities are involved in Seguin performance.

time went on the opinion only counted if it matched their own. Since autism became recognized as a severe disability by many governments, the lure of special education packages and other benefits begins to blur the true picture.

In 1966, the overall prevalence rate of autism in UK was estimated to be 4.5 per 10,000 children. In 1979, the figure was estimated to be 20 per 10,000, when the broader Autistic Spectrum Disorder (ASD) criteria were used. The equivalent estimate of the National Autistic Society in 1997 was at a similar level.[41]

According to the findings in a paper published in the Lancet in 2006, the prevalence of childhood autism in U.K. was estimated to be 116 per 10,000, but only 24.8 per 10,000 based on the narrower definition. The researchers found that prevalence of autism and related ASDs (autistic spectrum disorder) was substantially greater than previously recognised.[42]

---

[41] The changing prevalence of autism? Paul Shattock & Paul Whiteley
Autism Research Unit, University of Sunderland, UK

http://osiris.sunderland.ac.uk/autism/incidence.htm

Victor Lotter (1966) - Lotter published the first results of an epidemiological study of children with the behaviour pattern described by Kanner in the former county of Middlesex. He gave an overall prevalence rate of 4.5 per 10,000 children.

Wing & Gould (1979) - Using the definition of Kanner, Wing & Gould found the prevalence of autism in those with IQ under 70 was nearly 5 per 10,000. They also identified a group of children (15 per 10,000) who had the 'triad of impairments' identified as the broader 'autistic spectrum disorder (ASD)' (the total prevalence being 20 per 10,000). Further studies in different countries examining the prevalence of autism (but not the whole spectrum) found results ranging from 3.3 to 16 per 10,000.

NAS Summary figures (1997) - Estimated Prevalence Rates in the UK (NAS, 1997) = 91 per 10,000; % of children = 23%

[42] Prevalence of disorders of the autism spectrum in a population cohort of children in South Thames: the Special Needs and Autism Project (SNAP)

The Centre for Disease Control and Prevention (CDC) recently (February 2007) released new data on ASDs from multiple communities in the United States. Overall, the 2000 and 2002 studies found average prevalence rates of 66 to 67 per 10,000 eight-year olds.[43]

What has caused this marked increase? Could the increase be due to better ascertainment, broadening diagnostic criteria, or increased incidence?

The prevalence of childhood autism was 38.9 per 10,000 (95% CI 29.9-47.8) and that of other ASDs was 77.2 per 10,000 (52.1-102.3), making the total prevalence of all ASDs 116.1 per 10,000 (90.4-141.8). A narrower definition of childhood autism, which combined clinical consensus with instrument criteria for past and current presentation, provided a prevalence of 24.8 per 10,000 (17.6-32.0). The rate of previous local identification was lowest for children of less educated parents.

Prevalence of autism and related ASDs is substantially greater than previously recognised. Whether the increase is due to better ascertainment, broadening diagnostic criteria, or increased incidence is unclear. Services in health, education, and social care will need to recognise the needs of children with some form of ASD, who constitute 1% of the child population.
Lancet. 2006 Jul 15;368(9531):210-5

[43] CDC Releases New Data on Autism Spectrum Disorders (ASDs) from Multiple Communities in the United States – Press Release on February 8, 2007

http://www.cdc.gov/od/oc/media/pressrel/2007/r070208.htm

The Centers for Disease Control and Prevention (CDC) report: findings today from multiple U.S. communities. The results showed an average of 6.7 children out of 1,000 had an ASD in the six communities assessed in 2000, and an average of 6.6 children out of 1,000 having an ASD in the 14 communities included in the 2002 study. All children in the studies were eight years old.

For decades, the best estimate for the prevalence of autism was four to five per 10,000 children. More recent studies from multiple countries using current diagnostic criteria conducted with different methods have indicated that there is a range of ASD prevalence between 1 in 500 children and 1 in 166 children.

The 2000 study included approximately 4.5 percent of U.S. eight-year-old children born in 1992 from six states - Arizona, Georgia, Maryland, New Jersey, South Carolina and West Virginia. A total of 1,252 eight-year olds were identified as having an ASD.

The 2002 study included approximately 10 percent of U.S. eight-year-old children born in 1994 from 14 states - Alabama, Arizona, Arkansas, Colorado, Georgia, Maryland, Missouri, New Jersey, North Carolina, Pennsylvania, South Carolina, Utah, West Virginia and Wisconsin. A total of 2,685 eight-year-olds were identified as having an ASD.

In the spring of 1975 I found myself in a psychotherapy supervision session dedicated entirely to autism and attended by all trainees in the centre.

The supervisor, Frances Tustin[44], wore a head of thick pure white hair. Very short and of rather solid build, she used to wear only trousers, which seemed to be the only sensible wear for a child psychotherapist, and a very simple pinafore. She spoke with gesticulating arms in front of her. She was basically a Kleinian. Like many of them, I think she adapted. She must have been in her mid 60s and by then and for a long time her patients were mostly severely autistic children, the ones most people would gladly send to some god-forsaken place on the other side of the planet, at great expense to the local authority to ease their own guilt of not being able to offer much locally. She was thus naturally cuddly – cuddly enough to counter the world's most "un-cuddly", the "autists". I have no doubt she cuddled many of them - those who became frightened as she led them session after session through the dark underworld of their closed and rather terrifying mind. Nor have I any doubt that if she needed to break rules she would. After all, offering psychotherapy to autistic children was rule breaking in itself.

Many of her patients were at the High Wick hospital, a unit set up just for autistic children. People think a race is now on to decipher the brains of autists. All I can say is that the race was on

---

[44] Frances Tustin, born in Northern England in 1913, was a pioneering psychotherapist renowned for her work with children with autism in the 1950s.

then for perhaps a different aspect of the brain, and as long as we have autists the race continues.

It was not until some years later that I realised the significance of Tustin's influence, from the way she walked to the way she smiled. What is important is that she taught us not to be afraid. She was not afraid to challenge conventional views. She was not afraid because she did not think autism was such a terrible hopeless condition. She was therefore able to try all kinds of little tricks. She never went along completely with the tight defences of these little "autists". She got them to know and love her and then she would begin to dismantle their defences so that they could begin to adjust faster to a changing environment, namely to cope with life. She really was the pioneer of therapies that build in step-by-step challenges for these children. It is a principle that can indeed be applied to other psychiatric conditions such as anorexia, other eating disorders and addiction. Through therapy these children learn to laugh at their own silliness. They learn to cope with little frustrations and modify their demands when they find the therapist not giving in to them. Being afraid of one's child, whether normal or otherwise, is not a good idea. Strangely, many mothers found it hard to accept when their little "autist" changed.

Tustin's other great ability was her innate talent of simplifying things. Some of the greatest teachers I have met had the ability to use the simplest language to explain the most complex things. By the late 70s most others seemed to revel at the use of complex words to throw us simple folks off balance. Not so our supervisor.

Once in Paris I was in the presence of many eminent psychiatrists who were all deep into psychotherapy. I mentioned a few names - no real response. Then in another bit of conversation I mentioned casually that I had about two and a half years of weekly supervision from Frances Tustin. Everybody suddenly wanted to talk with me to find out more. That was the year 2000.

When I eventually left the Tavistock and became a Senior Registrar, I had the good fortune of working in a set-up for children and parents with three inpatient units. One unit was for the admission of the middle age group children of age nine to fourteen. Another unit was for the admission of, wait for this, whole families. The last unit, named The Pavillion, was dedicated to inpatient work with autistic children.

It was at The Pavillion that I first formulated my own view on entrenchment.

A mother was shocked on a lunch time visit to find her little Gerry eating peas.

"Darling, I thought you didn't like peas."

"I like them now."

Mother, now finding it difficult to save face, turned to one of the nurses and said, "Honest – he would be sick."

"He will be fine, he has been having peas for days," said the nurse.

"These are good," the autist added, without even looking up at mum.

Entrenchment is a trap into which so many parents can fall. They do not need an autistic child. The healthier children try to break out and we have rebelliousness. Others succumb and we have mental illness.

This is not the place to argue about the pros and cons of admitting autistic children as inpatients. The pea eating episode demonstrated to me the great value of inpatient observation. Many see separating the child from the family as cruel and yet I have seen many valuable changes in these children and their families that could not have been achieved by any other way.

Between 1977, when I started as a consultant, to when I left for Hong Kong in 1987 for a year of sabbatical, I did not see a single new case of Autism.

Where were they?

Chapter 17 Switch Off

I returned in the winter of 1989 from my one year sabbatical, not only to my old clinics in the South of England, but to a new one too. I was roped into covering for a colleague who had just retired after serving 27 years. She used to run two sessions a week in a clinic in a small town in the northern part of our county. As it proved to be virtually impossible to appoint another consultant, child psychiatry being a shortage specialty, a colleague and I agreed to cover a session each.

It was rumoured that for some reason this town was a centre of fringe Christian and other non Christian religious sects. Before long I realised that we did have to be careful when seeing someone and be aware that they might have turned up without their spouse knowing[45].

The clinic was reputed to provide an extremely friendly service that was amongst the best. The secretary I inherited was extremely pleasant and had top class short-hand skills, unusual by then as generally those with such skills no longer worked for the NHS. A consultant would be lucky if he had a secretary who could type from tape, or he would have to write out the notes in long hand. Nowadays some consultants may type their notes straight into the computer.

I was not in the habit of asking my secretaries to make me coffee. Here at this clinic, I was always presented with coffee and a piece of home-made cake as soon as I arrived. It would have been more offensive if I refused, so I thought I might as well enjoy it. One afternoon a week I was going to be looked after right and proper.

She also knew most people in the town and it was invaluable because I used to get real inside stories of the various characters that came to see me. One of these characters was the daughter of her cleaning lady.

"No, Dr Zhang does not put children on Largactil[46]. No, he does not dish out Ritalin left right and centre. No. No. No." I could hear her.

---

[45] Patients may turn up without their spouses knowing - It is against some belief to have psychiatric or medical treatments.

[46] Largactil – Chlorpromazine, a long standing antipsychotic medication that many families with a psychotic relative would know about.

I did not know what else the cleaning lady got out of my secretary but I suspected among other things, she heard there was no risk of her being Sectioned[47], nor being reported to Social Services. A medical secretary of the old school is indeed very helpful.

"I want Dr Zhang to tell me if my daughter is autistic."

Very cleverly my secretary did not book any other appointment for that afternoon. The session went on for over three hours. You must all think I was not very disciplined but it had been my principle to allow as much time as possible for a difficult case – and this might be the first case of autism to turn up in over a decade.

The child was wild and timid to the extreme.

As the story unfolded it became too clear that this was one of those cases that continued to turn up at clinics. This was about physical abuse. This was about severe sexual abuse. This was multigenerational and involved different members in a vast network of relatives. One of her daughters was already in care and had just run away to the Midlands where some part of the extended family lived. I would go no further than saying different things happened to different people in her family at different times. Mother was now so protective of the only child left with her and she was determined to make a go of it. She left school not knowing how to read or write but had in the last two years taught herself to do so as she was

---

[47] Section: Commit to a mental institution. British compulsory treatment terminology, denoting a particular Section of the Mental Health Act. The word has been verbalised to describe the act of applying the law. A patient admitted under the Mental Health Act is known as a Sectioned Patient.

trying to Home Educate[48] her daughter. She was already well known to Social Services and Education but nobody dared challenge her as she put up a good show in court and the case of her not sending her child to school was quietly dropped.

Considering the circumstances the child had done remarkably well. I had to conclude though that she was not autistic.

Anthony

One day a referral came of a boy called Anthony Wordsworth. He had just turned three.

"You will like Mrs Wordsworth." No reason was given. "Mr Wordsworth will probably not come to see you as he has a very important job in the City. Anthony is such a handsome boy, a bit quiet, and I think you will like him too."

The Wordsworths lived in one of these big houses and Mrs Wordsworth looked very young for a mother with two children, the older one being nine. I marvelled some years later how with all the hard work her two children put her through she still managed to look that young. The wonders of modern make-up together with smart dresses might have deceived me.

Anthony was truly autistic. At that time one of my juniors had just returned to work with me after having her twins. She sat through the first session.

She said to me afterwards, "I thought they did not make Kanner's classics anymore." Anthony was a Kanner's Classic. Leo

---

[48] Home Education - Home Education in recent years has become popular in the U.K. thanks mainly to the internet. Normally parents need to prove they are able to provide appropriate education.

Kanner first described the classical autistic child in 1943 and there had not been a better description since. Not many children have all the classical symptoms, but one finds the diagnosis of Autistic Spectrum Disorder (ASD) more and more common place[49].

I said, "Yes, even down to the good looks." I often wondered if our creator really has such a sense of humour or is everything just chance.

One could not but feel sorry for the mother. Later I found out that she came knowing that autism would be my diagnosis, and if I had come to anything different, I probably would have never seen her or Anthony again.

She knew of the diagnosis from very tragic personal experience. Her own brother was diagnosed such in London by our very eminent Professor who was the world's authority on autism.

In other words, she had lived, breathed and dreamed autism all her life and now her worst nightmare was realised. Her own child had turned out to be autistic like her own brother.

Perhaps her years of looking after her brother had prepared her for this day. Perhaps our creator made sure that for those who were going to have difficult children, they were made tough enough.

Anthony's older brother was smart and clever. She felt good then that perhaps genetics was not at play, and her worst fear was unfounded.

---

[49] Diagnosis of Autism Spectrum Disorder - There is a belief that Kanner's criteria remained the strictest, though other advocates for government funding of provisions for Autistics argue otherwise. Doctors can no longer rely on "clean" data.

I was once consulted by a grandmother on a very tragic situation. She had two daughters. One was severely autistic, and the other was very intelligent and a high achiever. The latter became an academic, married and received the best genetic counselling from the same university where she was a professor. Minimal chance, she was told. She went ahead and the first child was subsequently diagnosed as suffering from Retts Syndrome[50]. She was not really seeking any second opinion but wanted to know if Retts and Autism were the same. This case reminded me of the old Yiddish saying *"Men tracht un Got lacht"* – If you want to make God laugh, tell him your plans.

Anthony's mother went on to tell me she was going to take matters into her own hands because she would not want her son to deteriorate like her own brother, who was thirty five then and living in an institution.

"Mrs Wordsworth, I belong to that small group of doctors who believe that the brain is really capable of a good deal more. But we have to give it the right input."

This principle has been applied to the treatment of autism over the last fifteen years and the results are really quite exciting. We do not pretend to know the cause or causes of autism but I have been with some great pioneer workers and I believe that the old thinking that things cannot change is not entirely true.

She started crying and Anthony came towards her.

---

[50] Retts Syndrome - Andreas Rett first described the syndrome in 1965, first thought to be a severe form of Autism now known to be related to MECP2 mutation.

Even with the best breeding there was only so much one could hold back.

It was a moving sight, more because Anthony moved towards mum. What a positive sign.

"I would like to arrange for Anthony to see the same Professor that saw your brother. This is not because I do not trust my own diagnosis, but I think it may be what you would like but dare not request. It would be good for our future work together if you do go and see him.

"Before the appointment which could be a while, there is something you can start if you are not doing already. Do not stop talking to Anthony. Give him running commentaries on what you are doing even if it is about tidying the place, getting his dinner or doing his laundry."

"Don't wait for his response," I emphasized.

Many new parents tend to parent by responding to cues given to them. There is nothing wrong with that. We talk to our kids when they talk to us and we leave them alone if they want to play on their own. Sometimes parents insist that quiet play is actually good for their children when they themselves want some peace and quiet.

With autistic children one may have to wait a very long time for those cues and they may never come.

"To be honest, I have been doing quite a bit of that, but I was not sure if it was right or wrong and I never dare tell anyone, not even my husband."

It is always that much better to suggest something that a parent is already doing. First you are no longer instructing her and second you are more likely to succeed. She had been using her instinct and using it well.

She cried even more and told my secretary later that she was more moved because I seemed to know what she wanted and I saved her the embarrassment of having to ask me herself. She was planning to pluck up courage to ask me for a referral to the Professor towards the end of the session. It was not so much that she doubted my diagnosis but that she thought the Professor needed to know that there were now two cases in her family.

Mrs Wordsworth did get her appointment pretty quickly. No surprises. The diagnosis was confirmed. The Professor thought some of my suggestions seemed interesting enough and Anthony would be best served attending the clinic locally. He was grateful for the update on her brother's family history. He thought that Anthony's major long term handicap would probably be his speech.

With the Professor's blessing, we could now start.

We were aiming for very small changes but the feed would come from the parents and I wanted to get her husband involved if possible.

"I told him everything after our first meeting. It's a good job you referred us to London. I think he will be upset for a while but he will come round."

Denial is a useful if ineffectual defence, but now we needed to get results. It was time to have something for show.

"Do you think Anthony will have a speech impediment or handicap in that area?"

"You've heard the Professor but we are not going to stop doing things just because problem was predicted. The best doctors do not mind being proved wrong now and again."

Mother produced a video tape. A recording of a 90-minute period of her at home with Anthony.

"At this rate he will speak before three and a half, don't you think?" I joked.

"Like my brother you mean." She has already told me that her brother had a serious speech problem.

At three years and four months Anthony spoke. He did not just speak. He was in full sentences.

I said to mother, you have delivered.

Father came to see me the following session. I listened and picked out as many positive aspects as I could and encouraged him to just get on the floor and play with him. It was easy for me as I was already on the floor helping Anthony sort out a complex rail system that we had just acquired. In our work, you sometimes just have to have fun.

One little boy once observed, "Do you live here, Dr Zhang? It must be fun, with so many toys to play with."

We worked on entrenchment and we worked on expectation. We also ventured into something newer – putting challenges and obstacles through play into Anthony's life.

Then we tried something even more daring – introducing imagination.

Steven

About eight months after first seeing Anthony I had another full blown autism case referred to me at a different clinic.

Steven was the younger of two brothers. His older brother had been a bit of a model child who never gave mother any trouble. Father was a pilot. Mother used to fly but had now switched to ground work. They had help at home.

Mother realised that there was trouble when she found that Steven was counting lamp posts or rather reading the numbers on lamp posts. If for any reason she deviated from his normal route he would become very upset. Speech was otherwise minimal but he could read numbers from an early age, too early for mother to remember when. One day he was counting as he was piling up building blocks, one of these early learning ones with alphabets on them. He counted beyond twenty. But not much of anything else, no interest in colour, only numbers.

He liked lining up his brother's Dinky [51] cars. The main enjoyment was in the counting. One day the parents realised that it was the way the two brothers communicated and they felt his brother was responsible for helping him with the counting.

But then reading the numbers – do we have a genius or what?

The answer was we had a boy who suffered from autism.

I tried to be frank and open with the parents, but I was probably a bit too frank for them. Both parents admitted later to the initial shock but felt that because I put it so confidently they might as well accept it. They said it would have been worse if I had

---

[51] Dinky cars - Small models of real cars, now collectors' items.

suggested some tests to stall the time only to give them the diagnosis a week or two later. Those two weeks of "is he, is he not?" would have been more damaging.

What helped them was my positive attitude towards the future and they could not wait to get started.

One of Steven's problems was coping with change and mother often had to endure two to three hours of crying until he fell asleep from the exhaustion, only to have him wake up two hour later to resume the crying.

By then I had developed various strategies and tactics with which I could bring the parents on board. Steven's parents were exceptional, and they tried to come to appointments together, changing appointments if they clash with his flight schedule.

We had been working hard on imaginary things – of fake cups of tea that was too hot or too sweet; of food that burnt the baby; and of the hurt when a child fell. He was beginning to buy into a lot of that.

Coming to the clinic still posed some problems for Steven. He found it difficult that the doctor needed to see someone else. I was certainly responsible for his reluctance to leave. We had such fun together.

One day both parents arrived with big grins on their face. They told my secretary Marjorie that I had to wait till the end of the session but they hoped it would work.

I could hardly wait.

"Steven, five minutes," mother warned him as per usual practice.

No response.

"Two minutes."

No response.

The suspense was killing me.

"One minute."

Steven went over to his school bag. He took out something. I could not see what it was as it was imaginary. How stupid of me. He put in two batteries. I could not see those either.

With his other hand, he drew a big squarish thing in front of him that would have included most of me and my background. He aimed his thing and pressed.

"Swish-swosh-swish[52]."

"Ready. Mummy and daddy."

Steven had turned the session into a TV episode. He was now in control with his remote control. I was basically switched off.

Two very proud parents walked off very swiftly with Steven in tow.

"See you next time Marjorie," Steven waved to my secretary. She approved. No crying from Steven.

I was left standing there shell shocked.

They have done it!

---

[52] Swish-swosh-swish - the sound of statics as one switches off a television

Chapter 18 Bad, Mad, or Sad

It is singularly peculiar that in British psychiatry philosophy is more or less tabooed. I have never been able to understand this. Could it be that the organic approach is preferred and therefore philosophy is seen as too vague and woolly? Or could it be thought that we are dealing with enough mad people and therefore there is no point in adding more madness? Some people do consider philosophical ideas as formalized madness.

Consider James Joyce's question, "Why is it that when my daughter says the same things she is called a schizophrenic?"[53]

The few that dare to delve into the thought process of schizophrenics give us some idea of the strange world in which we

---

[53] James Joyce and schizophrenia - James Joyce's daughter Lucia was diagnosed Schizophrenic and 26 July was named Lucia Day for Schizophrenia Awareness in Ireland.

normal people seem to live. The illogical aspects of our daily language are enough to drive anyone mad. No wonder the likes of Autistics and Aspergers cannot cope with the ambiguities of our communication.

We did not have philosophers in ancient China, only poets. This solves a lot of problems, as it is all right to quote poets and even to study poetry.

Patrick

In August one year, two young boys disappeared in the Norfolk region of Britain. The story hit national news. The boys were on holiday with the family and went missing at the seaside. This was at the height of public awareness of paedophile cases and many in the media speculated that the two boys had been abducted. Patrick was on holiday with his parents in Cornwall. One Friday afternoon he walked into the local Police Station and surrendered himself as the paedophile who abducted the boys. The police detained him and got hold of the parents. They phoned his GP who confirmed that he was a psychiatric patient and had been on medication. At that point the bodies of the boys were found and the police released him.

Patrick was one of my patients. He had been suffering from schizophrenia and had been on antipsychotics for nearly a year. At the beginning of his holidays he came off his medication without telling anyone. His mother just thought he was livelier and felt that the holiday was doing him good.

By the time he returned from Cornwall he was in full blown relapse and had to be re-admitted to an inpatient unit for stabilization. He could not remember going to the police station.

Sometimes the mad ones think they are bad.

Sally

Sally was determined that there was something really wrong with her. The whole of her left leg was stiff and she could not bend it at all. She used a crutch to get herself up and about and around. She could not possibly attend school. She was worried that there were too many children at school who carried all kinds of germs and might infect her.

This concern was at first limited to school but later extended to shops as well so that her life became centred on just home and clinic. She attended regularly and I suspect that in her mind it was one way of authenticating her illness. I played along and tried to understand her. She had this recurrent nightmare that she would be infected by some serious germ and she would die.

I gained a fair bit of her confidence and one day managed to persuade her to go with her father to the newly opened supermarket next door to the clinic. I did not say as much but she worked out that a new place would be less likely to be full of germs. She had long rationalized that a clinic such as ours would not have germs as we did not have physically ill patients.

She was eventually able to accept a home tutor who must wash her hands and sit at the end of a long dining table for the one hour lesson.

Her leg remained stiff. Mother reassured me that in the middle of the night she could bend her leg when she tucked her back into her blanket.

One day she did not attend her usual appointment. Her father was very apologetic on the phone, saying that Sally's left arm went stiff and her glands swelled up. He would take her to the doctor as this could be a flare up of her glandular fever from five years back.

Two weeks later father called me to say that Sally had been diagnosed with Non Hodgkin Lymphoma and admitted to the Royal Marsden for chemotherapy. Interestingly, her stiff leg and arm got better overnight. He said that Sally told him she always knew that there was something wrong with her. We all thought she was mad but she was not.

How sad.

Sometimes it is better to be wrong.

Chapter 19 Who Is The Real Patient?

The early seventies was a very exciting time in London as the first ever course in Family Therapy in the U.K. was just launched.   Gregory Bateson[54] just published *Steps to an Ecology of Mind,* which to this day still manages to be exciting for anyone interested in family systems – a term coined to describe the interaction within a family or extended family.   Of course years before that, Ibsen[55] neatly observed family interactions in *Ghosts and*

---

[54] Gregory Bateson [1904 - 1980] - Anthropologist, Social Scientist, Cyberneticist - was one of the most important social scientists of this century. Strongly opposing those scientists who attempted to 'reduce' everything to mere matter, he was intent upon the task of re-introducing 'Mind' back into the scientific equations - writing two famous books Steps to an Ecology of Mind, and Mind & Nature as part of this task. Adopted by many thinkers in the anti-psychiatry movement because he provided a model and a new epistemology for developing a novel understanding of human madness, and also for his invention of the theory of the double bind.
http://www.oikos.org/batcn.htm

[55] Henrik Ibsen (1826-1906) Norwegian playwright generally acknowledged as the founder of modern prose drama.

Wild Duck. Both plays vividly captured family interaction that has hardly been bettered by any other modern writings.

Catherine

Catherine, aged fourteen, had not attended school for some time and all attempts by the school authority and educational psychologist failed to get her back to school. This was a pity as Catherine was really university material.

She had eleven older brothers and sisters. Two older sisters were married. One of them had a little baby of ten months. The other had two children at school. The youngest of the brothers attended a public school (i.e. an English private school) on a scholarship, and with financial assistance from the older siblings.

After an initial visit by the social worker, the team decided to approach the case in a family therapy sort of way – big family therapy in every sense of the word.

At that time, family therapy was a relatively new development and had probably grown out of some group therapy principles. One of the first courses was established at the Group Therapy Institute in London when I was still at the Tavistock. Little did I know then that it was history in the making. Of the people I was with then, either teachers or co-trainees, many have become prominent practitioners in the field.

Even the rather adventurous social worker was feeling a bit dubious. "Do you belong to the school that insists on everybody in the family attending?" She asked, hoping I would be a bit eclectic about it.

"Let's try and get everybody at least for the first session."

"I will do my best," she promised.

Good old Miss Kimble. She always got things done.

As some of the family were working, the session had to be organised for the evening. There is so much mystique attached to our kind of work that families often oblige without asking too many questions, at least at the early stage.

One of the older unmarried sisters took it upon herself to organise the meeting. The main one that caused some problem was the oldest brother who was a long distance lorry driver going all over Europe. The meeting needed to be on one of those nights when he was back from his delivery tour. The brother at the public school had a cricket match and he was apparently one of their best bowlers. One of the other brothers agreed to go to the match and bring him to the meeting as soon as the match was over. The sister with the baby would have to bring the little one but the older children would look after her at the meeting.

I told them that they could all join in.

Luckily with so many children the family had a reasonable sized council house and the family room was fairly long. They moved the dining chairs through to provide seating for everybody.

The scene was set. We just had to deliver the goods.

"We have come this far. We just have to do it," I told Miss Kimble. She probably had more faith in me than I had in myself.

Father looked after the parks and gardens for the council and had been with them since leaving school. Mother had not worked outside of home since the first child was born. She used to work in the Council Offices and that was where she met her husband.

All the unmarried children who had left school had jobs except for the one who organised the meeting. She was in fact the eldest sister. All hope was on the boy and Catherine, except now Catherine was not going to school and had not been for nearly a year. Two of the sisters worked in an insurance company, which was a very important local employer. Three boys worked for the Parks and Gardens department. One girl was a life guard at the local public Sports Complex that just opened and one boy looked after the gymnasium. The parents had done well and you could see that it was a very close knit and caring family.

Only the truck driver was absent. We chatted and waited. The baby in the meantime was crawling in the middle with the two older children fussing over her. Catherine sat close to mother and now and again would hold her hand. I was not too sure who was comforting whom but then family therapy was about observing the family interactions.

Cricket boy was busy devouring a plate of food mum left for him as he missed his school dinner.

Others were exchanging various gossips about boyfriends and girlfriends.

I thought that this was fun but there was also a lot to take in. The traditional approach would have allowed one to be more focused but it would probably have taken a long time to get to where we wanted to get to quickly.

When I heard air brakes, I knew that big brother had arrived. Everybody else knew as well. Swiftly Catherine let go of mum's hand and went to the door. One of the other sisters had the plate that had been kept warm in the oven set in a tray complete with a big can of beer. I declined the offer of beer as I was working.

Big brother was quite a big fellow but was friendly enough as he shook hands with me. After a few bites and some gulps of beer he turned to me and said, "We are all here now. What is this about?"

To this challenge, I explained in a very simple fashion why I wanted to see the whole family. I went on to use what I had since described to my juniors as a journalistic approach to history taking, as distinct from the traditional topic-by-topic approach. With the journalistic mantra – Who? What? When? Where? Why? How? – the patient or the family would just enter the conversation barely aware that you were taking a history. To keep focused, you do need to have clearly in your own mind the information you are seeking.

If you are not experienced, you can follow a printed questionnaire and take three hours of history but you will just end up with loads of seemingly unrelated information.

With my favoured journalistic approach you follow leads. The whole session becomes more integrated and it is easier for patients and families as you are not likely to appear to be jumping from one thing to another. It also comes across as more professional.

One thing led to another and my break came when one of the boys let slip that he remembered mother going into hospital after Catherine was born and big sister gave up a good job at the insurance company to stay home to look after the rest of them.

Mother was in the local mental hospital and had electrical shock treatment.

Mother started crying and big brother was rather upset and asked me what relevance this had except to upset mum.

At this point, the little baby who had been crawling around stopped in her track and crawled to Grandma and started touching one of her slippers. She started crying too.

I have my own theory that even before acquiring language, babies are able to retain emotional memory of early experiences. Later on in life it becomes difficult to grasp the source of the upset as there are no words to describe such emotional experiences. Traumas in early life have diffused effects; those happening later on in life are more focused and perhaps easier to deal with.

One famous psychiatrist once talked about his own experience of his mother's depression. He talked about having images of a wooden arm and it was through years of psychoanalysis that he reconstructed the whole image of his very depressed mother who had a rather catatonic posture in the deepest depth of her depression. He could remember himself as a toddler running into the house after play to be met with the wooden arm, sharply quietening down and then backing off. It was a rather moving seminar he gave at one of the conferences and a rare occasion when a British psychiatrist talked about psychoanalysis.

Back with the big family – all went rather quiet. A couple of the girls were sobbing. Catherine tried to comfort mum who said she knew it was all her fault. The eldest brother thanked me for making things clear for him.

All were relieved to hear that I would not be forcing Catherine back to school and that mother would not be prosecuted.

All agreed that Catherine would be wasting her brains if she did not have some form of education and I explained that I would be looking into alternatives.

Miss Kimble told me later that I was lucky to have that break and that it was a good job the baby was there.

It was uncanny that in my thirty plus years of experience, over half of the children who had problems attending school in a big way had mothers who had serious puerperal (post-natal) depression. Was the school refusal a clinical manifestation of genetically transmitted depression, or was it the psychological effect of living with a depressed mother? I really do not know.

Catherine never managed to return to "proper" school but with a fair bit of individual therapy we managed to get her to attend a tutorial unit. This we achieved by getting mother to find some part time work. Big sister too started working part time.

It was daunting for me to think that a single family session brought about so much change, but then I was reminded that the strength was with the family – we just tried to tap it.

Catherine had good exam results on the limited subjects she could sit but was immediately offered a trainee post at the insurance company.

Years later I bumped into one of the older sisters at the Sports Centre. She thanked me again for what I did for the family and told me that everybody was fine.

I told her I was scared by the lot of them especially her big brother. She told me I did all right. Catherine was his favourite sister.

I cannot remember seeing another big family since and with the disintegration of families it became increasingly difficult to do that type of family work.

Wayne

Wayne must have been about thirteen when he was referred to me. As with many similar cases he had not attended school for the better part of a year. I thought that this was another case of some degree of maternal depression rubbing off on the boy.

Wayne's father was a Sea Captain for years but for some years now he preferred to stay with Wayne's grand parents. "Who could blame him?" Wayne would remind me and himself. There was never a question of divorce and he did not want to involve the psychiatrists either. He preferred to just stay quiet about it.

Wayne had a very impressive crop of hair very much like that of Art Garfunkel. He was also very good looking, which immediately made him number one target for bullying. His favourite subject was English. He liked poetry and Shakespeare best – further cause for bullying. He enjoyed classical music as his father had a vast collection of records. But he kept this secret hobby to himself as the bullies already had too many reasons to pick on him. It was a rather sad reflection of our society.

The crisis came when his English teacher went on maternity leave. Before then, he was teased as the teacher's pet. His attendance at school was erratic at the best of times and when she went on leave he stopped going entirely. Then when he realised she was not coming back Wayne decided that school was finished as far as he was concerned.

To me Wayne had managed to find a good excuse to relieve himself of some rather petty and chronic bullying which could sometimes be worse than being severely beaten up. I condone neither, but both kinds occur with serious regularity in our schools although generally denied by school authorities. The side effect of this is that it is often a relief for all concerned when a request is made that the child should not attend school. It is when you start asking for other educational provision that troubles generally begin.

Wayne, once you got to know him, was the most pleasant boy you could wish to meet. He was not only courteous and well spoken, but also very knowledgeable about his subjects of poetry, Shakespeare and music. I do prefer to see more of the Wayne type than some other types I do not care to mention. It might be unprofessional but I know a few of my colleagues felt the same way too.

Some patients kept us interested.

Despite his age, Wayne was always brought to the clinic by his mother. They both cycled in. The reason was quite simple: Wayne needed protection, not from anyone in the clinic but from the possibility of bumping into someone on the journey to the clinic and back. When I realised this, we shifted the appointments to school hours and Wayne managed to turn up now and again without his mother.

His mother was always well turned out, always soft spoken and always waited in the waiting room through the whole session except when she saw our social worker. But those appointments were spaced out as nothing much came out of them.

After nine months, Wayne finally opened up to me.

Mother never threw away anything. Nothing at all!

Except wet waste, which was a relief.

This was a serious case of OCD (Obsessional Compulsive Disorder). It was still a great shock to have the full extent of the things that were kept detailed to you. Even a five bedroom house soon ran out of space.

Wayne told me that as far as he knew, mother had always been reluctant to throw away anything but it seemed to get out of control about five years ago when she discovered that father kept a woman in a port in the Far East. She moved out of the master bed-room and the rubbish moved in. Everything was neatly put in big rubbish bags and properly tied up. Some were in apple or other supermarket boxes. Even vacuum cleaner bags were kept.

Mother did a good job of it so that there was no bad smell at all, Wayne would reassure me. Just no space.

All these months, I had been thinking that the bullying was the cause of Wayne's problem. Did I get it wrong? All the time I spent trying to improve his self esteem, was it time wasted? Was there something I could have done earlier? Why did he take nine months?

Perhaps he needed that time to find out if I was going to send his mother to an asylum. Perhaps he needed all that time to trust me enough to talk about the sickest person in the family. Perhaps he never had any plan but the secret just came out.

Perhaps these were all valid explanations, but what could we as a clinic do?

It would be great if I were able to tell you that we carried out some wonderful therapeutic intervention. Mother was able to get rid of her "collection" and Wayne went back to school and eventually went to university and became a Professor in English or the Classics or something like that.

It would have been nice, but that would only have been a fairy tale.

We tried to arrange a couple of mother/son meetings but we really got nowhere. Wayne made vague promises in front of his mother that he would get back to school if this and that happened but I think he knew that neither he nor his mother could really initiate any change.

Could a mother or son in such a relationship make a bold move to get the other going? I fear not. It was a kind of symbiotic relationship that had gone too wrong for too long. By making a move to get "better", one party would be putting enormous pressure on the other to do likewise. Often either party would be afraid to become better in case the other one might become even sicker. It was just too risky to get better.

It is not uncommon for young and enthusiastic juniors to be attempting the bolder approach to force a change. I have come to realise and respect that many forms of mental illness are a kind of defence and in the end the mind or the gene that is the engine driving it knows best.

Similarly with drug addicts, alcoholics and many with sexual deviancy and perversion, our belief that they may change is perhaps misguided at the best of times and at worst, dangerous to others in society.

I was young then and a plan was soon hatched to somehow persuade mother that we would arrange for her "luggage" to be cleared. She indicated that she would find it difficult to watch. We managed to persuade her to go on a short break in her favourite seaside resort so that she would be away.

To our great surprise she agreed.

On the day, we had a phone call from the car that we had arranged to pick her up.

"She did not answer her door."

Our social worker rushed there. Wayne's mother refused to let her in but talked to her at the door. She had changed her mind. She did not want to go ahead with the plan. By then the firm we engaged to remove the rubbish had turned up too but she was adamant that she did not want it done. After an hour of hard negotiation everybody left.

She turned up for her next appointment to say that she could not sleep the night before thinking about what we offered to do for her (or perhaps to her). She felt it was such an imposition. She would need to dispose of those things herself when she was ready. When she was ready! I have a great admiration for the English way of understating things.

Wayne I never managed to get back to school. He never sat any examinations.

On the official school leaving day he asked me what he should do next. I told him that perhaps on leaving my clinic that day he should go to the local Job Centre to find a job.

To my great surprise he did. He was immediately offered a job at the local Water Works department as a receptionist/secretary. There they had problems keeping any female secretaries and Wayne fitted the bill. He had been typing since eleven and his English was good.

As far as I know, he is still with them. I do not think mother ever threw her things away.

Some cases you remember because of good dramatic changes. Others you just remember.

Chapter 20 Don't You Dare

Dominic was a boy of nearly three from a rather well-off middle class family. He had an older brother of five and a much older sister of nine. His father worked in the City and earned good money to support their comfortable lifestyle. Mother was often the only one that attended the clinic with Dominic. Sometimes the older ones attended as well if the appointment happened to be during school holidays.

I used to see many similar ones in my sleep clinic and early handling problem clinic. Wealth sometime detaches one from the extended family and with modern education and so on, mother's advice becomes old wives' tales. These young mothers much prefer to see their friendly child psychiatrist who is believed to be armed with the latest medical knowledge.

Dominic, like his siblings, was an angelic and smart child. There was one small problem. Since mother's rather late failed attempt to train him, he had taken to tearing off his large nappy and poo'ing behind a sofa in one of their grandest rooms – the one with the grand piano. He had refused to perform in the Mickey Mouse pot and umpteen other Disney inspired ones. Nor would he use the special attachment on the toilet seat or seats as there were four toilets he could use. No, he preferred the spot behind the sofa.

Mother was soft spoken and like many of the mothers with sleep problem children too gentle – too gentle in my book. Often these mothers tried to explain things to their six-month olds. They never shouted at their children. In fact they never shouted at anyone. Most were lucky to have a nice older daughter and in her case a nice older daughter and an older boy.

Knowing where the problem lies is often not the same as knowing what the solution is. It is virtually impossible to try and teach such parents to raise their voice. That would be like teaching them to be violent to their own child. They have to work it out for themselves.

You mean she became "violent"? My junior would ask me.

Well, I told mother that it was really not a psychiatric problem which of course was vaguely unbelievable to her. I started telling her stories about other mothers with similar but not exactly the same problem and how they managed to resolve things simply by becoming very "firm".

Very firm indeed!

"You mean you get them shouting?" My junior would ask.

"I never had to. But it worked."

"Invariably? So what happened?"

One day she turned up still in her riding gear. She told me she was too excited to go home to change.

"What happened?"

"Well, as you know my cleaning lady had great difficulty cleaning the yellow off the carpet. The different cleaning fluids have not really done the carpet any good. My husband is having his colleagues from his firm for a big Christmas do and so I have put in a new carpet. I have decided that all I needed to do is to keep an eye on the little devil and catch him before he could do any damage."

"And?"

"You know he was so crafty. I had to pretend to be reading my magazine but at roughly the right time I noticed he was edging towards the back of the sofa. I waited a few seconds for him to get to his favourite spot. When he tried to pull down his nappy, I did not know what got to me, I just saw red and shouted: don't you dare. Go to the toilet and do the 'poo' like everybody else."

"As if by magic, he looked at me, pulled his nappy up, went upstairs to his own toilet, the one with Mickey, and did the job." Mother was so proud. "He has been doing the same since."

We had one happy family again, with one happy grateful mother who had not got a psychiatric problem child.

I often used her story to help other mums.

Chapter 21 Autoeroticism

When I was at the Tavistock in the early 1970s, psychoanalysis was the new future. At last we could tap into the mind and perhaps the soul. This happened at a time of great progress in medicine. Medicine was moving into the modern era and advances in various imaging techniques meant that we could begin to see clearly the inside of the human body without having to be invasive. We could see the structure of the brain but not what was going on.

Psychoanalysis at last was beginning to make some inroads into mainstream British psychiatry with Anna Freud and Melanie Klein commanding a group of loyal followers in North London. Organic psychiatry would have to wait another twenty years before making the breakthrough with the new generations of psychotropic drugs. Kandel[56], Nobel Laureate, conceded that the 1970s was the era of psychoanalysis but his interest was soon diverted more to the cellular level of the working of the mind.

It was an exciting way of dealing with children and a challenge to reach inside their hopefully still quite unpolluted minds.

Very few parents were actually aware of what went on in those sessions and yet they were prepared to entrust their young child to the therapist. Many years later it emerged that therapy could indeed be harmful, and in cases of Post Traumatic Stress Disorder even just talking about the events could have the damaging effect of imprinting the trauma on the brain.

For those of us who had been on the other side the picture was quite different. One could get sex talk overload and after a while all the stuff about primal scene, good and bad breast, penis envy, castration complex and ultimately Oedipus complex could become too much. Some of us may re-read Sophocles to discover a different twist to the Oedipus Story. Put simply, Oedipus never knew his father or mother and could not have developed all those feelings. But Freud seemed to know about "branding" and "packaging". For years our minds were analysed according to a flawed theory and this will continue for a while yet.

Most of us trainees privately sensed that there was a flaw but no one would dare to voice any of our dissent. We were thinking of the next job and some hoped it would be within the same department. I can remember one of the trainees who was

[56] Kandel – In Search of Memory – The Emergence of a New Science of Mind, by Eric R. Kandel, Psychiatrist, 2000 Nobel Laureate for Physiology or Medicine

extremely fond of all that psychoanalytic sexual jargon and particularly those of Melanie Klein. It was rumoured that Melanie's daughter was so disgusted with her mother's lingo that she broke off relations with her and they did not speak to each other for the next forty years. The first subsequent "contact" was in the form of a public letter to mother published in a journal. Bad breasts indeed.

This particular Tavistock Registrar was a very tall guy. He was from one of the well known public schools. We often wondered what the kids made of his posh speak. Anyway for every case he presented there was something anal and autoerotic, i.e. getting sexual excitement from poking with one's anus or something of that nature. Once he presented a boy with soiling problem who drew a dog with a boy chasing after it. Some of us looked at one another and wondered what trick he was going to pull.

No problem – he managed to see the boy who was behind the dog as having his hand up the dogs back side.

I really had enough of this rubbish.

After moving away from the psychoanalytic environment I could look at my cases the way I saw fit and that meant not treading that Freudian or Kleinian path too often if at all.

Roy

Some time into my next job I had a boy referred to me because of soiling. I was not sure if the case should be seen at all, as he was only about two and a half then.

My social worker urged me to see him, saying it was a rather unusual case.

When mother brought Roy to see me he was like a little tornado. I had to double check his birthday to believe his was only thirty months old. Mother told me he was three stones and a half and was nearly half her weight. She was herself highly strung and like many mothers who came to see us for the first time, did not realise that they would have at least an hour of our time and more if necessary and therefore there was no rush at all.

Roy's size was from her husband's side of the family. Father was over six foot six, not fat but sturdy. Despite his size he was a very gentle man and so mother could not understand why Roy could be so aggressive. He himself was at a loss as to why his precious offspring was not tame as a lamb as he obviously was.

She felt that one problem could be because she could no longer hold him. Often when she was unloading any shopping he would run towards her and push her over. He had a very good appetite and would eat anything put in front of him.

The main reason for consulting us was that she had a new problem. They bought him a new bed about two weeks ago and since then he had started soiling again.

She said she never had any problem toilet-training him. She herself worked in a very tough environment, a builders' yard, where she had learned to cope with tough men. It was there she met her husband, as he was a builder.

It was however not the soiling she worried about. She could easily put him on nappies.

No, he dug his faeces out of the nappy, played with it and then smeared it all over the place. "Totally disgusting! I once saw him sticking his hand in his bottom when there was not enough to smear," Mum told me.

"I am also very house proud and I make sure that when my husband comes in all the work clothes are put in a basket and he takes a good shower. He fitted a powerful shower on my instruction when we got married and now I have to shower off Roy in it every morning."

We sometimes saw parents and could not understand why they had to come to see us. Some of them sounded so efficient that they must therefore have an extraordinary problem to get them beat. Roy's mother was one of these parents. She had stopped working since Roy was born and she said that if this went on she would rather go back to work and let someone else deal with it.

She also said that her husband was thinking of emigrating to Canada as his father and uncle were out there already, all in the construction business, and there was a great demand for someone like him. There was therefore double urgency to get Roy's problem sorted.

"So he was already going to the potty."

"He did, before we got him the new bed. After his first time I put him back on nappies and he started reaching inside his nappies and doing all these awful things."

In the meantime, Roy was playing happily in the corner. He found the spinning wheel and was happily pouring sand onto it over and over. Then he found the train set and was quite good at trying to arrange the tracks.

All the memories of the "anal" days at the Tavistock flooded back and it was very tempting to go down that route but I decided to try something different.

Since I arrived at the clinic I had started to run a mother-and-child group once a week on a Thursday afternoon. It lasted two hours and finished at a time when mothers could leave to fetch their other child or children from school if necessary. All the children were pre-school and basically it was quite an open group and parents could elect to come and go as they pleased. Most parents had handling problems other than sleep problems, which were dealt with separately in a monthly special sleep clinic. This group gave me more time to observe the children, and more time for the mothers to get to know us and to become comfortable enough to tell us some of their own painful stories, of which there were plenty. What was most important for me then was to find the time and space to sort out a way to help with specific problems.

Parents often did not want us to think badly of them and would perhaps white-wash their problems especially when they first met us. It was only when they got to know us that they started telling. With a limited session approach, sometimes it took them to the last session before they would reveal all.

With a group it was also easier to float ideas as if they were from another parent, and they often were, and this made it easier for parents to reject any suggestion if it proved difficult to stomach initially. They also found encouragement that perhaps children were made that way when other parents had experiences similar to their own. Many parents also became great friends and supported one another both within group time and outside of it.

I often told them that children, unlike other things bought from shops, did not come with instructions and they had to find out how to handle them by trial and error.

"So, you are the *help desk* then," I was once told.

There was at our clinic a big playroom complete with sand tray and various toys. As we were in an old house it was very impressive in terms of ceiling height and size. The smaller adjoining room was accessible by two doors and it was very useful for mothers to be able to sit there. We did not have to shut any doors and it allowed for observation of separation problems and so on, and mothers could talk with some privacy away from the kids. There were normally three of us and we took turns to look after the kids.

Over time many parents and their problem children came through the group and we were able to help many to achieve at least one small goal – the retrieval of parental control.

Modern parents are inclined to hand over control to the kids before they are ready, similarly with adolescents. I find that under these circumstances, whatever the problem, the important thing is for the parents to regain control.

I have often gone down on the floor myself to play with the children and many a time demonstrated how one could use *action* rather than *words* to effect control.

As Roy was much stronger than mum, it was impossible to use some of the old techniques that had stood the test of time. It was not even possible to get him to sit down unless he wanted to and mum found it difficult to put him in a high chair as he would get himself out of it. She tried to put him back in his old cot and put the cot in the middle of the room. That way if she did not wake up early enough he would not be able to reach the walls and the smearing would be limited to the cot and its contents. One day he managed to rock the cot to one wall and smear the wall.

The challenge was for me to come up with a solution. I suggested that perhaps if he had no access to his nappy or his bottom the playing and smearing would stop.

Forget about Klein. Forget about psychodynamics. We needed *action*.

"What does he wear to bed?"

"Pyjama top and bottom. Now that his nappy is under his pants, he needs something much bigger."

"Let's try this. Every night sew the top and bottom together so that it becomes impossible for him to access his parts."

The other mums looked astonished. That would be very bothersome.

"Not as bothersome as all the washing," I argued.

"Done." Mum said.

I knew she could not wait for that night to arrive. I could see the look on her face. She was going to retrieve control and she looked so satisfied.

She did not turn up the next week. I was disappointed. I knew it was only a simple measure but simple solutions were often the best. I was afraid that it did not work and mother had given us up for good.

One of the other mums then told me that Roy's parents had to go to the Canadian Embassy for an interview. She was sworn to secrecy though, as Roy's mum wanted to tell me what happened herself.

They had no idea that I already knew. I knew because that was my job. It could only be good news if she had wanted to tell me herself.

It was good news, and it was in fact more than good news.

Roy could not access his nappy but he did not put up any protest about it. After the third night he stopped soiling his nappies although mother continued to put a nappy on and sew his pyjamas together. She would not stop until I said so.

I told mother that she had regained control and it would be up to her to decide when to stop. "Perhaps when he becomes sixteen. Perhaps when he gets married," I joked.

There you are, a case of auto-eroticism that never was.

Mother continued to attend the group, more for companionship than for help as Roy was turning out to be a very well behaved boy and a very positive example of how well the group could do.

Then the news came that they were going to Canada. Some mums were in tears and others were already planning on a trip out there. For now they asked my permission to run a farewell party on one of the Thursdays, with home baked cakes and so.

Any excuse for a party. I said yes.

Mother turned up early, asking to speak to me on her own. Another mum was going to bring Roy later.

"Nothing serious, I hope."

"No, just a bit embarrassing; but I talked to Wendy (another mum who had become a good friend) and she said if I am worried I must talk to you because you are the doctor and you know how to handle these things."

Of course, it now dawned on me that was her last day and within a few days she would be half a world away. What better time to reveal everything?

"Do you think my son is going to be gay?"

This is an extremely serious question many mothers asked me. We may all want to be politically correct and all that but please do not let it be my son. How subtly magazines like Penthouse and Mayfair would miraculously appear where a growing teenage boy might easily find them. Hints are dropped as to whether or not so and so should be invited to the summer barbecue not because the parents are great pals but because they have an eligible daughter. If by the time they go to university and still do not have a girl friend, excuses would be made to other mothers that the boy works too hard and now that A levels are over he may have time on his hands.

"Why do you ask that?" She should know better by then that she would not get an immediate answer just like that.

"All the enjoyment he seemed to be getting out of fiddling with his back side, of course I am worried. There is something else I may not have been too clear with you about. You remember I told you in our first session that the first time he smeared faeces was when we put him on to a bed? It was not as simple as that. You see, my husband and I got on very well especially sexually. In fact when we were first dating, we mainly engaged in oral sex as he did not like wearing a condom and I could not take the pill and did not like the diaphragm. But I discovered that he actually enjoyed going down on me and liked all that came with it. It does mean that we do engage in it quite often. Roy sleeps in the afternoon and when my husband comes home we might spend a good half hour or an hour enjoying ourselves. We forgot that when we got him on a bed he could now climb off and that first afternoon while we were in the middle of it we heard his voice. It may sound funny. All he said was he wanted a drink. We managed to scramble something on and said nothing. The next morning he soiled. I was afraid that witnessing us doing all that might have damaged him and he may not want to be with a woman when he grows up."

Tavistock flashed before my eyes. All the time I thought this had nothing to do with autoeroticism and was about to congratulate myself on my brilliant practical treatment and now she gave me this information! I had to get out of this somehow, and with that thought I smiled.

"You are laughing at me. I wish I kept that secret and never told you."

"No. Sorry. The smile is not about you but about something I experienced when I was training."

"You mean your experience of children witnessing sex? Just tell me the truth."

"No, it was really about the soiling. Let me try and answer your questions now, as we do not have a lot of time before the party starts, and you will be busy with all your packing and will not be able to find time to come to see me again.

"You see, the current view is that if you are going to be gay you are going to be gay. It is not what parents did or did not do. Some years back we had this boy who loved wearing skirts. He was referred because his father was afraid he might be a transvestite or even gay. How can we tell at age four, I asked them and I told them what I am telling you now. They became more relaxed and the boy's fondness of skirts soon faded. For the last session the father came as well. My secretary had a good laugh and told me to be prepared. Father was himself a fireman and a burly one at that – muscular and macho. He was wearing a brightly coloured floral pair of pants."

"Was the boy OK?"

"He became very athletic and is now a personal trainer in one of the local sports centres and mum told me he now has a steady girl friend."

"So do you think my Roy is going to be all right? What about witnessing us making love and all that? Is that not going to be damaging?"

Primal Scene[57].

I had to come up with a quick response.

"I would say all the news on TV of horrible things going on in the world is possibly more damaging by comparison. Perhaps latching the door would be a good idea for a while."

The party went well. There were tears and hugs and good wishes. It was not everyday a patient's family emigrated. Mum whispered a thank you again as she left. It was a meaningful thank you and I thanked her in my heart. I thanked her for only telling me on her last day.

I may have to read Freud and Klein again.

---

[57] Primal scene - In psychoanalysis, the actual or fantasised observation by a child of sexual intercourse, particularly between the parents. Seen by Freud as a source of confusing psychological experience leading possibly to later neurosis. Later research showed that up to 41% of children have witnessed parental intercourse and neurosis may have origin other than witnessing primal scene itself.

Chapter 22 Family Tragedy

We found them! We found them! There was great excitement in the police car as the news broke through the radio.

"Are they all right?" Mr. Tanner shouted from the back of the police car.

"Just checking. They are not moving….. Yes there is a pulse. Yes, older girl too. … mmmm mother. Yes! They are all alive. We are getting them on the helicopter."

This high drama occurred on a Sussex beauty spot that is riddled with legend and stories of ghosts and the devil.

Chanctonbury Ring[58] was a truly man-made landmark. In 1760, a crown of beech trees were planted on top by a young man

---

[58] Chanctonbury Ring is a small Iron Age hill fort that was used in various periods of history and is still a notable Sussex landmark today, the subject of many paintings, postcards and photographs. It occupies a prominence on the northern edge of the South Downs, 783 feet above sea level and

named Charles Goring, who lived to eighty five and saw his trees grow to maturity.

Unfortunately it is also a spot where legend has it that you can trade your soul with the devil.

Mr Tanner was a very successful businessman who ran a number of very successful stores in the south of England. I was called to see his eldest daughter Tara following a massive overdose of painkillers. She survived because she took Aspirin instead of Paracetamol. There was perhaps some advantage in not being streetwise, namely not knowing which drug to take. Or perhaps she did not really want to die. It was not easy to tell after the event, as there is always an emotional rebound after an act like that. The lack of a suicide note was a positive indication and in truth, young people often want to draw attention to something going terribly wrong by attempting suicide.

I realised straight away that this was different to the kind of overdoses that we saw two or three times a week on the wards. She had not been involved in drugs, alcohol or boyfriends. She was not really worried about her exams. She was not at the top but within the top few percentages. No. She said it was not her exams that worried her.

---

overlooks a large portion of the weald below with the old ridgeway across the downs passing just to the south. After the abandonment of the hill fort, the ring was used by the Romans as a religious site. However, the fame of the Ring is due not to the hill fort but to the beech trees, which were planted in 1760 by Charles Goring within the earth bank of the fort, which is still prominent today. Local legend has it that Chanctonbury Ring was created by the Devil and that he can be summoned by running around the clump of trees seven times anti-clockwise. When he appears he will offer you a bowl of soup in exchange for your soul. The Ring is also rumoured to increase fertility in women who sleep underneath the trees for one night. If you come to the ring at summer solstice and recite Midsummer Night's Dream by Shakespeare, magic little people are said to appear in front of you.

http://www2.prestel.co.uk/aspen/sussex/chanctonbury.html

But she would not tell me what her fears were.

The meeting with both parents did not throw any light on the situation.

It was one of those meetings where you found yourself not being able to get anywhere inside the family. Everybody was well spoken, courteous and indeed unemotional. Mother was extremely pleasant and told her daughter that she would take her and the rest of the family on a Caribbean cruise after the exams. Tara was quite happy to stay on at the hospital despite mother's request for her to be discharged.

After the meeting, one of the nurses whispered to me that she knew the mother as she had seen her before on the adult ward when she worked nights there. Our nurses often worked nights or weekends in order to earn extra money. She went on to tell me that she in fact tried to jump onto the rail track a little while back but was somehow stopped. She also told me that the father was a very successful and wealthy man. She wondered why Tara was not in a private hospital.

I arranged to see father. In a one-to-one situation, he was a good deal more lucid and forthcoming.

Tara's mother came from a wealthy family and her own father was extremely successful. She was very pretty when he married her, although recently she had put on quite a bit of weight. She had a rather tragic family history. Her grandmother was in and out of a private psychiatric hospital where she eventually hanged herself. Her mother was diagnosed with manic-depressive disorder and killed herself by jumping onto a railway track. He felt that neither had the best treatment from the private hospitals.

His wife's first breakdown was shortly after the second daughter's birth. There was only a year's difference between the girls. She did get into a short funny phase after Tara's birth but she became pregnant again and the pregnancy seemed to settle her. He said it was not the blues but that she was more manic. She spent a lot of money on redecorating the whole house, decided she did not like the results and started all over again. Then she stopped sleeping at night. He realised that something was wrong and went to the doctor. She was admitted but was well after she was put on Lithium [59]. She did well for quite a while and he thought his nightmares were at last over. She decided she was well enough and decided to try for boys. Unfortunately the next baby was still a girl, followed by another baby girl a year later. She was very upset and stopped her medication. Not long after that she vanished from home and was seen to be behaving strangely at the local railway station. She had seldom used the trains and when questioned by the railway police could not give a good answer. She was brought home and he took her to the hospital where she confessed that she was going to kill herself. She was put on some new medication that had just come onto the market and that seemed to have worked well, except that made her put on a lot of weight.

They always had a nanny since the eldest was born and with the arrival of the younger girls they increased the staff to two

---

[59] Lithium Discovery: John Cade (1912-1980), an Australian psychiatrist, revolutionized the treatment of manic depression in 1949 by discovering lithium. It is regarded as the medical breakthrough that has led to the successful management of a mental condition which currently effects up to 2% of the world's population. It took about 20 years of struggle before lithium treatment for manic depression was accepted. But the work of Cade and his fellow supporters meant the chance for mental stability for hundreds of thousands of people around the world. Lithium remains the benchmark for bipolar treatments today.
Cade J (1949) Lithium salts in the treatment of psychotic excitement. Med J Australia 36 349

nannies and a house-keeper. He admitted he was wealthy but he did not want to use private healthcare because he felt his in-laws were badly treated. He thought his wife had been well cared for in the last ten years or so.

I am a traditionalist who believes that Lithium is still the drug of choice for Bipolar disorder (formerly Manic-Depressive Disorder)[60]. Tara's mother was well for ten years. She was taking only Lithium and no other medication.

Father was now extremely worried that Tara either had the same condition or was heading that way. He said he would have no problem with any treatment that I cared to recommend. He also told me that both his older daughters had phenomenal mood swings at the best of times and if they wanted something done it had to be done "now". He always thought that they were perhaps a bit spoiled and did not think much of it. They were both like their mother. He said he only mentioned to his wife that perhaps they could take the family on a Caribbean cruise and the next day she booked the cruise. Now he was wondering whether he might have to cancel it.

In the last three to four years it seemed to have become fashionable and even desirable for somebody to have Bipolar Disorder. The clinical landscape of child and adolescent psychiatric disorder was rapidly changing not as a result of solid research but a combination of the spread of often unsound information on the Internet and the surge of reliance on "chemicals" as the ultimate

---

[60] Bipolar disorder - Bipolar disorder, formerly called manic-depressive illness. People who have this illness tend to experience extreme mood swings, along with other specific symptoms and behaviours. These mood swings or "episodes" can take three forms: manic episodes, depressive episodes, or "mixed" episodes.

answer. Parents no longer had to feel guilty for being the cause of their child's ills and instead demanded that child psychiatrists gave their child one of the acceptable labels and suitable medication.

There was a touch of glamour to Bipolar Disorder too, as so many historical figures and modern day celebrities had been diagnosed either contemporaneously or posthumously with Bipolar Disorder[61]. A "coming out" of sorts. Many parents now are no longer satisfied with ADHD. They want Bipolar. It is helpful to de-stigmatise mental illness, but not so helpful that so many want to "catch" it.

These parents seem not to be aware that there is a serious downside to Bipolar Disorder: a very high mortality rate mainly from suicide[62].

Father however was right. Based on family history and current presentation, there was little doubt in my mind that Tara also suffered from Bipolar Disorder. Convincing the nursing staff was perhaps more difficult. Luckily the nurse that knew mother helped. Otherwise Tara would just have been branded a very

---

[61] Celebrities and Bipolar Disorder – celebrities who have this disorder or who are rumored to have this disorder include: actor Robert Downey, Jr., film maker Francis Ford Coppola, actress/writer Carrie Fisher, famed actress Vivien Leigh, Ben Stiller, poet Sylvia Plath (who committed suicide at age of 30), novelist Virginia Woolf (who drowned herself in 1941, aged 59), Thomas Jefferson, German-American entrepreneur Heinz Prechter (his death revealed a long-fought battle with manic depression that ultimately took his life), pop/country singer and actress Connie Francis.

http://bipolar.about.com/od/celebrities/Celebrities_with_Bipolar_Disorder.htm

[62] Bipolar Disorder and Suicide – People with bipolar disorder are at great risk for suicide if they are not getting treatment. The National Mental Health Association reports that 30%-70% of suicide victims have suffered from a form of depression. Men commit almost 75% of suicides, even though twice as many women attempt it.

http://www.webmd.com/content/article/102/106781.htm

spoiled child – spoiled seventeen year old and why, with such privilege, should she want to take her own life?

I started her on Lithium and within four weeks she was quite a different person. She had another four weeks before her first examination and we started trying her for some week-ends at home.

It was during one of these week-ends when mother asked Tara if she would go shopping with her. Tara declined as she was busy with her studies. Mother decided to take the younger two. For a long time father had not allowed mother to go out without one of the nannies. Somehow they were busy with other things and Tara was not really aware of the rule. Mother put the little ones in her new SUV.

When father came home, he threw a fit. Mother had been gone for three hours and was not answering her mobile. Tara told me that she realised later when mother said goodbye to her it was like a final farewell. She felt a bit strange but because of her exams she did not think twice about it.

They called the police and the Helicopter was summoned. Thanks to modern technology they were able to narrow the car down through the mobile phone signal transmission.

Mother had strapped the girls up, driven them up Chanctonbury Ring, attached a hose from the exhaust and put it through a narrow opening of one of the windows and left the car running. She left a suicide note saying she was a burden and caused Tara to be ill with her own Bipolar. Worst, she could not give her husband his heir. She took some gin and fell asleep at the back with the girls, who had probably been given drinks that were laced with gin as well.

Thank goodness for catalytic converters[63] and mobile phones – they did not come to much harm.

Unfortunately, mother had to be admitted compulsorily to a secure mental hospital and it was likely she would be there for a long time. The cruise had to be cancelled.

Tara's younger sister then took an overdose and she too was treated as a Bipolar Disorder patient. Tara managed to get the grades to get to the university she wanted.

I saw mother once walking in the garden of the secure wing of the hospital. She thanked me for all that I had done for her family.

What a tragedy. What a family tragedy!

---

[63] Cars with catalytic converters – The converter uses two different types of catalysts, a reduction catalyst and an oxidation catalyst. The reduction catalyst is the first stage of the catalytic converter. It uses platinum and rhodium to help reduce the NOx emissions to nitrogen and oxygen. The oxidation catalyst is the second stage of the catalytic converter. It reduces the unburned hydrocarbons and carbon monoxide by burning (oxidizing) them over a platinum and palladium catalyst. This catalyst aids the reaction of the CO and hydrocarbons with the remaining oxygen in the exhaust gas, turning carbon monoxide into carbon dioxide. Therefore attempting suicide by using gas from the exhaust of a modern car will not work as easily any more.

Chapter 23 Bullying

Margaret the Education Liaison Officer was about to retire. I wrote her a letter to send her my best wishes:

Dear Margaret,

For a change, I am not sending another letter asking for this or that for yet another deserving patient. It would be inappropriate for you to get such a letter within a week of your retirement.

Instead, contrary to what some other people might think, I am writing you a more personal letter to wish you a happy retirement.

You deserve it. You probably deserve it more for having to deal with the likes of me. I hope that in time you may remember bits of our communication more fondly than seem possible.

Yes, I do know you have a very limited budget as you have reminded me often enough. But then I am only a doctor and doctors are not very good managers.

It has occurred to me since I became Medical Director that most doctors are likely to make very bad managers and that is why those who tried at the CEO level in many NHS Trusts were soon displaced. It is not really because we are incapable, but because most of us still have our patients' welfare at heart.

There is an old Chinese saying: doctors have the hearts of parents. So for your own information, I doubt if I would want to stay in my manager's role for long either.

What inspired me to write is that I saw Emily today. I am sure you remember her. We must have broken the record on the number of letters and phone calls about a single patient. It is Christmas break and Emily could not wait to come to see me after her first term at university. I nearly fell off my chair when I saw her. She left me a little girl but came back with all the trimmings of sophistication. What a lot of difference three months made! She had a very good report and her essay on King Lear – why did she pick the one Shakespeare that I do not like, I wonder – received top honours and she was invited to read it to her class.

On top of that she wanted me to thank you for the support you somehow managed to find in some obscure petty cash pot funds for her travelling expenses. In spite of what you might think of all the letters I wrote on the subject, I too am slightly proud of what you came up with in the end.

I did promise you two years ago that she would be worth it and she is. So you should rightfully carry this good memory into your retirement. When you are sipping cocktail on your cruise ship or sunning in the Caribbean you might just remember: I once helped a janitor's daughter get to university.

Anyway, happy retirement and thanks also for your help with all the other patients as there are too many to mention. Nobody can say we did not try. One is in Lewis Jail awaiting trial; others are on probation, but no matter. No one has yet committed a murder.

Kind Regards
XXXXX

We had a simple rule at the clinic. All overdoses must have at least one follow-up a few weeks after the event. In our small clinic we got asked to see two to three overdoses a week on the Paediatric ward. The majority of these children were just following what was becoming fashionable and did not really require long term treatment in a psychiatric clinic. However, there was little doubt that by having a second psychiatric assessment two or three weeks after the event we could exclude treatable psychiatric conditions with confidence. We can proudly say that with this rule we had so far not missed a single one. Most overdose patients fortunately do not suffer from a serious mental illness.

Girls tended to outnumber boys by a factor of four and the commonest reason given was always: boyfriend. Overdose and other self harm behaviour such as wrist-slashing are very much a sociological phenomenon that many argue is not within the remit of psychiatrists.

Emily was first seen on the ward by one of my juniors following an overdose of a small number of Paracetamol tablets. It was vaguely about some problems with boys but she would not say much.

Two weeks later my junior saw her again and asked me to have a word. Emily had been discharged from hospital, had not returned to school and had not been very communicative with my junior. Her mother was with her and told us that Emily shut herself in her room most days, hardly ate much and only drank milk. When mother tried to talk to her she just burst into tears.

Mother took her to their General Practitioner who prescribed some antidepressants. Emily refused to take them so mother threw them away. She then decided to wait two weeks for the appointment instead of trying to get an earlier one.

I determined that it might be better if I saw Emily on her own. She was still refusing to say much. I told her that I was the consultant in charge and if she refused to say much I might not be able to get her the right treatment, which might also mean her getting the wrong treatment.

"I am not depressed for a start, and I do not need those pills the doctor gave me. Why should you care anyway? I am totally useless and I could not make a proper job of killing myself. If I had died, everybody would have been happy. See these marks? I couldn't even get a sharp enough knife to cut my wrists." She showed me her wrists and both had reddish scratch marks.

Emily was not by any description thin but seemed just right for a girl of fourteen after her two weeks of fasting.

"Also, I am so fat and nobody likes me."

"Is that why you wanted to kill yourself?"

"No, even when I tried my worst I still got top marks and everybody teased me."

"So you were not even successful in getting low marks then."

"I do not even think I am brainy because I am only the janitor's daughter."

Emily's father was the janitor at the school and had been there for years. Emily's mother was tall, slim and quite attractive. I found out later that she was a catalogue model and she had arranged for Emily to have a photo-shoot in London with the same company.

Life was not easy as the family lived within the school grounds. I sensed that Emily found life difficult to be pretty and brainy. Moreover, some girl found out that she was still a virgin and word soon got round the school. Many boys made offers, some made attempts and that was the last straw that led to the suicide attempt.

"How do you think I could get back to school?"

I quite agreed. And why should she be taking tablets for other people's perception of her?

She did not want to complain to the school especially as her father worked there and they would give him hell if they were not doing so already. She did not want to be publicly known as a victim – quite an interesting way of looking at it and I wanted to support her in that.

I thought about placing her at the local tutorial unit where they normally had timid children that found school too much. The teacher in charge, Sylvia, had become a good friend of mine through the many years we had worked together. In the early days she was given much autonomy and between us we had nursed some school phobic kids back to school or till they had done their examination. Since the new Education Act it was not as simple. A place at the tutorial unit required an "Education Statement" which involved recommendation by the Head Teacher of the school, followed by an assessment by an Educational Psychologist.

There lay the catch. Because there were too many children needing the "Statement" a long waiting list had built up for such assessments.

My suspicious mind told me that the waiting list was also a neat way for the Authority not to have to spend money on expensive Special Schools that were often private institutions charging three to five times as much as Eton[64]. Yet many of these children had nothing more than a non-psychiatric behavioural problem best described by Robert Goodman[65], who strongly argued that a number of behaviour problems were not within the remit of child psychiatry. A five-year placement cost between a quarter to half a million pounds, and often kids as young as nine were placed. More and more schools were concerned about league tables and performance targets and did not want to keep these disruptive children.

This is how the really needy were at a greater disadvantage than ever before. In the past the child psychiatrist's opinion was

---

[64] Eton – one of the top English public schools for boys. Both Princes William and Harry went there.

[65] Robert Goodman - BMJ:16 March,1988

paramount for the assessment before a child could be deemed "Maladjusted" and placed under the old Education Act. We saw ourselves as patients' advocate. However, the Education Department took exception to another professional department recommending something for which they had to fork out the finances as it is enshrined in law that they have to provide free education. Nobody seemed to ask: if the Education Department were required to organise education in hospital when a child had to spend some time in hospital, why should it be any different if a child suffering some known psychiatric condition had to be in a more specialised school?

The Education Department even took it upon their own hands to diagnose Autism – anything to be rid of conjoint working with the medical professionals.

As if that was not enough, they even banned meetings between our clinic and Educational Psychologists by decreeing that they could only meet us in their own time and they would not get paid travelling expenses. That was when one of the psychologists stopped having lunch with us and before long she decided to move to a catchment area nearer her home.

To me, to turn a professional person into a sort of form filling machine is rather destructive. There is every sign that the government is turning some part of child psychiatry that way too.

So with my friendly psychologist's departure, even my friend Sylvia could not do me the usual favour by admitting Emily first and getting the assessment done later. Everything had to be done according to strict rules. Once I was so annoyed I told someone that at Nuremberg they too followed rules. That did not go down well at all.

It soon became apparent that Emily had in fact been subjected to systemic bullying over a fairly extended period of time.

Now there is bullying and there is bullying. It is easy for most to understand the more dramatic acts. Yet chronic but persistent bullying occurs more often than people realise and it often involves some "bully" leader with a few hangers-on bullies. This may involve shoplifting for cigarettes, sweets or drinks. Or it may involve stealing money from home. Others are forced to succumb to sexual favours. More serious ones involve dealing in drugs and so on. Just when the victims think they are safe by giving in, new taunts or demands are invented. Having given sexual favours, a girl is teased as a slut and the bullying starts again.

Surprisingly very few parents are aware of this kind of bullying. Having dealt with many such cases over the years at the clinic I soon could smell what went on without the patient elaborating and I often wasted little time in taking the child off school.

This was not easy for Education Authorities to understand. I sometimes wonder if the life of murdered London headmaster, Philip Lawrence[66], could have been spared if there was a better understanding of this kind of bullying. It is an informal kind of

---

[66] Murder of London Headmaster Philip Lawrence – In March, 1996, Philip Lawrence, the popular and well-respected head of St George's School in Maida Vale, west London, died after being stabbed as he tried to protect one of his pupils from a gang attack outside his comprehensive school. A boy of 16 was subsequently convicted.

GANG. Some children are in serious danger and there have been many suicide attempts because of this kind of bullying.

Some would argue that it is a tough world out there and that we have no business keeping these children in a greenhouse.

Well, greenhouses are important for bringing on plants before you gently harden them.

There is also another argument for sending them back to school. How can we know that our diagnosis is correct? What if we were wrong? We would be wasting the authority's money.

With experience we soon know. In all branches of medicine, early diagnosis is the key and child psychiatry is no different. Subjecting a child to repeated bullying can often lead to tragedy and only those cases that result in deaths come to the public's notice. Personally I am not prepared to take that risk.

Others argue that going to school is very important for these children as they need to socialise.

There are drives to stamp out bullying but we all know that bullying on a bigger scale goes on in big corporations and even in government.

After a few sessions with Emily I realised that I was dealing with an exceptionally bright child. Going purely by family background and genetics, I would be hard pushed to explain how she was so intelligent. On the other hand growing up amongst refugee families in post war and post communist Hong Kong we learned from an early age to ignore parental occupation. If we only believed in genetics there were ample examples of these little break-outs. To me an enlightened government must be able to provide for these children as they too hold the future of the country.

Emily showed me from the beginning that she was a thinker. There was a big part of her who felt that she could not be just like any of the girls who would end up having a baby before sixteen and being on benefits. She had seen the disadvantage of the kind of work her father did.

She also talked to me about her near date rape experience which she felt taught her a good deal. She was only able to talk about that after making sure that I would not take any action. I took a chance as it had become impossible for us to give such assurances. However, someone's mental well being is more important than protocol and procedure. Over a period of time in both neighbouring counties roughly 400 sex abuse situations were reported, of which about 40 were investigated and only 4 were presented to the Director of Public Prosecution for consideration for going to trial. The legal system is unfortunately biased towards the protection of perpetrators not victims. If I could help it I would not turn one of my patients into a victim.

Medical Schools should remember to teach future doctors that without breaking rules and old dogma, no progress would ever be made in medicine. I went to an excellent medical school and one of the most impressive thing I learned in Gynaecology was how the great Professor Aleck Bourne[67] performed an abortion on a girl who was pregnant by rape because he felt that the girl's mental

---

[67] Aleck Bourne (1886-1974) MA, MB, FRCS, FRCOG, eminent gynaecologist, In 1938 Bourne came into the public eye when he operated to terminate the pregnancy of a girl aged 14 years and nine months, who had been criminally assaulted and raped by some soldiers in a London barracks. The operation was done in St. Mary's Hospital and Bourne himself drew the attention of the police to his intervention. He was tried at the Central Criminal Court in July, 1938, on a charge of procuring abortion and was acquitted. His action was described by the Lancet as "an example of disinterested conduct in consonance with the highest traditions of the profession".

health was more important than any law. It really started the whole modern day thinking on abortion and it also signalled the start of the hold religion had on the practice of Medicine. When Barnard performed the heart transplant in our final year of Medical School it was like discovering that the earth was round.

Emily would normally be entitled to home tuition but that would only be for five hours a week and most often home tuition is provided to children who are lagging at least two years behind in school. Trying to organise something for Emily proved to be practically impossible as she was way ahead of her year and she would need at least five home tutors with different subject skills to meet all her needs.

Then I remembered this rather delightful all girls state school at the corner of the county. Parents had a choice and could opt for their child to be educated in a single sex school. There was a boys school as well. The freedom to choose had one little catch. You had to get yourself there.

This school had become quite well sought after. It was more or less like the old grammar school without the name and a private girls school without the fee.

Emily jumped at the idea without even considering whether her parents could afford the travelling cost. It came as a big surprise to both the school and the authorities that one of Dr Zhang's school refusal patients would like to go to another school. The other bit of surprise to which they did not admit was that she was only the janitor's daughter. No doubt they also wondered if I thought she could cope with the rather demanding curriculum of the school.

"She would not cope if you took too long to decide and she had to miss many terms," I wanted to tell them. If my hunch was right she was definitely university material if not Oxbridge[68]. Even my secretary checked with me three times before sending the letter. I told my secretary that she knew I was always good at spotting the bright ones without testing them and "when was the last time I was wrong?" She said she was only concerned for my reputation as I had then risen to be the Medical Director.

I once saw a boy of three and a half and speculated that he was of genius quality. It took another five years before I could bribe a psychologist to test him privately. He turned out to have an IQ of 149 on the revised test[69] and I have not seen many scores above 130 on that scale.

Once you have established a good bond with a patient, the patient tends to want to make sure you succeed too. To go by public transport to that school Emily had to catch a bus, change to a train and then take another bus. She had to get up at four to make sure she could be at school by eight. This was rural England. Mother increased her cleaning commitment to pay for the fares. She would do anything to help their only child. She was one of those people who would never argue or question you. She was of the old school and had traditional values. She did not mind the sacrifices.

---

[68] Oxbridge – Oxford or Cambridge

[69] Wechsler Intelligence Scale for Children - III

Within about two weeks of Emily starting her new school her father had a heart attack. This caused quite a bit of concern especially it was early days for Emily's new regime. It turned out that father was also trying to earn some extra money doing other people's gardening and the physical stress proved too much.

Mother then revealed to me that they tried to cut down the journey time for Emily by paying for a taxi for part of the journey and now that her husband was in hospital they could no longer afford that.

That was when I thought there must be some way the authorities could help.

Children who are assessed as needing special education in a special school or even a tutorial unit get a taxi ride paid for wherever they live. In these cases, the authorities also pay for parents' transport to school meetings and so on. As you can imagine, special education involves the authorities a very substantial sum, counting the cost of transport, school fees for the privately run special schools and the high cost of running state ones. I knew the cost because I had been consultant to two state run special schools in my career.

This was how some of the exchanges went:

"As she opts to go to a normal school no such payment is allowed."

"But she was badly bullied at school."

"Maybe. But she was not prepared to name names."

"She did not want to be a victim."

"A procedure is a procedure. In any case how do we know Emily is telling the truth?"

I went to the top and many letters and phone calls later some special fund was found.

I just had to agree that it was a one-off. No precedent.

Sure.

Emily did not get her modelling job. They were looking for someone much wilder nowadays, mother told me in private, but she was glad that at least she tried it.

Father had a quadruple bypass and had to be retired on health grounds.

That in fact opened up a different opportunity for them. I found out later that Emily was leaving home earlier to avoid seeing anyone from school. Following father's retirement the council was obliged to re-house them as they could no longer live on school grounds.

God has mysterious ways.

They of course were delighted to leave the area and moved to a much better location for Emily's school. After the move, Emily only had to take one train in the morning. The authorities were delighted with the reduction in the cost of transportation and she could get on with her work.

Despite living quite far from my clinic after the move, Emily continued to see me for regular follow-ups.

Her school was extremely surprised at their new little gem. She proved quite an English scholar and was the only one in her year to be offered an interview at Oxford. She came to see me before and after the event and was thankful that she was better prepared than most on what to expect. Unfortunately she did not get a place but was offered one at Warwick[70].

"No, I did not get it wrong," I told my secretary as she typed the letter. "She was Oxbridge material. She had the interview, didn't she?"

"Perhaps Oxford should have asked your opinion," my secretary said.

"Perhaps."

---

[70] Warwick University – consistently ranked in the Top Ten UK Universities in the national league table.

Chapter 24 Ping Pong

It is the nature of life that now and again you have to do people favours. Sometimes you do it in case you need favours back. More often than not it is about doing the right thing.

One of my outpatient colleagues was female and ethnic. When she realised that I became in charge of the adolescent unit, she said to me, good, now I can get some of my patients admitted.

It was very difficult to decide if there was racism or sexism. It was true that many of her referrals did not get to be admitted and most of the time the nurses had justifiable reasons. One nurse in particular warned me from day one that I should not touch any of her cases.

Nurses are very powerful in an adolescent unit. They have front-end dealings with patients from pre-admission to admission to discharge. For someone new like me it would have been foolish not to take notice of such a clear cut warning. But anyone who knows me well enough would not expect me to be easily intimidated. I would not have an all out fight but I have my ways.

However, this consultant did not help herself in matters. Before my arrival she had been writing to the Health Authorities about her difficulties in getting patients admitted. Luckily for the nurses all the blame was laid on the previous consultant who was eventually suspended and dismissed.

By then, the nurses felt that they were in some position of authority and my emergence was not exactly met with fanfare, although there was for some a sense of relief as my success at the Children's Unit in the last ten months was beyond anybody's expectation except mine. The nurses working in the Children's Unit, including the wife of the charge nurse at the adolescent unit, warned me that adolescents were different.

It was also difficult to turn up at a place that had been running on auto-pilot for some time. The staff began to feel that doctors might not indeed be necessary except for this silly rule that they alone could prescribe.

The consultant in question was known to have an "over-understanding" approach to cases and she felt sorry for a number of patients where there was a strong social element to the problem. Due to shortage of beds, we did try to limit admission to genuine psychiatric cases.

However when I was asked by the Health Authorities handling her complaints to look at one of her cases again what choice did the nurses think I had? Quite simply, admit or else.

But the decision was always mine!

One of the boy's problems was that he lived with mum and had not been to school for nearly a year. As the consultant requested an assessment at a psychiatric unit, Education Department refused even to look at him until that had happened.

A stalemate.

In the meantime, Education Department had saved the better part of thirty thousand pounds and they had a legitimate reason. He was first kicked out of school because he used threatening language with a female teacher when asked to read his story.

Mother also reported how threatening he was to her at times.

From this bit of history he was definitely no good for our unit. The last time the unit had to be closed in the middle of the night was precisely because of violence to female staff.

We too had a legitimate reason not to admit him.

I took the charge nurse Martin on one side and asked him to tell me what he would think if we were dealing with a brand new referral.

I discovered months later that he found me genuine and really wanted to give me a chance to make a go of it. As such he had to tell me the problem.

The problem of anarchy.

There was amongst some staff a strong anti-authority feeling. There was no doubt they were let down by the previous consultant and some of the nurses could have been hurt. Following the incident, an outside consultant was employed to provide a report at great expense to the NHS Trust. I could have told them the problem free of charge.

Such is management nowadays that the dirty work has to be done by an outsider. We were still in the investigation period and no doubt everything I did would be under scrutiny. The survival of the unit would depend on the outside consultant's report. I had lunch with him on many occasions and luckily his NHS views were in fact very close to mine. Six weeks he had to be with the unit and six weeks was a long time.

So I was lucky in that there had to be a truce. We could not let personal prejudices override clinical decisions.

In the end and some thousands of pounds later we managed to keep our unit running and in some little way I changed my view about outside consultants. The good ones are good and this one was a practising inpatient child psychiatrist so there was no need really to say too much about politics and anarchism. He understood because he experienced it himself, and he found a way to deal with it.

So running an adolescent unit is like running a mini-country. In our democratic age, the wisest thing to do is to bring about the changes you want when you are riding high, and then leave. Do not wait to be kicked out.

As psychiatrists, we do have certain power conferred by the Mental Health Act and that is often a sore reminder of the difference between us and the other staff – more so as we still had two Sectioned patients in the unit at the time: one anorectic on tube feeding and one psychotic.

Martin the charge nurse said he would visit the boy Leroy at home to assess him and if I could agree to a time-limited admission we might have a "goer". He thought that Leroy was probably "all barks" only. His father was from the West Indies and the one time Martin met Leroy he was just loud and boastful and not as threatening as mother always made him out to be.

In the two years I lived on a Caribbean island, I discovered that many of the children there were in fact very gentle and timid, and they were never rude to their parents. I know not all the islands are the same and generalisation can be very dangerous.

"But you may have to speak with Kevin. He visited the last time."

Kevin was the one who warned me not to even think about it. There were many ways to deal with violence in our kind of unit. More often than not if the adolescent patients sensed that there was no leadership they ran wild.

I decided on a direct approach.

"I am going to be frank with you, Kevin. I want you to go out with Martin and see this boy again and I want him in a.s.a.p. unless you can convince me that there is a good reason why he should not have the benefit of a six week assessment. I know you think I am doing a favour and I can tell you now, I am. Sometimes in life you have to because not doing it is going to hurt a lot more people, including ourselves."

"Six weeks then."

My new junior, who was a very timid girl, decided to go out on the visit too when she realised that there would be protection. Leroy had just turned thirteen and she told me that she thought he might well have the King's disease.

"You mean what they claim King George VI had?" I thought it was very clever of the drug firms wanting to push the new drug for Social Phobia to involve the King. "Don't forget King George VI had lung cancer and metastasis could do strange things."

No problem. Leroy agreed to come in when he learned that we had two ping pong tables and that Martin played County Championship League. My junior said she was glad she went and she really did not understand what the fuss before was about. I told her that even in adult psychiatry, reports on patients could often paint an unreal picture and the mildest people could be made to appear like big monsters.

It was suggested that the only time there might be trouble would be when the boy came to be admitted, and therefore he should not come in his mother's car but in a hospital bus instead, accompanied by some of the big male nurses. I might have given in to the idea but my junior came to my rescue. She would go with the charge nurse and bring him in her car. Mum could drive down on her own.

"It is a hospital lease car anyway."

"The last time a male nurse offered to take a female patient home he was accused of touching her and he was suspended."

"Was he guilty?"

"No, but he died of a heart attack. We shall send our bus but you can be the medical escort."

I remember once escorting a Manic Depressive (Bipolar 1) from Hong Kong to London and I had to inject him en route, sitting right at the back of a BOAC[71] 707. That was an experience.

---

[71] BOAC – British Overseas Airways Corporation, now British Airways

So I reminded my junior, "Don't forget the rapid sedation pack – just kidding."

Why should all the fun be left to the nurses, I thought to myself but I was never going to let her drive, Crown Car or otherwise.

Leroy looked as if he was going to camp, with his new white trainers and sports outfit that father presented over the weekend together with the latest sunglasses.

Martin told me sometime later that father called him wanting to know if I was "Cool, man. You know what I mean, man."

"I told him you were actually Chinese. He said he did not want no white doctor putting no funny thing into his boy. I also told him the consultant would be happy to see him any time he liked."

Martin reckoned he was doped up heavy with something from the way he was slurring his speech. He was all right as long as I was not white.

"Good, no more racism. Not from us."

Father also gave Leroy a new sports-bag to carry all his stuff. It was really too big for him and my junior reported to me the verbal duel between mother and son.

"You are blocking the way with that stupid bag."

"Dad gave it to me."

"He is stupid."

"He is not."

"Why didn't you go live with him?"

"You took his house."

"He shouldn't hit me and you are copying him. Stupid bag, you are not going to Jamaica, you know, stupid sunglasses."

"Tag Heuer, they are the best."

"Move your stupid bag. Stupid Nike bag."

She turned to my junior, "He does not really want to go in, and that is why he is so slow."

With that he moved.

"Have you read Jay Haley[72]?" Jay Haley was a dominating figure in developing the Palo Alto Group's communications model and strategic family therapy, which became popular in the 1970's.

"I have read Bateson." Gregory Bateson was the well known social scientist who wrote *Steps to an Ecology of Mind*, and *Mind & Nature*.

I am beginning to like her. She is going to be a good psychiatrist.

So Leroy arrived and was at a bit of a loss standing outside the Nurses' Office.

It was time for mother to leave. We tended not to let mothers stay too long for admission for obvious reasons.

"Aren't you going to give me a kiss then? Why aren't you crying? I thought you did not want to come in."

---

[72] Jay Haley - A brilliant strategist and devastating critic, Jay Haley was a dominating figure in developing the Palo Alto Group's communications model and strategic family therapy, which became popular in the 1970's. He studied under three of the most influential pioneers in the evolution of family therapy - Gregory Bateson, Milton Erickson, and Salvador Minuchin, and combined ideas from each of these innovative thinkers to form his own unique brand of family therapy.

http://www.abacon.com/famtherapy/haley.html

Did she not realise that maybe the boy was not that stupid? After a year shut up in the house with a mother like that, he would take up any chance to be away for six weeks!

He did kiss her and started to cry.

My junior cried too. I thought she did because she felt sorry for the boy.

"Leroy is a lamb, isn't he?" Martin said to me later.

"So we shall be fine then."

He smiled.

For the first weekend inpatients were normally not granted home leave to allow for settling in and from then on the weekend leaves would be dependent on their performance at community meetings and on how they were assessed by their fellow patients. They had to ask for a grade and if the grade was not good enough they were not allowed home. This system had been running for years and I really did not want to rock the boat at such an early stage.

It was all stage-managed by the teaching staff, who unfortunately found this the only way whereby they could have any control over the children's behaviour.

The first weekend Leroy was fine except when mother visited. There was some silly argument and he took himself to the toilet and did not come out until he was assured mum was gone.

Then he said he missed his dad, who did not have a car and mum refused to drive him down as the last time she drove him somewhere he hit her after some argument.

"He wanted a new game from dad and dad promised he would get him one if he could get home leave," Kevin told me the real reason he wanted to be home.

That is very much the modern way a parent relates to a child. They do not know any other way.

"Psychology, you see," he told Kevin over the phone. "I want to help the China Man."

"I need everybody's help!"

"Do you agree that Leroy has Social Phobia[73]? Everything fitted in with the criteria in DSM IV." My junior plucked up courage to ask me during supervision.

It was good to keep oneself on one's toes with juniors who had just arrived from London and who read up on everything.

"What's wrong with shyness?" I joked, "Do you want me to put him on SSRI (Selective serotonin reuptake inhibitors)?"

"It is supposed to work."

---

[73] Social Phobia (now renamed Social Anxiety Disorder): Everyone feels nervous from time to time. Going on a first date or giving a speech often causes that butterflies-in-your-stomach feeling, for example. Or maybe you feel shy at a party among a group of strangers, but then slowly warm up to them and have a great time.

For some people, though, this normal nervousness is magnified into extreme anxiety, fear and self-consciousness. Everyday social activities, even the most mundane, are virtually impossible. They may avoid dating, giving speeches or attending parties altogether. They may not even be able to eat with others or write a check at the grocery store.

When someone's anxiety is so extreme that it disrupts their life and they avoid certain situations, they may have social anxiety disorder. Social anxiety disorder is a chronic condition that causes an irrational anxiety or fear of activities or situations in which the sufferer feels others may be watching or judging him/her. They also fear that they will embarrass or humiliate themselves. Social anxiety disorder can be so debilitating that it interferes with work, school and other routine activities.

http://www.mayoclinic.com/health/social-anxiety-disorder/DS00595

"If he starts taking SSRI at thirteen, what is he going to do for the rest of his life?!"

"The newer short acting ones are supposed to be better."

"Take one advice from me; think the opposite, the opposite to what the big Pharmas tell you. In pharmacology, shorter acting drugs are more addictive. That was what I learned in Medical School and is still true if you think carefully about it."

By Community Meeting time nobody had a hard word to say about Leroy, but they all noticed he did not socialise much. He had to ask for his grade as per time-honoured ritual. He could not. Everybody tried to urge him. My junior sat next to him and tried to hold his hand. He rushed off to the toilet and locked himself in again.

"To lock yourself in a toilet is a down-gradable offence and to do it twice in a week is just not on. And, Doctor, we have to be very strict with these rules. Otherwise we shall start having problems again," said a teacher.

So, I was warned. My junior got rather emotional and said that was just too much for her. It was her first case and why couldn't they be more understanding?

Martin interjected and said that of course if there were psychological reasons the consultant could grant a special home visit like half a day so that everybody could save face.

I liked that. Saving face. But then how popular would I be with the teachers?

What about Leroy's face?

I knew whose face I wanted to save.

So I arranged to see Leroy straight away. No, I did not ask him why he could not speak up for himself. I knew already.

"I hear you are a very good ping pong player."

"Table Tennis, you mean." He was speaking to me.

"O.K. Table Tennis. You know he is good." I said, pointing to Martin.

"Yeah, that is why I am not playing him. I played with Gerry." Gerry was his nurse.

"The fat one."

He smiled a little, thinking I was rude.

"He was a bit slow."

"You must have given him a good run."

Smile again.

"I hear you did not play with the kids though."

"How did you know? They are no good."

"Well, how about this? Have you ever played a Chinese?"

"No."

"We hold the bat differently, you know."

"Weird."

"We'll play three games and if you win you can go home for half a day and if you don't, you stay."

The look on my junior's face was something to be seen. Martin put on a look to pretend that he knew I would come up with something, although he admitted later that what I suggested was the last thing on his mind.

The scene was set for a three game match between the consultant and his patient to decide if his patient could go for a short week-end leave.

Even the headmaster came out to watch, shaking his head in disbelief.

It was spring, still cold but sunny. The sun was streaming in. I lost the first game. I had not played for fifteen years. I took off my jacket. I barely managed the second. That brought some cheers.

From certain quarters.

He beat me bad on the last one. I did not get past 9 and that was bad for ping pong – sorry, Table Tennis.

I thought everybody forgave me. I did not give the game to him. He beat me fair and square. The situation was too surreal for anyone to remember to get cross.

The girls clapped as they all loved him and wanted to mother him, especially the older ones, even when many of them did not have a chance of home leave as their weight was not good.

I became their hero. Nobody reported me to the General Medical Council. Not that time, anyway.

Mother was horrified but thought that if he had been good and had not attacked any female he would be fine. She would just take him to his father, who would buy him his game.

On Saturday I was there for a new admission. My junior rushed in saying there was a disaster. Leroy would not go with mum because she did not want to buy him a Diet Coke from the Petrol Station next door. She said there was a pack from Tesco sitting at home and the Coke from the Petrol Station was too expensive.

"After all that!" I exclaimed to myself.

He just sat near the door. I went out, waved my arm in a table tennis move and asked him to follow me to the car.

"Cool wheels," he said, "but it's for old people though."

I ignored him, opened the car boot and gave him a can of Diet Coke – still cool from the overnight frost.

I knew where his problem was.

Chapter 25 Crying and Sleep

Do you think babies should be allowed to cry?
My sister in-law-asked me on the plane as we flew in together to Hong Kong for a wedding.

"Why do you ask that?"

"My sister lives in California and there her paediatrician told her that she should never allow her baby to cry."

Fashion was moving into child care. Not crying is this year's new BLACK. I thought to myself.

Doctors are notorious for making the wrong recommendations over the ages.

"Remember the days when breast feeding was considered bad by the same doctors and babies were fed goat milk only to be infected because of contamination?"

"I did not know that," my sister-in-law admitted. "I did hear that some sunshine is now said to be good for you[74]."

"I know, Australia has been so successful with the Sunscreen campaign that they now have a vitamin D deficiency problem[75]."

"What about margarine?"

"All the years of people being taken in! Stay with good old olive oil and butter. Just not too much."

"What about baby food? I used to give my babies my own home prepared food."

"In some societies, preference is still given to tinned or bottled baby food that has high sugar content. No wonder we have problems with obesity in children and adults, but they have tried to blame it on genes. It is interesting to visit some countries where babies are not fed canned or bottled baby food and see how small the people generally are."

"And the question of crying?" My sister-in-law was not that easy to distract.

"There is something fundamentally wrong if a baby cries all the time. To me, that is a sure indication of pain or discomfort. Years ago we did not need child psychiatrists because we had grandparents. Now we either do not live close to grandparents or we feel that their ideas are too old fashioned. Mothers prefer to turn to doctors for advice."

---

[74] Scientists say vitamin D from ultraviolet rays may fight cancer. It helped protect against lymphoma and cancers of the prostate, lung and, ironically, the skin. The strongest evidence is for colon cancer. http://www.msnbc.msn.com/ID/7875140/

[75] Robinson et al.: The re-emerging burden of rickets: a decade of experience from Sydney. Archives of Disease in Childhood 2006;91:564-568

"She is not close to any relatives."

"There are different kinds of parents. Overall it may be useful to look at three main types: the over-reacting, the under-reacting and the normal-reacting. It is beginning to sound quite simple once you have been told, isn't it? It also makes child psychiatry interesting. When parents come to see us, it is our job to decipher to which type they belong. Now you think that is straightforward enough. Let me tell you this, the same parents can be all three types under different circumstances and in different situations."

"I think she is definitely the over-reacting type."

"There are parents who are totally obsessed with the right foods and healthiness for their babies but have no second thought about pumping cigarette smokes around them."

"She does not smoke."

"In an interesting way one cannot learn to bring up a child just by reading books. Humans survived over 74 million years because they learn from their parents and ancestors. Modern education has one major side effect – it takes away some of our instinctual capabilities. Think about it, instinct only surfaces when needed. Mothers usually have the instinct to respond to their infants in an appropriate way. Observational studies of the animal kingdom inform us that their parenting skills cannot have come by books."

"But books are what mark us out from animals."

"I grant you that, but many well-educated parents have so much trouble with bringing up children because they trust books more than they trust their own instincts. Books can be good references for illness of all kinds, but beyond that instinct will help a mother to decide if a piece of advice is good or not. The most tragic example of a public health campaign that had gone wrong in modern child rearing is that concerning sudden infant death syndrome (SIDS) or Cot Death."

"Oh. She is worried about that too. But I know that happens rarely amongst the Chinese."

"There was a time when paediatricians advised mothers to put babies to sleep on their tummies for the reason that if a baby vomits, it is less likely to choke. This went on for quite a while and nobody thought much about it if not for some rather bizarre events that followed the publication of a paper by paediatricians from Hong Kong[76]."

"When was that?"

"1985 Lancet."

"I thought it was 1992 when they recommended sleeping babies on the back."

"That is a long story. Apart from low infant mortality figures, Hong Kong also enjoyed a very low SIDS incident. In fact most recorded cases were expatriate Caucasians. The 1985 paper put forward several theories including the fact that the majority of

---

[76] 1985 Cot Death paper from Hong Kong - Cot death is very rare in Hong Kong; this may be an important contributory factor to the low postneonatal mortality (3.1 per 1000). Over the 5 years 1980-84 only 15 cases of cot death were documented by forensic pathologists--an approximate incidence of 0.036 per 1000 live births. If the incidence was similar to that in western countries (2-3 per 1000), 800-1200 cot deaths might have been expected over this period. It is argued that this rare occurrence is real and not cot death masquerading as other causes of death. It is speculated that perhaps life-style (including crowded living conditions), the practice of placing babies supine in their cots rather than prone, and a lower frequency of preterm birth could contribute.
Davies,D.P. Lancet. 1985 Dec 14;2(8468):1346–1349. Cot death in Hong Kong: a rare problem?

http://www.ncbi.nlm.nih.gov/sites/entrez?db=PubMed&cmd=Retrieve&list_uids=2866397
http://www.pubmedcentral.nih.gov/picrender.fcgi?artid=1835990&blobtype=pdf

Chinese parents in Hong Kong ignored the advice to put babies to sleep on their tummies. My own speculative view is that the unclean air, high background noise level and crowded living conditions may have been contributing factors to a different arousal level so that infants have a much lighter sleep pattern and are therefore less likely to just fade away as in quiet country suburbs."

"What happened in 1992?"

"Because such findings came out of the small British colony of Hong Kong three prominent Professors challenged the findings in a prestigious medical journal. They even suggested that the Chinese were probably hiding and secretly disposing of their dead babies."

"We do get very bad press for lots of things!"

"Fortunately a group from Tasmania[77], of all places, decided to carry out a control study, by suggesting to prospective parents randomly how to place their babies, on their tummies or on their back. It is amazing how under-reactive some parents really are and do not mind subjecting their precious babies to a life and death situation. Now it is considered unethical to conduct a control study in such a way. If a drug is so obviously life-saving another way of assessing its value has to be found, rather than denying half the patients the chance of survival."

---

[77] Prospective cohort study of prone sleeping position and sudden infant death syndrome. Dwyer. (*Lancet* 1991; 337: 1244-1247). Lancet. 1985 Dec 14;2(8468):1346–1349. The "Island State" provided a perfect source population for unbiased selection of cases and comparison samples or controls. Further, the land area and population size (around 500 000 people) made follow-up of cohorts relatively easy. Thus, Tasmania had important advantages for the two major strategies used to search for environmental and lifestyle causes of disease — case-control and cohort studies. *Terence Dwyer, MD, FAFPHM, Director.*

"I am surprised too.   So what were the results of the research?"

"Nearly 50% fewer Cot Death in the sleep on back group. That was 1991. The rest is history"

"I thought it was 1992."

"That was when the view was taken up in U.S."

"I see."

"In 1991 British news anchor Anne Diamond's son Norman died of SIDS and she only found out about the Tasmania research when she travelled to New Zealand[78]. She was furious. The story did not end there. There are still paediatricians who insist that premature infants have better oxygenation if they sleep on their tummies."

"Now back to the question of whether one should let a baby cry."

"Did I not answer that?"

"You mean parents should understand the importance of trusting one's instinct?"

---

[78] Anne Diamond and SIDS - In THIS WEEK [31/10/91] Anne Diamond reported on the research in New Zealand. Significant factors include babies sleeping on their stomachs, over-heating and not being breast fed. Research in New Zealand and Avon has reduced SIDS incidence by up to 50% but the programme suggests the UK Government has done nothing. Audience includes parents who have lost children in cot deaths and some mothers in tears describe what happened.

In 1969, when Beckwith proposed the now universally accepted definition of the sudden infant death syndrome, there were around 1200 sudden infant deaths in England and Wales each year. Through the 1970s and 1980s this annual total remained at about 1000 until the "back to sleep" campaign at the beginning of this decade. This campaign was reinforced by the death of the child of a well known and popular TV presenter and its attendant publicity. Since then, the annual totals, although they vary slightly from year to year, now hover around the 400 mark.

http://www.bmj.com/cgi/content/full/319/7211/697

I used to run a fortnightly sleep clinic – a parent and child group for parents with sleep problem infants. There the parents were empowered to trust their own instinct and to feel that they were doing a great job already. All they needed was an understanding of the science of sleep and the majority of parents no longer felt that they had a problem after just one visit. Yet often there really was no point by point advice from me on what to do. Of course a small group of parents continued to have a problem but they are in the minority.

"Yes – if the advice fits in with the instinct then we should follow it."

"The advice to put babies on their tummies seems to be the single most deadly medical advice of all time."

"And the advice to lie on the back in the BACK TO SLEEP campaign has remained the single most successful one in the UK and a number of other countries."

Chapter 26 Forgiveness

KING CLAUDIUS
….My fault is past. But, O, what form of prayer
Can serve my turn? 'Forgive me my foul murder'?...

HAMLET
Now might I do it pat, now he is praying;
And now I'll do't. And so he goes to heaven;

Hamlet Act 3, Scene 3.
William Shakespeare

Sometimes we are reminded of our patients in the most unusual way. One summer we had the opportunity to go on a Baltic Cruise which started and finished in Copenhagen. It is unavoidable on such tours to come across tragic stories in history. The different Baltic countries had their fair share of wars, sieges, slaughters and some of the most macabre murders in the history of mankind.

Our last stop was outside Elsinore and those of us who were interested were tendered to visit Kronborg Castle, the setting for Shakespeare's Hamlet.

Hamlet reminded me of Anita. She refused to attend school because of Hamlet. In my work I have come across many unusual patients but it has never occurred to me that someone would refuse school because of Hamlet.

I can still remember being called to see her on a Domiciliary Visit as she had refused to come to the clinic. The parents were not very forthcoming and felt that at seventeen, she should be able to talk to me herself.

She reluctantly agreed. We then had a most interesting discussion about Hamlet. She was upset because her English teacher did not like what she wrote about Hamlet. The essay was about Hamlet and forgiveness. She felt that Hamlet indeed should have been more "forgiving" and killed his uncle when he was praying.

"So what if the uncle goes to Heaven? Big deal!"

"Instead," she added, "he got himself killed as well."

Our sweet prince was no hero to her and that upset her teacher. He really wanted the class to write about Hamlet and Laertes exchanging forgiveness[79].

She then refused to return to school. At least that was what appeared to be the problem.

---

[79] LAERTES
Exchange forgiveness with me, noble Hamlet:
Mine and my father's death come not upon thee,
Nor thine on me.
Hamlet, Act 5, Scene 2

I eventually got her back to school and persuaded her to see me at the clinic regularly for the next eight months or so. She wrote a good deal and told me that she kept a diary that was kept under lock and key. She said whatever happened she would never let anyone see it, not even her psychiatrist, as she would probably have to kill that person afterwards. I did not ask to see it and told her that I had no intention of asking to see it in future.

Teenagers have their secrets and I certainly want to respect that, I thought. She did show me some other writings and she had some very interesting and unusual things to say.

Looking back, I often wondered about the challenges we faced, having to base our diagnosis and treatment on some of the most subjective things related to us by our often very disturbed patients. We could hardly expect to get any "truth" from them, and yet various psychiatric professional bodies seem to accept psychiatric diagnosis made in this way as infallible. She probably did give me a clue but unfortunately I missed it.

One day she was very distressed, saying she thought she might have caught something from a Spanish Waiter that she slept with. I was a bit puzzled as she did not appear to be the promiscuous type and certainly not the type who would sleep with someone she hardly knew.

We had some discussion and I advised her to go to the Special STD[80] Clinic to have it seen to.

She never turned up again despite several reminders.

---

[80] STD - Sexually Transmitted Diseases Clinics are set up to encourage patients to attend without fear of stigma.

Then she came to the notice of the adult psychiatric department following a serious overdose. This was on the day of her father's death. She saw a lady psychiatrist and disclosed to her that her father had been abusing her since she was eleven. She never kept any follow-up appointments though and there had not been any further episodes of self harm.

Nearly a quarter of a century later we had four boys referred because of serious sleep disturbance. One of my colleagues at the clinic made an initial home visit and afterwards asked to see me in a distressed state.

She said it was one of the worst cases she had ever come across and asked me to see the mother, who happened to be my patient twenty some years prior.

It was Anita.

She, who should be in her early 40s then, appeared worn and exhausted, and looked much older than her age.

When her father died it was all too much for her. She said she was very confused by what happened to her. She admitted that there never was a Spanish Waiter but she was hoping that I would enquire further. She was desperate to understand what was going on then.

"The overdose woke me up," she recalled, "I felt I had to forgive what my father did to me."

She decided to go into journalism. One of her assignments was to do an article on a notorious murderer. For that, she had to interview that murderer in prison.

"That was the start of all my troubles."

Fascinated by her first case experience, she became a voluntary prison visitor for those prisoners who did not have any visitor of their own.

"We live in a very forgiving society."

Then she met this man that was to become her husband. He was serving time for murder.

"He killed his father who abused him for as long as he knew," Anita recalled, "I could identify with him and I felt so sorry for him."

Was it the process of reparation? I too struggled to understand her.

She found herself falling in love with him.

Prisons allowed conjugal visits and before long she had two boys by him. Because of her and the children the parole board soon granted him day release passes.

A murderer granted day release! Not long after he was out on license.

We indeed do have a rather forgiving penal system.

"But he never even knew his father, let alone killed him!"

By age nineteen he was doing time in a borstal and soon after his release he killed the landlord who took pity on him and gave him board and lodging. The landlord was unfortunate enough to catch him trying to steal from him.

"I did not know until the trial."

It is amazing how protective we are of convicted criminals. I could never understand why the probation service did not warn her.

No wonder the public has little faith in our rather liberal judicial and parole system. People sitting on parole boards seem to continue to fail to see into the darker side of the human psyche. Often those trained to understand the human mind also appear not to understand, or are they so driven by performance targets and results that they just want another successful treatment to add to their credit?

This man had "anger management" therapy when he was doing time. The truth is a psychopathic personality is capable of adapting to suit his ulterior motive. We do have too many psychiatric casualties from such unfortunate releases from maximum security mental hospitals and I am not even referring to psychotic patients.

He could not hold his job as a security guard and started to do break-ins. He was open to his wife and she said she did not understand why she never informed his probation officer.

"Perhaps I was afraid of him but he convinced me that these people would get their money back from insurance and he was never going to hurt anyone as he loved her and the children and did not want to be locked up again."

One cannot help wondering how much the wives of "famous" serial killers actually knew and to what extent they were convinced by the arguments put forward by their spouses.

She had two more boys.

One day he decided that they could make more money if he set her up as a prostitute. He would stop the house break-ins as it was getting more dangerous with the alarms set up by people.

Surprisingly she went along.

"I had to do something to stop his burglary activities. I did not want to lose him."

"I was sick over the first client. As it reminded me so much of what my father did, I told him I could not do it."

The next day he said he was resuming his break-in business.

"The rest is in the papers."

He came home when the children were having tea. He was covered in blood.

"The idiots tried to stop me!" he told her.

The children were screaming. Suddenly she felt a strong repulsion and called the police.

Even the most forgiving philanthropist had her limits.

"I was thinking more of my children. I was not going to be like my mother. I was sure she knew all along."

I had to agree.

How could this ever have been allowed to happen? What did her forgiveness do to her? Could I have done anything?

He was tried for murder and sentenced to life imprisonment without parole. What he did was much worse than what he told her on the day he came home covered in blood, but that was by and by. Hopefully no one will think it unkind to lock him away forever. You never know.

Anita had to pick up the pieces of her life again, having had her long held belief in good human nature and forgiveness totally demolished.

It was probably destroyed a long time ago by someone she should have been able to trust.

Chapter 27 Sadness

And your experience makes you sad:
I had rather have a fool to make me merry
than experience to make me sad.....

As You Like It - Act II, Scene 7
William Shakespeare

With so many quotable quotes from As You Like It you may wonder why I would chose to pick this one.

Perhaps it is a warning to young doctors to enjoy the blessings of inexperience. Luckily for me sadness brought about by experience from my clinical work is mercifully little but I would be either dishonest or heartless to say that there has been none.

As You Like It happens to be one of the few popular plays of Shakespeare that are often performed in schools, maybe apart from Dreams, and for most it is basically a comedy with a happy ending.

My wife and I went to a recent production at BAM (Brooklyn Academy of Music) by none other than Peter Hall with his daughter playing Rosalind – their New York debut. Few would imagine Sir Peter picking Brooklyn for his debut but in the end it was a great experience. The New York Times said that it was more reviving than spending a week in the Caribbean. Having been an accidental resident in the Caribbean for two years I would dispute the comparison but totally agreed with the sentiments expressed.

At the BAM, it was like walking into a renovation site and in many ways I hope they leave it that way as it was rather charming. It was a most fitting setting for Shakespeare. I accept that they have to make sure it is safe.

It was at the start of my psychiatric training in England when I asked one of my gurus about reading matter. Apart from Shakespeare, he recommended Ibsen. I have since read Ibsen's plays but still come back to Shakespeare, who seemed to be able to pick up so many strands of human experience.

My ideal Shakespeare is indeed one that can be performed on a bed sheet with a few broomsticks for prop and without wanting to sound derogatory, I would say that this was exactly the approach adopted by this production.

Much was left to the imagination and it worked.

Mrs Coleman

Now and again in our work we get an indescribably sad case. Sometimes what started out as a rather straightforward case might begin to roll downhill so fast that we would be forever taking deep breaths thinking: can it get any worse? We would question if what we were doing was making any difference at all to what seemed like a predetermined course where no intervention would be able to make any impact on the final outcome.

One thing is for sure, real life is not like a play – you have only one chance to perform it and often not everything is clear.

Mrs Coleman came to see me about her daughter within months of my appointment as a consultant. With my new job came advantages and disadvantages. I used to be able to ask my seniors about cases, especially the difficult ones. Suddenly I was supposed to know it all. I used to have a big team working on a case, to the point that when the patient came to me there was hardly anything left for me to discover. Single-handed consultants are "on their own". They are lucky to have a social worker and perhaps a psychologist. I had both but the psychologist was not really part of our team – she happened to be sharing the same building. She belonged to the old school, which meant she knew her field and she did not try to be a social worker. For a while it became fashionable to blame everything on background and upbringing. Any disturbed child not performing well at school had nothing to do with teaching methods or intelligence but everything to do with social background. What were the implications for the social background of bright high achieving children?

There was some excitement in the clinic when it was known that a shepherd's family had been referred.

Shepherds? "As You Like It" sprang into my mind.

We have lambs so we must have shepherds – so I thought. It is true that we seldom had referrals from the farming community. I can only remember one other case and that was when I was a trainee. Shepherds also conjure up scenes of nativity and there is a sort of biblical romantic feel to it.

What we did have was something quite different. As it was unfortunately the lambing season, the shepherd Mr Coleman, though making a valiant appearance, was as good as asleep during most of the session. Mrs Coleman talked through the session with her rather charming old Sussex accent.

Mrs Coleman at the time had two children but it was the older daughter Laura of nine with whom she was having trouble. Tom, some eighteen months younger, was a happy-go-lucky sort of boy. Laura had a whole range of behavioural problems. She had recently taken to soiling in her pants.

It was often our practice for the social worker to do a preliminary home visit, and my social worker told me that she was most impressed with their home when she visited. They lived in a tied cottage on the farm. The children's grandfather was a shepherd and he had two sons, the older one working on the dairy side. There was also a daughter, the children's aunt, and her husband was the local milkman. The aunt had children similar in age to Laura and Tom. She worked part time in the local greengrocer's and between her and Laura's mother they split the fetching from school and childcare. The aunt unfortunately was recently diagnosed with breast cancer and was having different kinds of treatment at the local hospital. Luckily her husband was a milkman and could take over the afternoon part of the childcare arrangement whenever necessary. Mrs Coleman took the children to school on the days when the aunt had to go to hospital.

The aunt was a strong lady, Mrs Coleman told me, and she was sure she would outlive her.

It was an old cottage they lived in and my social worker told me that Mrs Coleman kept the place clean and tidy. It was therefore most upsetting to her when her nine year old daughter started soiling herself.

It was mostly in the afternoon but not everyday.

As my social worker had just started her training at the Tavistock Clinic on child therapy it was a good chance for her to take the girl on for some individual therapy sessions. Like my old consultant did when I was in training, it was now my turn to see mother.

This seemed to be a simple enough family and I did wonder at the beginning if there was much to unfold.

I was proved wrong.

Within two to three weeks of Laura starting therapy, Tom the younger brother refused to go to school. It was natural for everybody to think that there was some jealousy involved. So I arranged for mother to bring him to see me. It was rather obvious from the start that he was not very bright and that his not going to school had little or nothing to do with Laura but more to do with the fact that he could not keep up with the work and was being teased at school very badly. He tried to hit back at one particular boy and was told off by one of the teachers on duty at play-time. He did not want to go back. I arranged for the psychologist to assess him.

Yes, he was functioning at a much younger age and yes, he needed to go to a special school. In those days it was called an ESN school – school for the Educationally Subnormal. The SSN school was for the Severely Subnormal. In the 90s, it was deemed more polite to call the subnormal children "special".

Both schools were local and extremely well run. Tom was transferred and seemed to have settled down well there.

Not bad. I congratulated myself.

Laura was getting on well with her new therapist. She was attending without any problem and was doing nice drawings, according to my social worker.

Mrs Coleman was grateful that I sorted out her son. Tom, who had always been a Daddy's boy, had upset father very much with his escapade but as he had now settled in his new school father was rather pleased. He in fact went to the same school so he made it a point to turn up to thank me once everything settled.

Mmmm, perhaps we are not escaping the genetics theory.

As a precaution, we also tested Laura but she turned out to be rather bright.

Genetics, you are wrong.

Not so, Mrs Colman must have thought. She was rather perturbed when I told her. She started crying and pleaded with me to keep the secret she was about to tell me.

Her husband was not Laura's father.

Mrs Coleman had worked at the local butcher's since she left school and he was always all over her. Before long he was having intercourse with her at the back of the shop. He always gave her extra for that part of the service and she was happy with the extra bit of money. The butcher's wife had a stroke a few years back and had been bed ridden.

"It was not the money," Mrs Coleman assured me. She did not want me to think of her as a slut.

None of the mothers I saw wanted me to think badly of them and it often took a while before they would reveal their secrets.

Mrs Coleman had also been seeing the shepherd but never gave him much thought as she felt he was rather stupid. The butcher was much brighter.

Then one day some accident happened and she found herself pregnant. But the butcher was not going to divorce his wife. She was the one with the money.

She decided that the next best thing was to let the shepherd sleep with her as long as he married her. He was so pleased with himself and they had a big white wedding in the local church.

So Laura was the butcher's daughter and not her husband's. Now that I had proved Laura was clever, she was afraid I might ask awkward questions although she doubted if her husband would ever really work it out for himself.

Once a parent realised that you had ways to get to the truth, they often started revealing things that you wished they never did.

The butcher had some idea that Laura was his and had been slipping even more extra money for mother to buy her things. He never had any other children.

I never broke my promise and to this day I do not think that her husband ever knew.

What was to unfold was what caused most sadness.

I attended some special seminar on sexual abuse and at the time some rather ugly looking anatomical dolls were produced for the sole purpose of diagnosing Sexual Abuse. They were anatomical in that a whole family set including parents and grandparents, children and adolescent all had what was described as anatomically correct parts - females with breasts, nipples, vagina and anus; and males with penis and anus; and all the orifices were so to speak fully functional. These dolls all had proper clothes on and yet all the clothes could come off.

The idea was that normal children played with them as normal dolls but abused children would perform with the anatomical parts.

I had a full set ordered, having spent sometime persuading the managers that others had labs and X-rays and so on, but these were the only tools we required for the specific job.

Laura was the first to discover them and before my social worker's eyes one of the male figure's penis was in the girl's mouth. She told my social worker that was what Uncle Tom liked.

What followed were special "disclosure" interviews conducted under camera. Uncle Tom was the milkman. It happened to both girls. When the boys were in the kitchen playing computer games on the TV, slowly the girls were made to suck him. That was when Laura started soiling.

Mrs Coleman went berserk. Arrangements had to be made for alternative child care which really meant she had to cut short her hours at the butcher's. Uncle Tom moved to his mother's as a temporary measure pending Social Service investigation and Police enquiry.

Mrs Coleman could not sleep at night and called her GP. He asked her to pray with him as she had to be forgiving. She was so angry and when she was cleaning around the house she managed to get some caustic liquid all over herself and had to be admitted to hospital. She was also referred to the adult psychiatric department.

She started attending an anger management group at the hospital. It was thought to be the best way to help her deal with recent events.

One day when I went in to work, my social worker was already there and in tears. Mrs Coleman had just taken a massive overdose of Paracetamol and her liver was thought to be too far gone to survive. She died a rather painful death and we were all deeply saddened.

Could we have done any better? Was the truth too much for Mrs Coleman to bear? Would she still be alive if we had not discovered the sex abuse? We would never know. We might have rescued Laura from sex abuse but now she had lost her mother. Mrs Coleman was right about one thing though, her sister-in-law did outlive her.

As Shakespeare said, ".......And your experience makes you sad....."

I wanted to hide the dolls.

Chapter 28 Airline boy

"We shan't save all we should like to,
but we shall save a great deal more than if we had never tried."

Sir Peter Scott (1909-89)
WWF founder 1961

I had an hour to kill before my flight to Finland and who should I bump into but Richard. Was it because he was still wearing the same dark rimmed glasses that made him so recognisable from a distance, or was it because he was one of the patients that would be hard for anyone to forget?

"So what are you doing now, Richard?"

"I am now working in the luggage handling department at the airport."

Now Richard was only five foot four or six and very slim. It was hard to imagine that he would be handling luggage. He, being Richard, read my mind and said very quickly, "I am doing a desk job."

How silly. I should have guessed as he was in a suit that was far too big and carrying an attaché case.

"I thought you might be running Virgin by now." Naughty, naughty. It was not nice but I could not help myself.

"No, Dr Zhang, you know I would not, trust me."

Well, TRUST is a word I had been telling parents with teenage children to delete from their vocabulary. I will stick with WHAT YOU SEE IS WHAT YOU GET.

"I am glad you are settling down. How are your parents?"

"Dad has his old job back and is travelling to Africa a lot. Dad said he did not want to see me but mum meets me at the airport now and again before picking up dad or after dropping him off. I know they are upset about what I did but mum is O. K. really."

"I am glad for that and I am sure your father will come round."

"I hope so too. You have been right about most things and I hope you are with this one. Anyway thank you for all that you have done for me. I know I probably don't deserve it but somehow you have stuck by me and so I must thank you. I am sorry for letting you down but I am sure you understand."

We see dolphins and whales beaching and dying for reasons we do not understand and men make all the effort to save them and nearly all the time fail. Some good friends of mine went down to the animal refuge to pick up a poor dog which had been abused and beaten and was worm ridden. They struggled to give the dog a new home only to find furniture damaged and children infested with Toxocara canis[81] worm and they eventually gave up.

I too have seen many adoptions bring untold misery of a magnitude that was beyond all imagination.

But if we never tried we would never know if our effort would do some good.

It was good to see Richard having a proper job. Perhaps he was reformed. It was still disconcerting to find him working at an airport. Why, Richard? Why still an airport?

To understand this question of mine, you will need to know a bit more about Richard's history.

I knew Richard from when he was first referred to the clinic for a medical report as part of his educational assessment. It was the days of the old Education Act where child psychiatrists were actively involved in assessing children for placement in special schools. Not many eleven year olds were placed in special schools for the simple reason that they would not yet have started at secondary school, where trouble normally began.

Richard was at a private school. His father was a senior executive in a multi-national company and had been based in Kenya for many years. Richard was adopted and placed with them when he was about six months old. They had many servants and a nanny in Africa and Richard was particularly liked because he was small, white and looked very intelligent even as a baby. Mother

---

[81] Toxocariasis – Toxocariasis is an infection caused by the dog roundworm, Toxocara canis. Infective stages of this parasite can be found in the environment - particularly in areas frequented by large numbers of dogs - kennels, public parks and exercise areas. Children can be infected by picking up the disease from the environment or from handling dogs.

recounted all this to me with tears in her eyes. She could not understand what could have gone wrong. They lived a life of luxury. They travelled first class. They went on expensive holidays and the boy had all the latest in toys and gadgetry. He had his own computer and it was in the days when computer games were just becoming the latest fad. He had always been brilliant at those games especially flight simulation and airport management.

From an early age he had been fascinated by planes and although flight simulation was normally for fathers, he had mastered several versions of them. Again, Airport Management game was a rather curious choice for a boy, although at the time games like Sync City was among the top sellers.

The reason why he was referred was because the local state school refused to admit him, advising that he should be placed in a special school instead.

"Well, he burned down a whole wing of his last private school," Father told me abruptly and waited to see how shocked I was.

As I already had that bit of information from the school, I could not pretend to be shocked. Yet I could not quite connect the figure of this boy with a school arsonist.

We have this sad stereotype of school arsonists – a big, rude and often crude yob of a boy who would hate to see a shrink. I have in my work seen a couple of them. One even tried to throw a chair at me when I told his parents that what they did not see they could not leave to trust – a point I made earlier.

This was not Richard. Richard looked like a scholar. That would be how Hollywood would cast them – bespectacled, timid, small.

He could not have been a school arsonist.

"We were surprised that the school asked us to seek help, saying that it might be a deep seated problem."

"And the school did not even know he was adopted," mother assured me, "so they could not even blame that."

It is not unusual for parents to be defensive especially when events took them by surprise.

The parents were obviously not aware of the confidential report that the state school obtained from the private school. The report mentioned the fire and stated in no uncertain terms that had Richard decided to stay in the school, he would have been reported to the Police or referred to a psychiatrist or both. The school was of the opinion that no other school should take him in without referring him to a psychiatrist.

Richard's previous school appeared to have treated the fire as an accident. It was Richard's version anyway when he was challenged. The fire started somewhere in the chemistry laboratory after school. Richard was fascinated by chemistry and did very well in exams. One of his two teachers in chemistry really liked him and gave him permission to do extra experiments after school unsupervised. That went on for about three months, before the mysterious fire started one day shortly after Richard finished there.

"We would have believed that it was an innocent accident if we had not found his diary. There were a number of entries in it about how he hated the other chemistry teacher and that one day he, the teacher, would be in trouble."

"They did not know about the diary," mother assured me.

The school had already made their decision as they did not want any adverse publicity. They decided not to take any further action as long as Richard did not move up to their sister senior school.

At that time the father's employer moved their headquarters and they decided to ask for a transfer back to the company headquarters in U.K. They hoped to just register Richard at the local state school and let him have a fresh start. As he was a high achiever they thought any school would snap him up.

Then mother told me about some trouble a few years back when Richard was just eight. They were home in Scotland for a month in August. Mother invariably came home for the month of August, when Scotland was at its best. They always had the best corporate tickets for the Edinburgh Festival.

Father used to join the family in Scotland for only about a week. When he was home early one day because golf was rained off, he had a phone call from one of the airlines.

"Just checking that Master Richard will be met by his aunt in London," said the airline staff at the other end.

"First of all Richard's only aunt is eighty six years old and lives in a home in the suburb of Edinburgh. Second Master Richard is not travelling anywhere."

"But we have his first class ticket booking. As he is an unaccompanied minor we need to check."

Our Richard was used to luxury.

There followed some frantic searches and investigation and questioning. Luckily there was a whole detailed record kept by Richard of what went on. He planned to attend a World Wildlife Fund Congress in London. He had paid the conference fees and booked the hotel and the plane tickets. The fees were paid for by mother's credit card, and so was the hotel booking. With some imagination a young boy of Richard's age could make himself sound like a woman. He had a whole envelope full of cash for him to spend in London. He could hardly have used his mother's credit card in person.

But where did he get his cash from?

There was a sort of account book of donations from a large number of people in their neighbourhood. It was not an insubstantial amount.

He was keen on wildlife, having lived in Africa, and was serious about going to the conference, which would be attended by big shots and by many African government ministers.

Richard used his Kenyan address for the conference and apparently it was an important address, so to speak, and nobody realised he was only eight.

He had a detailed brochure prepared for showing to the neighbourhood people from whom he collected money and he even showed them the ledger record of who had donated what amount.

Father decided that all the money must be returned and took him round the houses to explain and return the money. To the father's amazement some of the old ladies did not believe him and did not want their money back!

The parents were worried for Richard's future and decided not to report him to the police or to anyone.

Hearing this fascinating tale, I sat there trying hard to hide my astonishment and even admiration. This boy would go far, I thought. One day when he was a multi-billionaire I could write an account of this. I was sure he would love it.

For now, I must try and help this boy by whatever means possible.

When confronted with a patient who may be a menace to society, a psychiatrist often finds it difficult to balance his loyalty to his patient against his duty to society. There are indeed so few good predictors available that it becomes painful when one needs to jump a few steps and suggest a management program that may in the end be detrimental to the patient. We now acknowledge that we have a public duty and patient-doctor confidentiality holds no sway even in a court of law. Sadly many in our profession still hide behind patient-doctor confidentiality and do not consider their wider duty to the public. Mistakes are likely to be made one way or the other, but to err on the patient's side could mean that innocent people might be hurt or even murdered.

Richard was barely twelve. How could I possibly be sure how he would turn out?

I could not. Yet there was enough information for me to realise that we were not dealing with an ordinary case. This boy kept a detailed record of all the things he was doing and at eight was able to become a major fund-raiser. More to the point, he was convincing and that was what worried me. I was sure he had just started the train and more would be taken for a ride. Luckily, no pronouncement was required from me. Reading between the lines, I gathered that the referral was more about finding the right school for him.

You might have guessed that he had superior intelligence and he was totally meticulous in his daily life. So highly disciplined was he that his room at home was not like that of any youngster. Perhaps parents could console themselves that having untidy children might not be that bad after all. He knew everything about planes and flying and through his simulator games many airports in the world. The walls of his room were covered with pictures of planes and engines and airports.

We already knew that he had a deep interest in wildlife. This was not surprising as he had been going to safaris from an early age and Kenya probably had the world's finest. However since the WWF incident, aeroplanes had taken over and his collection of animal pictures and wildlife information had been securely filed away. Painstakingly, mother assured me. Richard supervised the packing himself when they moved.

Richard got on with me extremely well as I am interested in wildlife and in aircrafts. I knew then Richard was going to be "big time", but I did not realise how big it was going to be.

I was able to find somewhere in the West Country for him. It was a small private special boarding school that catered for the very bright but disturbed children and they would be able to get him to university entrance level for a limited number of subjects.

Mother felt relieved and for Richard, being away at school was something he had been used to and there was not a drop of tears. Mother cried, not because of the separation but because she hoped it would work, and yet feared maybe it would not and that he might still be destined to be a monster.

Adoption can do funny things to parents when things go wrong. On the one hand they feel it is their fault. On the other hand they are secretly glad that the child does not carry any of their genes. It is always painful though that God cannot be argued with. Far too many families felt that they were dealt a very bad hand.

The next three years went by without much incident. Richard became a model pupil.

The headmaster hinted in every report that perhaps it was unfair that Richard could not be at a school nearer home. He thought I might have been too harsh and worst, made the wrong judgment.

I did wonder then if I had been too harsh.

After all I liked him.

Richard did well in every single subject and his father kept him well occupied with aviation magazines and the like. He spent half-term breaks and Easter in Kenya and Christmas and summer in England punctuated with times in Scotland in August and New Year.

I secretly congratulated myself for getting the right placement for him. I kept up my duty of seeing him once a term and I brushed up on my knowledge on planes and aviation on the whole.

I had to continue to make the case for him to stay where he was as it was quite an expensive school. It was not a big problem in those days as it was quite difficult to de-assess someone who was deemed to be maladjusted. Now and again I wondered if I did the right thing. Seeing that he was achieving and thriving at his special boarding school, I too was beginning to have my doubts.

Then Richard was sent home a week early before the summer break and the parents asked me to see him urgently. Father flew in from Kenya especially for the appointment with me.

It must be serious.

First they drove down to the school to collect him. School insisted that they should pack all his belongings. It was always a bad sign when that happened. They probably did not want him back.

Father gave me two thick folders.

I started looking through them.

"My goodness. This is good." I thought.

The work was really good.

In the two folders was a detailed record of what Richard had been doing for at least two and a half years, with intensified activities in the last month or so.

Richard was in the process of setting up an AIRLINE!

The quality of planning and execution was admirable. Any business management consultant would have been proud.

There were detailed pricing schedules of major plane manufacturers and they were going out of their way to offer special packages.

"How did he get all those top secret pricing schedules?"

"Obviously not difficult," father commented, "as the industry is going through a difficult time, what with Laker[82] folding and so on."

What upset the school most was it all started with the Headmaster kindly suggesting that the hardworking model pupil, Richard, could work in his office after school, unsupervised.

No, nothing went missing.

In any boarding school, theft was often the main reason for a pupil to get thrown out. Even some degree of violence might be tolerated.

"But perhaps he did steal," mother interjected.

The school had just had a phone bill that was over five hundred pounds mostly for calls to the U.S. and Holland.

"Not to Kenya."

"No, these were calls to the plane manufacturers and one European airline"

Richard had got himself registered for free pilot training with this European airline.

"All the phones in schools were blocked for national and international calls but not the direct line from the headmaster's office," father explained. "We wrote a cheque to the school."

---

[82] Laker Airways – Sir Freddie Laker pioneered the concept of cheap fares for the masses, and although his Skytrain venture eventually collapsed in 1982, owing £270 million to banks and other creditors, he laid the foundations for low-cost carriers that proliferate today.

After winning hard-fought approval from governments on both sides of the Atlantic, the first Laker Skytrain from London to New York took off in 1977 in a blaze of positive publicity. As with today's low-cost flights, passengers had to pay extra for food and drink.

http://news.bbc.co.uk/onthisday/hi/dates/stories/february/5/newsid_2535000/2535297.stm

What was disturbing was that Richard was able to open a bank account with one of the big four national banks and had personalised cheques printed for him. He was able to make use of those cheques for his "project". Father went to see the manager of the bank who simply said that some other bank would have let him have an account if they had not. Richard was very convincing, they added.

Richard claimed that he had enough money to pay for the calls but that he had not yet got round to it.

He was going to start an airline between Gatwick and Chicago, Business Class only as there was a demand.

It took some phone calls and swift footwork to get the headmaster to take Richard back. He claimed he had not expelled him but wanted some action. I gently reminded him that it was he who thought that we got it wrong in the first place and now he had first hand personal experience of what Richard could be capable of. We never pretended to him that Richard was going to be straightforward and in my opinion, the state was paying the school a not insubstantial amount for their trouble, although I never quite put it like that. It would have been impossible to find him another school at that stage.

Richard would have to agree to very tight supervision from then on.

Also, he would have to work with the other children, not in the headmaster's office.

There was relief all round. I did not get it too wrong after all, but like in many cases, I wish I did.

He finished the rest of his school up to O-levels without further incident. He decided not to go to university and the last formal appointment he had with me was a rather sad one. His father had just been made redundant. It was the usual story — a solid company became good value when the Stock Market took a dive and it was bought up by a multinational based in Texas. Those who were not prepared to move to Texas were made redundant but offered a good package. Father was not sure if the company would really keep the senior people for long and decided to take the package and look for another job. The exchanges between Richard and father were rather painful and it was impossible to convince Richard that going to university was going to be any good.

"You have a Ph. D. and you are without a job!" was the line I can always remember. Mother cried and father looked away trying to suppress his desire to just strike the boy.

"Anyway, all the very successful people never went to university," said Richard, and he started to reel off names in the airline and other industries and in show business.

"So, which one are you going to be?" Mother retorted, getting rather annoyed with Richard for insulting her husband.

"Never you mind. Perhaps the one running an airline."

He obviously had not given up that idea.

I sensed that there was unfinished business and offered a follow-up in six months' time. It seemed a good way all round to deal with the impasse and I made some vague suggestion that although most people took a year off after A-levels, Richard might want to reconsider A-levels and university after a break.

They never turned up for the appointment.

Not because they forgot or that they felt it would be useless.

Richard was in a local prison awaiting trial.

In the intermediate six months, Richard had gone about, supercharged, trying to establish his airline. With redundancies in the industry, he signed up pilots that had no job. He held a press conference at a well known airport hotel. Some big names in the industry were roped in to be the founding directors, and businessmen flew in from Chicago and the Middle East. The event was reported in the local papers. Richard offered to buy all the aircrafts from an airline that went out of business at that time. He had financial backing from the Middle-East.

His downfall was not caused by any mistake he made, but by his honest unpaid assistant.

He never expected that. It was not in any of his private MBA studies.

Richard had managed to use a photocopier to fade out the yellow wording – SAMPLE DOCUMENT from some financial pre-approval documents before sending them off to the Middle Eastern financier. When the financier requested the originals, Richard's assistant duly sent the original sample documents.

He was soon in jail.

It was a great surprise for his social worker as it was unusual for a first offender of a non-violent crime to be remanded in prison pending trial. I could only speculate that perhaps large sums of money were involved or that he embarrassed too many "successful" entrepreneurs who might have political clout.

Who would want to admit to being conned by a boy barely eighteen?

But our Richard had a lucky break!

The judge at the Crown Court noted that Richard's remand in prison was rather unnecessary and decided against further custodial sentence. I wrote a factual report for Richard trying to steer away from being too "prophetic" and that probably helped him. The judge put him on probation for two years.

Richard's probation officer told me when I met her at another meeting, "Richard was lucky. The judge was an ex-RAF pilot and he liked some of his ideas."

Since then we have seen major frauds in big corporations: Maxwell[83] in England and Enron[84] in the U.S. to name a few.

---

[83] Maxwell Pension scandal: On the 5th Nov., 1991, the body of the millionaire newspaper publisher, Robert Maxwell, was found in the sea off the coast of Tenerife. After Robert Maxwell's death it emerged that the Mirror Group's debts vastly outweighed its assets and £440m was missing from the company's pension funds.

In 1996, after an eight-month trial, Kevin and Ian Maxwell and another man, Larry Trachtenberg, were cleared of conspiracy to defraud Mirror Group pensioners. In 2001 the Department of Trade and Industry released a report into the Maxwell affair which said "primary responsibility" for the collapse of the Maxwell business empire lay with its founder. But it added that Kevin Maxwell and some leading City financial institutions also bore a "heavy responsibility" for the company's failure.

After Robert Maxwell's death campaigners for the 30,000 Mirror Group pensioners mounted a three-year campaign for compensation. Their funds were largely recovered thanks to a £100m government payout and a £276m out-of-court settlement with City institutions and the remnants of Robert Maxwell's media group.

http://news.bbc.co.uk/onthisday/hi/dates/stories/november/5/newsid_2514000/2514649.stm

[84] Enron: the most spectacular collapse of a major US Blue Chip company that is well known to all in the post 9/11 world of commerce.

For years, the Enron Corporation used its political muscle to build the markets in which it thrived, pushing relentlessly on Capitol Hill and in bureaucratic backwaters to deregulate the nation's natural gas and electricity businesses. Its achievement, as one Enron executive said today, in creating a "regulatory black hole" fit nicely with what he called the company's "core management philosophy, which was to be the first mover into a market and to make money in the initial chaos and lack of transparency."

Jeff Gerth and Richard A. Oppel Jr. "Regulators struggle with a marketplace created by Enron.", The New York Times, Nov 10, 2001

"To educate a man in mind, and not in morals,
is to educate a menace to society."
"A man who has never gone to school may steal from a freight car;
but if he has a university education, he may steal the whole railroad."

Theodore Roosevelt   26th President, United States

Chapter 29 The Power of Prayers

According to old Chinese advice, it is wise never to discuss politics or religion even amongst best friends. Religious belief can often blur judgement in the wisest of people. In psychiatry it is sometimes not easy. This is particularly true in cases of florid psychosis, which often presents with symptoms of hallucination, delusion and even vision.

I remember my early days of psychiatry in a mental hospital in Hong Kong. Yes, it was the days of 2000-bed hospitals. Yes, it was the days of Medical Superintendents who had supreme power and all doctors of whatever rank and experience were Mental Health Officers with special authority to sign papers for compulsory admissions. The forensic unit was contained within the same complex.

Those were the days when we encountered psychosis in the raw so to speak. All the colony's really mad people were admitted to this one place set in the furthest corner of the colony. In our year seven of us decided without much discussion that we all wanted to go into psychiatry. That was over 10% and all had quite idealistic reasons. It was perhaps a bit of a disappointment to our parents that we did not pursue a more conventional specialty that might provide us with more status and financial reward. Then there was the fear of contamination that somehow one might become mad too. Recent day medical students are said to shy away from psychiatry for these same reasons.

Education seems to have little effect on superstition.

I can vividly remember the day when three coach loads of a particular church descended at the front entrance to our hospital. We had one of those grand gates which somehow were never locked. Those that needed to be locked up would have been detained in their individual hospital wards. The hospital had extensive grounds, and was the only non-high rise public hospital in Hong Kong. Wards were individual self-contained buildings spread like a horseshoe, and in all there were eighteen of them. The wards were given numbers without names but the numbers served the same purpose: 3 was for acute male, 11 for GPI[85]'s and so on and so forth.

Only the maximum security wards were air-conditioned to satisfy prison standards.

---

[85] GPI - General paresis of the insane. A now-rare neuropsychiatric disorder affecting the brain and central nervous system. A late complication of syphilis.

In the middle of the horseshoe was the main medical block — the Medical Superintendent's suite and the different staff rooms. Then there was the administration block where the kitchens were located. Laundry, refuse disposal etc. were a bit away from the main buildings, so was the Mortuary. Yes, there was a Mort. On call doctors carried out post mortems and very rarely would any outside pathologist be called in. There was much trust in doctors then. As there were dementia wards, people did die of natural causes especially when the weather changed.

In a matter of a few weeks we learned a good deal. We learned a good deal about acute psychosis. We also learned a good deal about the other end of the spectrum, that of chronicity and dementia. We also became aware that suddenly we were no longer lowly medical students. Even though we were still junior we had certain status. Now someone cleaned our car every day for a small fee. The guards at the gate saluted you. The local restaurants knew there was a new group of doctors who would lunch regularly. Even the local shopkeepers gave us special treatment.

Imagine the shock when three coach loads of church people descended upon this Institution to challenge one of its doctors. The patient in question was a girl, and amongst other psychotic symptoms she had a vision. She was admitted the night before as she became unmanageable at home. She was sectioned and was now in the care of the team to which one of my good friends belonged. As luck would have it he was a devout Christian and managed to defuse the situation. Yes, she could be having a vision. Yes all necessary investigation would be carried out including that of the nervous system as she might have a brain tumour. Yes, please continue to pray for her. Yes, it could be the work of the devil.

There was no brain tumour.

There was no religious vision.

The prayers worked. She had a good doctor – my friend. She was put on Stelazine[86].

Some time in early February of 1978 I was called to do a Home Visit on a thirteen year old girl by Dr Pinkerton, a paediatric consultant. Dr Pinkerton had been the local Paed for years and was generally well regarded. She had, in my short time as consultant, referred a couple of cases, most notably that of a Tourette[87] syndrome and a boy with non-stoppable hiccups. Both cases put me in her A-list and I gathered that not many were on that list. Needless to say I realised too that her cases were never straightforward or simple. Those she would have dealt with herself. The girl had upper arm stiffness on the left side and Dr Pinkerton could not find much else wrong with her, and so it crossed her mind that perhaps there was something psychiatrically wrong. The

---

[86] Stelazine - trifluoperazine hydrochloride, an antipsychotic widely used for schizophrenia before the new generation of drugs came on the market.

[87] Tourette syndrome - Over 100 years ago, the French physician Georges Gilles de la Tourette wrote an article in which he described nine individuals who, since childhood, had suffered from involuntary movements and sounds and compulsive rituals or behaviours. In his honor, this constellation of symptoms was named Gilles de la Tourette's Syndrome. Today, we recognize that Tourette's is a spectrum disorder, with some people having a few tics and others having tics plus features of other conditions such as obsessions, compulsions, inattention, impulsivity, mood variability. Once thought to be a rare condition, Tourette's is a fairly common childhood-onset condition.

http://www.tourettesyndrome.net/tourette.htm

girl was also carrying out some strange rituals around the house and Dr Pinkerton did wonder about psychosis or even catatonia[88].

One of my two clinics was in this so called "new town". Basically it was an idea conceived after the war in about 1949. The idea was that if people were moved out of the inner city their life would improve. Because they often moved the same people from the same area to the exact same street in the new town the problems travelled with them. Old foes stayed in the same streets as warring neighbours. Yet generations of Local Councils continued to move people into newer housing estates, not understanding why they never managed to solve the problem. I had visited a few of these new towns.

The family I had to visit luckily did not have any enemies but they only moved three months ago and felt very isolated. They moved from a very tough neighbourhood in London not to get away from difficult neighbours. They moved because their daughter did not fit in. She was a timid shy adolescent who did not do normal South London teenage things and was becoming ostracised. She was not into drugs, smoking or drinking or even sex. To her peers she was a weirdo. After the move, father was able to find a job at the local airport and mother worked part time as a dinner lady at the local school. Feeling isolated, they went with a

---

[88] Catatonia - Catatonia is a disturbance of motor behaviour that can have either a psychological or neurological cause. Its most well-known form involves a rigid, immobile position that is held by a person for a considerable length of time— often days, weeks, or longer. It can also refer to agitated, purposeless motor activity that is not stimulated by something in the environment. A less extreme form of catatonia involves very slow motor activity. Often, the physical posture of a catatonic individual is unusual and/or inappropriate, and the individual may hold a posture if placed in it by someone else.

http://www.minddisorders.com/Br-Del/Catatonia.html

neighbour to a local church group and both parents had recently been converted.

I was asked very early on by mother, although father did try to stop her, if this might be the work of the devil. She heard that the devil was always trying to do nasty things to anyone who had just become a Christian although she also heard that it could sometimes be God himself wanting to test her faith.

Memories about my friend and the vision girl flooded back and I had not even had a chance to see what the problem was.

I saw what mum meant. The girl was ignoring my presence. She was mumbling to herself and pacing around the room with a semi-fixed gaze. She held her left arm stiff in a half-raised position and was going round the room as if looking for bits of dirt on the wall and rubbing it. It started about two days before when the parents came home from a church prayer meeting to find her non responsive. Since then she had had sips of water but hardly ate anything. Dr Pinkerton came out straight away to see her and called me in.

There was really no significant medical or psychiatric history in the family. She was an only child with the history of the usual childhood ailments. She was average at school though the year before she was not performing well because of problems with other girls. Both parents were healthy although I noticed that mum was nursing a cold sore.

I did wonder if catatonia was making a come back but the golden rule in psychiatry, as in General Medicine, is: if in doubt, observe.

I told mother that it might be better if we got her into hospital for observation. After all they probably needed a break as they did not have any sleep properly since this started. The parents did try to take turns to catch some sleep but as father still had to go into work it was very exhausting.

"But it would not be the mental hospital."

"No, it would be one of my beds in the paediatric ward, although it would not be the same hospital as Dr Pinkerton's."

"Anything would do, Doctor. We leave it in your hands."

Even when we did not know what was going on, we had learned how to keep that from our patients. Was it cheating or was it just good doctoring? Patient's confidence in you is as important as your medical knowledge. Perhaps that is why doctors are not doing so well nowadays.

"You will sort her out, won't you, doctor?"

"Sure we shall. In hospital we can run a few tests including those on the brain just in case and then we can proceed with treatment."

"Have you seen cases like this before?"

"Sure, not that many but we sure have."

What else could I have said? To be honest, I am only a junior consultant and I have never seen anything like this before, any further question?

"I know you are good. You have helped the boy with the swearing at our church. He now hardly swears."

My goodness. It is a small place. I have been here only three months and people already know.

All I knew was it would be easy enough if it was indeed the start of a psychotic illness and all would be all right though sad.

I must first exclude rare but serious neurological conditions.

I had no idea what was to hit me in the next twenty four hours.

The hospital to which she was admitted was built during the war by Canadian soldiers. It was unusual for an English Hospital as all the wards were built of Red Cedar. All the wards were linked by covered walkways. Over time we all became very fond of it - a true cottage hospital. Everybody was friendly. Consultations were easy to arrange in such a place; I had used my two bed allocation regularly and had developed a good working relationship with the paediatric nursing staff. In fact the Tourette boy was one of the first admitted for observation and proved to be a great hit. Most had never heard of such cases and the few that had had never seen one. Then I had the boy who refused to eat what most others liked and I soon became the psychiatrist that brought interesting cases.

They could not wait for my next case. Maybe not.

Sister Clark used to be at University College Hospital in London where I had the good fortune of gaining some paediatric training. She moved here to look after her eighty eight year old mother. We knew we were in safe hands as there was nothing to replace a good Sister on any ward. They reminded us of important things to look out for and basically if we were not too pompous they would look after us. That way we tended not to miss a thing clinically.

When I reached the ward after my day's clinic, Sister took me to the nursing station. She said the girl was either pregnant or she had a full bladder. A quick examination revealed a soft mass up her umbilical level.

How stupid of me. Remember: every female of child bearing age is pregnant until proved otherwise. Mother's reassurance that she was not like the other girls fooled me. She must have found it difficult to tell her parents and therefore was in such a difficult psychiatric state. Faking mental illness would be one good way out.

I thought: great! At least I could deliver. Pregnancy test and OB consult and that would be it.

But hang on. Would mother not notice her sickness if she was this big? Would she not have complained about other symptoms? Something was not fitting in. And she still looked pre-pubescent.

Perhaps we should catheterise her. She had not been seen to use the toilet for hours although she was not drinking much. She was still going round in her room – we gave her the side room and a nurse – and we put on an input output chart so we knew. The new junior doctor's car broke down so she was late in examining her.

Bother, I forgot it was changeover time, when new doctors came in for their new six-month rotation. This is one of the days of the year not to be ill.

"Good work Sister. What do we do without you?"

Sister did the catheterisation but only got about 150ml. The mass was still there.

I phoned Ob-Gyn. The consultant had left for home, but I got her Senior Registrar.

He came over. Yes, it was possible that she was pregnant but unlikely as there were no breast changes. He would hate to do an X-ray but that seemed justified in the case of an undiagnosed abdominal mass.

My mind was racing now. Sometimes you do have to believe what you see. Sometimes you have to believe the parents. She was not one of those girls. She could not be pregnant. So now we had to go through the differential diagnosis for abdominal mass in a young girl of thirteen.

Ovarian cyst was the obvious one.

This big?

Possible.

No. It cannot be.

The x-ray came back. The tell tale tooth was there and yes – a Teratoma[89], the distinctive type of tumour that can include teeth, hair, sometimes, even a jaw and tongue. I guessed just a split second before the results came back. How annoying.

Working diagnosis: Teratoma with possible toxic psychosis.

Emergency operation was arranged. Yes, she would be fine a little while after the operation, I reassured the parents.

The paediatric junior arrived and took some history and did a quick physical before she was prepared for the theatre. This petite doctor with a very babyish face told me that on her first day in her last job she had to do an emergency tracheotomy. This time she

---

[89] Teratoma – Teratomas are tumors comprising more than a single cell type derived from more than one germ layer. Usually, dermoid cysts contain representative tissues of the three embryonic germ cell layers: ectoderm, mesoderm and endoderm. Sebaceous material, hairs, cartilages, teeth, even thyroid tissue are frequently observed. A well-formed jaw and tongue has been reported. Teratomas of other organs have also been reported to contain teeth.

had been on call for the last three nights and the battery in her old Mini could not cope with the heavy frost so she had to wait for AA before coming. She was most apologetic for not having got in earlier.

She asked if I had seen many toxic psychosis cases and I asked if she had come across any in her psychiatric placement. As with all good psychiatrists answering a question with another is in our blood and here it worked well.

Neither of us knew what was to hit us next.

At 2 A.M. I had a call from her.

"Your patient – I mean our patient could not be aroused after the operation. Yes they removed the teratoma, complete and intact. It is bigger than any specimen I have seen but she could not be aroused. Any ideas?"

"Call the paediatrician on call in the regional paediatric unit and I will be in."

What happened? I asked myself as I drove to the hospital.

What had we done? This was fast becoming a nightmare situation.

What was I going to say to the parents?

Something else was going on here, and I was not happy because I did not know what it was. I was supposed to know and I generally did. After all I was the consultant now.

Thank goodness she could breathe without assistance. That was the first thing I noticed. I saw mother in the corner obviously in tears. She asked if her daughter would be all right. I cannot remember what I said but knowing myself I could not have said anything too discouraging. But then I knew I was in tricky territory and it was unlikely to be the territory of a child psychiatrist.

A good doctor is one who is not afraid to ask for help but he must also know where to ask.

"Get me Great Ormond Street."

"I already did."

She is going to be a good doctor.

"Well, the Regional unit said that they had no beds so I thought I should ring up my classmate at GOS and she talked to her SR who said "send her in"."

Who needs consultants when juniors have that kind of network? This girl will do well.

"Everything has been set up. The ambulance will be here in about half an hour and if it is all right I would like to go with her."

"Yes, you do and thanks a lot."

I told mother that we were transferring her daughter to the best children's hospital in England if not in the world and the doctor would stay with her in the ambulance. She would be fine.

When I got into work later that day, my secretary asked how my patient was as she heard from her friend that the church was going to hold a 24-hour vigil for her.

Trust my secretary. She knew someone from the same church and she always had the knack of extracting information first hand.

"They say this may be the work of the devil as the doctors and surgeons all did the right things and removed this big tumour but the devil must have got to her."

I did have a vague fear that there might have been some anaesthetic accident but quickly told myself off for thinking along that line. I knew all the anaesthetists and such a thing could never have happened.

I was back at the hospital to deal with an overdose case. The junior was there and we had a chat in Sister's office.

They had to ventilate her. That was the first thing she told me. I thanked her for going up there and she said it was scary but she felt important and the mother who was in the ambulance could not thank her enough.

She was impressed with mother's faith and trust in God.

She said mother was near to tears. It was bad enough to have such a large Teratoma and then to have the patient unconscious with no one knowing what was going on was very frightening.

"I have seen some deaths as a medical student but never since I was registered. I do not want this to be my first."

I knew the feeling well but what could I say? A doctor has to face it some time.

"Do you believe there is God?" She asked

"Do you really think I can answer that one?"

"Well, you have more experience."

"To me it is like reading a good book. You would not know until the end."

"So you mean I am not going to know until then."

"Interpret whichever way you like. I remember Jung in his Memoir gave quite an account on the Holy Trinity. There were seventeen bishops in Jung's family including his own father. Jung had always been puzzled by deity and the bible and most of all by the concept of the Holy Trinity. I know many religious philosophers struggle with that too. By some accident he had access to his father's inner library. He saw this folder clearly marked Holy Trinity. The relief was phenomenal. He could now have the answer. He hesitated before opening the folder."

"What did the folder contain?"

"See, you want the last chapter. I wanted to know as well. The folder contained pieces of blank paper."

"That was it?"

"That was it."

"Well. My view is this. We are here. We live. We help others to live and maybe we do not ask too many questions and we might or might not in the end know the answer."

"But do you think this girl is going to live though? I do not want this girl to be my first death. It would be so awful."

"Neither do I. I keep saying to myself that it is now over seventy two hours and she is still alive and I do know that some cases of viral encephalitis can be very dramatic in presentation and recovery."

"But which virus?"

"The nearest I have is Herpes."

"Mother's cold sore."

"You have noticed that too."

"I was with her for a long time."

We had our own prayer for her too. Let it be Herpes encephalitis and all would be well.

I left the hospital feeling slightly strange. I just had a philosophical encounter with a young doctor. How strange it is that threats of death always get one thinking about these things.

The girl remained unconscious although the word was that the EEG was more hopeful than was first thought. GOS decided to transfer her next door to Queen Square - National Hospital for Nervous Diseases. A lumber puncture[90] was done and the initial findings were in keeping with viral encephalitis. They were now trying to grow the virus. They also wanted Queen Square to decide on assisted ventilation.

There was now a candlelight vigil at the church and it was hoped that there would always be a lit candle until she came home. The story was in the local paper and radio. Faith was now on field test if not on trial. The doctors were not. They had done their best.

On the 10th day the ventilator came off, and she was able to breathe without support.

They then started a vigil in the girl's home.

By the 23rd day, as my optimism was about to give in, word came from the hospital that she became conscious. It became big news in the papers.

When mother came home from London, she came to see my secretary to give her the details. She told my secretary that she always knew that her daughter would live.

No virus was ever isolated and her diagnosis on discharge was that she had a variant of Encephalitis Lethargica[91].

---

[90] lumbar puncture – A lumbar puncture (also called a spinal tap) is a procedure to collect and look at the fluid (cerebrospinal fluid, or CSF) surrounding the brain and spinal cord.

[91] Encephalitis Lethargica - a disease characterized by high fever, headache, double vision, delayed physical and mental response, and lethargy. In acute cases, patients may enter coma.

http://www.ninds.nih.gov/disorders/encephalitis_lethargica/encephalitis_lethargica.htm

"Did you agree with the diagnosis?" The junior asked me when I saw her next.

"Why should I be arguing with the best neurological centre in the world? It is harder to argue with a variant of Lethargica. However the next few months or years will be important. If she is well then Herpes fits in better and often it is an allergic type of reaction on first exposure. But if she is like those in Awakenings[92], then Encephalitis Lethargica."

I saw her at the local hospital rehab a couple of times. Initially there were a good deal of residual symptoms including awkward gait and dis-inhibition. She became better and was moved to a specialised centre and that was the last I heard of her.

Ten years later mother came to see my secretary and left a photo. It was a photo of her daughter and her new baby. She had been working at the local bank since she left school, met a very nice man and now she had a baby. Mother thought I might remember them and perhaps I would be pleased with the outcome.

I was very pleased for them too but I would hate for anyone to put faith or god to such a test too often.

---

[92] Awakenings – Oliver Sacks' remarkable account of a group of patients who contracted sleeping-sickness during the great epidemic just after World War I. Frozen in a decades-long sleep, these men and women were given up as hopeless until 1969, when Dr. Sacks gave them the then-new drug L-DOPA, which had an astonishing, explosive, "awakening" effect. This account inspired the 1990 film of the same name, starring Robert De Niro and Robin Williams.

http://www.oliversacks.com/awake.htm

Chapter 30 Religious Fanaticism

In our work we have some unusual referrals now and again and sometimes they require unusual handling.

I had an urgent call to deal with a serious suicide attempt at a well known local boarding school.

No, the child was not admitted to hospital as would be the usual practice, but was kept at the infirmary at the school instead. I arranged to make an immediate visit to see her there. She was only twelve.

This was one of the few Church Schools that catered for able children who could not afford expensive private schools. Part of the intake were bright children of church personnel from all over the country. It still had rather medieval costumes for uniform and you could spot the school children a mile away with their long dark blue gowns. Boys and girls had the same outer costumes, but different belts and buckles according to the pupil's year group.

The school had the feel of a monastery and was quite overpowering as you entered. Individual boarding houses lined up neatly. It read: "We mean business. You are here to learn."

The infirmary was even more imposing. It was part of the main block. The main door as you could imagine was at least 15 ft tall and weighed a ton. The old wrought iron handle had seen a few centuries of use and yet its hinges were well oiled so that when the matron greeted me, she had no problem opening it and it did not produce the squeak I expected.

The dark double height ceiling made darker by a few centuries of candle and oil smoke would make you think twice before falling ill. I was led through a couple of archways before I reached the infirmary. There were glass cabinets with all kinds of ancient medical equipments. I was once fortunate enough to archive by photo the small museum at our psychiatric hospital and had since been interested in ancient medical tools. This place seemed to have more and one wondered what they used those tools for. Then I realised that this was a hospital before it became a school, and during the war it was a military hospital.

At least I am in good company today, I thought, and I had better not let down my colleagues from the Hippocratic past.

It was early March and spring had not quite arrived in southern England that year. There was not much light coming through the small oval windows. Matron seemed to have read my mind.

"This was not in fact a proper hospital ward as the main hospital buildings are now the dormitory. This was the staff chapel, but as we all now use the main chapel, it seems such a good idea to turn this into an infirmary. Very good for migraines and headaches and that is normally what we deal with." Matron said.

I thought - mmmmm, neither condition can be confirmed by any medical investigation.

Still it was quite a big room and with the neatly made beds and their white sheets, was speaking loudly – this is an infirmary; you are here to be ill and hopefully to recover.

Ruth was sitting in one of the middle beds and with her nurse.

"We have kept a nurse with her since last night, doctor." Matron assured me.

There we were, a rather petite looking girl in her hospital outfit sitting on the rather high bed trying to read. She had a small face and as I approached, slipped off the bed and stood to attention. That said a lot about what kind of school this was. She was reading a French novel but I could not really tell which one it was. She looked cheerful, certainly too cheerful for someone who had tried to get to the other side less than twelve hours ago.

It was a job to persuade matron to let me speak to Ruth on my own. When she realised that I meant what I said she sent the nurse to sit outside the door just in case and still hoped that I would let her keep it ajar an inch or so. She eventually agreed to have it closed but the nurse would just be outside.

Ruth herself was not too bothered and I suspected that when you lived in a big dormitory, privacy was not a big concern.

It was not my style to jump straight to what happened. This disappointed her a bit.

"Don't you want to know what happened?" she asked.

But she agreed to do it my way and in fact it was a better idea, she later agreed. She thought I was going to ask about the night before and then send her to a mental institution.

Matron had informed the parents of my visit and mother, who was a social worker, was driving up from the coast and hoped to meet me within the hour.

There is a very simple rule when we assess attempted suicide. We have to decide if this is the usual or the unusual.

The usual – probably late teenage, made up to look twenty one, argument with boyfriend, got drunk and took eighteen Paracetamol or whatever was handy including the rest of the month's pill. Most survived but now and again they were unlucky, were found too late and died a rather painful death. I was lucky – I never had to deal with those. I heard of one though, but she was dead when found. She left mum a note but mum was out with her boyfriend all night and the next day she came home to find a dead girl. Luckily these cases were rare and for that we had to thank our lucky stars. The virtual disappearance of barbiturates and tricyclic antidepressants meant that we had to deal with fewer accidental deaths, though Paracetamol remained the most potent killing agent.

This girl was not like the usual. She tried to hang herself with the very belt with which she was meant to tie her cloak. Luckily for her the light to which she tied the belt did not hold her weight and she fell to her bed and tripped out the mains. Most of the other girls were asleep but her best friend saw her. She was too scared to say anything at first but now she could not stop crying and had been kept in her own dorm away from my patient's influence.

She was one of the star pupils of her year. Her father was the chaplain at a church near the coast. She was the only child. She was also a very good swimmer and represented the school in competitions. She was very talkative and despite what happened was quite at ease telling me about herself and her views of life.

For three nights before going to sleep she heard a voice telling her to hang herself. The previous night she actually saw a shadow telling her she must do it to keep her parents from harm. She thought it would not matter as her parents were more important.

I did not think she was making it up. She did try to hang herself.

What should I do? Was this the start of a psychotic illness? Did she have a fast growing brain tumour? If I made the wrong decision, she might end up dead one way or another.

No, there was no other sign of either a depressive illness or psychosis. Why were the parents not here for something so serious? Why was mother still at work? Why was father not on his way here? Perhaps they did not take this seriously and maybe I should not either.

This was an otherwise well put together girl, clever, good looking and had a good prospect of achieving well.

Would this be someone you put on an antidepressant or antipsychotic? Would I need to send her to a mental institution?

One of the most important things we learned in medicine is: *when in doubt, do nothing.*

To be more precise, *do not do anything that is not reversible*. What was the rush?

I had for years an arrangement to admit my patients, if necessary, to our paediatric ward which normally took in tonsils and dental patients. The hot cases were appendicitis, and then there were my patients who did not require psychiatric inpatient treatment; they had mostly been anorectic patients who, incidentally, had done well over the years. They were often there without other anorectics and that was perhaps one of the reasons they did well.

A number of O/Ds (overdoses) used to go through the paediatricians, and I would be consulted before any of them could be discharged – a sort of safety valve approach. There were no seriously ill patients. The nurses were a fairly stable group. It was an ideal place for mothers returning to a nursing career. Over the years, they had got to like my special group of patients, including infants with a sleep problem.

That would be the ideal place for Ruth. It was a modern hospital. And we could observe her. Like they say, something is going to give.

Mother turned up. She did look like a social worker. She explained that if this was a hysterical gesture she did not want the girl to think that she could do something like this and get her attention.

But that was not how I saw it. No, this was no textbook case.

It was very interesting talking to mother. Half the time I was talking to a colleague and the other half to a very frustrated modern woman married to a very strictly religious man.

She and her husband were at college together. They were idealists. They were CND members. They marched against this war and that and eventually he studied theology and she, social work. Ruth was a perfect baby, bright and cheerful. She was their only child. She obeyed all rules and she was diligent. She was every mother's dream. She was cute, charming, clever and full of life, never demanding in any way and had always been the top achiever in everything she did, academic or sport. She had quite a following in school and what happened came as a shock, and a serious shock to a boarding school.

A religious boarding school.

Such behaviour could be infectious and more so when a natural leader did it.

This is particularly true of psychiatric patients and more so adolescents in an institution. Some years ago a colleague's two daughters sadly committed suicide one after another in a boarding school.

I had to come up with a solution.

A friend once said to me, "You often have to do certain things when a patient is referred to you, not because it is necessary for the patient, but because it is important for the referrer, the parents or the people around the patient."

I could not leave Ruth in the boarding school. I could not send her to a mental institution. So I had to admit her to the paediatric ward.

Mother agreed. Matron was most relieved. Ruth of course would not object. I felt happier getting her out of that rather imposing place.

An MRI did not reveal any lurking growth and you would be surprised how many parents would have been disappointed with that. Luckily not this mother.

Ruth became extremely helpful on the ward assisting with the younger kids distressed by their ops and she would be patiently reading them stories. Schoolwork was sent in regularly and I did not think she suffered much from being absent.

Visiting was rather restricted, not by the hospital but by the school for obvious fear of contamination, contamination of the minds of the innocent ones.

She soon revealed the figure she saw was that of her father. She said she was afraid to tell me before.

Now I understood the reasons I never once saw father.

She told me that over an extended period of time she would be shut in with him in an under-stairway cupboard when he would recount biblical passages of hell and damnation. The idea was to give her a real taste of hell.

"Why was it necessary?" I wondered to myself, "Why do this to a girl who by all standards is perfect?"

I wish I knew and I wish I had made up the story. But real life could be very strange indeed.

With her permission, I brought mother in and she started crying when Ruth said, "I told him."

Mother assured me later that she did not think there was any sex abuse but it did cross her mind that all the dramatic teaching of Revelation might have something to do with her daughter's hearing voices and especially those of her father.

At that time I had just come back from Peru, with images of Juanita[93] still fresh in my mind. The tribal rituals of virgin sacrifice in the Andes, visions and religious fanaticism suddenly took on a new meaning.

She respected her father and what he said had to be done, even if it was hallucination. Sacrifice would be nothing and if she was to go to heaven anyway, she would have avoided the torture of hell.

I continued to see her and her mother. We seldom talked about religious matters, but more about studies, literature, sport and current affairs. Father never came to any of the appointments. I did not force him to come to see me. I believe it was sometimes more revealing to let things unfold. Often things that did not happen told a story too.

There were two more sightings of the devil but she was not distressed.

I never pronounced any judgment on the origin of her symptoms and school soon gave up asking me. There was an unspoken understanding with Ruth and mother and I preferred to leave it that way. I felt that my job was not to destroy but to help recovery.

Was it ethical? Could I have missed what is called Satanic Abuse? We do know what happened to some of those who were so

---

[93] Juanita (also known as "The Ice Maiden") was discovered on the top of Mount Ampato near Arequipa, Peru, on September 8, 1995 by Johan Reinhard. She was 12 to 14 years old when she was sacrificed and is believed to have died about 500 years ago.

Although she was frozen in the frigid temperatures on Mount Ampato, her body was discovered because a nearby volcano had caused Ampato's snowcap to melt. The undisturbed site of her burial included many items left as offerings to the gods. Two other children's bodies were discovered near her.

sure of their views of abuse. How much harm was caused? How many children were wrongfully taken away never to return to their parents?

Of course doctors could be wrong and of course my views might change in time but for now things were working out.

Bad parents are generally easier to deal with. It is easier for children to know from early on that they are better off not taking any notice of them and they will, at least the resilient ones will, survive. Many children of psychotic parents become independent and tough from an early age. "Good parents", on the other hand, are more difficult to handle and if they already have a position in society, what are the poor children supposed to do?

Ruth had been sheltered in her upbringing. She was not streetwise and staying in a highly religious institution, she did not have the chance to mix with any rebellious children.

As a first born, she followed rules and orders.

I continued to see them. Later, without any direct instruction by me, mother worked out that it would be better to move her from her current school to another church school. This one was less austere and the focus was more on education than on religion. She blossomed and now as she was not boarding, she began to go out and meet boys. Soon enough she was dating a boy. With mother's help they kept this from father whom I still had not met. She achieved some exceptional GCSE results, moved on to a state sixth form college which her now boyfriend also attended. He wanted to be an engineer and she was aiming for languages.

She went on the pill and father still had no idea she had this boyfriend.

Her A Level results were straight A's and she got her place at a top university. She came to see me during the Christmas break. She settled in very well and was enjoying her course. I did not ask her about her hallucinations. Sometimes we need to know what not to say.

Mother left father as soon as Ruth got to university and continued to work as a social worker. Father was transferred to the north.

Perhaps I should have raised alarms about father.

Perhaps.

I was lucky she came to no harm.

Sometimes one may not be so lucky.

Chapter 31 Adapting To Guidelines

As we move into the new century child psychiatrists are faced with more and more guidelines and protocols.

Since Maria Colwell [94] Social Services have been working under revised Guidelines and Child Protection Procedures. The sad

---

[94] Maria Colwell - Maria Colwell died on 6th January 1973, aged 7. Maria, removed from her mother's care due to neglect, had been living happily with an aunt after her father's death, but was returned to her mother at the mother's request. Despite warnings of abuse, and 30 calls to social services from neighbours, she was left in a violent household. One neighbour reported the child being hit for being dirty, and saw her at a window with a blackened face "and one eye just a pool of blood." The neighbour asked NSPCC and Social Services: "What protection does a child have against her parents? Does she have to be killed before they take her away?" In Maria's case the answer was yes. Maria was taken to hospital in a pram, after being beaten by her stepfather the night before. She was found to be dead on arrival. She had two bruised eyes, bruising on neck, back, arms and legs, severe internal injuries and brain damage. Her stomach was empty.

http://archive.theargus.co.uk/2003/1/31/141384.html
http://society.guardian.co.uk/climbie/comment/0,,882568,00.html

truth is that more children continue to be abused and killed despite these tighter guidelines and procedures.

My hunch is that despite media coverage[95] many of us still fail to grasp the dark side – the dark side of human nature. Until we do, we shall continue to read about child abuse, abductions and murders of the worst kind.

In our work, it is sometimes necessary not to follow strictly some of these protocols. One thing I have learned is that the anger in separated/divorced parents is often vented onto us and from an early stage I had set up certain unwritten rules for my own benefit and for the benefit of my trainees. One of these was not to see estranged parents who no longer had custody of the child, and I was often challenged upon this. Refusing to see estranged parents went against all that was being proposed in the NHS as good practice and seemed totally unacceptable in the modern era where it is "rights" and "rights" all the time.

You would not be able to hear the other side of the story – I was told.

Did I really need the other side of the story? What was wrong with assessing the child as he or she was?

---

[95] example of media coverage: 10th August 2007 – Two people have today been found guilty of the murder of four year-old Leticia Wright in Huddersfield. A four-year-old girl was murdered after a horrific four-week period of sustained violence, just weeks after social services had shut the file on her case. Social workers called at the home in Huddersfield four weeks before the girl's body was found. They saw no injuries, found her weight normal, and noted she was registered with a local nursery. Soon afterwards, the court was told, she must have been subjected to a vicious attack which left her with 100 separate injuries.
http://www.westyorkshire.police.uk/section-item.asp?sid=12&iid=3800

Rebecca

Rebecca was nearly sixteen but she had suffered very badly from her parents' divorce. She loved her father but every time she saw him he would bombard her with all the "nasties" about mother. She wanted him to stop and pleaded with me that I should see him. Mother agreed and in fact pleaded with me to do so when I told her about my little rule. He had by then moved to Dorset some distance away and I made arrangements for him to come and see me. Rebecca wanted to be there so mother drove her to the clinic. Rebecca came in to see me first as I wanted to know if she still felt fine about me seeing her father.

Then I heard commotions and shouts and fights in the waiting room. My secretary rushed in saying she had just called the police.

Apparently the parents started some argument in the waiting area and a fight broke out. Mother's nose was bleeding and father quickly drove off.

This had become my standard story for some years whenever I refused to see the other parent.

Isabella

The most undervalued person in a clinic is probably the secretary, a good secretary. In fact the same can be said of many organisations. Medical secretaries used to have to be specially trained. Eventually people at the top decided that doctors should no longer have that privilege. In some places doctors phone in their letters to a pool of typists. Before long these typists will be located in some far distant countries. Typed letters can then be emailed back to the clinic for printing and signatures. It is possible to save the NHS a lot of money. I believe some Imaging set-ups have already been outsourced. Have your PET scan read at the best possible rate in some other country.

Those were the days when doctors in U.K. were amongst the top three most respected professions and Members of Parliament shared the bottom ranking with Estate Agents.

The doctor's position had over the last ten years moved nearer the bottom end with no such counter moves by politicians. Some argued that the rot started with Shipman[96] and the move to check on doctors' competence will soon become law. The sad truth is that incompetence was not Shipman's problem as he was able to shield the deaths that he created with his expert medical knowledge. The incompetence was with those that regulated him. He was probably more up-to-date with medicine than most, and expert at euthanasia. Recent scandals relating *to Cleveland*[97], *Bristol*[98], *Alder*

---

[96] Shipman - Harold Frederick Shipman (January 14, 1946–January 13, 2004) was an English general practitioner who was one of the most prolific known serial killers in modern history. He was convicted on 15 sample charges in 2000 and sentenced to 15 consecutive life sentences. He committed suicide in 2004 at HMP Wakefield, West Riding of Yorkshire, without admitting or explaining his crimes.

After his trial, an inquest decided that there was enough evidence to suggest that Shipman had killed a total of 215 people, about four out of five of them women.

[97] Cleveland Child Sex Abuse scandal - In early summer 1987, the United Kingdom and the world were rocked by allegations of child sexual abuse occurring in Cleveland, a major industrial conurbation in the North-East of England.

Allegations of child sexual abuse were being made by Marietta Higgs, a paediatrician at a Middlesbrough hospital. Using a novel technique known as reflex anal dilatation, in 1987 she diagnosed 121 children as victims of sexual abuse. Once the allegations had been made, social workers were compelled by law to remove the children from their families and place them in foster care. Initially public opinion favoured the doctor and the social workers but, as the number of cases increased, parents decided to hold a protest march from the hospital to the offices of the local newspaper, where they planned to tell their versions of events. The media slowly turned to support the parents and a public inquiry was enacted, led by Elizabeth Butler-Sloss. Cases involving 96 of the 121 children alleged to be victims of sexual abuse were dismissed by the courts.

Hey[99], *Kent Authority*[100], *and MMR*[101] all help to erode people's trust in their doctors and their regulator, the GMC[102].

---

[98] Bristol Royal Infirmary scandal - Between 30 and 35 children who underwent heart surgery at the Bristol Royal Infirmary between 1991 and 1995 died unnecessarily as a result of sub-standard care. The heart unit was split between two sites, with no dedicated children's intensive care beds and no way of monitoring quality and poor organisation.
http://news.bbc.co.uk/2/low/health/1444983.stm

[99] Alder Hey scandal – At Alder Hay Hospital, a Dutch histopathologist Dick van Velzen, who was in charge of pediatric autopsies. was found to have issued diagnoses not borne out by tissue examination and to have retained portions of autopsy materials not specifically authorized for retention between 1988 and 1994. In June 20, 2005 - General Medical Council ruled that he should be permanently banned from practising medicine permanently in the UK.

[100] Kent Authority scandal - In February 1996 Kent and Canterbury hospital was forced to admit that its cervical screening programme was in serious trouble. It was discovered that mistakes by cervical screeners missed cancers in hundreds of women. The failures in the cervical screening programme there are believed to have led to the deaths of eight women, and forced 30 to undergo hysterectomies which might have been avoided by earlier diagnosis. A report into the events blamed staff shortages, poor morale, insufficient training and the failure of doctors to respond to warning signs about bad quality work at the laboratory. However, the Royal College, which was brought in to look at the laboratory's work involving other cancers, found mistakes in diagnosing cancer at the hospital were "within the expected range" of error.
http://news.bbc.co.uk/1/hi/health/307165.stm
http://news.bbc.co.uk/1/hi/health/515733.stm

[101] MMR scandal - Since the early 1970s in the United States, and 1988 in the United Kingdom, the three-in-one live virus measles, mumps and rubella vaccine has been routinely administered to almost all children, soon after they're one year old. Along with other immunisations, such as that against polio, and the combined diphtheria, tetanus and pertussis shot, the triple MMR has become a mainstay of public health, protecting against infectious diseases.
But in 1998 a UK medical journal, the Lancet, unleashed a devastating assault on confidence in the vaccine: suggesting that independent researchers at London's Royal Free Hospital had discovered a possible link with the development of bowel disease and regressive autism. It triggered a slump in immunizations and a rise in outbreaks of infectious diseases. But the key finding was a sham: laundering anonymized allegations against MMR by claimants in a lawsuit against the vaccine's makers - which the researcher had been paid huge sums to back. Investigative journalists from Sunday Times also discovered a string of patent applications - for a vaccine and products that could only have succeeded if MMR's reputation was damaged. From July 2007, Andrew Wakefield and two other British doctors face an estimated four-month disciplinary hearing before a panel of the UK General Medical Council over charges of serious professional misconduct, arising from the launch of a worldwide scare over the safety of the MMR vaccine, and the treatment of developmentally-challenged children.
http://briandeer.com/mmr-lancet.htm

[102] The General Medical Council (GMC) Gynaecologist Richard Neale faces being struck off after he was found guilty of botching operations and failing to obtain proper consent from patients.
The GMC must explain why the doctor was allowed to practise in the UK for 14 years despite being barred in Canada.
http://news.bbc.co.uk/1/hi/health/843501.stm

Nowadays in hospital and clinics there is in prominent display guidance on how patients and relatives can complain – not where they can "compliment".

The trust between the doctor and the patient has been responsible for, as long as medicine is in existence, that mysterious force that brings about healing and often cures. That is all but gone. Now doctors have to act according to guidelines, protocols and rules, written or otherwise. Interestingly there is as yet no guideline for guideline writers. Two of the most commonly used drugs recommended by NICE for diabetes, which were taken by hundreds of thousands of mostly overweight people in the U.K. last year, were shown to cause widespread heart failure[103]. The embarrassing alarm was raised by a "maverick" doctor[104].

There is a place in medicine to continually question. After all most drug trials only last six weeks and problems may not emerge for a good three decades.

---

[103] Diabetes drugs recommended by National Institute for Health and Clinical Excellence (NICE) were linked by scientists to heart failure. Last year 1.8m prescriptions were written across the UK, which scientists say equates to several hundred thousand patients taking the drugs which are recommended for use across the NHS by NICE. But researchers today call on NICE to think again, revealing that as many as one in every 50 patients taking the drugs Avandia (rosiglitazone) and Actos (pioglitazone) over a period of 26 months will have to be hospitalised for heart failure.
http://business.guardian.co.uk/story/0,,2136076,00.html

[104] Dr Steven E. Nissen - Drug Safety Critic Hurls Darts From the Inside

Dr. Nissen is shaking up the nation's pharmaceutical industry. His questioning of the safety of the Avandia diabetes medication in late May, for example, prompted a federal safety alert and led to a sales decline of about 30 percent for the drug, which brought in $3.2 billion for GlaxoSmithKline last year. Now, with a federal panel soon to decide whether it can remain on the market, Avandia's future is uncertain.

The drug is the latest example of why Dr. Nissen, 58, whose day job is chairman of cardiovascular medicine at the Cleveland Clinic, has emerged as a Naderesque figure and the nation's unofficial arbiter of drug safety.
http://www.nytimes.com/2007/07/22/business/22nissen.html?adxnnl=1&adxnnlx=1185550813-HvntBJ4JOPGWXK5iwVC0/A

With Isabella, my rule of not seeing an estranged parent again landed me in some trouble.

I turned up one morning at the clinic and my secretary immediately informed me that a man who claimed that he was an important person demanded to see me about his daughter. He was of course Isabella's father.

I had been asked to see Isabella urgently by his GP, but had not seen her yet. Having read the GP's account, I wrote back to say that knowing there would be court proceedings, I would only see her on the understanding that the consultation was not for the purpose of providing a court report but purely for clinical reasons. That was a new tactic I had started using since many referrals turned out to be a sort of back-door way for Court Welfare Officers to secure a psychiatric report. There is a place for forensic psychiatric practice but this often interferes with day to day therapeutic work. The GP understood and wrote to the courts and it was agreed by the courts that this should be so and I was due to see Isabella that morning.

Father probably got wind of that and turned up. Isabella, her mother and grandmother had arrived earlier and were seated in my consulting room by my efficient secretary, who now asked me what I wanted to do with father.

I told my secretary that I would not be able to see him. She went and told him so. He was not having it, saying that he was a local councillor and he knew his rights. My secretary came back and I told her to tell him to look at the complaints procedure posted on the board outside and if he did not leave we would call the police.

He said that we would be hearing from his lawyer but my secretary said that she had never seen anyone go off so abruptly when the police was mentioned.

I realised why when I saw Isabella, her mother and her grandmother. Isabella's father was from Eastern Europe and made quite a success of himself running a building business. Considering he arrived in the country as a refugee he had done well. He married his secretary at the firm and for a while things were going fine. Isabella was born and to both sides of the family it was a dream that came true. Isabella was not only beautiful but also intelligent.

Then things started going wrong as father was a bit of a womaniser and one day Isabella's mother found out quite by chance and challenged him.

He blew his top, hit her and tried to strangle her in the presence of Isabella. Luckily mother's parents happened to call and they called the police. There was now a restraining order and a non-molestation order on him and he was not supposed to come within 500 metres of her.

Yes, he was on the local council.

But at least I knew why he ran off so quickly.

Holly

Holly was a very gentle person. Sometimes one could be too gentle. For years she had suffered from her husband's violence, physical and mental, and it was quite a miracle when she finally walked into the court house and obtained an injunction. Her two girls were having nightmares and were referred to me.

Soon after the initial interview father demanded to see me. He saw the girls every other week for three hours, at his parents' house, under the supervision of a social worker. He claimed that whatever problem his wife was having with the children he had a right to know. My usual spiel did not work as it only invited a complaint to the managers.

My then immediate manager belonged to the old school. She was there when the hospital was a mental institution holding 800 patients. Some had been there for over 60 years. I knew as I was invited to do some photographic portraits of the oldest patient for the in-house magazine, with full permission of course. I always helped her out with the magazine for which she was responsible and it was a bit of an embarrassment for both of us when I was "un-cooperative".

We had to find a way.

"Only if you will see him with me," I conceded.

"Fine," she said.

"But I still will not divulge what mother said to me."

"I understand," she said

It was a tense meeting. The man was of small build, contrary to my fantasy that wife beaters were big and burly.

He tried to have a go at me for my initial refusal, telling me it was against the Patient's Charter – a Government initiative under John Major, 1991. He was not too pleased when I told him he was not my patient. He turned visibly green when I refused to discuss his wife's session with me and I could sense the hostility building up.

My manager, who was very experienced in dealing with long term psychiatric patients, began to feel that she might well have made a mistake.

"You are going to hear from my lawyer," and with that he moved so violently out of his chair that it fell against my bookcase and nearly broke the glass doors.

I looked at the manager and she put her hand on my arm and said she understood.

Getting one's lawyer to write is of course a controlled form of violence and I knew then that it would not really happen, but my manager would not force me to see another parent against my will again.

Holly managed to take the two girls to her parents for the up coming half term.

When she returned she found her house was broken into. All the things that were of important emotional value such as photos and cards were torn. He took her car, crashed it into the fields and set fire to it. He was later arrested but Holly would not press charges.

I never heard from him or his lawyer but I did tell my manager.

She said she knew I was right but we had to be seen to be doing the right thing.

Two rights could make some peculiar wrongs and we could both have been hurt.

Chapter 32 Let Her Die

C an a patient be allowed to die? This is a dilemma sometimes
faced by doctors, even child psychiatrists.

Nicola

Nicola was not sure of me. Suddenly she was eating enough
and within three weeks of my arriving reached her target weight to
be sent home.

What a relief, I thought. Talk about flight to health. How
many others were going to do it?

Admitting anorectics all to the same place was never my
favourite idea of treating them. But right then there was no good
alternative.

Why? They would talk and build up their repertoire of tricks, and they would help each other. Not always in the way we wanted them to.

Those who earned home leaves met to gossip.

Word got round that I was cute and cool.

Four weeks later, Nicola was back. This time she was below the weight she was admitted before. There was an agreement that she would be re-admitted if that happened, to appease the parents. It was all in the contract.

Luckily, some of these girls could not keep the secret and confided in me. As a matter of fact, most girls cannot keep a secret – I have worked this one out. Not the anorectics anyway. Not if the secret is not about themselves.

Imagine working amongst the most intelligent girls without an insider!

Without wanting to upset the nurses, the same old contract was put into place and hopefully Nicola would be gone as quickly as she came.

At my age, there was a certain reward to be regarded as cool by teenagers and as cool by just being myself. Yes, I played ping-pong with them and home leave could depend on whether they won or not. But I still played in my work suit and leather shoes. Yes, I tuned the cello of one of the girls. She did not know that I phoned my daughter to get an A. Yes, I got Candy to eat when no one else could.

But I did not go round looking like a hippie or pretending that I liked the music the teenagers listened to. I told them to me it was trash. I did not pierce my ear or have a tattoo. I certainly did not wear trainers to work.

But I did drive a cool car, a cool car for old men, one boy remarked when I gave him a Diet Coke from my boot.

In short, you do not have to gain respect by becoming like them or worse, by pretending that you are like them.

It appeared that Nicola decided that I was her man.

It was really quite painful to sit there and talk to someone who looked worse than the worst they showed from Auswitz. Why could Nicola not realise that if she wanted any man to like her she would need to look a lot better, which involved doubling her weight for starters.

She was determined to stay. This was a family given up even by Dr Hillman, my most fervent supporter of family therapy. Father used to run a business security agency specialising in industrial counter espionage. Or was it espionage? I cannot be sure.

I spent one session with them and agreed with Dr Hillman. They were good. We looked like a bunch of amateurs dealing with professionals. None of the family therapy tricks work, Minuchin or Haley.

Impenetrable!

Why, you may well ask.

Too often there is this bizarre desire by some parents to make sure that if they cannot do it, no one else should either. We need to recognise it early enough. We are doomed otherwise, and so is the patient.

I was glad though that I realised early enough.

There really was no need for me to compete with the parents. My concern was of course for my patient. I must come up with some new ideas.

To these parents this was a medical condition and we, the medical people, would have to deal with it.

A month went by – nothing happened. Another one – nothing.

She was eating, I was told, just not putting on weight.

She claimed too that she was eating but her body was not "responding".

"I am sending her home!" I told her nurse one bright spring morning.

"What? At her weight? She will die!"

The nurse was most reluctant but grudgingly agreed when I told her my reasoning. It would be on my head anyway.

To me, suspension on full pay is a risk every doctor takes nowadays, as the basis is no longer limited to bad practice. It is no longer a reflection on whether you are good or bad clinically. Many psychiatrists are no longer prepared to use techniques that might upset their patients or parents of their patients.

A family meeting was called and it lasted only a few minutes.

I was in top form.

"Nicola has been eating but after two months has not put on any weight. I cannot see any reason for her to continue to stay here. She might as well do the eating at home. She can then sort out for herself why she is not gaining weight without the pressure from us."

I tried to put it in the calmest way possible.

"You mean you will let her die?" Father sounded a bit annoyed.

Everybody in the room looked at me – mother, Nicola, her nurse and Dr Hillman.

They all seemed to be saying one thing, "Now how do you respond to that?"

I decided to use the oldest trick in psychiatry – I just repeated myself. I thought, "I am a psychiatrist, you know, and this is not my first Anorexia Nervosa either."

"You are going to let her die!" With that father got up and left the room without saying another word.

"What do I do now? You have upset him!" said mother.

Good, something got to him at last, but I did not say it.

Nicola gave a wry smile to me as if to say, "You found me out."

She turned to mum, "Let's pack and leave this dump."

We all kept still.

Six months later, one of the nurses bumped into Nicola in a nearby town. She was kicked out by father and moved in with another ex-anorectic. She was with a boy friend. More importantly she was wearing a very sexy dress to show off her then very good figure.

She did not die.

Chapter 33 The Peril of Diagnosis

It is probably too late as so many doctors and psychiatrists are brought up on empirical diagnosis that sheds little light on the sufferings of the individual. The more powerful the diagnosis is, the easier it is to ignore the person as an individual and not to take into account his life history that may have a strong bearing on his treatment.

In physical medicine we all understand that pain is a symptom and not in itself a diagnosis. When we move on to stroke or heart attack, it may be more problematic. Even in these cases, most clinicians will still be looking at or for the underlying cause or causes and will not rest until that is identified. Hopefully it may have important bearing on the treatment. Underlying hypertension or diabetes, for example, will have to be treated.

In psychiatry, attempted suicide is not in itself a diagnosis and that is simple enough.

When we come to Anorexia Nervosa, psychiatrists are suddenly blinded. It is what I call a powerful diagnosis because it overshadows everything else.

I am not arguing against the "pure" form of Anorexia Nervosa and I am sure it exists.

Why?

Because I have seen these cases myself.

What I really want to alert readers to is the inherent danger in following blindly DSM (Diagnostic and Statistical Manual of Mental Disorders) or ICD (International Classification of Diseases) classifications. The danger is in seeing an Anorexia Nervosa patient as someone who has caught the "virus" that causes it.

A great disservice will be done to the patient if this distinction between what is the manifestation and what is the underlying pathology is not recognised.

The same is of course true of Drug and Alcohol Abuse. It is however a lot easier for most people to understand that there is an underlying cause for these. Pearl Harbour star Kate Beckensale[105] was recently reported to have the view that Anorexia Nervosa sufferers were not different to Cocaine junkies – an observation

---

[105] Miss Beckinsale, whose weight once plummeted to five stones, said: "I believe anorexia, alcoholism and drug abuse in teens are more about what is happening in the home than a problem with images in the media.

"It is the nice girl's way of becoming a crack whore."

http://www.dailymail.co.uk/pages/live/articles/showbiz/showbiznews.html?in_article_id=450464&in_page_id=1773

that stirred much controversy but was probably closer to the truth than most would care to admit.

Amanda

My old secretary Karen went to work for a plastic surgeon in the local hospital specializing in burns. Out of the blue she gave me a call.

"It is about Amanda. You should see her. She has all these scars on her."

It had been over two years since I last saw Amanda. It was rather sad as she had a real talent in art and I managed to secure the last ever support from the Education Authorities for accommodation for her at the Art College. But she dropped out after a year. Nevertheless she still managed to make appointments to see me a couple of times before disappearing.

"Why don't you ask her to arrange to see me next time she has a follow up at the clinic."

"That should not be a problem."

"But only if she wants to."

"I think you may still be of some help."

Well, Karen actually drove Amanda to my clinic late that afternoon and I stayed on to see her. Luckily Karen was still in the room with me when Amanda simply decided to lift her T-shirt. She was not wearing anything else underneath and what she revealed was a body covered in a number of three to four inches long keloidal scars. Some were actually over her breasts.

Karen stayed as chaperone and Amanda did not seem to mind. In our work there are certain risks when you see young people on their own and more so when you see someone like Amanda. I sometimes felt rather unsafe with some of the mothers too.

Amanda was first presented to me as a severe anorectic who more or less required immediate hospital admission. I put her in the paediatric ward rather than referred her to the hospital as at that time we were having some trouble with the quality of care there.

At the time, her weight was dangerously low. She was the only patient that I had to keep in the hospital over Christmas. It was rather strange that she seemed quite happy to do so. There were no protests from the parents either. It meant that I had to see her on Christmas day and I even bought her a nice soft toy for a present, something I had never done before or after.

Her body weight gradually picked up and it was time for some trial home leave. She pleaded with me not to let her go home even for half a day.

I did not want her to become dependent on us and there was every sign that she had now settled in on the ward.

She came back from home leave and decided not to follow our agreed contract. It was popular in those days to have a weight gain contract and we had one too. Of course now I realise how rigidity with a contract can have drawbacks. In fact in child psychiatry too rigid an approach often causes problems one way or another and it is one of the few medical disciplines with which strict guidelines are not a good idea.

At the time, another patient was on the ward after a serious suicide attempt. She had been abused by her step-father and step-brother over the years. She had had enough and decided to end it all. I was trying to sort out where she could go as there were all the child protection issues. She became very friendly with Amanda.

One day when I arrived on the ward, the Sister-in-charge handed me an envelope and said that Amanda would like me to read it first.

I have since used the same two pages she wrote as teaching material. Most female junior doctors could not go through with reading it aloud. It is nice to think that years of medical training do not really harden someone. Or was it something too horrible to be faced with? It was particularly upsetting when the abuser was Amanda's father.

Amanda was by then fourteen but her father had been abusing her since she was about eleven. Her mother worked night shifts and father would come to her bed room to tuck her in. This had been going on for as long as she could remember. She started to have budding breasts and her father would at first accidentally brush them and Amanda would be quite annoyed with that. Then one night he started fondling with her breasts and also outside her pants. She was so scared she froze and did not say anything. He went further and further until he penetrated her. She was bleeding quite badly and told her mother, who told her that was what happened to girls when they grew up. She knew what menstrual period was but she said this was different; but mum did not want to know and gave her a box of sanitary pads. Then her period started and she started to worry about becoming pregnant. Her father said it was not a problem and asked her to suck him instead. She recorded that she was sick every time. Then one day her father decided to try her "back-side". It caused so much bleeding it stained her school skirt and when she told her mother she was bleeding from her "back side" she just said, "Don't be silly. It is only a heavy period."

It is disturbing even for me to give you the details now. But this is what is happening to many children and is happening all around the world. If anything, I probably have toned down the content of that letter. What has gone wrong with mankind? I cannot say I know any better since my early cockroach catching days.

Then on the day I "forced" her to go home he picked her up and made her go down on him in the car on the way home when he parked on a lay-by.

In the end it was the other girl in the ward who encouraged her to write to me. She told her that she suffered the same for a long time and was stupid enough to try and hurt herself before she could tell anyone.

There was no time to waste to report this to Social Services. However, Amanda's father, who worked at the local mental hospital, had a "breakdown" and was admitted under the Mental Health Act the night before all of this came out. Amanda was not aware of this. When I showed mother what Amanda wrote, she just said to me, "He is in a mental hospital," and walked out.

It has taken me years to grasp that maternal failure plays a major role in family sexual abuse. This mother's action says it all. Can't you see he is mad?

It was a most peculiar case. His psychiatrist refused to even let me know of his problem, citing patient doctor confidentiality. He obviously had not worked with child abuse. Mother denied all knowledge of the bleeding incidents and claimed that it was all in Amanda's imagination and it became very hard trying to place Amanda because her mother would not acknowledge that there was a problem. At this time West[106] was arrested and it helped me at least to understand the unfathomable.

One of the nurses who got on well with Amanda told me that I should look at her examination portfolio for art. Every picture was morbid. One struck me with the René Magritte[107] style of surrealism. A body of a girl with a penis floating over what looked like a classical stone grave. The head was covered in cloth and separated from the body. There were many daggers on the upper body of this half-man half-woman. There was a sort of school in the distance with small figures of school children. The sky was normal blue with white clouds which contrasted dramatically with the central theme. There was no question that the sky was a Magritte sky, and so was the cloth covered head. The rest was original Amanda.

I knew then from what I remembered of Erickson that the picture was not just about the past with which one naturally associated but also about the future. Yet it took me a few years to realise that it was about the cutting.

---

[106] West – Frederick West was a British serial killer. He and his wife Rosemary are believed to have murdered at least 12 young women, many at the couple's home in Gloucester. He even raped his own 13-year old daughter. On 1 January 1995, he committed suicide in his cell at Winson Green Prison while awaiting trial for murder.

[107] René Magritte - was a Belgian surrealist artist. He became well known for a number of witty and amusing images. A consummate technician, his work frequently displays a juxtaposition of ordinary objects in an unusual context, giving new meanings to familiar things. The representational use of objects as other than what they seem is typified in his painting.

She said she was now working as a waitress. Her teacher at college did not want her to do all the morbid paintings, so she quit. She had been sleeping with virtually any man she came across and every time she would cut herself afterwards. She wanted to feel something, she told me. What was worst was that whenever she was with a man she saw her father.

What an outcome. I had spent so much time with this girl and this was in the end what happened. She said one day she would be in a mental hospital like her father, but she hoped to kill herself before then.

I no longer remember Amanda as a severe anorectic but rather a very talented artist who suffered serious abuse. Yet in a society which prides itself in social care, she did not become a famous artist with a high income, telling all about her history of abuse in front of a famous chat show host. Nor did she become a movie star telling all after drug and alcohol rehab.

Instead she was on benefits and I am struggling hard to find something uplifting to end this story. It has taught me one thing: Anorexia Nervosa may be just a manifestation.

Jane

Jane was never abused by anyone. Not as far as I know unless self abuse is counted.

She was every bit a classical Anorexia Nervosa. Or that was what I thought.

She was a very attractive girl, more so when she was skinny. Her older sister was slightly overweight and looked ...

well…unattractive. It is amazing how that Hepburn look is so attractive and was desired then and still is now.

She was very intelligent and studied the cello with a famous cellist.

I was never quite sure if she liked the cello or not. If truth be told, being that middle class in an adolescent unit does not bode well.

Most of the others knew nothing about classical music and preferred pop. Nobody read quality newspapers and that went for the staff as well. However, a number of the admitted anorectics came from the upper middle class background. Most if not all.

You guess right. There was an undercurrent of "dumbing" down. It was everywhere. It was in keeping with government policy.

With Jane I tried every ploy available to me.

Everybody was waiting for me to pull another trick, especially after the "Seven minute cure".

Some thought it was hard work going to a private school. Not just going to one, but being at the top of your year with a scholarship.

One day mother confessed to me in private that she too went through a phase of Anorexia. Nobody knew. Not even her own doctor, and could I keep it a secret?

Jane got on well with me.

She had to, as nobody understood that to her achieving was not a hardship but something she secretly enjoyed. She was no longer allowed to pick up her books as she had not put on any weight since her admission.

She missed the cello too, the only thing she could use to shut out her worries.

Fourteen and carrying the burden of the world.

Cello would be banned too, if her nurse was to have her way.

For the unit to function the nurse must have her way. After all I was not there all the time to watch her. To watch if she was eating, vomiting, exercising or whatever else they did to avoid gaining weight.

But I was determined that it would be the first privilege she would get if she put on half a gram. Or any excuse I could think of.

Brutal confrontation is often what happened in many adolescent units dealing with Anorexia Nervosa. The brutality is not physical.

But these patients are intelligent and have such strong will power that confrontation generally fails and the failure can be a miserable one. Yet it is the kind of condition that hurts. It hurts those trying to help. It hurts because these patients deserve better for themselves. It hurts because they are not drop-outs of society.

Was it too hard for Jane to keep at the top academically? Someone offered that as an explanation. Perhaps she should be moved to a state school.

The idea horrified me.

A fourteen year old non-smoking, non-drinking, non-drug taking, intelligent Audrey Hepburn look alike virgin turning up at your local comprehensive. It sounded like a major disaster to me.

I had to take the matter into my own hands. She did put on some weight and at the earliest opportunity I decided she should get back to the cello which had always been by her bed at the unit.

"I cannot tune it."

"What?"

But why should I be surprised? It was quite an expensive Cello, an heirloom from her grandmother on father's side. She had been a good cellist in her time although she stopped playing when she married Jane's grandfather and went to South Africa. That was where her father was born.

Jane's teacher had kept the cello in tune and although my children tuned their violins now, it was the teacher who did it for Jane.

Luckily it only needed minor adjustment but we had no A reference.

But I was not to be defeated having come this far.

She was not going to play unless it got tuned.

"Dad used to tune it, and he was very good."

I phoned my daughter and she played an A on the piano at home, which I recorded on my cell phone. We got the cello to sound a little bit decent.

"I am not going to be as good as your teacher, but I hope this will do."

She played a couple of scales and we made some fine tuning. It was not quite the same as the violin, but at least I knew not to overdo the pegs. Then she started playing.

"Ah. The Bach G-major"

"So you know it"

Of course I do. The hours I spent listening to Yo Yo Ma and it was such amazing music, melancholic and uplifting at the same time. For a moment I forgot that I was her psychiatrist and she forgot she was my patient.

"My grandma gave me Casals."

I knew Casals was even more emotional than Ma, but Ma is Chinese and he was less affecting, allowing the listener to tune in to his own mood.

She played from memory. What talent! What went wrong?

"I wish my dad could hear me."

It was the first time she could talk about her father. They had a very comfortable life in South Africa when father was alive. It was very difficult to imagine what he would have looked like. It was never clear what he did but he was involved in a number of ventures. The plantation Jane's grandfather ran was sold when apartheid came to an end. He was involved in some private reserve and he was a photographer of sorts but my junior told me that mum started to cry when she talked about him so she did not pursue too deeply.

He died of lung cancer. That much we knew. The family came back to England where mother's family lived. There were educational trust funds set up by the grandparents and mother bought an old Victorian House just across the street from where I used to live. The only time mother stopped me was when she told me about her own Anorexia.

We had for a while adopted a policy of no weight gain no talk. Looking back now, it was probably a rebound from previous experience with a girl who never really got any better from hours of psychotherapy. Rules can be dangerous in psychiatry as every individual is different, and the assumption that the patient wants to put on weight and talk may be wrong.

She gained enough weight to get home and soon I put her back on outpatient care. One of my juniors started to provide a weekly time. I did not use the term psychotherapy as it was more to see if she would click with someone other than me. I was too much of an authority figure for her.

We were only able to "hover" her. Her weight would go up for a couple of weeks and then down and then up again.

Then I retired and after a year or so my junior left too.

In one of the letters from my contacts at the clinic, I was told that Jane had to be admitted to a hospital in London. Her weight was so low that she was on tube feeding.

News of a famous heiress just flashed through this morning's news [108] and the psychodynamics of Jane's Anorexia Nervosa suddenly became clearer. The heiress witnessed her uncle's murder and was anorectic ever since[109]. Jane was home when her father died in mother's arms with a massive haemoptysis (coughing up of blood, a rare but not unknown effect of lung cancer, generally a massive bleed). It must have been very traumatic.

---

[108] Donatella Versace's 20-year-old daughter, Allegra, is undergoing treatment for anorexia, the fashion designer said Tuesday. "Our daughter, Allegra, has been battling anorexia, a very serious disease, for many years," Versace and Paul Beck said in a statement released by spokesman Robert Zimmerman.

http://tv.msn.com/tv/article.aspx?news=256482&GT1=7703

[109] Allegra Versace, the girl Versace called his "little princess" was only 11 when he was shot dead outside his Miami Beach mansion by serial killer Andrew Cunanan.
http://news.scotsman.com/topics.cfm?tid=1470&id=483912007

How dim of me. That was bereavement, a slow suicide by someone who felt less worthy to survive.

.

Chapter 34 Failure?

It is not easy to admit to failures and harder still for doctors to do so especially if they did everything right and according to protocol.

Doing the "right" thing is not an indication of success.

Hardly.

Yes. I am coming back to Anorexia Nervosa again and I do not apologise for it. I am apologising for our failures though.

The British Daily Mail reported in March 2007[110]:

"It is thought there are between 60,000 and 90,000 adults being treated for eating disorders at any one time in the UK. The average age of diagnosis is

---

[110] Daily Mail report on 26th March 2007 – Children as young as six suffering from aneroxia. http://www.dailymail.co.uk/pages/live/articles/health/healthmain.html?in_article_id=444646&in_page_id=1774

between 16 and 18between 60,000 and 90,000 adults are estimated to be treated for eating disorders at any one time in the UK.

Over a 13-month period from March 2005, 206 preteenage children across Britain and Ireland were newly diagnosed with serious disorders ranging from bulimia and anorexia to binge eating.

Half were admitted to hospitals for in-patient treatment. Some were showing symptoms of starvation such as a low temperature and a slow heart rate, while 10 per cent had to be fed by tube."

In the same month, the British Independent[111] reported:

"Anorexia Nervosa has the highest death rate of any psychiatric condition. In ten years 3% of these patients died, and although half were by suicide, the rest were related to the starvation process.

Just this week in Rome a 27-year-old model identified only as Ilaria died of Anorexia after an illness lasting ten years. She weighed 35kg at her death. Luisel Ramos, 22-year-old Uruguayan model died at a fashion show in August, 2006 after suffering a fatal heart attack that was thought to be the result of Anorexia. Ana Carolina Reston Marcan, the Brazilian catwalk queen died only three months later in a Sao Paulo hospital."

When I took over the adolescent unit as its consultant in charge there were six Anorexia Nervosa patients in varying stages of emaciation or weight gain depending on from which side you want to look at it. It is not always wise to have so many anorectic

---

[111] Independent report on 29th March 2007: The Versace family: Allegra and the curse of anorexia
http://www.independent.co.uk/news/europe/the-versace-family-allegra-and-the-curse-of-anorexia-442347.html

patients together as they do share tricks with each other and it is often more difficult to customise treatment.

What needed my urgent attention was of course Sammy. Sammy had a very feminine name but preferred the nickname Sammy. Sammy's Section was due to expire in less than 14 days and I had to compile a report for the Tribunal which would be sitting to decide on her fate.

It was perhaps a sign of our failure as psychiatrists to effectively treat Anorexia Nervosa that eventually case law was established to regard food in Anorexia Nervosa as medicine. Therefore food may be used forcibly to treat Anorexia Nervosa when the condition becomes life threatening.

The usual test of mental capacity no longer applies. Instead the law is used forcibly to feed a generally bright and intelligent person "over-doing" what most consider to be "good". They try to eat less and eat healthily by avoiding fat and the like and *wham* we have the law on them.

I have to admit that I have not liked this aspect of Sectioning. Unfortunately it is used often, judging by the high numbers of tube fed patients.

On the other hand not everybody is able to treat Anorexia Nervosa patients or, in reality, do battle with them. It requires experience, energy, time, wit, charisma and often impeccable timing. However, sometimes I do wonder if we are indeed doing a disservice when we take things out of parents' hands by agreeing to take over.

With hindsight and upon reflecting on a number of cases I have dealt with, I often wonder: if hospitalisation had not been an option at all, would improvement rate and, more importantly, mortality rate have been any different.

We do not section people for smoking, drinking, or doing drugs, which all endanger life. Nor do we stop people running the Marathon or eating raw oysters when these activities regularly lead to mortalities.

Society is coming round to do something about over-eating in children but it will take some time before they apply the Mental Health Acts.

To me, the moment a psychiatrist turns to the law he is admitting that he has failed.

At least that is my view and if I perpetuated the Compulsory Order with Sammy, I too would be part of that failure.

There had been no weight gain in Sammy despite the tube feeding and the debate was: shall we increase the feed or shall we wait? Everybody just assumed that she would stay on as a compulsory patient.

Despite bed rests and even more embarrassingly the use of bedpans, many Anorexia Nervosa patients managed not to gain weight whatever we pumped into them. The balanced feeds were in fact quite expensive. There was no secret that they were aware of the exercises they could perform even on bed rest and the determination not to put on weight had to be seen to be believed. If such determination was applied elsewhere I was sure these young girls could be very successful.

I had to find an answer, an answer for Sammy and an answer for myself.

Being forced to eat by the State remained the treatment of choice for everybody except for one stubborn consultant.

"At least we did all we could," my staff constantly reminded me.

"And she is the most determined of all the Anorectics we have right now."

More reason to show the others that this new psychiatrist had some other means than brute force, I thought to myself.

Yes, I could be as determined as they were.

The hours of family therapy only brought about accusations and counter accusations with hardly any resolution. Middle class families have certain ways of dealing with things where some branches of family therapy are not particularly good at all.

The modern trend is certainly moving away from blaming families. Or that is the rhetoric of most who write publicly about it.

Whatever the official line, families cannot help feeling blamed.

"If we are not to blame, why do we need family therapy?"

"There are so many other families like ours. Why do they not have the same problem?"

We may reassure them that there are and that is the truth, but the truth is that there are also Anorexia-free families.

Yes, it might help if they do find a gene like they did with obesity. Yet that cannot explain why there are more extremely obese people in say the U.S. which collects gene pools from across the globe.

So Sammy's family had the full benefit of eight sessions of family therapy by two very experienced therapists. In the end, there was just a lot of recrimination between all parties including the therapists and all agreed it would not be the way forward. That was when tube-feeding started.

Minuchin[112] dealt with over-involvement, over-protectiveness and conflict avoidance in these families with no special apology on whether he blamed the family or not. He used to start with a meal session with the family. His success, like many such methods, probably had more to do with his charisma than his method and is thus difficult to replicate.

For Sammy and her family the message was simple and clear enough, no matter how hard we lied.

The family had failed and the hospital had to take over.

That was the blunt truth.

But the hospital had failed too and we had to resort to the Mental Health Act on one of society's most sensible and decent and safest citizens.

I decided enough was enough. I could no longer perpetuate the no-blame approach. I could no longer continue to hide behind the power conferred onto me by the law. In short, I had to reverse just about everything that had gone on before, and more.

Just two weeks before the tribunal sat we had the big review meeting. To most at the unit, the review was fairly routine as there was hardly any choice – a full Section for Hospital Treatment primarily intended for difficult to treat Schizophrenics and difficult

---

[112] Salvador Minuchin: (born 1921 in Argentina), in 1965 became the director of the Philadelphia Child Guidance Clinic, which eventually became the world's leading center for family therapy and training. He is author of a number of books including Families and Family Therapy and Family Kaleidoscope and coauthor of Psychosomatic Families: Anorexia Nervosa in Context and Mastering Family Therapy.

to control Bipolars in the acute manic phase. Sammy would be "detained at Her Majesty's pleasure", and classed with the likes of the few psychotics who had committed the most heinous murders. To save Sammy's life, it would be natural to continue with the Mental Health Act.

Yes there would be weeks of tube feeding and bed rest, but the State had to take over the complete care of this bright young thing for her own sake.

I could not see any other way either.

Unless ....I could reverse everything that had gone on before.

If our work is to be therapeutic then a sort of therapeutic alliance is important, even if tentative. Some people do not realise that you can fight with your patient and still have a sort of therapeutic alliance.

I had a plan.

These meetings were attended by just about everybody who had anything to do with the patient. They were held at school times so that most of the teaching staff could be present as well. These meetings also had a tendency to drag on as everybody seemed to have a lot to say about very little, a trait not just limited to psychiatrists but also seen in social workers, therapists, nurses, junior grade doctors, teachers and visiting professionals. People always seemed to have a lot to say on cases where there was the least progress.

My personal view is that this was a sure sign of anarchy which had unfortunately drifted into our Health Service, encouraged in part by the numerous re-organisations that had gradually eroded the authority of the doctor.

Saul Wurman[113], an architect by training but also an author of business and tour books, famously wrote that meetings really do not always need to be an hour long. Why can it not be ten or twenty minutes?

Could I achieve that?

After briefly explaining to all the purpose of the meeting, I turned to Sammy, who still had the nasal feeding tube "Micropore'd[114]" securely and said, "What do you think?"

"It is so unfair. Now I shall not be able to go to Harvard."

It is generally perceived as a given that a U.K. citizen who has been Sectioned will not be able to use the Visa Waiver to visit the U.S. If that person then has to apply for a Visa, having been detained under the Mental Health Act must be a major hindrance, although I have never seen this applied in practice. One of my patients did have to cancel a horse trial trip to Kentucky because she was sectioned at the height of a manic episode.

I did not know she had aspirations to get to Harvard but I was not surprised given what I already knew about mother.

"Before I say anything else, can I ask you a few things?"

"What? Sure!"

"Do you smoke, drink, take Ecstasy or go out clubbing?"

---

[113] Richard Saul Wurman: (born 1936) an architect by training, published over 81 books including his best-selling book Information Anxiety and his award winning ACCESS Travel Guides. His latest books are UNDERSTANDING Children and UNDERSTANDING Healthcare (January 2004). http://www.wurman.com/rsw/

[114] Micropore™: Micropore consists of a conformable, non-extensible non-woven fabric manufactured by 3M from 100% viscose, coated with a layer of an acrylic adhesive.

"No. Why?"

"Do you have piercings and tattoos on you?"

"Tattoos—yuk! Yes, I having my ears pierced. That is all."

"Do you like Pop music?"

"No way. I play the violin and I like Bach and Bartok!"

Everybody was attentive now.

"Do you shoot heroin or smoke Cannabis?"

"No way!"

She was getting annoyed.

"What about boys and sex?" I felt bad even to ask especially in front of her mother, who I thought would faint if we knew something she did not.

"How can you even ask and in front of my parents? You know I don't do things like that!"

I can remember my own adolescence. I did not do any of those things either and I did not even have pierced ears.

I then turned to the parents. Mother was a history teacher at a famous private school in one of England's most middle class town. She also spent a year at Harvard, hence Sammy's ambition to follow her. Father was a prominent city lawyer.

"You have always provided well for her, a good education, European and U.S. holidays, a comfortable home and expensive music lessons."

"We are fortunate enough to be able to do that. She is our only child." Mother replied in a tone implying, "what's wrong with that?"

"And she has always been a bright child, strong willed and single minded. She passed her Grade 8 violin with distinction at 14 and could have become a musician. But she wanted to do International Studies." Mother added.

"So she always had her way."

"She has always got on with everything, studying and practising the violin. And she keeps a tidy bedroom!"

A tidy bedroom! My goodness, everything was falling into place.

"Sammy......"

"Yes......"

"You know what? You are the first adolescent I know that keeps a tidy bedroom, do not do drugs, do not drink, do not smoke and you do not do a load of other things I asked you about. You are by modern standards a FAILED adolescent!"

Then I turned to the parents.

"And you, FAILED parents!"

"And we FAILED you. We failed you because we had to hide behind the law and force fed you."

Sammy said, "I can't do all those things even if you make me."

Ah, the turning point.

"No, don't get me wrong. I don't want you to either."

I then told her that I would like to take the tube off her despite lack of progress, or because of it.

It simply had not worked.

I wanted her to take over, do what she needed to do and I would decide in about ten days if I had to extend the Treatment Order.

Forty five minutes. The meeting took forty five minutes as people had to present summaries of different reports, the details of which were irrelevant here.

The battle was over. Sammy looked relaxed. Nobody was fighting her now. She was back in control.

I took her off the Section as she started to put on weight and before long she was discharged.

We forget how easy it is to entrench. To entrench is a sure way to perpetuate a problem.

Chapter 35 Like Father, Like Son

New discoveries in genetics seem to hit the headlines at increasing frequency, and probably the most eye-catching and controversial are those dealing with human behaviour. Thus, there has been popular media interest in reports of genes conferring susceptibility to bad behaviour and to traits such as aggression, intelligence, and neuroticism. The scope for sensationalism and oversimplification is great. As my safeguard to our patients we tend to shy away from any consideration that behaviour could have been so specifically transmitted genetically, especially not in a single generation. The theory of Morphic Resonance has been used to explain the very new ability of butterflies (new in evolutionary terms) to duck under cars.

Gordon

Gordon was one of the first cases about which I had to write a psychiatric report. A copy was sent to the probation officer who took issue with my recommendation. He thought I was too harsh as it was the boy's first offence.

It was an unusual offence. The boy knocked on some neighbour's door and asked if he could use the toilet. It was a quiet neighbourhood and the lady did not think much of it although most boys would probably just do it behind a tree. In fact he was not even that far from home.

He did not go to the toilet but instead looked through her wardrobe and masturbated into her underwear. The police were called and now they wanted a report.

To me, this probably was not the first time. There was some planning and it might be an indication of a deeper disturbance. I thought my recommendations were appropriate.

His probation officer said that he lived with his father who was divorced from his mother. He was a travelling salesman and was away a lot. I did manage to see him before finalising the report. He was not very forthcoming and said that Gordon was just a boy growing up and I should not see too much into it. Later he tried to put pressure on the probation officer to influence me to recommend that Gordon should be let off with a caution instead of being put on probation for two years or so.

I would have taken advice from other professionals but as I was contemplating that, my secretary showed me the local paper.

A man was found guilty of gross indecency. He was caught masturbating in his car by a school gate. In his defence, he pleaded that it was his birthday. He had been divorced from his wife and he felt lonely. However, he had two similar offences to be taken into consideration. The court adjourned for a psychiatric report.

I thought to myself: the case was already pending and yet nobody told me.

"I did not want to influence your decision," said Gordon's probation officer, who happened to be the father's probation officer as well.

I did not change my recommendation. The probation officer changed his job three moths later.

Nigel

Nigel's first appointment was not short of drama.

His father was accompanied by two prison officers, as he was serving time at a local prison for drug offences. He was using crutches but he told me he would tell me why later. The fact that I agreed to see him had already set me up as high as he could put me on his pedestal but not really where I wanted to be, considering that I hardly knew him. Yet here was a man who had done his research. His wife was as nice as any wife of a "criminal" could get, long suffering and accepting, no doubt because of all the luxuries she would never have enjoyed if there had not been the money that came with the territory. She had an accent that is best described as Estuarial and much loved by TV nowadays – I am not talking just about the reality shows as lately it has been creeping into mainstream broadcasting.

Yes, they had moved from Essex and bought a house in Sussex. Then the law caught up with him. I suspect they were greedy, and on the way upset a few people, people with influence. He had three more years to serve. That meant that that he was involved in a fairly massive operation.

He had checked with the locals. "One of our neighbours said I should ask to see you. You helped his son a lot."

Beware of the man that flatters. Yes, I knew who he was referring to.

I asked the Prison escorts to wait outside my consulting room, once I realised that he was not going to do me harm. I was not too concerned about him running away. How far could he go?

Nigel had been branded as naughty. The parents felt that he was simply out of control because father was in prison.

Nigel was foul mouthed and he had many suspensions from school which suited him. Suspension might be a good punishment for the middle-class children, as that might interfere with mum's coffee mornings, charity work or horse riding. It is a godsend for kids like Nigel. "I don't need school; my dad has money," had been his attitude.

If anyone had seen Nigel, they would have known that he was no ordinary difficult bad boy. He was suffering from very severe Tourette's Disorder[115]. He had very severe tics and he twitched his left shoulder blade so much that he looked like the Hunchback of Notre Dame. His swearing was bad but rhythmic too. The more he tried to control his facial tics the more he became self conscious. He then thought he was watched and the expletives came out.

[115] Tourette's Disorder (DSM-IV-TR), Tourette's Disorder may be diagnosed when a person exhibits both multiple motor and one or more vocal tics (although these do not need to be concurrent) over the period of a year, with no more than three consecutive tic-free months.

During the session he tried a few times to cover his mouth. His mother said that sometimes he would stick his fingers down his throat – a fairly common tactic used by a number of Tourettes I have seen. He tried to smile at me all through the session between the twitchings. He had it bad.

I have never worked out why Tourettes swear but good old Gilles de la Tourette[116] belonged to that old school of medical pioneers who were taught to observe and observe without preconceived ideas. Tourette himself unfortunately suffered from Bipolar disorder and died in a psychiatric hospital.

Imagine the relief on Nigel's father's face when told that his son had a "famous name" illness. To him it would be his salvation. He could apply for earlier parole to help look after him. I noticed he had very similar twitches but I did not say much as I felt that there was enough for them to digest in one day.

As they were leaving he told me he was suing the Prison as he sustained a head injury from being beaten up by "person or persons unknown" when first transferred to the present place. One night he was dragged out and beaten unconscious. He had some idea what happened but thought it would be better not to tell me. He thought he might have sustained brain or spinal injury or both. He was

---

[116] Gilles de la Tourette - Georges Albert Édouard Brutus Gilles de la Tourette (October 30, 1857 - May 26, 1904) was a French neurologist who is the eponym of Tourette syndrome, a neurological condition. Tourette studied and lectured in psychotherapy, hysteria and medical and legal ramifications of mesmerism (modern-day hypnosis). Tourette described the symptoms of Tourette syndrome in nine patients in 1884, using the name "maladie des tics". Charcot renamed the syndrome "Gilles de la Tourette's illness" in his honour. In 1893 (or 1896) a former female patient shot Tourette in the head, claiming he had hypnotized her against her will. Both Tourette and many modern hypnologists state that this is impossible. His mentor, Charcot, had recently died, and his young son had also recently died tragically. After these events he began to have mood swings between depression and hypomania, and eventually died in a psychiatric hospital in Lausanne, Switzerland.

320 • The Cockroach Catcher

awaiting an appointment with a neurologist. He had serious weakness in his legs ever since, hence the crutches.

Nigel could not go to regular school at the time – medication could only control some of the symptoms. He was placed at the local special school. His father managed an early parole. It is a sad reflection of our penal system that the authorities will use any excuse not to keep someone behind bars. I was neutral in this and had no interest in whether he was kept in or let out. In any case his son worshipped him as a hero and there was little anyone could do to dampen that feeling. His lawsuit might succeed and there might be a good chance he would get compensation.

Substantial compensation.

Nigel's father saw the neurologist. He in turn referred him to a psychiatrist. He saw the psychiatrist and was diagnosed with – surprise, surprise, Tourette's Disorder. He was to go on the same medication as his son.

That put a hold on his claim for compensation. He reacted badly to the medication, with very serious side effects of tremor and stiffness. He now turned up in a wheel chair to see me. However he was able to get a specially adapted car and a special disability allowance. How fantastic our welfare system was, he remarked to me, although he was still very upset by the beating in prison.

Nigel gave the teachers at special school a good run for their money which to be fair was not that much for what they had to put up with. His twitches had gone down but his hump was still there.

Because of further weakening of Nigel's father's legs, to the extent that he seemed unable to walk, his psychiatrist decided to send him back to the neurologist. This time he did a lumbar puncture.

Multiple Sclerosis.

"Life is unfair," he said to me. "I just hope my son does not catch it from me."

"Life is unfair." I concurred. But I knew he was referring more to his failed compensation claim.

Chapter 36 Entrepreneur

It would not surprise anyone to find that in our work we come across some rather peculiar cases which are indeed stranger than fiction. You often saw the life story of some child unfold in front of you and there appeared little you could do to effect any change in the course it was going to take.

Alan

Alan you could not help but like the first time you met him. He was hardly eleven when he first came to see me. He would not sit still. He explored everything in the room and showed most interest in anything but the material set up for such consultations. He would look outside the window and name all the cars he could see and gave me a good run down on the specification of the different cars. He would particularly like a Mini though. Cooper S to be exact.

"That is my mother's Mini. But it is only an 850".

He wanted to know what car I drove.

He wanted to know if one of the buttons on the phone connected to the police in case some patient attacked me.

- Where is your home?
- How fast do you drive?
- Have you been caught speeding?
- Do you have a wife?
- How many children have you got?

He was controlling the session.

He wanted to be Richard Branson and have lots of money.

These were the wonderful days when ADHD had not really been invented, when Hyperkinetic Disorder was a rarity, to the point that Ritalin at one time was withdrawn from the British market due to lack of demand. Very few of us considered the diagnosis and we struggled on with seeing parents, listening and then seeing them again.

Alan's family moved from South London as part of the "new town" scheme. Inner city problems were to be solved by moving families out to new towns. What nobody realised was that people were the problem, not the buildings. Also without good co-ordination families at loggerheads with each other in the inner city got moved to the same town by different social workers in the same office. Old inner-city ghettos became slightly better looking new town ghettos.

Alan's father I suspect was serving time somewhere but the official story from mother was that he was dead. Mother was hardly twenty six but looked at least ten years older. She had some part-time cleaning job but could not work more or she would lose her Social Security benefits.

Alan was on the verge of being sent away but the housing department came up with the goods in time and Alan was sort of spared. Within a month of moving down here she found out that the boy with whom Alan was in trouble had also moved to the same street.

A street with a beautiful flower name.

Have you noticed how planners give wonderful botanical names to these Council Housing developments? Most people in the know now tend to avoid moving into those streets.

Alan was very close to mother's brother who was a car mechanic and Alan used to spend hours at his garage when he was doing up cars. He was a stabilising influence as he kept telling Alan to stay out of trouble.

He knew that Alan's father had done time as mother confessed once she got to know me. It was some major scam and afterwards he went back to Ireland and never surfaced again. He was thought to have a family over there as well.

Once Alan found that this other boy was at his school he refused to go.

It was a time when there were EWOs (Education Welfare Officers) who would be called in when a child refused to attend school and generally these children would be referred to us. You may ask why they were not referred to an Educational Psychologist.

Well, they had a long waiting list. This was more so since the new Education Act came into force and they had to do these "Statement of Need" which involved a good deal of paper work. For a short while during the transition, Education Department would still honour our recommendations.

Alan's EWO was an ex-policeman who had decided to change his job. He had to deal with these children in his role as a community police officer, but felt very much limited by being a policeman. He had a way of getting the trust of the children and their parents.

He told me that Alan's mother kept a very clean and tidy house. She did indulge in Alan quite a bit and having been hurt by quite a few male friends, was not involved then with any men. She wanted to get Alan sorted out.

Alan said he could not see the point of school. Many successful people as far as he knew did not have much of an education. In an age when there was high publicity for lottery millionaires, entrepreneurs and pop stars, and when stories abounded of people earning lots of money without having to go through higher education, it was difficult to justify schooling to Alan.

As a temporary measure, the EWO organised home tuition for him. This involved a teacher coming to his house for five hours a week.

Five hours a week.

If you think carefully about it, that is probably more than any child in school will ever get from their teacher considering the abandonment of class teaching a long time ago.

Mother saw me regularly about specific ways to handle Alan but regrettably made questionable progress. She persevered and so did I.

Then we managed to get him to a specific tutorial unit that took on his type of school refusers.

I continued to see him and I had regular contact with the lead teacher at the tutorial unit.

He was not moving on from there and I did not see the point of forcing him to school. Our sessions were changed to about once a term.

Then one day the EWO called me and asked if I could see Alan urgently.

Alan came with his mother. He was quite bubbly and very proud, saying he now owned a Mini Cooper.

Not long ago Mum found the car in the back garden. Alan and a friend found it abandoned on the street and pushed it home. It was in quite a bad state and the engine would not start as the carburettors had been taken out, probably by someone else for parts. Alan said that a policeman saw them, checked and agreed that it was abandoned and since they were not driving it there was nothing he could do.

What really upset mother was that one day when she tried to start her car it would not start – nothing happened. She knew it must be Alan. He had transferred mother's carburettor to his car and even managed to start it. Mother had to call his brother from South London to fix things. He towed the car away and said he would let Alan have it when he became old enough.

When Alan reached sixteen he stopped going to the tutorial unit. There is a clause in the Education Act which allows children like Alan to leave education as soon as they reach sixteen. Mother was not too happy with that. I agreed to see mother and Alan every six months or so.

It is amazing that in this modern era parenting seems to be about how to be scared of your children. Modern parents like to think they have to respect their children's privacy.

Once two boys under ten were referred to the clinic. Together they tried to burn down a barn in a local farm. One boy saw me and the other boy's family refused psychiatric involvement for fear of stigmatisation. Father asked me what my views were and I simply said that if he wanted to keep his son, he should never let him out of his sight. His social worker thought I was far too strict and it was morally wrong.

A year later the other boy with others tried to burn down a school. My patient was fishing with his father at the time. The other boys were sent away. My patient's father asked to see me so that he could thank me. His boy was happy being restricted because he was now doing things with father.

Alan pinned up very stern notices outside his door and mother was only allowed to knock on his door if she wanted to speak to him or get him to the phone. Alan had not been in any trouble with the law. One day mother realised that Alan's window had been changed to UPVC. This was done in the time mother was out cleaning. Apparently Alan signed in mother's name for a mortgage to pay for the new window. This was the first story I heard at one of the first appointments after he left school.

Alan now had to clean mother's car to pay off that mortgage and I worked out that at the going rate, it would take him the next ten years to do that.

Parents always thought that the latest episode would be the last. In fact the opposite was true.

The next time I saw him he had set up an office at home and one day mother found thousands of wine bottles delivered and stacked outside his window. He was seen driving the fork lift truck although he had no licence.

He had somehow secured a loan on a credit card and when the bank was challenged by mother they said that if they did not do it, someone else would.

The next thing was more serious. For some reason, Alan was not answering his door and this time mother went in.

Shock! Horror! Admiration!

She did not know what to say. She was aghast.

Alan had cut an opening in the ceiling and set up a spiral staircase to his "new office" up in the loft space. I asked the EWO to go and have a look. He said it was well built and safe. If they reported it to the council mother would have to pay for it to be made good. If not it looked like a good use of the space.

What could I say?

Mother would have to decide on her course of action.

Perhaps she needed to be less open-minded and be more vigilant.

Chapter 37 Good Intentions

It is important for our own sanity to assume that government policies in a democratic country have good intentions.

Following the Kent [117] success in special fostering, many counties pushed fostering as a direct substitute for Children's

---

[117] Special Fostering in Kent – The Kent County Council recognised that children in need of foster care can have many complexities in their lives that need a focused response and developed specialist schemes to match such needs. The main schemes are: Therapeutic Reparenting Programme (This scheme helps young people with emotional problems arising from lack of attention and stimulation in their early years. It provides specialised care for children aged between 4 and 13 who are showing signs of immature psychological development); Treatment Foster Care (Teenagers displaying challenging and anti-social behaviour are offered tailored treatment and support to encourage them to develop useful skills and attitudes); Remand Foster Care (This type of fostering involves providing a supportive environment for young people on remand while awaiting sentencing); Assessment Foster Care (Sometimes foster care needs to be provided for children with very little notice or background information. This scheme involves coordinated and rapid multi-agency assessments of needs so that effective decisions can be made quickly about each child's future care). In addition to the standard fees for the younger and older children age groups, carers are assessed against competencies and paid an enhanced fee dependent on their assessed skill level.

http://www.kent.gov.uk/SocialCare/children/fostering/specialist-schemes.htm

Home. But special fostering still cost money and many foster parents were then "persuaded" to adopt.

In 2000, Tony Blair, British Prime Minister brought in an initiative with rewards for local councils who employed social workers to meet targets for adoption, with the intention to help the older difficult-to-adopt children settle into good families[118].

Jim and Delia

I came across Jim and Delia at the peak of the enforcement of Social Services' policy to receive children into care for the

---

[118] UK targets set to speed adoption – As part of the government's £375m Quality Protects shake-up of services for children in care, the Children's Social Services framework set local authorities clear targets to improve the safety and wellbeing of children in care. The intention is that vulnerable children will spend less time waiting to be adopted under these new targets.

Government figures reveal the number of children being looked after rose to 55,300 - up 4% on 1998 and 11% on 1995. In some 34,100 of these cases - 2,000 more than the previous year, local authorities were forced to go to court to obtain a care order to protect the child. 44% were under 10 years old.
http://news.bbc.co.uk/1/hi/uk_politics/467876.stm

As expected, these targets influenced behaviours, not always in a desirable way, as seen in the following extracts.

Babies 'removed to meet targets' - In an Early Day Motion, with cross-party support from 12 MPs, Lib Dem MP John Hemming, warns of "increasing numbers of babies being taken into care, not for the safety of the infant, but because they are easy to get adopted".
http://news.bbc.co.uk/1/hi/uk_politics/6297573.stm

"Tony Blair set a goal in 2000 for a 50 per cent increase in adoptions, to reduce the time children spent in foster care. In the last round of targets, councils were offered bonuses totalling £36 million for increasing the number and speed of adoptions.

Cash rewards for councils which put up more babies for adoption could be scrapped in a shake-up of government targets.

Campaigners blame the incentives for a sharp rise in adoptions, some of which they claim involve babies taken from their parents for no good reason.

More than 2,000 babies aged under 12 months were taken for adoption last year, almost three times the level of a decade ago."

The rate for older children adoption actually dropped in that period. That was Tony Blair's original intention.

They were good intentions.
http://www.telegraph.co.uk/news/main.jhtml?xml=/news/2007/07/22/nadopt222.xml

shortest possible time and then quickly place them into foster care with a view to adoption.

It is often nerve wracking for secretaries when there is a referral of a consultant's child or children as in this case. Statistics dictate that doctors too may have medical and psychiatric problems and, as parents, problems with their children.

This referral came from another NHS Trust and I did not know the consultant concerned.

We had the tradition of helping the staff of a neighbouring Trust with their psychiatric problems but this was the first time I had been consulted about the children of one of their staff members. It made good sense. The fact remained that there was still a stigma attached to seeking psychiatric help.

The wife came to see me on her own for the initial interview.

The consultant must have been very busy or he might have found it too embarrassing to talk to another colleague about what was still taboo in medicine – psychiatry. Later in the session his wife confirmed the latter, although initially she said he could not get any time off his busy clinics.

Jim and Delia were not their own.

She was quick to point this out to me from the beginning.

Over the years I have observed how many parents were secretly relieved that the problem of their disturbed/maladjusted child could not be blamed on their genes. Could this be why so many big movie stars are adopting children?

Jim and Delia were natural brothers and sisters. Their history could be summed up with one simple phrase: multiple abuses, physical, sexual and emotional. Whatever that has been written about abuse, these children had endured. At the time the family came to see me, they had had the children for nearly a whole year. The consultant just got his appointment and moved south from the north. They planned to adopt these two as they did not have children of their own.

The reason for seeing me was to seek my advice on whether they should proceed with adoption.

They had been under great pressure from their social workers up north. She found it difficult as she found Jim extremely hard work. Initially Jim and Delia were extremely compliant children, so good that they wondered what the warnings given by their friends and their social workers were about.

The children were in poor heath, emaciated and frightened. These foster parents nursed them back to health. They could not have been in better hands. The couple's medical credentials put them in an advantageous position. They had tried for a long time to adopt "white" children but all they had been offered were "coloured" children or "imports".

There was every reason they would want to adopt.

For a start Jim was particularly intelligent and had been soaking up everything he could glean in and out of school. The abuses he suffered did not seem to have dented him in any way.

Delia on the other hand was not half as bright as Jim but she was very pretty like her natural mother.

Jim's father was a professor at the university. Jim's mother dropped out of university and later met Delia's father, who was a construction worker. He used to get drunk on Fridays and beat up her and the children and she left him.

She then met a much older man who turned out to be a paedophile but his activities were not discovered until nearly a year later and it turned out that he had a previous conviction. He simply changed his name and managed to avoid detection.

Mother had since drifted in and out of mental hospitals with numerous attempts of overdoses and wrist-cutting.

Some are of the view that abuse does damage to intelligence. If it was so we did not see it with Jim. Research was said to back this up. Well I can only think that this research was dubious or they had dubious motives. There are researchers who like to believe that intelligence is not innate and every now and then research papers pop up to "prove" the case.

But there was a dark side to Jim. He tried to poison Delia at least on three occasions and on the last one with garden pesticide that luckily did not cause much damage because of the tell-tale foul taste. Jim each time denied point blank. But there could not have been anyone else except the parents. Delia, despite what happened to her, loved her brother to bits and idolised him.

Delia on the other hand did not show any obvious signs of disturbance. Foster mother had been warned to watch out for promiscuity and so on and so forth but none was forthcoming.

This I have found again and again in child psychiatric practice. I can only say that it probably boils down to individual resilience. It is a good illustration of how differently two children could react under virtually similar conditions.

There was little doubt that Delia was vulnerable as she adored her half brother despite what he tried to do.

Now foster mother was very torn. Should they only adopt the girl thus separating the two siblings, or half siblings, or should she not adopt at all, as after several meetings with me, she was feeling less inclined to adopt the boy.

The crunch finally came when on a week-end walk the boy somehow managed to pick up a fairly large piece of stone and threw it at Delia's head without any provocation. Delia sustained a cut and required some stitching but no major injury to the brain.

The foster parents' minds were made up: they would like to negotiate to adopt the girl only or not at all.

Shortly after, I received a phone call from the social worker more or less telling me off for not helping them place such "difficult to place" children. No way would they entertain separating the two of them but they doubted if they could place them as similar things had happened at the previous foster home.

Now they told me.

Jeff's son

I always have a great admiration for people who are prepared to offer not just help but a home to children with the most horrendous early life experience. Even recently Social Services were advertising for families to foster drug abusers.[119]

"We are looking for people who are resilient, have good support networks and able to deal with young people with very challenging behaviour.

---

[119] Advertisement by Lincolnshire Social Services for carers to look after young drug users

http://news.bbc.co.uk/2/hi/uk_news/england/2821365.stm

The placements will be for a maximum of 13 weeks.

The programme is a partnership between Lincolnshire County Council and the Lincolnshire Drug Action Team.

The organisers want foster carers who are based at home and have spare bedrooms and no children under 16 of their own at home.

Carers would be paid an allowance for their work."

Some years ago a good friend of mine left her husband and came to live in England. Her husband Jeff was a successful attorney in U.S., earning a very good living. I knew their children from when they were born. The oldest boy decided to stay with mum and go to school in England. When he was in the last two years of secondary school, mother took in and fostered a girl about the same age as the boy. This girl had been badly abused sexually and physically from a young age and later went into drugs. Mother took pity on her and took her in. Unfortunately the boy fell in love with her. Before long he gave up his medical studies as the university was too far away from home and he could not face not seeing her. Soon she became pregnant and he married her. He found a job with a local vet, although his father continued to support him. But the marriage did not last long, and he and his mother ended up looking after the child. The divorce was a highly acrimonious one with the result that the little boy was not allowed to leave the country, which meant that he could no longer be taken to visit his grandfather in U.S. The boy's mother then disappeared and did not see the boy for over five years. The court order could not be changed because she could not be traced. It was unclear if she was even alive.

I became involved when they moved to within my area.

It was such a waste – a highly capable and intelligent boy who could have become a brilliant doctor was struggling to make ends meet. He tried to make a go of running a garage with the help of his father but was not happy to be under father's control. His son had severe epilepsy and it was never clear if it was the result of mother's drug use or physical shaking.

It took quite some doing to get the injunction lifted and the full divorce finalised. Substantial financial settlement obviously worked. The cost of grandmother's philanthropy was immeasurable.

On the morning of July 1, 2005, an adoptive mother grabbed her adopted child around the neck, shook her and then dropped her to the floor, where she kicked her repeatedly before dragging her up to her room, punching her as they went. The adoptive mother is now serving a 19-year sentence for second-degree murder in a maximum-security prison[120].

---

[120] Newsweek: When Adoption Goes Wrong. Pat Wingert. Dec.,17 2007.

Chapter 38 Adoption

In the Spring of 1975, I started my Senior Registrar placement at a child psychiatric department.

The department, located in the South of England, consisted of three discrete inpatient units and one outpatient unit. There were two lady consultants and the "Chief". The "Chief" was an Austrian émigré, six foot six and a very formidable figure that most people were scared of. He was a highly intelligent man with a French wife and two highly intelligent children. Fortunately we hit it off from the very start.

He fed you cases. Just as you thought you had some breathing space more would come. That he fed you interesting ones was a sure sign he approved of what you had been doing. One day I was late after some family session. It must have been around seven or seven thirty. There he was in the secretaries' office. A few filing drawers were open.

The "Chief" was looking through our files.

Then I knew and I have learned since that that is what "Chiefs" do.

One of the first cases he gave me was Sabrina. Sabrina he had to give to someone he could trust. Sabrina was one of his favourite patients.

Sabrina was my first professional encounter of the adoption problem.

Years ago when I was lodging with a family in my fourth year at medical school the landlady had a cousin who desperately wanted a baby.

She bought one. One that had not yet been born.

She pretended she was pregnant first so that none of her relatives knew. It was possible to use a private midwife in those days so registering the baby was not difficult.

I was totally shocked at the time but said nothing. It was not my business. She never planned to tell the child and thank goodness, DNA tests were not around.

As far as I know, the boy grew up to be a very nice young man without all the hang-ups and attachment problems we now see with a high proportion of adopted children.

She did what she thought was right. Telling your adopted child that he or she is not yours is the worst thunderbolt and if done at the wrong age probably causes more damage than the adoption itself. But who would believe me?

Sabrina was a very troubled girl who tried to set fire to her parents' bedroom at the age of seven, followed by more extreme acts against her parents. Her crashing of the family car one night when both parents were asleep led to her admission to our inpatient unit. By then she was nearly fourteen and in those days one would not be criminally responsible until fourteen and that could mean Borstal, but girls were generally treated more leniently. Borstal for girls was rare and tough and one tried to hold off such a placement.

Sabrina was bright and pretty and she knew it. One day one of the male staff got into trouble for sitting outside in the garden with her for the whole night talking to her.

She had charisma and everybody liked her. It was a puzzle to me in those days as to why she was so disturbed and I suppose I still do not understand it today despite all the things that have been written, mostly to do with the phenomenon of Reactive Attachment (I prefer reactive detachment but so be it) but with not much insight otherwise.

She was adopted at six months. Her adoptive parents were around forty by then and were quite wealthy so she was sent to private schools all her life. As was the practice, she was told at the first opportunity meaning as soon as she could understand. I find that concept difficult as children do not understand much about the biological significance of copulation and fertilisation and would find the difference between natural and adoptive baffling.

She did well at school. The fire was more or less seen as an accident by her social worker and parents but then she became more and more difficult. When she was in junior school she would go up to another set of parents at parents' evening and she would ask:

"Are you my parents?"

"No."

"Can you be my parents?"

The adoptive parents struggled on but when she eventually crashed one of the family cars they had to get her admitted.

The "Chief" had a special view about adoption. He was against it. He would ask some question like "how do you like so and so's work?" and then he would go on to slaughter every bit that was in his article or book.

It was the first time I learnt that you did not need to go with "accepted" views, and yet he would be so oblique in the way he presented it that very few could "read" him.

I could and I was grateful.

He was the first to criticise questionnaire psychiatry and psychology. His main complaint was "valency", a term I had not heard used since chemistry days. It seems simple enough that the answer to each question cannot carry the same weighting.

It made important sense. Yet questionnaires became the be all and end all of most of psychiatry.

One day, "Chief" asked if I had a minute. I always had a minute for "Chief", I thought.

I had never seen "Chief" looking so glum.

"Sabrina was killed. She drove the school's Range Rover and crashed it some hundred miles away from school. She and a school friend were both killed."

Oh. No.

"You know, her real father was a perpetual car thief and was in jail when she was born. Her real mother had four children and she was persuaded by her social worker to have Sabrina adopted. What a tragedy!"

"Could we have done anything different?"

"Perhaps she should never have been told that she was adopted. You know many adoptive parents are secretly thankful that their *bad* child has nothing genetic to do with them. I am sure adoptive mother will say, like father, like daughter."

I dared not tell "Chief" about my knowledge of one Chinese adoptive mother. It really was a far cry from what was "correct" but twenty five years on I began to have my doubts.

Chapter 39 Three Different Mothers

It is an undeniable fact that we saw mothers more often than fathers at our clinic. The practical fact is that in many families it is the fathers who work and mothers who deal with everyday matters.

Fathers did try and attended the initial appointments but with more and more marriage break-ups, many mothers became single parents, outnumbering single fathers by a factor in excess of 20 to 1, at least of those that were referred to the clinic.

About half way through my 25-year career as a consultant child psychiatrist, referrals of broken homes and in particular single parents outnumbered those of intact families. It may be surprising for me to say that those from intact families were in general more disturbed and might indeed be suffering from a more serious mental illness. In the absence of any external causes for a child's psychiatric problems, it was probably genetics at play.

Still, marriage break-up represents a single most significant risk factor in terms of the mental health of the growing child. Often it is the dynamics in the new family structure that cause stress which in turn lead to disturbed behaviour. It is the lack of outlets for the stresses these mothers suffer that perpetuates the problems in such new family settings.

In time, I realised that I had a collection of mothers who never missed a single appointment. It gradually became clear that my role was less of a psychiatrist but more of a surrogate grandfather, father, husband or uncle. There were a few couples who stayed with me a long time too.

This fact suddenly dawned on me in a very strange situation. I was attending a good friend's son's Bar Mitzvah[121]. It was a great honour as a Chinese to be invited to such an occasion. In the course of the day's event, I talked to some of the relatives. One uncle who was obviously a successful merchant was very interested in my work. He told me that he did have some trouble with his eldest son but he never needed to use a child psychiatrist like myself. He just took him to the Rabbi.

I was therefore father confessional and rabbi and medicine man and whatever else they have in other societies with a culture that has not been fractured by modernisation.

Do not get me wrong, as I have no real complaints about such work. Over time one gets to understand psychodynamics

---

[121] Bar Mitzvah - A Jewish boy becomes a bar mitzvah automatically upon turning 13 years old. No ceremony is needed but it has become customary to mark the occasion.

more than from the usual two or three appointments most clinics offer.

Mothers with boys have a serious problem of identification. There is no running away from the basic facts of genetics. When the boys look like their fathers, there is a big problem as it creates a huge conflict. How are you going to love a son who is by the day looking more and more like the man you once loved and now hate? The child picks up the vibes and before you know he is behaving exactly like the now much hated father.

The worst part of it is that you cannot admit this to anyone.

This is where I came in. Interpretation in psychotherapy is often about the therapist articulating the unspeakable.

Daughters somehow fare better from my own observation despite the fact that they have a tendency to look like their fathers. Mothers somehow can find comfort in their daughters especially if they manage to be a victim like they have been.

Solidarity of the sexes.

I was also lucky enough to be working in an era when the actual practice of medicine was left to the clinicians. There was minimal state interference in the guise of targets and standards and guidelines. Patients got a better service in those days. Why else did they keep turning up?

And turn up they did. There were a number of mothers who never seemed to go away. One couple with an adopted son was among my first patients when I started as a consultant, and they continued seeing me all through my consultant career.

Three particular mothers can be conveniently grouped together. They were different in their own right and yet they had some tenuous link that makes it easier for me to describe them together.

They all had a single child and all were single parents. Two of them had boys and one had a girl.

These mothers had little trust in men and it took them a while to trust me. Until the trust was developed they would not talk about their past. There was also a sense of betrayal. Victims feel that they have betrayed their own kind and blame no one except themselves for what has happened in their lives.

It is often very tricky to work with them because they notice every little reaction and response from you, especially indirect ones. They are forever looking out for hints of criticism from you – an assumption that all men criticise. In psychotherapy terms it is euphemistically termed "transference" and "counter-transference" (interpreted simply, the patient's feeling towards you and your feeling towards the patient). The wise ones among us would try to make full use of it instead of dreading it.

The other side of the coin is that once they decided that you were not like other men they knew, they became attached to you. It then became a struggle to discharge them.

Daryl

There was not much that was the matter with Daryl. That was the impression I had when I first met him. He was a healthy looking boy, charming and very courteous.

Mother thought he was deceitful and dishonest. He lied a lot and she could never get any truthful answer from him.

It was a shock to me as I thought I was normally quite a good judge of character. In our work we had to rely heavily on parent's report. There was no reliable psychological test for these things. Whether a child improved or not was also dependent on parent's report. It took me a while to realise that it did not matter all that much as it was more the parent's perception we had to work on. It needed not have too much of a bearing on reality. It was only when we admitted a child that we could observe and assess for ourselves. Often we saw a totally different child to what was described to us.

Daryl's father though was an expert in finding out about other people's deceptions. He was a Private Eye and a very good one. So good that he even appeared on television. His main work had been to track down and photograph unfaithful husbands for divorce proceedings. Mother used to work for him and that was how they met. They used to have a comfortable home.

The great Private Eye turned out to have been a master in deception himself. He kept another wife and two sons in another part of the country. His fame through the television programme brought the whole thing to a head. I shall not divulge the details here but suffice to say Daryl's mother found out.

"I thought bigamy was a thing of the past," she told me.

So did I. Many men have mistresses but would not go as far as polygamy. In our work we met strange cases.

When mum was ready to tell me more of what happened, the whole thing made sense to me.

She inherited some money when her single aunt died and with that money she bought the family home after she got married to

Daryl's father. Although nearly all the money was from her, she had the house in joint names.

She was in love.

Her mother did advise against having the house in joint names, but she said it would otherwise upset him. He agreed to pay for legal fees and other fees related to the purchase. They had a nice home in a sought after London suburb where he had his office.

His work would take him all over the country and sometimes Europe and he was spending more and more time away from home. Mother would be lucky to see him for more than a weekend in a month.

But it never clicked until suddenly one day bailiffs turned up.

He had re-mortgaged the house and had not re-paid a single penny in months.

He then promptly disappeared.

He had managed to get another woman to go to the bank to sign the necessary documents, pretending that she was his wife. Mother managed to find out more from another Private Eye who was disgusted with what her husband did. He was married before with two teenage children. He never really divorced his first wife and in all his so-called trips he was more or less with his other wife. It was rumoured that he was now somewhere outside British jurisdiction.

Mother had to move back in with her mother who was widowed and obviously she had to eat humble pie and put up with many "I told you so"s. She had to survive on benefits and her mother's charity and was still in the process of getting a judgment on the bank.

Daryl reminded her so much of her husband even when in fact he had not done much to deserve it. She was eventually able to work through that; but up to my retirement she had not tried to find another man and she failed in her attempt to get anything out of the bank.

Sara

Sara was luckier. Her mother identified with her so had never hated her. She too was healthy looking, charming and very courteous. To her advantage she looked like her mother.

Sara's mother was always well turned out when she came to see me. It was rather unusual at our clinic for mothers to turn up well groomed and well dressed.

This was the NHS after all.

Her hair would be nicely coloured and done up. She would put nice scent on and would come in a very smart outfit. She looked like she was going on a date.

Everybody else in the clinic thought so except me. As she had just returned from Australia, I thought that was just normal. You want to impress your doctor, was my impression.

Yet the more I knew about her the more I appreciated the effort she made to come to the clinic.

Since coming back from Australia, she had been more or less house-bound except for the attendance at the clinic. Everything else was done by her own mother, Sara's grandmother.

She had lived in Australia for nearly ten years. Sara was by then nearly seven. They used to live in a rather grand house on the beach. During the last six months before moving back to England they had been moving from one refuge to another. That her husband only served three months of a three year sentence for abusing his own daughter meant that she felt totally unsafe as soon as he was released. On top of that her belief in herself was totally destroyed or at least her belief in her own ability to judge character. He started stalking her and despite an injunction she did not feel safe and in desperation went to a refuge. Eventually she was advised to return to England. She was lucky her mother lived here. This way she was able to get some sleep and hopefully get her life back together.

It was her wisest move as Sara really blossomed. She was five when the abuse started and she had serious perineal injuries. It was at a time where Sex Abuse was not a highly talked about subject. Talk show hosts and celebrities had not yet come out with their own experiences and juries often faced cases with their own prejudices and bewilderment, leading to inappropriate judgments and sentences. Victims were often abused a second time.

Without help, self blame continues. Many find it difficult to return to normal life. Sara's mother had totally abandoned the idea of doing the daily chores outside of the house. Her only time out of the house was to see me at the clinic. I was her only route to re-establish her faith.

Her faith in herself and in others, especially in men.

Others at the clinic were often puzzled why I was seeing her. She looked so well.

Well, looks could be deceptive.

Chris

That Chris' mother should have been the patient was obvious from the first time I met her. She indeed saw a psychiatrist before moving from Dorset. She had been hospitalised for Anorexia Nervosa.

She was cured. She got married. Then she had Chris.

If she did not tell me, I never would have guessed she had Anorexia Nervosa.

At first I did not even know how I knew.

"She was a very good looking woman," my secretary told me one day, "she hasn't got a bad figure either."

Doctors are not supposed to notice these things and if they do they have to keep it to themselves.

That was the discordance. She had a good figure. Many recovered anorectics cannot maintain a nice balanced figure and I am quite sure it is to do with the various hormonal upsets from the extreme dieting, a sort of gonadotrophin stimulating hormone problem.

She did have fertility treatment in order to have Chris. She would feed me with information now and again. Perhaps that had something to do with it.

Chris was difficult, but no more than the average single parent child. His father had long since disappeared.

Was Chris' behaviour one of the reasons she consulted me?

She was one of those mothers with lots of questions, and I am one of those psychiatrists who wanted parents to find their own answers.

In psychiatry knowing the answer is no guarantee to a cure. In fact it is the same in many branches of medicine as we still have so many incurable diseases. Parents do want to have the answer and of course in the commercial world there are now doctors that cater for that desire. A nice label, be it ADHD, ME, Autism or Asperger. As long as there is a technical sounding name people are happy. If you can have a specific drug, so much the better. If not you may get special education, benefits or both.

As long as it has nothing to do with "upbringing".

But upbringing could be trans-generational. What happens to one generation can have an impact on the next generation.

Many parents want to look at the here and now and a quick fix answer.

One day mother told me, "I am bulimic!"

Then she took out some capsules and said that she could not have those as she could not have an orgasm. She had been seeing an adult psychiatrist but came to me for the problems she found too embarrassing to discuss with her own psychiatrist.

She had a new boy friend who was much older than she was and he was a pilot.

She wanted me to see him to explain about the side effect of her medication.

"I am taking 60 mg." she told me.

I did wonder, as the 20 mg dosage might have been less problematic.

I declined the request and she was rather disappointed. She accepted my reasoning – I did not initiate the treatment.

Three weeks later she told me she broke up with him.

Then she told me she normally could not have an orgasm unless she imagined she was having sex with an older man. She then thought it might work with having an older boyfriend.

As I listened mother decided to tell me more.

She had been abused by her father from about the age of twelve and the awful thing for her was that she actually enjoyed the sexual side of things. It was an abuse she found hard to come to terms with. She could not hate her father because when she came out of hospital after her Anorexia, she had no breasts to speak of. Her father paid for implants, twice.

When Chris's father left he bought a house for them.

He paid for her private treatment for Bulimia.

Worst of all, she had to imagine her father whenever she made love to have any chance of an orgasm.

No. She had never told anyone else before.

Three different mothers, three different kinds of abuse.

Chapter 40 It May Not Be All In The Mind

I have often wondered if it would be such a disservice to mankind if doctors were not so understanding of the psychological side of things.

The possibility of a serious illness being missed is of course a major concern when a patient seeks help for one reason or another.[122] To put psychological conditions at the top of the list of possible diagnosis is dangerous. Given the concern over cost in most health care systems, the need to restrict the use of expensive investigation is understandable. However, with clinical reliance on sophisticated investigations especially in modern medical training,

---

[122] Example of missed diagnosis: BBC news on 30th December 2007. Stroke victim 'was misdiagnosed as mad' – When Steve Hall had a stroke four years ago he lost the ability to speak - but that was just the start of his troubles. Doctors feared he was suffering mental health problems and he was placed in a secure unit, where his stroke went undetected. Steve, whose symptoms were later recognised as aphasia (speech loss following stroke), was terrified. He did not understand what was happening and felt abandoned by the health professionals who could have helped him.

the art of physical examination is perhaps lost to this generation of newly qualified doctors. Moreover, the reliance on the internet for information removes the need to make use of the still most powerful computer of them all – the brain. No more effort is made to attempt to download the information into our brain for future parallel processing. As a result, vital and glaring clues are often missed and, worse, dismissed because of over-saturation of information.

The idea that modern medical training requires some time spent in far-flung places where even the stethoscope is a luxury item is a neat attempt to remind future doctors of the importance of clinical judgement based on physical examination. Unfortunately feedback from medical students that I had the good fortune to teach only confirmed my worst fears. Such attachments are more a chance for them to visit exotic places in the midst of a busy course than to hone the skills of medicine on which their seniors were brought up.

It was an eye opener for me to witness in 1971 a case presentation at Queen Square where a "blind" case was presented to the Professor. I believe it was the tradition then for one of the senior lecturers to present a difficult case that would have been totally unknown to the Professor. A bit like wine tasting. The Professor had no recourse to sophisticated investigations that were widely available today – no MRI and PET scan (PET was at least three years away and MRI, first called NMR, was even later). It was an important lesson for us on clinical skills. The jealous ones had of course dubbed Neurology as 99% diagnosis and 1% cure. Evolutionists proclaim that it is encoded in our genes to self-destruct in cases of nervous system damage. Neurologists are faced with this scenario day in and day out. No wonder some of them get a bit strange. The odd Stephen Hawking[123] does not compensate for the thousands that perish from Motor Neurone Disease everywhere in the world.

The lecture hall was packed with many visiting clinicians from other countries. I was sitting between an American and an Australian.

The "blind" case was a woman with pain in the toe as the presenting symptom. Nowadays she would most likely be given a psychiatric diagnosis and might even be started on Olanzapine or Prozac or both. However, at the end of the session she was given a diagnosis of a lesion in the Thalamus area. It was later confirmed – I knew because I was working there at the time. Whether the lesion was treatable or not was not really the point and it certainly was not the point of Neurology. At least she was spared of the side effects of some of the psychiatric drugs.

The advent of PCT (Primary Care Trust) is so divisive for the National Health Service in U.K. Referrals to specialists are now vetted by a group of doctors. I doubt if a patient with pain in the toe will ever be referred. To us specialists, there is a need to limit prescription of specialist medication such as those in psychiatry to

---

[123] Stephen Hawking - Author: A Brief History of Time, first published in 1988. As soon as he arrived at Cambridge, he started developing symptoms of Motor Neurone Disease (known in the US as Lou Gehrig's disease), a type of motor neuron disease which would cost him the loss of almost all neuromuscular control. Motor Neurone Disease is typically fatal within 2-5 years. Around 50% die within 14 months of diagnosis. The remaining 50% will not necessarily die within the next 14 months as the distribution is significantly skewed. As a rough estimate, 1 in 5 patients survive for 5 years, and 1 in 10 patients survive 10 years. Stephen Hawking is a well-known example of a person with MND, and has lived for more than 40 years with the disease.

the specialists themselves. There have been some restrictions but often not for clinical reasons. Such measure will be more beneficial to patients than the proposed validation by the General Medical Council.

In a recently published book, the author described how she 'was dismissed as an alcoholic when her symptoms were blatantly that of multiple sclerosis.' [124]

Too often, instead of keeping an open mind, one finds it too easy and necessary to try and fit things into one's narrow way of thinking. That could become dangerous when it is the doctor who is doing it.

When I first started in psychiatry in Hong Kong, I was fortunate enough to work with a consultant who had a very firm grounding in General Medicine. A case I shall never forget was a thirty-five year old man presenting with very sudden phobic symptoms. At the time we had just opened in Kowloon our new District General Hospital Acute Psychiatric Unit with thirty acute beds, shared equally between Males and Female admissions. This allowed for some acute screening before the long trek to the only mental hospital in the colony, which was twenty two miles away in the New Territories. To many visiting relatives, twenty two miles is a long way, especially in the seventies. As we were all part of one

---

[124] The Guardian, Monday December 18 2006 - ...She suggested I was an alcoholic on the back of one or two business lunches a week and as many nights out. I gave her medical expertise 30 seconds' serious thought before leaving the surgery deflated and without so much as a prescription for how to deal with sanctimonious doctors. Two weeks later, and nearly £1,500 poorer, I was staring at my MRI scan while a private neurologist told me I had multiple sclerosis. I knew it wasn't the drinking - so somebody pour me a glass. Michelle Mullen
http://www.guardian.co.uk/society/2006/dec/18/health.medicineandhealth)

big organisation, it was not really a problem to have screening and then transfer only if it became necessary.

It was important to carry out a thorough physical examination on all patients including a thorough neurological test. This particular patient checked out normal on most things except for a positive Babinski (a reflex that can identify disease of the spinal cord and brain)[125]. I was totally baffled but instead of dismissing it I asked my consultant to have a look on the morning round. He carried out a full Neurological.

"Yes, positive Babinski."

Now how on earth can positive Babinski be related to phobic symptoms?

"We shall need an X-ray urgently, but whatever it is it is not psychiatric", he declared.

The patient was found to have a special type of very aggressive lung cancer, with extensive metastasis.

He died within six weeks despite some very aggressive treatment at the time.

The sad thing about the case was that being right may not in the end change the outcome. It bore witness to how little we do know and how little we can do even when we do identify the problem.

---

[125] Babinski - Babinski's reflex occurs when the great toe flexes toward the top of the foot and the other toes fan out after the sole of the foot has been firmly stroked. This is normal in younger children, but abnormal after the age of 2. In medicine (neurology), the Babinski reflex or Babinski sign is a reflex that can identify disease of the spinal cord and brain. It is more properly called the plantar reflex, as Babinski's sign in reality only refers to the pathological form.

This case definitely established a principle for my clinical practice. Psychological diagnosis need not be the first diagnosis. Rule out organics first.

Modern medical schools on the other hand pride themselves in concentrating on the role of psychology in bodily dysfunction. It is arguably true that most family doctors do not get to see all the obscure cases we spent so much time studying as a medical student. Yet in time these cases do get to the hospital to be seen by the specialists. Where indeed do they come from? Are they not referred by the family doctors, or are they simply missed and then picked up by the specialists?

Do we as psychiatrists think that it is such a brilliant idea to think "psychology" all the time? Do we really think that people want to see their doctor even when there is fundamentally nothing wrong with them? Is there a grave danger in that assumption?

Health planners seem to assume that most who turn up at Family Surgeries have nothing seriously wrong, and similarly those who turn up at A & E. The latter group are just there because they could not be bothered to see their Family Doctors earlier.

Do we need to apply the money test? Charge a small fee for every consultation for any new condition to exclude malingerers, a sort of "deductible", in insurance terminology?

Would it not be safer for all concerned that we should remember: "*It may not be all in the mind!*"

Rachel

Rachel could not get to school. She was having such bad back pain. Her family doctor wrote an urgent referral. As she would not see the psychologist at school, school was considering taking mother to court.

There was a change in managing school refusal. Education Authorities suddenly turned trigger happy and all over the country parents were taken to court. I did wonder if this was due to a shortage of Educational Psychologists who were now too busy dealing with Formal Assessments as a result of the new Education Act, or whether it was due to years of public criticism of the inadequacy of the softly softly approach to the problem. There is some truth that there is a hard core of children whom no teacher really wants to see at school and the authorities are quite happy they are absent. These are children who are entitled to free meals and the hidden saving of them not attending school adds up to a pretty substantial sum. To assess them would take up precious Psychologist time and also may generate expenses in terms of ferrying these children by taxi to special tutorial units or schools.

But Rachel came from a professional family. Mother was a lawyer and father an insurance executive commuting to London. Yes, Rachel had some problems a year earlier because of her height. She did stop attending school for a while, claiming she had pain in her back. She was way over the 98th percentile for height. Some strong pain killer prescribed by her doctor seemed to have done the trick and she had not been absent until the present attack of pain.

Clinical judgment is indeed a kind of "profiling". We judge our patients from a variety of information and we "profile" them. It may not be correct but we do.

I had my suspicion that the Educational Psychologist never got to see her record to realise that she was not really the type anyone should ever dream of prosecuting.

The family doctor thought that I should be given a shot before anyone should have a go. Mother was told in no uncertain term that she needed to get Rachel to see me.

"But she was in such pain!" mother said. She did protest but in the end succumbed. With the help of a neighbour, they managed to get her to the clinic and she was lying down in our waiting area.

I had one look at Rachel, perhaps 6 ft tall, lying flat in the waiting area and asked my secretary to call an ambulance whilst I talked to the Radiology Consultant. An X-ray examination was ordered and if necessary an MRI scan.

How could I come to such a decision without even spending half a minute with mother or the patient? Was I being over dramatic? Or was it what we have been trained for? Was it why psychiatrists are trained as doctors first?

I could of course have been entirely wrong and the girl might really have been school phobic. Would I have subjected her to an unnecessary X-ray examination? Would my reputation suffer as a result?

The ambulance came. The paramedics were excellent. They treated it as potential spinal injury and transported her that way. I accompanied her onto the ambulance. You had to see her face to know you were right. She was grateful someone believed her. For me it was worth all the drama. My only wish was we were not too late that she might not be able to walk.

Mother too shook my hand as the ambulance got ready to go. I always told my juniors. "Trust them, most of the time."

I left a message for the radiologist to call me.

The call came back from the radiologist. She had two collapsed vertebrae, a common condition among very tall children who have just had a growth spurt. The Orthopaedic Surgeon was preparing for an emergency operation.

"Good work." The radiologist said.

I knew. He meant: "Good work for a psychiatrist, and a child psychiatrist at that."

Some time later mother arranged to see me to tell me in detail what was done.

"She wants to thank you for believing her."

I was just doing my job.

Chapter 41 Elective Mute

I have never really come to terms with Elective Mutes or, if preferred, Selective Mutes.

Where do they really fit in the schema of various diagnostic categories, or more precisely, in what way can we understand them? In terms of Freudian, Jungian or Kleinian theories, or Erikson's or Mahler's more child friendly models, or modern neuro-transmitter bio-physiology?

Yet we have all seen them in our career as psychiatrists. Because we are essentially rendered ineffectual in our therapeutic approach, they are often treated as a novelty and one's hope is that either the family come to terms with what might best be described as a quirk of nature, for which little can be done, or the patient grows older and never really commits anything that requires hospitalisation.

I can also see how in time, guideline controlled health practice will allow little room for anyone practising child psychiatry to be spending any time at all with these cases.

We do not get to see them that often and I can remember three cases in my three decades of work with children, or at least, three that stuck in my mind.

To put it simply, Elective Mutes (a term I prefer as it gives a hint of election by the patient) are not true mutes as they speak at home, often to only one person such as the mother, but not to anyone else, especially at school. At some point in the history of child psychiatry someone changed the diagnosis to Selective Mute and so it was included here in case anyone thought I was talking about a non-existent condition.

A Chinese Patient

An exceptional consultation was requested by a psychiatrist friend of mine in a nearby town. He had a patient, a Chinese mother who spoke little English and she was very concerned about her son. Exceptional consultations are allowed within the NHS when the need arises to call on the expertise of another consultant not working for the authority, for a specified fee. In this case the expertise was not clinical but language; although by asking a child psychiatrist instead of just an interpreter he was killing two birds with one stone.

The family ran a Chinese Fish and Chips shop and lived in the flat above the shop in the older part of the town. There was an

older daughter and a young baby. The referred patient had turned
five and just started school. Five is generally the age when these
patients get referred. I was offered a seat by a small table in a
corner near the rear window of the flat. Some steps led from the
shop to this sitting area at the back of the flat. Whiffs of frying oil
crept through the tightly shut windows. On the wall was the
traditional Buddhist shrine with remnants of the previous day's
incense sticks. I was not entirely sure if I preferred the smell of
incense stick or frying oil. On the bench across from me, the older
girl was diligently doing her home work. My patient was playing
with his new looking power ranger, possibly a bribe so that he
would stay and see the doctor. The baby was in mother's arms
sound asleep. She apologised that her husband was busy getting
ready for the shop to open in about an hour's time.

This was fairly typical of Chinese families in similar take away
businesses. They probably made a reasonable living but some of the
money might have to be sent to their folks back in their home
village. Décor at home would be basic although most would have
the latest model of television set and video recorder.

Mother was relieved that I could speak fluent Cantonese, but
her daughter would barge in now and again in perfect English
about her brother.

The boy conversed at home with both parents and sister,
although I could sense that with his sister's talkativeness he would
hardly stand a chance.

Both my patient and his sister spoke fluent Cantonese with
the parents and mother did not notice anything unusual about the
boy until the school complained.

To prove that he could really speak, mother said that they had a video recording made during the last Chinese New Year when they took the family to Hong Kong. He was even speaking to other relatives in Hong Kong. Dutifully the daughter put the tape into the video machine and played the video. There were also bits of English spoken between him and his sister.

What worried mother was that after father received the complaint letter from school, he stood the boy in front of him with a cane and said that he would cane him if he did not talk to his teacher the next day. The boy did not wait and put out his hands.

His father did not hit him. He only wanted to threaten him.

A week went by and another letter came. The boy was again summoned before father. His sister urged him in English not to be afraid of his teachers and to speak in school or he would be punished. This time father held a clever and threatened to chop his hands off if he were to receive another letter from school.

The boy put out his hands again.

Suddenly I was extremely worried for the parents. The town they lived in was hot on Child Abuse at the time. Although I had no fear at all that these parents would chop their son's hands off, some over vigilant social workers might take it upon themselves to act. I took it upon myself to advise the parents that any such threat might bring the wrath of Social Service upon them.

Chinese families and perhaps oriental ones in general want little to do with authorities. The parents had in fact resisted the involvement of Educational Psychologists and I was only let in because I was Chinese. Now I understand why it was an adult psychiatrist who consulted me. He was more a regular customer than mother's psychiatrist.

Now, mother was worried.

"Would they take him away?"

She asked if they should send him to a private school or do something else. They just did not want to lose him. She assured me that her husband loved him as he was his first son but he just did not want to upset school in any way.

I suggested that it was probably too early to act, as the boy might soon decide to speak. It would be important to check if he was making any progress, but on the video recording, he was reading with his sister. If it became necessary for them to see a Psychologist I would help to facilitate. I suggested that three months might be a good time for me to see him again.

Two month later, I received a call from my psychiatrist friend. No follow up appointment would be necessary.

"Did the boy speak?"

I was anxious to know.

"No, they sent him back to Hong Kong to live with the grandparents. They said he was doing well at school there."

How stupid of me! I should have guessed from the tape and from what I know of the Eastern way: avoid authorities more than you need to avoid tigers.

And who is to say that the boy would have done better if he had continued here.

Who knows?

Norman

Paper darts or planes were one of my favourite pastimes as a child and from a plain piece of paper I am able to build one that will be able to do nice aerobatics in a small room by minute tweaking of the under-wing rudder. Now and again with the appropriate child I might resort to building one to start a therapeutic relationship and most times it worked like a treat.

So it was after weeks of struggling with an elective mute that I decided to try my luck.

Little Norman was a handsome looking boy of six and never spoke to anyone outside of the house. He would speak to his parents indoors but not out. Of all other relatives he would only speak to his maternal grandparents who lived nearby but only in his own home, never theirs.

He had made reasonable progress at school as mother was an infant teacher before she had him and regularly checked his progress.

He just would not speak to anyone else.

He looked like an autistic child and certainly had the tendency to avoid eye contacts. However he acquired his language at the usual times and mother had a normal uneventful birth. Father was an accountant working in London, of the quiet type as mother put it. I only met him once on their first appointment.

Norman was their pride and joy, being the first grand child on both sides of the family. The paternal grandparents lived in the West Country and did not see Norman too often.

So, there we were, one of my first mutes since I became a consultant. Despite all recorded difficulties with Elective Mutes, I decided to try my luck with some therapy sessions.

The boy got quite used to me after a while. He would draw, write and often look at all the story books I had around. He would play with Lego, assemble and dissemble the train set but he just would not speak.

I was young then and had the mistaken belief that getting him to speak with me would be counted as some sort of cure. This has not been written up anywhere and we had little knowledge of the long term outcome of these cases.

I was determined, determined to get him to speak, at least with me.

Paper plane.

I hit on the idea of my faithful friend.

I built one, then two. He had one and I had the other. They flew, made beautiful loops, did aerobatics and he was thoroughly enjoying it.

I sensed that he wanted to take them home to show his dad.

"You will have to ask me for them."

How nasty could I be?

He turned solemn, then pale, then red.

I was beginning to hate myself. How could I? He was my little friend. We could have gone on for months playing.

"Please may I have the planes?"

I was shocked, so was mum when she heard what happened. I was not pleased with myself. I had tricked the little boy to give up his principles, whatever they were.

Mum on the other hand thought I was brilliant.

Simone

Little Simone, aged five, had a beautiful crop of blonde hair with the cute little face and blue eyes to go with it. I was wondering if it was a genetic thing. Good looks and mutism. She had a brother four years older. He was smart, too smart sometimes as he always seemed to know what she wanted and would speak up for her.

Simone did not even talk to her father or brother. Only to her mother and only when no one else was around.

Her brother was doing extremely well at school and they were thinking of sending him to a private school.

Father was a pilot and was hardly home which might explain in part why Simone did not speak to him. At least that was how mother tried to help me understand. Also, her brother might be too old for her, especially as he had his own friends and she was a girl. "Boys of that age don't talk to girls" was the other lesson I received.

I hardly needed to do any talking from the first time I met mother as she would ask the questions and answer them. Most were sensible answers and I was sure many child psychiatrists would not have such a deep understanding of children.

No, mother was not worried, as she could check on Simone's progress.

At the time, we had just moved to our new clinic and we had a video link and recording facility in our playroom.

What an opportunity to test out our equipment.

So we had Simone set in a routine of spending some time first with mother and then one of my female junior doctors would join us in the second half of the session to talk to mother.

At first Simone would stay quiet throughout.

After about three months, the breakthrough came. Simone started talking to mother when she was alone playing with her. When the door handle turned, she switched off. This continued for some sessions. Simone by now would be reading story books with mother and she was an avid and good reader for her age.

One day, watching the proceedings, I hit on an idea, a very naughty idea.

What if my junior doctor played back the video recording to her? It might disclose the secret. We knew she could speak.

As if by magic, it worked. The rest you might have guessed.

Was it the right thing to do? Did making an elective mute speak represent a cure? I do not know.

On one cold April morning in 2007 in Virginia a former mute went on a shooting rampage and many innocent lives were lost.

Chapter 42 What If …

I am sure we all have been asked the great "what if….." question.
I was fortunate enough in my practice to have had some "lucky"
breaks.

Given my interest in the very young, now and again we had
some strange cases that tested our ingenuity to the limit. No
amount of SSRI (Selective serotonin reuptake inhibitors) would be
able to help. Often it was a clear battle of wills, a battle between
the consultant and someone barely one sixth his age.

That this particular child had already beaten two adults with a
combined age well over ten times hers should have been a clear
warning to me on what I was to take on.

The contestant was a little girl nearing five years of age who
had developed an addiction to Huggies. Yes, Huggies.

It could well be the success of advertising or it could be the future of the human race, I joked to the nursing staff as the desperate parents agreed that the girl should be admitted to the children's ward for "nappy withdrawal".

The problem was simply this. She needed to put on a disposable nappy in order to pass urine, or do No. 1, as she put it. At her age, she required the biggest size available. The cost had been piling up. As it seemed so trivial, the parents never sought help until now when school days were imminent. It would not be possible to contemplate her going to school with nappies.

With our enlightened staff, admission to the paediatric ward was no longer the traumatic experience it used to be. This little girl soon settled in and was promoted to be the No. 1 helper around the ward.

However, whenever she needed to, she helped herself to a nappy, and after performing, took it off and put it in the appropriate bin. She worked that one out in no time at all.

One nil.

I needed to come up with a battle plan quickly. The ward was fast running out of the giant nappies and I had no intention to make a special requisition.

"That is it. I HAVE AN IDEA."

I found a large clean plastic bag and put all the nappies in it. There were three. I gave it to my opponent and said, "These are the last three and, when you have finished, there will be no more.

Unperturbed she snatched the bag from me as if to say, "Not a problem, doc."

I went on with the rest of the morning round and went to the clinic.

After the day's main clinics, I decided to have a peep.

"She used two of the nappies and is now down to the last. She carries it around with her. It is becoming quite a sight." Sister told me.

Everybody knew I was not going to win this one, but were prepared to see it to the end.

By now she was quite urgent and you could see she was struggling a bit. Her last performance was over three hours ago.

She looked at her nappy, thought about it, and then something curious happened.

She went to her favourite nurse and took her by the hand, "Will you take me?"

She sat on the toilet and passed urine, still holding on to the nappy. There was a sudden cheer from all the mothers. My head was visibly doubling in size.

"Well done!"

 Shortly after, Sister took me to the side and asked, "What if she did use the last nappy? What would you have done?"

"Sometimes there just is no *what if*. You have to do certain thing as if it were the only way."

Her family went on their planned camping holiday in the South of France and from there they sent a post card.

"Yes! It is still working. We have truly cracked it or you have. Thanks a million. We are all having a lovely time."

In early 2007, a female astronaut wore a nappy in order to drive non stop to threaten another woman, a rival in love.

No, she was not my patient.

Chapter 43 A New Era

I was early as usual, because of the number of acute admissions we had had recently. As I turned right into this leafy country lane with a few nice big houses along the way, I knew I was no more than five minutes from the inpatient unit.

That was when I spotted somebody who looked like Craig. He was in a yellow Jersey trying to climb up a trellis into someone's garden. Then he disappeared. Of course it was him. How could I not recognize him especially after he sprayed my car with another boy's shaving foam in big letters – DOC? I was never quite sure if he meant to spray DOG, but I was inclined to think it was not vandalism but part of his acute breakdown.

I thought the nurses were supposed to have him under observation. That was what they wanted to do, but I had no doubt in my mind about the diagnosis.

After parking some distance away from the hospital at the Post Graduate Centre, which was totally out of view from the street, I rushed into the unit's dining room where some of the children were still having their breakfast.

Breakfast was an interesting sight. The six anorectics were at one table playing the staring game. They were the group that had achieved some independence for breakfast. Those who achieved certain weight gain could take an extra ten minutes. They all stared at their cereals and toasts as if delaying the eating was going to be of some help. Or was it a matter of not swallowing the EVIL that was food?

The two anorectics who had not achieved that status had to sit with the Anorexia Nurse. They were being timed and they had to finish within a set time. If they missed the second hand by even a second, they would have to have an extra helping. They too played the game and tried to leave it till the last second. Sometimes they would have an audience urging them on but not that day.

The rationale of this regime I never managed to grasp, but it was, as the nurses put it, a NURSING THING and if it was not important I would stick to the DOCTOR thing.

The biggest girl was asking for her third helping. She could not help it. It was the Olanzapine she was on. Now she looked nothing like the slim girl she once was, having put on as much as her original body weight.

But her symptoms had disappeared.

She needed three helpings of cereals and six slices of toast complete with thick layers of jam and butter – butter that was from the EEC and only for hospital use by patients, all part of the huge mountain[126] that even the might of the Vatican could not consume.

The rest seemed to have finished. The boys normally took less than five minutes to "do" breakfast and made use of the rest of the time for their Game Boys. The few girls that finished just gossiped about Spice Girls and whatever was the latest.

But no Craig!

"Where is Craig?" I asked, knowing exactly where he was.
"He pee'ed into his breakfast again and we sent him to his room to think about it."

His nurse sensed that something was terribly wrong, rushed to his room and came back within seconds.

"He's gone."

Craig was a very clever boy. He had managed to undo the security lock in his bedroom window and climbed out. The windows were all of Perspex and unbreakable.

Only two weeks earlier a young adult psychotic managed to scale a modern supposedly un-scaleable twenty foot soft fence from the Acute Observation Ward and committed suicide by jumping onto the Rail track. He was very strong and by some very fast

---

[126] Butter mountain – Under the Common Agricultural Policy of the European Economic Community, farmers in Germany, UK, Holland and other countries were encouraged to produce subsidised products in quantities that ended up dwarfing demand, and enormous dairy subsidies had made milk and butter lucrative on paper but impossible to actually sell once produced. At the rate going from the early 1970s until the mid-1980s, EEC was running out of storage space before running out of butter. In 1975, there were about half a million tons of unwanted butter waiting to be sold off for next to nothing.

In January 1971 EEC statisticians noticed that butter exports to the Vatican had hit 160 tons a year—suspiciously high for a place with a population of only 700.

moves was able to overcome the fence. As Medical Director, I had to be informed. In the old days, before the days of CEOs, Managers and Directors, it would have been the Medical Superintendent. These modern fences looked less oppressive than the old style walls.

I told them I thought I saw him climbing up someone's trellis trying to get into their back garden.

At that point we saw that a police car had arrived.

Phew. He was safe.

Some lady reported that she found this boy in her garden asking her for food as the hospital would not let him eat.

"The boy is having his first major psychotic breakdown and we are still trying the behavioural approach?"

No. I did not say that aloud.

Many years ago when I started psychiatry, I started at the deep end. It was an eye-opening experience for a newly qualified doctor. The Psychiatric Hospital catered for the very ill. The patients were so different that it was not at all difficult for us to tell between the psychotic and the non-psychotics. Treatment options were very few and because of side effects it was not difficult to spot the ones who were on medication.

We were now in the late 1990s, having just woken up from the mistakes of the 70s – the mistakes of over-medication, institutionalization, and problems with ignoring rehabilitation. Whether the activities of the anti-psychiatry movement [127] had

---

[127] Anti psychiatry movement - R. D. Laing with a number of popular books was the most influential. Their views could be summed up as follows:
  • Psychiatric categories are labels for unacceptable forms of behaviour.

anything to do with the eventual demise of mental institutions or not, I am not entirely sure. I suspect that money eventually played a greater role.

Until the arrival of the newer antipsychotics, we had to struggle with the effect of the older type of medications.

By then we had moved into the new era. The Australians led the way with aggressive treatment of First Episode Psychosis, which is necessary if we are to stand a better chance of preventing relapses, reducing morbidity, preserving social skills and hopefully maintaining family support that is so essential since we want to be rid of the asylums. This trend had just begun to spread to Europe, notably the Scandinavian Countries and Germany and lately U.K.

The few of us who made the effort to attend International Conferences were made aware of these new practices and could keep a step ahead. It became then a matter of selling the newer and more aggressive treatment approach to the rest of the team who were used to the older ways and did not know anything better.

To convince them, I called a meeting of the most senior medical and nursing staff at the unit, turned on my laptop and gave a PowerPoint presentation that I prepared for the juniors on the

---

- 'Psychopathology' can be seen as intelligible human reactions to situations.
- To learn about people we should use hermeneutic methods – listening, trying to understand the sense of behaviour from the point of view of the agents themselves. It may seem hard to believe, but this was a fairly revolutionary proposal in British psychiatry at the time.
- The struggle against classical psychiatry was part of wider struggle against authoritarian, oppressive forms of power, which rested on unquestioned assumptions. These assumptions were enshrined in 'common sense', so that those who had 'lost touch with reality' had perhaps only come to their senses.

http://www.laingsociety.org/biograph.htm
http://www.rcpsych.ac.uk/Docs/Bulletin%20Winter%202005.doc.

new approach in the management of First Episode Psychosis. We agreed that there was some urgency in initiating treatment. Close supervision had proved to be an ineffective observational and diagnostic tool, although until the effect of treatment kicked in, anything less could be dangerous.

Living with hallucinations is a traumatizing experience, and acting on them even more so. Normal behaviour approach is often perceived as further persecution by the psychotic. Accidents could happen and life could be in danger. We already lost a young adult not too long ago.

The parents were informed of the incident and they were on their way to the unit. I gave them my professional view and outlined the treatment plan. They listened and were receptive.

Mother said to me afterwards, "I knew he was not naughty. I kept telling the school."

He did well on a mood stabilizer and one of the newer anti-psychotics. One of my juniors who had good training in family therapy was excellent in psycho-education and was able to help the parents through a very trying time. Their hands needed holding through the difficult time until the mood stabilizers took effect.

There were still a few stubborn ones amongst the staff who felt that given time, they could have "cured" the boy without medication.

I knew it was not true and I knew we had to move on.

But I did not want to make a song and dance of it. It was not a game. It was about patients – the safety of patients.

A new era had arrived.

Chapter 44 Madness and Ethnicity

The idea that all men are created equal is a very attractive one. It is also politically correct and it pleases every modern open-minded person.

When I at last visited the great nation of South Africa, I realised how real the concept of a superior race was in our own time and in our own generation. The one thing Apartheid (supposedly good neighbourliness) did for the black people was to unite them, most of them anyway, in South Africa. One only has to look at the neighbouring countries to realise how indirectly Apartheid strengthened the resolve of the South African people.

It is a generally held view that world wide the rate of schizophrenia stays the same regardless. However, according to some reports, in England the ETHNIC population has twice as high a rate for developing psychosis than white Caucasians[128]. Why should that be?

Could it be that doctors and especially psychiatrists in England are reluctant to diagnose the most serious of mental illness in the white population, but not so for the ethnic groups? Could it be that ethnic people by virtue of their migratorial history inadvertently put their descendants at risk[129]? Could the rate of drug abuse be a contributory factor?

---

[128] Detention figures in England & Wales – Using datasets for the purpose of examining detentions under Part II of the Mental Health Act 1983 in England, a study reported that Black people were over *six times* more likely to be detained than White people. In the cases of Black men this rose to an *eight-fold* increase, while Asian people were 65% more frequently detained under Part II (Audini and Lelliott 2002). This study analysed 31,702 incidences of Part II detention over the period 1988-99 from areas with a combined population of 9.2 million.

Previous studies have placed the figure for detentions for Black people at closer to *three times* more likely than for White people although one article that reported this statistic included Asian in its definition of Black (Keating et al 2003).

An update on current literature relating to Chinese mental health reported returns to the Mental Health Act Commission detentions for Chinese as 0.3% for the period from 1996-98 (Cowan 2001). This percentage detained is exactly the same as the proportion of Chinese people in the England & Wales national population with 40% residing in Greater London.

A study which conducted a retrospective case note analysis on hospital records and clinical notes of restricted hospital order patients conditionally discharged from a large medium secure unit in England between 1987-2000, compared data on those of Black African-Caribbean race and origin with all other ethnic categories (Riordan et al 2004). Most of the subjects in both groups had a diagnosis of schizophrenia and there was an *over-representation* of Black people (36%) as compared to the general population.

http://www.scotland.gov.uk/Publications/2005/07/1595204/52295

[129] Migration and schizophrenia, a paper published in Social Psychiatry and Psychiatric Epidemiology - The last decade of the twentieth century has seen an unprecedented increase in the number of reports in the psychiatric literature documenting increased rates of psychotic illness among migrants in a range of European countries. In countries where high rates of immigration have been long-standing such as Britain and the Netherlands, these increased rates have also been seen in the second generation of migrants. This has impacted on psychiatry significantly with regard to the aetiology, diagnosis, and treatment of schizophrenia.

http://www.ingentaconnect.com/content/klu/127/2004/00000039/00000005/art00002?crawler=true

Although puzzling, it cannot be denied that at any one time half of our psychotic patients were Ethnic, and all of our eating disorders were white.

Thomas

Thomas was a white boy with loving and doting parents. He was the only child. His mother must have been a ballerina at some point in her life as the house was adorned with black and white ballet photos. His father worked hard as one of these young store managers for a big national supermarket.

Thomas had a good pocket money allowance. He had all the latest gadgets a boy could want.   PS2[130] was his latest Christmas present. He used to have wall posters of Ferraris and Porsches as he could not quite decide on which one he liked better. No pop stars, no girl posters, no, that was not Thomas. Mother did let on later her worries that he might be gay.

Then during the summer school break, he suddenly tore off all his posters, stopped playing with his PS2, as mother could no longer hear the racing car noise, and started writing copious amounts. He used to get food for himself as both parents had a busy social life and he was sixteen and liked to get his own food. Mother noticed that he went through the ice creams, Mars bars and biscuits but not much else. He was often up till the small hours, writing. He did not sleep much and when the family finally saw him he looked dreadful.

---

[130] PS2: Play Station 2. A Computer based game console made by Sony.

One day mother decided to go into his room to check. That was when she found all the posters torn off.

His bed was unmade and his dirty clothing and sweet wrappers and paper were all over the place. She thought the room had a funny smell too. Not the usual boy smell.

She looked at the pages and pages of his writings. It was the Bible, the Bible according to Thomas! Her son had turned into the new Saviour and was writing a new version of the Bible.

She looked under his bed. No, no Playboy or Penthouse or worse. No such luck. Instead she found three strange glass structures.

It is simply astonishing how little parents know of the youth culture of today. Perhaps I should modify this and say white middle class youth culture.

Thomas had been taking marijuana for some time and just had his first psychotic episode. He had been having MUNCHIES[131] and those strange glass structures were BONGS[132]

Drug and sex education should be for parents not the children, I have always maintained, but nobody would listen to me. U.K. has now the worst teenage pregnancy problem in Europe despite its vigorous Sex Education program and not far behind in teenage drug problem.

---

[131] Munchies - Smoking cannabis often triggers an urge to eat - what smokers sometimes refer to as "the munchies".

[132] Bong - A bong, also known as a water pipe, is a smoking device, generally used to smoke marijuana.

Father in his neat modern management way wanted to know how it happened, what Thomas should take and how long it would be before he could recover, what his chances of relapse were and what he should do to prevent future relapses. Mother just cried, listened and cried.

"My nice boy uses drugs and is now psychotic and the two are probably related! What have I done wrong?" wailed mother.

There really was no family history I could find. Even in my cautious way I had to concede that this white Caucasian teenager had drug induced psychosis but the prognosis might not be as bad as the parents feared. Only time would tell.

Sohan

I cannot forget Sohan. I should not have asked what his name meant in Punjab when he was brought to see me by his mother and grandmother. I was told Sohan meant "beautiful".

Sohan came to see me because he was afraid. He was afraid he was turning into a woman. He was polite and rational and told me that he had this dream that he was turning into a woman. He was about to finish school and would be going to India for a holiday with his grandmother. After the holiday he would start work with one of the airport caterers which already employed both his parents.

I was not able to work out what his fears were but said I would be happy to talk to him again when he returned from his vacation. As he would be working shifts it would not be such a problem.

He never did keep his appointment but I was called to the hospital by my adult psychiatrist colleagues as Sohan was admitted to the acute psychiatric ward. He had swallowed a large number of coins but as they were being excreted no operation would be necessary. He wanted to see me because he said I would understand.

I went up to see him the same day they called. He was quite pleased to see me. The next thing that happened he pulled up his top. He had a big one-sided breast.

"You see, Doctor, that was what I told you."

My colleague came round at the time.

"Sorry, old chap. Forgot to tell you. We put him on the usual[133] but in four days he came up with that. We have asked a surgeon to look at it and he reckoned a mastectomy would be required. We have now switched him to one of these new drugs. But no question, he is schizophrenic."

How sad. Did he predict the future or did doctors re-create his future?

Masud

That Masud was having his Manic episode was not in dispute. He was missing from home and then the police called the parents who both worked at the airport. He tried to board a plane with his father's passport and a first class ticket to Karachi. The passport had a different forename and a keen eyed staff at check-in spotted

---

[133] At that time Adult Psychiatrists were not allowed to use the newer antipsychotics except as a second line. Largactil was the "usual" first line drug and in young people can lead to quite dramatic breast enlargement

the anomaly. He looked much too young anyhow, but he was well dressed in a brand new Armani outfit and Gucci shoes carrying a new Apple. He looked like a young executive. He became rather abusive saying he was a CEO of a big company and he was going to sue.

In less than 24 hours he managed to spend more than six thousand pounds that he had saved and by the time he reached us he could hardly tell the time of the day or his mother's name.

By then, no one in the unit had any problem with the diagnosis of bipolar disorder, current episode manic.

He was indeed quite confused when we got him but it probably was more due to the lack of sleep for some days than anything else we could think of. To be on the safe side an MRI was done and it did not reveal any space-occupying lesion.

He was put on Lithium and made an uneventful recovery. As it was a first class ticket unused we managed to get his refund. His parents were happy to have him back and they put money into his account to compensate for what he wasted. At any rate a nice outfit and a nice computer could not be such a waste.

He was back to his job at the airport and luckily his boss was one of father's relations.

The family saw to it that he took his medication religiously and he stayed well for over nine months.

One day father called the unit to say that Masud was confused and speaking gibberish and they thought he might be having a relapse. They got hold of me and the story of confusion at his first episode crossed my mind but I asked the parents to check his temperature. 40 degrees C.

"Get him to the hospital. Whatever it is he is not ours, not this time. But wait. Has he overdosed on the Lithium?"

"No. my wife is very careful and she puts it out every morning, and the rest is in her bag."

Phew, at least I warned them of the danger. It gave me perpetual nightmare to put so many of my Bipolars on Lithium but from my experience it was otherwise the best.

"Get him admitted and I shall talk to the doctor there."

He was in fact delirious by the time they got him into hospital and he was admitted to the local Neurological hospital. He was unconscious for at least ten days but no, his lithium level was within therapeutic range.

He had one of the worst encephalitis they had seen in recent times and they were surprised he survived.

Then I asked the Neurologist who was new, as my good friend had retired by then, if the lithium had in fact protected him. He said he was glad I asked as he was just reading some article on the neuroprotectiveness of lithium[134].

Well, you never know. One does get lucky sometimes. What lithium might do to Masud in the years to come would be another matter.

I found that people from the Indian subcontinent were very loyal once they realised they had a good doctor – loyalty taking the

---

[134] Neuroprotectiveness of Lithium - Lithium has emerged as a neuroprotective agent efficacious in preventing apoptosis-dependent cellular death. Lithium neuroprotection is provided through multiple, intersecting mechanisms, although how lithium interacts with these mechanisms is still under investigation.

http://journals.cambridge.org/action/displayAbstract;jsessionid=6523D307A035A220FBB10393053B7CF1.tomcat1?fromPage=online&aid=252359

form of doing exactly what you told them, like keeping medicine safe; and also insisting that they saw only you, not one of your juniors even if they were from their own country. It must have been hard when I retired.

Yosef

Yosef's family was from Morocco, but he was born and brought up in England. He had been acting strange for some time and the last straw came when his mother tried to stop him going to this "no good" place in the East End of London. He went most Fridays, not returning until late Saturday afternoon. His mother had no idea where he slept on those Friday nights and decided one day to stop him. He attacked her and the two older sisters called the police. At the time father was in Morocco seeing to some family matter.

There was no question he was having a psychotic breakdown. The family was not very forthcoming with any family history but said they wanted to wait for father to return from Morocco. They seemed to be afraid to say much, which I later worked out to be very much a cultural thing. Women cooked and did the chores and the rest was left to the men. They could not even tell me what the family business was.

Yosef managed to run away from our unit the following Friday and was brought back in the early hours of Saturday by the London police, who had a call from the club. He was too wild for the club to handle. When he started arguing with the bouncers, they called the police. He still had the hospital band on his wrist and that was why the Police brought him back.

Now, I really cannot tell you the exact club as they would be very upset. But some of our nursing staff did know of people who went there. It was a very trendy place and it was very much public knowledge that people did drugs there and they did it in a big way. Not just Ecstasy, but all things imaginable. This was despite the fact that they searched people before they were allowed in. I had absolutely no idea where the drugs came from and the official line was that they did not tolerate drugs.

Out of interest and for his sake we ran a drug screen on him, quite an exhaustive one as I felt it was important to know if he was suffering from drug induced psychosis. The screen came back all negative. There was no alcohol either.

Perhaps some of them do not need drugs, just the wrong genes.

So he was too weird for the club to handle. That must be a first.

He had refused medication since admission which meant his psychosis was not going to disappear overnight. Luckily we had an arrangement with the adult secure ward and they would take over any young psychotic patient who needed to be detained under the Mental Health Act. Our ward was very much an open ward and the perimeters were impossible to secure.

We did not have any rights to restrain him. If he decided to leave he could as he had his rights, and he reminded the staff of this in his most psychotic phase.

So we were basically babysitting him until a bed could be found in the adult secure ward. He walked out twice but became cold and hungry and came back. Thank goodness for British weather.

It also made me wonder about human rights – for some patients their rights were also their handicap. We certainly could not secretly dope him by putting tasteless antipsychotic in his food or drink.

It is a good rule and protects people against bad doctors and perhaps dictatorial tyrants, but the latter would probably just change the law.

In the mean time our teenage psychotic would have to go over to a Secure Acute Adult Mental Heath Ward after sedation.

The Nurse sent by the adult secure ward for him was like an animal tamer, a version of horse whisperer for humans. The necessary papers were signed, and the injection was ready. They now had the power of reasonable restraint and as they pulled his trousers down for his injection he cried out like a baby,

"Doctor, Doctor, save me!"

I just did.

He did not give them any trouble at all.

He was put on depot[135] medication as he could not be trusted to take any other.

Horses for courses or was it the other way round?

Over the years I have not really shifted from the view that sometimes the old fashioned secured ward is good. The idea of an

---

[135] Depot medication - A depot antipsychotic is essentially an injectable antipsychotic medication that is released into the body slowly over an extended period of time.

open place for Yosef would horrify me. What if something happened to him when he ran away?

Father came back from Morocco. He was not too surprised. His own uncle had been in a mental hospital in Morocco for years and he had just gone to Morocco to sign the papers for his younger brother's admission to the same hospital as his uncle's. Schizophrenia.

Martina

Martina was already at the adolescent inpatient unit when I arrived. She was supposed to be schizophrenic. The family were refugees from Sudan. They were a small Sect of Catholics that were said to be persecuted.

Martina was not very communicative but her records and observations by her outpatient psychiatrist indicated that the diagnosis was robust enough. However, after over a year in hospital she was not improving and we had tried the newer antipsychotic without making much headway.

There was one thing left to do – to put her on Clozapine[136].

I was once at one of these big drug firm meetings when all the big boys on the newer antipsychotics were there.

Having filled my plate from the delicious buffet, I sat next to two nicely clad representatives.

---

[136] Clozapine – Clozapine was the first of the atypical antipsychotics to be developed. It is used principally in treating treatment-resistant schizophrenia, a term generally used for the failure of symptoms to respond satisfactorily to at least two different antipsychotics. Safe use of clozapine requires weekly blood monitoring for around five months followed by four weekly testing thereafter. Echocardiograms are recommended every 6 months to exclude cardiac damage. It is often hailed as one of three major medical breakthroughs of the last thirty years. (The other two are Helicobacter discovery and Stent cardiac treatment.)

"So you ladies are from Novartis?" I did my usual stunt.

"How did you work that one out?"

"Well, you two have the best designer outfits and I guessed you must be from the makers of Clozapine."

They were there to see what the opposition might come up with but as far as I was concerned no other pharmaceutical would touch them for decades.

When they have a drug that works so well, even research is sometimes redundant. The U.S. was very slow in approving the drug even when the rest of Europe has been using it. At an APA conference I once sat next to a doctor of Chinese ethnic origin. He was employed in the U.S. to carry out the first research into Clozapine.

The blood problem could have been a disaster. (A small percentage of patients will develop leucopaenia, a lowering of white cells, and die if unchecked. Stopping the medication as soon as possible will reverse the process – hence the regular blood test.) But for a drug so definitely superior Novartis have managed to turn the potential disaster into a perpetual gold mine. The need for regular blood test and a national registry for the supply depending on the result of the blood test mean that Novartis will have the monopoly for a long, long time to come. I heard stories of the drug being smuggled into the U.S. before it was approved by the FDA. How could it have been done?

With Clozapine, the change in Martina was almost miraculous. At least, the family thought so. We were able to get her into one of these special shelter places run by Catholic nuns. Her

negativity literally disappeared and my junior continued to give me glowing reports on her.

At the time of the lunch meeting, Martina was already at the special shelter. I asked the reps what the youngest age on Clozapine was and learned that at that time in England there were two eleven year olds on Clozapine. Black ethnic groups are often prescribed a higher dose and very often with another antipsychotic. Asians have a slightly higher incidence of blood problem.

You learn something new every day and it started me thinking about another aspect of psychosis, drug use and ethnicity.

It has been a concern of mine that we have been told that globally the rate for schizophrenia has been stable. Recent concerns over cannabis and psychosis highlight certain anomalies.

If Cannabis is "causing" psychosis, and the overall rate for psychosis is stable, then some part of the population must be spared of the psychosis to balance out. Some consider this to be a good enough reason not to do much about the increased use of cannabis.

By the same token, if ethnic minorities are experiencing a higher rate of psychosis, then the local non ethnic group must have a correspondingly lower rate to balance out the figures.

The answer came in a thorough research in Australia[137]:

---

[137] Australian research on Schizophrenia – findings are from a Queensland Centre for Mental Health Research (QCMHR) report, published in the American-based journal Public Library of Science Medicine

http://www.medicalnewstoday.com/articles/25389.php

"The University of Queensland's Professor John McGrath, who led the research team, said the 21-page-report was the biggest and most comprehensive survey of schizophrenia rates around the globe.

His team collected 188 schizophrenia studies dating from 1965 to 2002 from 46 countries.

The report debunks a popular textbook definition that schizophrenia will affect 10 in every 1000 people no matter where patients live.

It says this rate is too high and more likely, between seven and eight in 1000 people, although this varied from region to region

Our data shows that the incidence and prevalence of schizophrenia varies much more around the world than previously acknowledged."

Chapter 45 Born Good?

After many years of dealing with disturbed people, it would be insincere of me to say that I would be prepared to give a straight answer to the most fundamental question of them all:

Do I believe that men are born good?[138]

The animal kingdom has ways that may at times seem extremely brutal. The first observations of how the newborn cuckoo commits genocide of the first order were met with great

---

[138] Are men born good or bad?

Mencius (Chinese, c.371-c.289 B.C), Chinese philosopher and sage, developed his entire philosophy from two basic propositions: the first, that Man's original nature is good; and the second, that Man's original nature becomes evil when his wishes are not fulfilled.

Hsun Tzu (300–230 BC), Chinese philosopher, a sceptical rationalist. He argued that human nature is essentially evil and needs to be constrained into moral behaviour by laws and punishments.

disbelief when Jenner first published his findings.[139] In Africa when a male lion comes into a new family where there are cubs from another male, he will proceed to kill all these cubs.

I learned my lesson soon after becoming a consultant.

Nathan

Within weeks of starting my position as a consultant, I was asked to see a family very urgently on a domiciliary visit. Their teenage boy was sent down from a very expensive private school. He was not present when I called but both parents were.

It was quite an eye-opener to call on such a grand house in the middle of the Sussex country side. There was a black Bentley in the front porch. Entering the house was like entering a classic BBC film set of a period drama. Hunting trophies gave an impression that this was old money indeed.

Nathan was their only child. He was adopted and placed with them before he was six months old. They had no end of trouble with him and in the end sent him away to a private school. Mother had spent periods at a private psychiatric hospital for her agoraphobia (abnormal and persistent fear of public areas or open spaces) and was still on medication. She was the one who inherited the money and the house from her parents, who made their money in Rhodesia. Father was in the wine business and dealt mainly in

---

[139] Jenner's observations of cuckoos' unusual behaviour of laying their eggs in the nests of hedge sparrows with the subsequent ejection of host sparrows' eggs by the young cuckoos on hatching were most accurate.
http://www.jcu.edu.au/jrtph/vol/v02saunders.pdf

German wines. During the week he stayed in London, but he travelled down especially for my visit.

It was in many ways an eye-opening as well as an intimidating visit. I was often offered tea or coffee on my visits but as a rule I had a way of not really drinking it. This time I was offered a glass of wine. German wines are not my favourites and yet I must admit that I have not tasted a better Spätlese since.

Back to the more serious subject of their adopted son, it was clear that he had already been in trouble a number of times, including leaving some obscene graffiti on the school front door just the night before speech day. The latest was extremely serious as he had defaced the portrait of the current head, on one of a series of expensive oil paintings commissioned for every head.

It did not look likely that they would have him back for the Sixth Forms, father pronounced.

I did not think so either, but as father was an alumnus and had donated much over the years, he might be able to pull some strings. He had of course offered to get his restorer to restore the painting.

Their question was whether he should just be sent to the local Sixth Form College. They needed to know as they were due to fly out to South Africa to visit mother's family the following day. As a punishment, Nathan was not allowed to go with them and instead he would stay with one of his friends.

It was not unusual with these cases that the decision had already been made and it was a simple matter for me to work out what they would like to hear and concur with their wishes.

Even though Nathan was adopted he was still very much seen as an heir and the talk of sending him to a State school was more a threat to bring him in line. Could he really survive the State system after years of private schooling?

I did not think so. Not if he spoke like they did.

No further visit was planned. They would call me after their trip to let me know of their decision.

Some weeks later I had a call from mother. They had just returned from South Africa.

They had been burgled, by their own son.

When they were away, neighbours saw removal trucks and did not think much of it. Some of their favourite paintings and hunting trophies had vanished and they could not locate their son. Her husband was livid and was determined that he would disown him.

Perhaps they were lucky. News broke of a couple in Southern England killed by their adopted son in his plot to get his inheritance early.

Lions may not be so foolish.

Damien

Damien too was adopted but not into a rich family like Nathan. I only met him once and he was brought to me by his probation officer.

I have often marvelled at how unfailingly understanding probation officers are. They could always see and understand the reason for a child to commit an offence. It was their background. It was their upbringing. Poor things.

My rather unsympathetic report did not go down well with this probation officer at all.

What else did she expect me to do? This was Damien's eighteenth T & D, taking and driving without permission.

Without permission! He was not even old enough to have a licence. The English language is such a gem.

I have never understood how a well-educated girl wants to be dealing with offenders but this one was tough. She would not let me include details of his previous offences in my report.

But that was past history and my Psychiatric Report would not be complete without past history.

But she was right. Of course I knew that. I was not going to change my recommendation though. He had to be sent away.

"But he had a very abusive adoptive father."

"Still, it was no excuse to steal a car and crash it."

"In fact, I cannot see how stealing a car is a psychiatrist's concern."

"Crime is crime, and it has to be dealt with."

She was not pleased.

"I thought psychiatrists are supposed to be understanding."

She was not going to include my report.

As the report was paid for by Public Funds, a copy would always be sent to the Clerk of Court.

She was livid.

It would not be a surprise to you that I was not called to the hearing.

I was sitting at my clinic making use of the bonus free time to sort out some paper work when I heard a knock on the door.

It was the probation officer. She was in tears.

"What happened? Did they send him away?"

"I wish. He ran away from the court and took my car. The police are now after him."

"And after all you did for him!"

"Yes, after all I did for him!"

Chapter 46 Yellow Card

Communication is everything, nowhere more so than in child psychiatry. Yet most failings in families are to do with communication.

Autistics, Aspergers and of course Psychotic patients have fundamental difficulties with what most of us find straightforward. Sanity, some would argue, is the ability to hold and perhaps live with opposing ideas in one's head without distress or disturbance.

I have described in another chapter how one autistic child made good use of modern-day gadgets to communicate and manage what might have been distressing.

In an adolescent unit there are certain rules, but these rules are regularly broken. The extent of tolerance is in part dependant on the degree of annoyance such rule-breaking causes.

With regard to dangerous acts, the rules are applied without ambiguity and these rules tend not to be broken. There are therefore very few murders or rapes in such places. Transgressions involving cigarettes and alcohol pose some problems, but drugs are easier to deal with, as they are simply not allowed. It remains true that some members of the staff are still trying to work through their own adolescent difficulties, but then this is true of most institutions including none other than the parliament. Even there, gross transgressions of rules and even the laws of the land are often tolerated to serve some other political end.

The reason for saying this is not so much to embarrass the government but to forestall any criticism of how such units were run during my time as their consultant.

I have argued valiantly that some tolerance of transgression is indeed the hallmark of all good parenting. If every child is punished at every transgression, we would probably have very little spending at birthdays and Christmas, and a very busy Social Services Department. Maybe a few chopped hands too.

Some places did apply rules rigidly and those have mainly been shut down in the last two decades. They were children's homes.

Some of us may wish for a less tolerant approach, especially in the prison services, but often tolerances are for the warders' benefit, as stricter application of rules often lead to riots.

Too liberal an approach and trouble of a different kind will inevitably follow.

A delicate balance is required for the smooth running of such a place and it is important to have the right balance of different types of cases. The same goes for adult psychiatric wards. The modern approach of only admitting the severely disturbed to a hospital changed the whole therapeutic milieu of the mental hospital ward of old. Admitting only acutely psychotic patients to a ward full of other acutely psychotics is a sure recipe for disaster. It is bad for patients and it is bad for the morale of the staff[140].

Some children have been over-tolerated all their lives, to the point that they become wild and un-manageable. Modern parents no longer know when and where to draw the line, and when in doubt, they give in by buying the latest in sports or electronic gadgets.

One such child was the result of a long awaited pregnancy of a mother I have come to know since the boy was three. He was an angelic boy who was a model on the catwalk before he was five. But he gave her hell from when he was born. A bad forceps delivery left her with serious stress incontinence. She wore an adult nappy all the time; and she was in the fashion business and a successful one at that.

Money bought her reprieves now and again and she had been a loyal attendant at the outpatient clinic over the years until the boy became a fully fledged teenager. He turned out as handsome as he promised to be, if he had not marred his looks by various unsightly piercing and peculiar hair colours. Fortunately, tattoos were not popular then.

---

[140] Inside the violent, chaotic world of our mental wards by Amelia Hill, Observer, Sunday April 8, 2007
http://www.guardian.co.uk/medicine/story/0,,2052528,00.html

Not having seen him for a while in the in-between years when only mother attended the clinic, I was visibly shocked by the turn of events and fully sympathetic of mother's serious misgivings on how far she should continue to be tolerant.

My early bond with the boy at least allowed me to have some reasonable communication with him. He had then become a keen football fan of a well known club featuring the red shirt. He wore one most of the time he came to see me.

It became clear enough that he needed to be assessed at the adolescent unit.

I was dubious about him becoming a day patient, not knowing how well he might cope. Yet within a short while of being a day patient, he begged for a change of status. He wanted to be admitted as an inpatient.

Since it was my intention to admit him at some point as an inpatient, I thought it might not be an entirely bad idea. I perhaps temporarily forgot my own golden rule of never giving the patient what they want as this would invariably imply a loss of control on my part.

He bought his way up the pecking order and one could speculate how many games and football memorabilia he traded. But soon he was top dog and he started bringing in cigarettes and vodka in different guises.

I had to act, but it was no good giving him a list of rules. It does not operate like that in an adolescent unit for the reasons I explained above.

I had to come up with something else.

I looked at his football shirt and his new hair style which was a direct copy of one famous footballer and without doubt cost mum a fair bit over the weekend.

Right! Yellow card and god forbid, Red one too.

Now the boy understood.

My staff looked at me – you don't even like football and you are using football lingo!

This was where I found the advantage of having a fully equipped school on site. Fully plasticised yellow cards were made and distributed to the staff and I was the only one with the RED one.

We did have peace for a while and the cards did not have to be used.

One day there was pandemonium when I got in. Out of some trivial argument when he could not get his own way, he started defacing other children's posters, his main target being those of opposing football clubs. The yellow card did not work and two of the staff had to hold on to him to prevent further damage. They could otherwise not guarantee his safety.

I walked into the room where he was held.

The horror on his face when I reached for my top pocket was quite a sight. Top footballer in disgrace.

RED CARD.

So in the end it did not work but I was glad it lasted as long as it did.

Chapter 47 Going To The Moon

Time and again I have been asked why I decided to pursue child psychiatry as my career. This question was often posed by my juniors who were at the point of their life when they had to choose their career path. It would have been dishonest of me to tell them that I knew exactly why. In life certain events seem to just happen and hopefully they gel together well enough so that one does not have to say at the end of one's working life that a wrong decision was made.

After passing my finals, I did my internship in Internal Medicine and Obstetrics and Gynaecology.

In our final year the first reports came through of cures in Leukaemia. People's hopes were rekindled and Medicine moved into a new era.

Needless to say cancer touches every family in more ways than one can imagine and especially when it hits at one's prime in life it is a highly emotive thing. In other words, no one is immune, not even if you are a doctor. At the time of my internship we had to deal with all those over the age of twelve and a number of inpatients were young Oncology cases. One of the boys I can remember was having the full VAMP treatment. Someone had a dry sense of humour to borrow from the word Vampire and with good reasons. Blood samples had to be drawn often and it was years later that I appreciated the work of some psychiatrists who recommend the limiting of daily blood drawing to before 10 A.M. every morning. This simple enforceable rule greatly reduced the emotional stress of the children involved. Patients were by and large compliant and they knew that the blood drawing was important. When they were able to work out that it would not happen after 10 A.M. they had at least a good ten hours of relative peace.

I had this highly intelligent boy on the ward with Leukaemia on treatment. He was barely thirteen and looked nine-ish. He was my most helpful assistant and would follow me on the lab trolley when I was doing my blood sample rounds. He would fill in the forms and match the numbers on the sample bottles. He never made a single mistake as far as I can remember. Most of my contemporaries had some pet patient like that. How else could we have got through the day's work? Most sisters and matrons turned a blind eye and the consultants and professors had been there so they did not mind either. Considering that we were then spending the major part of our waking life on the ward, we got closer to these patients than to anyone else in our life at that point.

This boy was beginning to show the effect of steroids and he had some of the most frightening nightmares when he would scream in the middle of the night and nothing much would comfort him. He would sit up and say something about going to the moon and that was probably the only thing of which anyone could make some sense. The regular night nurse who had children of his age was most fond of him and would give me detailed reports of the timing of such occurrences. At other times I could see her playing her mother rather than nurse role and just holding him while he sobbed.

He had the Number 1 bed which was right by the nurse's station and it was a rather cosy one as the bed opposite was generally the last one to be used. If I had not been on call, he would give me a quick run down on who was new and who was unconscious and who had insecticide poisoning from suicidal ingestion. In any case, one could smell the insecticide as one walked in as these survivors breathed it out.

We all so hoped that the cure would extend to him and he would certainly make a good doctor or a good nurse.

One day when I returned from weekend leave – the one in four weekend that we got to catch up with our sleep, our romance and our family – I could smell something but it was not Malathion[141]. Something was wrong. All his things were gone and

---

[141] Malathion – an insecticide often ingested in attempted suicides at the time.

the bed was now stripped bare. Night nurse was still around, waiting for me to turn up.

"He has gone to the moon," she said.

Oh no. He had a massive bleed in the brain and passed away during the weekend. His last words were: I am going to the moon.

I more or less decided at that moment that although we were brought up on the first day of Medical School to confront death, this just might be too much for me. Dealing with the death of a good friend's father following a cerebral haemorrhage was hard enough but the passing of a young thirteen year old was going to leave its mark and I did not want too many of those.

It was a bit of a relief when I had my next six months at an obstetrics teaching hospital. We had top class training there – we still had very high birth rates and high number of patients meant lots of experience. This was a contributing factor to Hong Kong's world class position of low infant mortality – joint lead shared with Japan. We lived on the top floor of a seven-storey hospital dedicated to obstetrics. In an emergency situation, we were geared to get a baby out by Caesarean Section in less than four minutes. Here we confronted life instead of death. We had to work closely with the midwives and apart from a couple of rather formidable matrons the rest were some of the nicest medical staff one would hope to work with. Even the formidable matrons were there for a good reason. They drove the fear of God into the young medical students, making sure that they were professional from the very beginning. It was said that once you got invited to the midnight feast by the matron you had passed the test.

From early on in my medical student days I had developed the knack of delivering babies without much need for cutting the perineum. I probably would have enjoyed a career in Obstetrics except in those days Obstetrics was always combined with gynaecology, which of course meant oncology and some rather heroic surgical operations for pelvic spread of tumours. But the crunch really came when I had to deliver the baby of an eleven year old mother. Yes, eleven. It was a smooth event but the complex case situation of the uncle abusing her and so on probably sowed some seeds for my eventual move into child psychiatry.

At the time we had an eminent Professor of Psychiatry whose work on transcultural psychiatry fascinated quite a few of us, to the point that over one in ten of our class decided to go into psychiatry – a shock to the department though I did not think it contributed to the Professor's sudden death in Mexico City when he was attending a World Psychiatric Organisation conference. It was the altitude.

With the loss of the professor, some of us left Hong Kong to seek training in other countries including Canada, Australia, United States and England. It was in England that against stiff competition I won the offer of a training post with the world famous Tavistock Clinic and my most understanding wife agreed it would be a pity if I did not take it up.

In England I met a few very inspiring teachers and was able to further my career. At that time, child psychiatry was a virtually unknown discipline in Hong Kong. I was so to speak their first ever. I came to enjoy the rich cultural life of England. Our two daughters were both born in England and as the saying goes, home is where your children are, I stayed until I retired.

In the spring of 1984, I was fortunate enough to attend the 2nd Infant Psychiatry Congress held in the beautiful town of Cannes, more famous for its film festival. Having found the first congress to be rather exciting and ego-syntonic[142] I decided to attend the second one. The first one was a rather smaller affair where one got to know most people through the four days of meetings, meals and Gala. I had since been to visit some of their hospitals and clinics to learn from their practices. What impressed me most was the general attitude across the Atlantic that one should never be shy to try new approaches in treatment and management of cases.

What I did not realise at the time was that I was about to witness the passing of the older generation of great thinkers in child psychiatry. I was fortunate enough when I was at the Tavistock Clinic to have attended some seminars held by Anna Freud, Sigmund Freud's daughter. In Cannes I went to presentations by Margaret Mahler and Erik Erikson[143].

That was the golden era for psychoanalysis and also for child psychoanalysis. It was hard to believe that thirty years on we are back to a biochemical approach. It is not difficult to see the attractions as the implied blame on parents, especially on mothers,

---

[142] Ego-syntonic - a medical term referring to behaviours, values, feelings, which are in harmony with or acceptable to the needs and goals of the ego, or consistent with one's ideal self-image.

[143] Erik Erikson - Erik Homburger Erikson (June 15, 1902 – May 12, 1994) was a German developmental psychologist and psychoanalyst known for his theory on social development of human beings, and for coining the phrase identity crisis.

disappeared overnight - whether you like it or not my son has ADD (attention deficit disorder). ADHD (attention deficit/hyperactivity disorder) is slightly difficult for parents and some do get confused. Most like the idea that they do not even need to be hyperactive. Some have never caught up with the American Psychiatric Association's change of name and that includes some psychiatrists and psychologists.

Margaret Mahler at eighty six must qualify as the grandmother figure to psychoanalysis and her understanding of child development was superb if you could get past the first hurdle of her own terminology.

Erik Erikson was also rather complex in his staging of development. Put it another way they were not the easiest to understand. However, Erikson's books became very popular; and Margaret Mahler's use of terms like autistic [144] phase and symbiotic[145] phase helped a couple of generations of psychiatrists in their understanding of the complex world of child development.

It was Mahler's use of the term Rapprochement[146] that caused me most problems. The meaning of this First World War left-over

---

[144] Autistic phase – In Mahler's Theory of Child Development, first few weeks of life. The infant is detached and self absorbed. Spends most of his/her time sleeping. Mahler later abandoned this phase, based on new findings from her infant research. She believed it to be non-existent. The phase still appears in many books on her theories.

[145] Symbiotic phase - In Mahler's Theory of Child Development, lasts until about 5 months of age. The child is now aware of his/her mother but there is not a sense of individuality. The infant and the mother are one, and there is a barrier between them and the rest of the world.

[146] Rapprochement - In Mahler's Theory of Child Development, 15-24 months. The infant once again becomes close to the mother. The child realizes that his physical mobility demonstrates psychic separateness from his mother. The toddler may become tentative, wanting his mother to be in sight so that, through eye contact and action, he can explore his world. The risk is that the mother will misread this need and respond with impatience or unavailability. This can lead to an anxious fear of abandonment in the toddler. A basic 'mood predisposition' may be established at this point.

terminology that was barely used post Second World War had become unintelligible as wars of the modern world had turned so religion based that rapprochement never came into it.

Imagine my excitement when I realised that Mahler was due to talk about Rapprochement Phase in a keynote lecture. She must have realised that it was a term most of her students had difficulties with. The rather grand modern Cannes Auditorium – famed for being the venue for the Cannes Film Festival presentation of prizes – was packed. There was standing room only, and some attendees had to sit on the steps. The short diminutive figure with her heavy European accent commanded a fully attentive audience, and she treated us to some old film footage as well. She was no doubt the star and well deserved the heart-felt standing ovation that was normally reserved for those going up to the stage for their life-time achievement in the film industry. I was glad I was there.

Erikson's lecture was probably a closing day event but I cannot be sure. Whether people entirely agreed with his view or not no longer mattered on such an important historical event. What was more important was that the talk he delivered was a new one about his life-time's work, namely the follow-up of his patients thirty five years on. With meticulous note and history taking that was a European obsession, Erikson was able to refer back to notes kept on the first session of his little patients all those years ago. He managed to track down a number of them and made a thorough study of how they had fared in the intervening years. The essence of the presentation was how for the majority, material collected in the first session from either the play activities, or drawings or conversation, revealed a life plan that many of them followed closely. It was uncanny but there was no reason why Erikson would want to make it up.

Mahler and Erikson reminded me of a boy with hydrocephalous that was referred to the clinic at the start of all the fuss about stimulants and ADD/ADHD

Most things that are popular across the Atlantic can cause two opposing reactions: one an unreserved acceptance that if it is from America, it must be good; the other outright rejection that if it is from America, it cannot be any good. Look at the Cuban boy who was sent back to Cuba because the father did not want anything to do with the U.S. What can the boy do apart from getting obese, take drugs and learn to shoot people? It is a sad indictment of not just America but of the free world that National Guards were needed, with the threat of machine guns, to retrieve the boy. Would they really shoot? Would they really obey orders even if the orders were inhumane and unreasonable? They must have been very relieved that in the end they were not compelled to take that decision.

A treatment that had a history of over fifty years, starting life under fairly relaxed FDA rules, was approved for a different purpose in 1980 under fairly dubious circumstances, based on minimal research data on some very small samples. The treatment never caught the imagination of the child psychiatrists of the time and was so rarely used that in 1986 the drug was withdrawn from the British market. Then suddenly it took off and if I say anymore about my personal view on how and why it took off, I might be faced with libel action from the main parties concerned.

The drug concerned is still hardly prescribed in France, a country well endowed with child psychiatric services and the French are rather fond of their *medicament*. There is no market yet in China which has a fifth of the world's population and presumably also roughly a fifth of the world's child population. It probably would not take long for China to adopt it though. Contrary to popular belief, admiration for all things American is endemic in China if not epidemic. You may not think so considering the rhetoric of the leaders. On a recent visit, I noticed one of their bottled water advertisements proudly saying "using the latest US reverse osmosis technology". For now there are countries both in the first world and in the developing world that have not found it necessary to use the drug.

Most research showed that Ritalin would eventually lead to addiction; but there are some who prefer to insist there is no truth in that. The U.S. is the world's No.1 prescriber of Ritalin and is also the world's No.1 consumer of Cocaine. The other listed use of Ritalin is for Cocaine withdrawal.

Why then is there such a renewed demand and interest in diagnosis and drug treatment of ADHD?

It is a sad reflection of our times that we demand fast responses. Being patient is no longer seen as a virtue. Have you not noticed that with faster and faster computers we still consider them slow and therefore manufacturers can continue to sell us "faster" ones? TV and computer games have conditioned kids so that they can rarely hold their concentration for more than three seconds. Even the term "three minute culture" is now out of date – no modern day television or film scene must last longer than ten seconds. How many children nowadays can withstand five hours of waiting at the fishing rod without catching anything? How many mothers have to cope with lines like: I am thirsty, mummy, I want my juice now, please. Are they really going to die of dehydration if mother makes them wait a bit?

Concentration like most other things in our modern society is no longer something that is packaged by our Maker. People need to acquire it and one way is by taking a stimulant such as Ritalin.

Ritalin has also become popular because it takes the blame away from those responsible for the child – the parents and often the teachers as well. Some parents who do not wish for their child to go on Ritalin are often put under tremendous pressure by the teachers. Very few have even bothered to find out if there is any non drug related method at all.

Thus James was referred to me by his doctor. He had just started school and his teacher considered him hyperactive and wondered if he had this new disease called ADD and should he be on Ritalin. What my secretary did not tell me was that mother was a friend of hers and that mother had already extracted out of her that I did not prescribe stimulants "willy nilly" and it was on that basis that she made the appointment.

What my secretary did not tell me either was that James had hydrocephalous and had a shunt. There had been trips to the hospital and mother was in a way not looking forward to the clinic appointment until she realised that we did not wear white coats.

James decided to hold mother's hand when I collected them from the waiting area and was merrily swinging her hand as he skipped down our corridor. Seemingly happy mother-child pair, I thought. It could also be that faced with an outsider like myself, James found mother the safer bet.

Very often when the so-called hyperactive children came to see us, they were so well behaved that it upset the parents.

This, I thought, might well turn out to be one of those cases.

In our play-room we had a sand pit complete with beach toys. I often wondered if I should get rid of it as it had the major drawback of so absorbing the visiting children that they forgot they were there to show me how badly behaved they were.

Not our James – he ignored the sandpit!

Instead he was taken up by some simple wood building blocks. The kind of toy I really like - timeless and priceless.

These allow the child's fantasy to run wild and anything can then be anything.

Mother started describing to me how she had to go up to London for James's follow-ups although nowadays the appointments were quite a bit apart and James tended to doze off to sleep on the train. At other times he seemed to be totally contrary and mother just had to fight with him on most things. This considering the fact that he had turned five was a bit trying for mother. Unfortunately this had extended to school where his class teacher was also a woman of mother's age. James would behave in front of his father but as father worked for himself as a builder he worked all the hours God gave him and mother was really his main parenting figure. There was an older sister who by comparison was an angel. She was ten years older and would often give mum a break and look after him.

Simple things including getting ready for school would be a battle to the point that mother would pretend to be busy and then he would let big sister get him ready. Mother felt that there should really be no need for this kind of play acting. After all she brought up the older child without much problem.

Mothers tended to look to us to say something professionally which pointed out that they were not really at fault. Most actually came to us feeling that they had been so. Such guilt was an added burden on top of the difficult child they had to deal with. This is not to say that I thought all mothers were innocent. Far from it. But it was getting more and more non politically correct to blame mothers. Some mothers do goad and entrench their kids. But that is another problem.

"I do not really want him to be on drugs if I can help it." Mother declared at last. "I would never forgive myself if something should happen to him. His father would never forgive me."

Mother was afraid that James was in fact backward and that he was behaving like a two-year-old.

Observant mothers tend to know. They do not need a lecture form Mahler or Erikson. They are well versed in the developmental stages. They just do not use our terminology.

I helped James build a sort of tower. He would then knock it down and tried to build a taller one. He would go higher and higher. Mother was rather nervous about him knocking down the building and asked me if it was OK.

In our work we have to bear in mind always that we must not take away a parent's authority. It is of course so easy to do. So I said that if mummy thought it was OK then it was OK.

James now looked at mum after finishing a taller tower to see if it was all right to knock it down. Mum nodded her head and I could see tears in her eyes.

"Sorry, but he has never asked me before." Mum said to me with a shaky voice.

James looked at mum and decided that he really wanted mum to knock it down.

Thank you, Margaret Mahler - RAPPROCHEMENT.

James then built a bigger and taller building. He put a plane with a little boy on top and said, "he is going to the moon."

He found one of the soft sponge balls that we had and put it up on a shelf. Then he took mum's hand and together they flew the little boy round the room and eventually landed on the moon.

James was never prescribed Ritalin. They came to see me regularly and mother reported within a short while how much easier life was for her and for everybody. Her daughter could give more attention to her exam work and mother had taken on some evening work at the local supermarket. I concentrated on helping mother retrieve her authority. I have often said that children tend to see through parents. If the parents do not believe in themselves then the child will not either. It reminded me of that terrible SARS epidemic in Hong Kong. Everybody was wearing a mask - babies and children alike. It was not the most comfortable thing to wear but on checking with friends and family I found that every child wore one, with no protest. It was not negotiable. It was life and death.

If a child will do that he or she will obey other orders too.

James turned out to be one of those likeable children that charmed everybody at the clinic when he was waiting and he became so used to the routine of playing with mum talking to me that he was a real pleasure to see. You will be surprised how some simple suggestions from me meant a lot to many mothers, and sometimes even changed their lives, and for that they showed eternal gratitude. Mother was so pleased that James got better without medication. Father tried to have Sundays off so that he could take James fishing, that being his only hobby. I started getting tales of how big a fish father caught every time I saw James.

Then one day when I turned up for my afternoon clinic and expected to see James waiting in the waiting area reading a book with mum, he was not there.

They never failed a single appointment before.

When I reached my room I could see that Marjorie my secretary had been crying.

What's wrong?

She couldn't say.

My social worker pulled me to her room.

James had some sort of fit and died on the way to the children's hospital the night before.

It all flashed before my eyes – the leukaemia boy, James, the moon.

I muttered something like: he has gone to the moon.

Luckily, my staff all knew me well. It was months later that I told them the story of my leukaemia patient and the moon. Now the same social worker is fighting her own battle with Hodgkin's.

Life can be cruel.

Eric Erikson, I wish you were wrong.

No, maybe we should not record my patient's first meeting.

Some months later, mum arranged to see me to thank me for all that I did and for giving her some quality months with James. I could hardly hold back my emotions.

Chapter 48 The Last Cook

One of the few things I learned working in some inpatient units was to be appreciative of the ancillary staff. What a cleaner might reveal to us was often more telling than a formal interview. It could well be that often parents were unguarded and more able to reveal things to someone like the cleaner or indeed the cook.

I was fortunate enough to experience one of the last NHS cooks when I was Senior Registrar at an inpatient unit. The inpatient unit catered for a middle age group spanning the older children to the younger adolescents. It was one of a kind in the U.K. and indeed it was the first to start a national training course for Psychiatric nurses in inpatient care, a good three years before anywhere else.

The unit was in the middle of town and was considered to be too far from the Hospital for catering purposes. Instead a cook was employed to cater for the needs of the children and nursing staff. We doctors were not supposed to eat there. But we did. Mainly for lunch.

If we arrived at mid-morning we used to get a nice cup of tea. But that was only since I started bringing in my own tea leaves. We also got served home-made scones and the like.

All very homely.

I had since wondered if our great success rate was more to do with having our own cook than all the other therapies and tit bits that we did.

You never know as people do not really research these things.

Looking back now, I feel my time at that unit probably stood me in good stead for what was to come years later, looking after both a Children and an Adolescent unit.

Alas, catering in the last two units were impersonal with huge grey metal trolleys wheeled from the main hospital. If there was a competition, I am sure our food would beat school dinners anytime for poor quality.

I often arrived late at lunch time after the children and nurses had eaten as morning clinics had a habit of running late. With less than ten minutes to spare, the cook would still manage to serve me a bit of some of the things she knew I preferred. Often she felt compelled to sit with me to tell me about her grandchildren or about what the government should really be doing to help the likes of her, a war widow bringing up two sons in this Naval town. I always admired the resilience shining through her stories.

She also provided me with her down to earth views of what we should do with whichever patient that had come in. I listened. I took note. You never know.

One of her grandsons wanted to join the Navy. She could not understand as his grandfather died during the Normandy landing.

Nor did I, I told her, but that was life.

She worked out my likes and dislikes and everything would just be ready for my lunch complete with my Darjeeling Tea brewed to perfection, 20 seconds and out.

Sometimes I got in early enough to eat with everybody. The noise was unbelievable. Everybody seemed to get exactly what they wanted. Psychiatric patients were amongst the fussiest eaters in the world.

I once had this boy of twelve whose diet consisted of nothing but milk, cheddar cheese, Cadbury's Milk Chocolate and strawberries in season.

Our cook soon sorted him out and he left with a balanced repertoire of around twelve items. We all agreed that it was the cook who did it. He was one of the healthiest looking kids I had ever met. Just shows we may have all got it wrong in our quest for the best diet. But he was back on the right track when he left, eating broccoli and carrots and even fish.

Then we had Sheena.

Sheena was the mother of two girls we had to admit. They were both soilers and they would never touch vegetables at home or anywhere.

Sheena was petite, worn and a chain smoker.

But she had two lovely looking girls.

We knew from the start there were handling issues and most likely diet ones too.

One of the other reasons for their admission was that by and large there were very few girl soilers.

It was always a good sign when a child flourished in an inpatient setting, and away from home some mothers were more capable of telling you more of what went on. Some mothers found it easier to talk to one of the non-medical staff, perhaps the cook.

Mothers got fed too on their visits. More often than not the children preferred their mother to go home than to stay and watch them. That was a different issue. With the money spent on cigarettes and drinks not much was left for food either for the children or the parents. I knew that if we checked for vitamin and other deficiencies we would find them, a problem that had taken Public Health a long time to wake up to. Increasing tax for cigarettes and drinks did not change people's habit one little bit.

With a simple routine the girls were clean in no time.   At least during the week as they all went home week-ends, when the unit was closed.

We were at a loss as to what was going on. We had never seen father but we knew he had a diagnosis of Schizophrenia and was on Modecate[147] injection. Mother had always insisted that he was so

---

[147] Modecate - Fluphenazine decanoate belongs to a group of medicines known as the phenothiazine antipsychotics. It is sometimes described as a 'major tranquilliser'. It acts by blocking a variety of receptors in the brain, particularly dopamine receptors. Dopamine is involved in transmitting signals between brain cells. When there is an excess amount of dopamine in the brain it causes over-stimulation of dopamine receptors. These receptors normally act to modify behaviour and over-

"out of it" that there would not be any point in the unit involving him. We did have reports from his day-hospital social worker and we left it at that.

The girls would get worse over the week-end and soil. This went on for quite a while.

Then one day the cook talked to me.

"Sheena never stays Mondays," she told me.

I listened.

"Have you noticed she is always in dark glasses on Mondays?"

How stupid of me. Now and again I saw her at the door seeing the girls off and yes, she wore huge sunglasses.

Sheena was not a movie star.

I arranged to see Sheena.

She said, "You knew."

I nodded.

"But I cannot leave him. I have nowhere to go and I shall not get enough benefit money if I am divorced from him. He now goes to the day hospital. Fridays he gets drunk and beats me up. It is like a routine. I try not to get hurt and hide it from the girls. If I walk out, he will find me even if I have somewhere to go. I shall still get beaten up. Now at least I know when it will happen and I can live with that."

I suggested that I should speak to him but she looked terrified.

---

stimulation may result in psychotic illness. Fluphenazine decanoate blocks these receptors and stops them becoming over-stimulated, thereby helping to control psychotic illness.
http://www.healthyplace.com/medications/fluphenazine.asp

She felt he might even kill her if I did and last time he threw a chair at a male nurse who tried to say something.

She was probably right. We often had no idea what people and particularly women put up with. It would be too easy for us to bulldoze in. We had to think twice before intervening unless we had something better to offer. His Schizophrenia diagnosis allowed for a higher level of benefit she would not otherwise get. Who would she meet up with next? Another violent man most likely.

Was it such a cop-out on my part?

Maybe it was, but in a strange way the girls stopped soiling after that one meeting I had with mum. The case left me with some unease - unease not just about what I did or did not do but about keeping patients in the community. Three other lives were affected here and who knows, one day he might go too far. That was before Maria Colwell.

The unit had long since been closed.

The last cook in the NHS retired[148] .

---

[148] Wide dissatisfaction with NHS hospital food – A survey of catering at 97 health trusts in 2006 revealed that NHS hospitals were slowing patients' recovery by serving meals that were tepid, unappetising or downright inedible.

The research was conducted by patient forums - official bodies set up by the government to represent the interests of NHS users. They interviewed a sample of 2,240 patients in hospitals across England and discovered widespread dissatisfaction.

http://www.guardian.co.uk/food/Story/0,,1923345,00.html

Chapter 49 Definitely Not All In The Mind

It would not be a great surprise to anyone who has any inkling of the history of medicine that sooner or later any medical condition with an alleged aetiology of pure psychological origin will prove to have a non psychological cause. This is particularly true of those conditions classified by non-psychiatrists.

In the past, ignorance has led to belief that certain conditions are either punishment by god, visions of great religious significance or simply madness. Accordingly you might be burnt, become a saint or simply be given one of the psychiatric medications.

Pork with tapeworm infestation was observed to be associated with manifestation of madness (resulting from cerebral invasion) so that some wise early religious leaders banned their believers from ingesting this meat.

Leprosy was distinctly a punishment by God and it was not until the discovery of the infesting agent that the whole treatment approach was changed.

Certain conditions were said to be linked to morality. Once upon a time cervical cancer was considered a sign of promiscuity and multiple partners. In medical school we were taught that circumcision was definitely related to very low or zero incidence of this amongst the Jews. It was a convenient way of fitting findings to a view. Little was said of other religious groups with similar circumcision rituals that had the same cancer rate as non circumcised communities. Now that high risk HPVs[149] (a virus) have been identified and a vaccine manufactured, we can look forward to a complete eradication of the condition.

You might think modern medicine has changed after nearly two and a half millennia of quasi-science. Not so much.

Take Legionnaire. It was first declared a form of "mass hysteria". [150] "Mass hysteria" leading to deaths! One of the

---

[149] HUMAN PAPILLOMAVIRUS (HPV) – Over 100 different human papillomavirus (HPV) types have been characterized. Some HPV types cause benign skin warts, or papillomas, for which the virus family is named. HPVs associated with the development of such "common warts" are transmitted environmentally or by casual skin-to-skin contact. A group of about 30-40 HPVs are typically transmitted through sexual contact and infect the anogenital region. Some sexually transmitted HPVs, such as types 6 and 11, can cause genital warts. However, most HPV types that infect the genitals tend not to cause noticeable symptoms.
Persistent infection with a subset of about 13 so-called "high-risk" sexually transmitted HPVs, can lead to the development of cervical dyskaryosis, or precancerous lesions, which may in turn lead to cancer of the cervix among women, or in men, cancer of the penis aka penile cancer. HPV infection is a necessary factor in the development of nearly all cases of cervical cancer.
http://en.wikipedia.org/wiki/Human_papillomavirus

[150] Legionnaires' disease - Legionnaires' disease acquired its name in 1976 when an outbreak of pneumonia occurred among ex-service personnel attending a convention of the American Legion in Philadelphia during the US Bicentennial celebration in July 1976. A total of 221 people contracted the disease and 34 died. At first, the outbreak was thought to be one of mass hysteria. On January 18, 1977 scientists identified the causative agent as a previously unknown bacterium, subsequently named Legionella.

psychologists proclaiming such was carried out horizontally three days later with the same "hysteria". Then a little germ was found.

The jury is still not out for Morgellon[151] (a peculiar skin condition that has been prevalent in California and Texas, with constant extrusion of black fibre looking substance) and many sufferers are deemed "delusional" and treated accordingly with strong anti-psychotic medication.

To this day, ME (Myalgic Encephalomyopathy) remains controversial as a disease entity and many still believe in it being a purely psychological anomaly.

Chantal

In the August of the same year when I started at the inpatient unit Chantal was referred to us. She was at the local children's hospital with paralysis of both lower limbs. The hospital paediatrician was reluctant to refer her to the London Neurology Department as he thought that Chantal's problem was most likely psychological. It is always difficult when some other doctor has made the diagnosis for you. My preference would be for a

---

[151] Morgellons Disease – "Imagine your body pocked by erupting sores. The sensation of little bugs crawling all over you. And worst of all, mysterious red and blue fibers sprouting from your skin." It may sound like a macabre science fiction movie, but a growing legion of Americans say they suffer from this condition. And now the U.S. Centers for Disease Control and Prevention is investigating. Some psychiatrists consider it as part of a wider phenomenon-delusional parasitosis.

http://www.foxnews.com/story/0,2933,207497,00.html

consultation so that I could advise on whether the parent's request was reasonable and that a Neurological referral was necessary.

No matter - I felt that I would be competent enough to make some of my own neurological assessments.

The case was more complex than I was led to believe. Mother turned out to be an established head mistress of a local school and father a rather well-known London Architect. They were told that after a spell at our hospital, I would be the one to decide if Chantal needed to be referred. I am sure the unfortunate funding problem started by the then Tory government had something to do with this but I was determined not to let that get in the way.

The charge nurse who visited the patient at the children's hospital briefed me that the parents were not too pleased with the transfer but they sold me as the doctor who could deal with obscure cases and had solved a couple of theirs since my arrival.

I had experience of dealing with the headmistress of England's most famous Girls school as well as some successful architects, and I am not normally put off by so called "high powered" people. In fact I find them easier to talk to as I am closer to them in interests and so on. Many find me difficult to place in their usual class-conscious context and luckily I have always been given the benefit of doubt.

Meeting with the consultant at such an inpatient unit is always an event, especially for junior medical and nursing staff. It is indeed a sort of assessment but an assessment from both sides and the whole thing is of course unscripted. I particularly enjoyed this part of my work and was noted for my unusual ability to quote from medical and other material at will. Some of my staff often asked how I managed to commit so much to memory and it was some time later when I discovered from the Nobel prize winning psychiatrist Kandel[152] that it was possibly a defect that led some of us not to forget things.

Mother, a small but elegant figure, remained well composed throughout the long session. Father I can only remember as a huge tall figure, the sort of man that I sometimes meet on golf courses who has all the theories about swings and will normally fade his first tee into the rough or water.

---

[152] Kandel – Eric R. Kandel, University Professor of Physiology and Cell Biophysics, Psychiatry, Biochemistry and Molecular Biophysics at Columbia University, shares the 2000 Nobel Prize for Medicine with Arvid Carlsson of the University of Goteborg, Sweden and Paul Greengard of The Rockefeller University, New York, for their contributions to the field of neuroscience. Kandel's seminal work with the sea slug Aplysia, a creature with relatively few nerve cells and clearly delineated behavioural circuitry compared with vertebrates, demonstrated fundamental ways in which nerve cells alter their responsiveness to chemical signals to produce a coordinated change in behaviour. The work has been essential not only for our understanding of the basic processes of learning and memory, but also for highlighting many of the cellular processes that are targets of psychoactive drugs.

Kandel's research has been pivotal in relating three psychologically defined forms of learning (habituation, sensitization, and classical conditioning) to subcellular processes and intercellular signaling. In his studies, Dr. Kandel found that simple behaviours could be accounted for by distinctive sets of nerve cells connected in invariant circuits. Dr. Kandel and colleagues found that learning produces changes in behaviour not by altering basic circuitry, but by adjusting the strength of particular connections between nerve cells. Dr. Kandel and co-workers also defined sets of genes and proteins that stabilize synaptic connections and trigger growth of new ones. Kandel's lab has extended this approach from simple forms of memory in the Aplysia to more complex forms of spatial learning in mammals, and identified a key brain protein involved in retaining memories, which could help explain why some are stored away and some are not. CREB (cAMP response element binding protein) operates in the nucleus of brain cells and helps to activate genes which are thought to be possibly involved in the formation of long-term memory. To look at what the protein does, the researchers looked at a process called long-term potentiation (LTP). LTP is an alteration in the communication between nerve cells in a part of the brain concerned with memory storage. Cells were given an electrical stimulus and then tested for LTP by giving a second stimulus after some time had passed. The research found if CREB was activated all the time, long-lasting memories were created.

Kandel wins Nobel prize in medicine:
http://www.columbia.edu/cu/pr/00/10/ericKandel.html

How the brain remembers: http://news.bbc.co.uk/1/hi/health/1862819.stm

Mother had a note pad which was normally a bad sign. With her the pad was not just for taking notes but she had a list of questions to ask.

As a good friend of mine used to live in the small village they lived in, I was soon able to relax everybody by talking about their village and who had a nice swimming pool and so on. She was a good friend of the headmistress at my daughters' old school and they were impressed that one of them went to a famous Architecture School and the other to Cambridge.

Some may consider it un-kosher to reveal too much of one's personal life but in this cutting edge work everything counts and the trust and respect of your patients and their parents is of paramount importance, just like the trust and respect my parents used to have for the Traditional Chinese herbal doctor that they used to take me to.

Some people assume that you know what you are doing and others need to find out. With the gradual deterioration in the public's trust of doctors we now have little choice but to make use of every little bit of what we have.

Having some months earlier dealt with a similar case and established the diagnosis that led to some red faces, I had a good idea what I wanted to do with Chantal. This time I was not going to reveal anything to anyone until I was sure.

Mother turned out to be a great opera lover and we exchanged notes on Glyndebourne and the operas we had seen and the ones we were going to see that season. I knew that it was a meeting where most others were just observers. But they knew I was getting somewhere with these parents and it would be good for the reputation of the unit. The discussion was so intense and absorbing that it was getting dark and no one remembered to switch on the lights and I noticed that mother stopped taking notes.

They were happy for Chantal to stay and they awaited the results of my investigations.

The staff had for so long dealt with cases from deprived backgrounds that they needed to be reprogrammed. Soon that was done. Chantal was herself a charming girl with a great outgoing personality. Various theories were put forward by just about everybody on the psychological basis of her paralysis. Most eventually returned to the conjecture that it was her way of getting at her influential and controlling parents. I listened courteously but I had my own thought. I had mixed feelings about modern day psychological theories. If you subscribed to them you had better not be a parent at all, or rather not a successful upper middle class parent. We are what we are and we do what we do. There is no good or bad, right or wrong way. There is only love, care and concern.

Following the junior's thorough examination, I performed my Queen Square style neurological examination on Chantal, much to the amazement of the juniors watching. Queen Square trained us to a style that was at once elegant and thorough and I was vaguely pleased that I went through everything that my tutor taught me some thirty years ago.

The juniors were sworn to secrecy and special blood tests were rushed to the laboratory. They both kept their fingers crossed as there was only an off chance of the diagnosis being confirmed.

Chantal was a great athlete and a county level swimmer. She was at a friend's birthday swimming party in the house I knew of and was in the water the whole of the time. She was very annoyed that soon summer would be over and she could not go there to swim.

A routine was soon set up as she needed good physiotherapy to prevent any wasting of her muscle. Those who thought it was all psychological felt that it would be important for her to shuffle downstairs instead of being carried. She would then be allowed to use the wheelchair. She was happy to be with us. She played cricket from the wheelchair and I even had it videotaped. Arrangements were made for her vegetarian diet but she looked healthy enough.

The blood tests had to be sent to a major centre and required at least ten days, the pathologist told my juniors when they took the samples to him as my special request needed his approval.

Chantal was in a good routine. Mother visited daily and father every few days as he often stayed in his London flat during the week. There were theories afloat that maybe the marriage was on the rocks as father was not home all the time. Perhaps Chantal wanted to see more of her father. It was really difficult to convince some staff that certain professional people had to live the way they did to get the best of both worlds - one in the city and one in the country. One could read too much into things.

A call came through during one of our morning meetings. No, the consultant insisted on talking to me. He was calling from home as he was on leave. Fortunately my secretary knew the etiquette. When another consultant called she must get me out of meetings. It was the pathologist. He said he would be brief as I was in a meeting but "I had a double whammy" were his exact words. Campylobacter titre[153] was very high indicating there was a recent infection so was that for ECHO[154] virus. Either would have caused the Guillain-Barré syndrome[155] (temporary paralysis being the main symptom) but two were overloading it a bit.

I thanked him for going along with my hunch and approving the tests (which would not have been a problem in the old days and which must have been the problem in the Children's hospital). Some months later when I became medical director we had to work together when we discovered on routine testing Legionnaire in the water system of the acute ward. We had a certain mutual respect for each other.

It was a relief for me and my juniors and of course the parents and Chantal. Luckily most such cases recover spontaneously. There remained one little problem: Chantal was vegetarian and so she did not eat chicken which of course was the commonest source of the infection. I desperately looked for clues on the websites and found that one of the world's most publicized outbreak occurred after a swimming expedition when a large

---

[153] Campylobacter titre - Campylobacter is a genus of Gram-negative bacteria.

[154] Enteric cytopathic human orphan (ECHO) viruses are a group of enteroviruses, which are viruses that enter the body through the gastrointestinal tract and thrive there, often moving on to attack the nervous system.

[155] Guillain-Barré syndrome - is a disorder in which the body's immune system attacks part of the peripheral nervous system. The first symptoms of this disorder include varying degrees of weakness or tingling sensations in the legs. In many instances, the weakness and abnormal sensations spread to the arms and upper body. These symptoms can increase in intensity until the muscles cannot be used at all and the patient is almost totally paralyzed.

http://www.ninds.nih.gov/disorders/gbs/gbs.htm

number of children were infected. It was perhaps a hazard of domestic pools where normally it would not be a big problem until a large number of children used it. That was my theory but I never put it to a test. I left it to mother's discretion as to what she might want to do. In any case Chantal was not going there to swim again.

The other trick I pulled was rather dramatic. Chantal was pleased I found the little creatures that caused her problem but she wanted to know when she would be better. I had a quick calculation in my head and blurted out something like another four weeks.

A day before the four weeks were up, I had a phone call from Max, one of the few male nurses in the unit, who had been with me on this case from the beginning. He said, "Guess what, Doctor Zhang, Chantal walked this morning."

No, I did not want to be a prophet, but it was a good feeling. On Chantal's discharge, I had a case of very good wine which I shared out with the staff. Mother hugged everybody but shook hands with me. See you some time at Glyndebourne.

No, there was no marital discord. No pending divorce. Just middle class.

Chapter 50 Trauma and Human Resilience

One early lunch time in June, 2001 I attended the usual seminar at the hospital postgraduate centre. At that time, such meetings were quite serious affairs sponsored by at least three drug firms to avoid accusations of impropriety.

The lunch was always of very high quality catered by three young ladies who would also come to cater in our homes for those psychiatric meetings hosted at different consultants' homes.

You had to sign in – all part of continuing education.

It was quite a packed house and I was a little bit surprised as I vaguely remembered that the topic was psychiatric and this was a meeting for the whole hospital which included all the mainstream specialties.

Then when I looked at the title again, I understood immediately the attraction of the talk.

"What have we learnt from King's Cross?"

The speaker was a Senior Registrar from the Maudsley.

He was a Registrar at the time of the King's Cross[156] fire. He was just coming out of the station when the accident happened, and so was at the front line so to speak not just as a pedestrian but also as a psychiatrist. He became interested in PTSD (Post Traumatic Stress Disorder) and did a fair bit of research on King's Cross and other disasters.

He quoted a number of cases, including the Herald of Free Enterprise disaster[157]. There were those who despite help of all kinds would commit suicide. Many were heroes in that they saved many lives. Yet the feeling that they did not deserve to live eventually overtook them and they committed suicide.

What was most surprising was how the group that had counselling generally faired worse, much worse than those without any counselling. The group that did best were the ones that drank, and drank a fair amount.

---

[156] King's Cross St Pancras Underground Station Fire: a fatal underground fire at approximately 19:30 on November 18, 1987, killing 31 people.
http://news.bbc.co.uk/onthisday/hi/dates/stories/november/18/newsid_2519000/2519675.stm

[157] Herald of Free Enterprise Disaster: At 6:30pm on Friday 6 March 1987, the British cross-Channel roll on-roll off ferry 'Herald of Free Enterprise', operated by Townsend Thoresen, left Zeebrugge in Belgium with 533 passengers and crew abroad. Some five minute later she had capsized in shallow water outside the harbour and lay half-submerged on her port side in complete darkness and extremely cold water .

193 people perished in the United Kingdom's worst peace-time marine tragedy since the sinking of the 'Titanic' in 1912. Some 340 people were saved, in large part due to the actions of the crew and the heroic and efficient operation of the Belgian rescue and hospital services.
http://www.dover-kent.co.uk/transport/herald_disaster.htm
http://news.bbc.co.uk/onthisday/hi/dates/stories/october/8/newsid_2626000/2626265.stm

It was not his intention to promote vodka but he thought we could not be kept from the truth. He added that some new treatments were showing great promise.

His research showed that talking about the incident seemed to make things worse, much worse than anyone ever imagined. He postulated that this might have something to do with the "kindling effect"[158], normally seen in epilepsy. But it all seemed to make sense.

Hopefully none of us will have to face the kind of trauma like King's Cross and Herald of Free Enterprise but if we did at least I would know what not to do.

It reminded me of the girl on the front page of Time Magazine at the height of the Vietnam War.

Kim Phuc.

By rights possibly one of the most damaged psychologically and physically. She underwent no fewer than seventeen operations. The photo of her running down the street of Saigon naked probably changed the course of the Vietnam War and the world's perception of good and bad. Then came her dramatic escape in 1992 to Newfoundland and her eventual settling down in Canada. Human resilience is not to be underestimated and the imposition of psychological intervention could represent a great under-estimation of our genetical endowment. At one of her public lectures, one of the war veterans who was a helicopter gunner broke down.

---

[158] Kindling effect - G.V. Goddard and his associates in 1969 reported a peculiar kindling effect generated by repeated, periodic, low-intensity stimulation of the limbic region of mammalian brains. Goddard, G.V. (1967). Development of epileptic seizures through brain stimulation at low intensity. Nature, 214, 1020-1021.
http://homepages.nyu.edu/~eh597/kindle.htm

Crying, he told her he had regular nightmares.

He was possibly more damaged than Kim.

She told him she forgave him[159]. That was it.

He had control over his and her fate and she did not. Could it be that when one did not have control, it would be psychologically less damaging?

Then came September 11. I remembered I was on holiday in Spain when it happened. I had just finished golf. I put my clubs away and went to the club house for a drink with my playing partners. As I approached their table, I sensed that something was wrong. There were no drinks.

Then one of them said, "One of the World Trade Centre Towers is down!"

I was trying to see if I heard right.

"In New York?"

"New York."

Then moments later, the Spanish waitress came out and said to us, the second tower was down too.

I rushed back to our villa and shouted to my wife to turn on CNN and tried to contact our children, one of whom worked in Manhattan.

Lines were dead.

---

[159] In 1996, Kim was invited to attend the Veterans Day ceremonies at the Vietnam Memorial in Washington, D.C. Kim spoke to a group of several thousand Vietnam War veterans about her experiences after the napalm attack on her village. She used that opportunity to share with the veterans how she finally found happiness and freedom after years of pain and suffering. She even met a pilot who coordinated the air strike on her village - she forgave him!
http://www.kimfoundation.com/modules/contentpage/index.php?file=story.htm&ma=10&subid=101

Luckily, an Email came through our other daughter who was in England: Sis OK, at a meeting on 55th Street. Now trying to walk home to Brooklyn.

What a shock. Unlike my parents' generation we have had a long period of peace and prosperity but now everything was shattered.

The following day my office put a call through and I talked to my Associate Specialist.

The clinic just had an urgent referral. A local girl was referred. Very disturbed by what happened as one of her father's good friends was one of the pilots whose plane went down. The family spent many holidays with them in their Florida home and she was now most upset.

"Whatever you do, by all means talk to the parents but not to the girl. No one should see her. They should not turn on the TV and avoid any reminder of what happened."

I then nearly said, "Give her Vodka, Gin or similar," but I did not.

I gave the next best thing.

"Put her on a short course of Benzodiazepine to let her sleep for a few days."

It shocked my Associate Specialist. It was not a drug I normally used, if at all, and why now?

Well, whatever happened, all I could say was that the family was in total agreement and months later my Associate Specialist told me that it was brave of me but it seemed to have worked for this girl.

In July last year I met a young couple at the swimming pool of our holiday condo. I thought they were Chinese but it turned out they were Vietnamese Chinese.

We started chatting. He said he left Nam (Vietnam) on the last day.

Jokingly, I said, you mean you were on the Helicopter?

"Yeah, how did you know?"

"You looked too young to be working for the Embassy."

"My mum worked there. But my story was nothing, you should hear hers."

His wife, an elegant looking petite Chinese swam closer.

"So, tell me."

Well, she came out later. Her mother put her and four sisters on a junk (a Chinese fishing boat), one of those that took refugees out of Nam for an exorbitant fee and generally it had to be gold. Their boat sank outside Hong Kong but they swam ashore. She spent the next three years in one of the Hong Kong camps.

"Yes, I remember those."

"I know - the stench. We got used to it."

Those camps were run under the auspices of the United Nations but the UN never really paid Hong Kong a single dollar. However that is beside the point. Conditions were very poor and one could hardly decide if it was Hong Kong's or UN's fault. Every time we drove past it was like passing a local authority rubbish tip. We had to wind up the windows. Yet there were politicians who felt they needed to keep it bad to deter people. They continued to flow in right up to the handover. As it was still under British rule,

Britain tried its best to keep people from going to Britain. They needed not have worried. Most wanted to go to U.S. An irony really.

I said something that sounded like an apology, an apology for Hong Kong, and for mankind.

"No. It's fine. I am not bitter. We waited and we got to the U.S. There was nothing you could have done anyway."

She told me someone suggested that she should have some therapy. She never did.

"Some things you can never change. If it happened it happened."

But she managed to get most of her family out of camps and settled in the US. She was very successful in her business and her only regret was that her parents never made it.

What a story of human resilience and triumph over adversities.

And I can still remember that lunch time meeting and the learning from King's Cross.

Now mountains are once again mountains,
and waters once again waters.

Index

A

B

C

D

E

F

I

J

K

L

M